Essential

ESSENTIAL

The Selected Writings of
KATHY ACKER

Edited by Amy Scholder and Dennis Cooper

with an Introduction by Jeanette Winterson

Grove Press/New York

Selections from "Politics" (1968), "New York City in 1979" (1981), "Translations of the Diaries of Laure the Schoolgirl" (1983), "Algeria" (1984), and "Lust" (1988), excerpted here, are published in full in *Hannibal Lecter, My Father* (Semiotexte Native Agents, 2002) and are reprinted here with the cooperation of Semiotexte.

"Hello, I'm Erica Jong" was published as a chapbook by Contact II Publications, New York in 1982.

Implosion was published as a chapbook by Wedge Press, New York in 1983.

"Low" was published on the occasion of a Nayland Blake exhibition at Petersburg Gallery, New York in 1990.

All the other works have been previously published by Grove Press.

Published simultaneously in Canada
Printed in the United States of America

FIRST EDITION

Library of Congress Cataloging-in-Publication Data
Acker, Kathy, 1948–1997
    [Selections. 2002]
    Essential Acker : the selected writings of Kathy Acker / edited by Amy Scholder and Dennis Cooper ; with an introduction by Jeanette Winterson.
    p. cm.
    ISBN 0-8021-3921-3
    I. Scholder, Amy. II. Cooper, Dennis, 1953– III. Title.
PS3551.C44 A6 2002
813'.54—dc21   2002016446

Design by Laura Hammond Hough

Grove Press
841 Broadway
New York, NY 10003

02 03 04 05 10 9 8 7 6 5 4 3 2 1

Contents

Contents

Introduction

Jeanette Winterson

There are three things to say about Acker:

1) She was ahead of her time.
2) Her fiction is closer to the European literary tradition of Borges and Calvino, than it is to the Anglo-American narrative drive of Salinger or Roth or Amis.
3) She was a woman—therefore she was locked out of tradition and time.

I know it is usual to talk about Acker in relation to Burroughs and Ginsberg, but while Kathy was a true New Yorker, her sensibility and her sense of exile were European. Her family on her mother's side was German, and Acker lived in Germany and France, as well as in England, for significant periods of her life.

Acker positioned herself on the outside—on the side of exile— not only out of disaffection with the United States but also because her cultural and literary interests were wider than any single tradition could offer. Acker the wild girl was Acker the well-educated and voracious reader. I have seen her in her piercings and leopardskin, suddenly put on her reading glasses and look exactly like perfect casting for *The Prime of Miss Jean Brodie*.

In the 1970s Acker began a series of experiments with form and language, many of which included herself as a character. I have noticed that when women include themselves as a character in their own work, the work is read as autobiography.

When men do it—say Milan Kundera or Paul Auster—it is read as metafiction.

Women can only write from their own experience. Men are imaginative. Women write testimony and confessional. Men write the big picture . . .—or so we're told.

Acker hated all that. She believed that a writer could be a vibrant amalgam of confession and imagination. She worked on the difficult boundary of formal experiment and naked desire.

A book she loved was De Quincey's *Confessions of an English Opium Eater.* She felt, and she was right, that the English literary tradition changed radically around 1830, as the Romantic movement dissolved into the nineteenth-century obsession with realism.

Acker was seeking something freer, but not less disciplined.

Acker was one of the most disciplined writers I have met—not only in her habits, but in her defense of form as the necessary buffer against chaos. Those who criticize her writing as a kind of bathetic splurge don't know how to read it.

She often chose a literary or legendary figure, like Don Quixote or Pasolini or Toulouse-Lautrec, as a basic shape for her inquiries, both subjective and formal. She merged her identity with these characters, creating an autonomous being who could speak personally and also without any personal agenda. She roamed these beings through time.

Do not underestimate how radical this was when Acker started doing it. Nowadays it has become a commonplace of fiction to merge the past and the present and to use real and imaginary figures in the same narrative.

Acker was doing this in the 1970s, along with Calvino and Angela Carter, but this was pioneer work of the kind that had hardly been attempted since Virginia Woolf's *Orlando* in 1928.

Acker was not alone, but she was one of the few, and she was one of the few I was able to look to in the 1980s, when I wanted to put myself into my work in *Oranges Are Not the Only Fruit,* and, later, to use invented worlds, outside of the confines of realism.

Now, everything you read that is not a novel in the realist tradition is some ghastly creative writing school attempt at colliding history, geography, and time, or a dull memoir where the author slips themselves in as a character. Dear Reader, it was not always so . . .

Acker saw herself as dispossessed—from her homeland, because of its politics, and from literature, because she was a woman. Harold Bloom's seminal *The Anxiety of Influence* is fine if you are the son overthrowing the father, but what if you are the daughter? Many of the daughters in Acker fiction end up fucking their fathers. Some castrate him later because they have no other hope of freedom, no other means of revenge.

Acker took revenge on a male literary tradition by raiding it mercilessly; her so-called plagiarism is a way of appropriating what is otherwise denied. As a woman, she can't inherit. As a pirate, she can take all the treasure for herself.

Acker was never a woman writer, but she was a writer who was a woman. Her vulnerability as a woman in a man's world set her to use her body as text. She would be a writer—fuck 'em—but she would write from the place denied, despised, and desired by men. She would not deny her own body, indeed she treated it like a fetish item, adorning, tattooing, and piercing it, feeling directly the power of the image—the image of femaleness used and abused by men for centuries.

Her female characters are both dispossessed and abused, but they are strong too, and full of hope that is not disgust. Acker may be the true mother of Brat Pack writers like Bret Easton Ellis, but there is no disgust in her work. Vomit, shit, urine, cocks, cunts, assholes, blood, the body are intimately described, and not in the language of cloudy romance. Yet there is no disgust. Disgust is reserved for the hypocrites, the morons, the authority figures, the moneymen, the politicians. Transgression is never disgust—it is a way of surviving.

"'I want love—the love I can only dream about or read in books. I'll make the world into love.' This was the way Don Quixote transformed sickness into a knightly tool."

Acker believed that desire is the only honest part of us, and she believed that art is authentic desire. She never expected that art itself could transform the world, but she knew art could awaken in us the authentic desire buried under the meaninglessness of modern life. The responsibility to act on that desire is up to us.

* * *

Acker took the garbage, the waste, the revolt, the sickness and made it into a knightly tool—that is, something shining and bright, piercing and free, to cut life loose from its manacles.

She was edging fiction forward, just as she was trying to jab humanity into a little bit of consciousness. She was a moral writer— she had high ideals and a cause.

At the end of *Empire of the Senseless,* her character Abhor says:

"And then I thought that, one day, maybe, there'd be a human society in a world which is beautiful, a society which wasn't just disgust."

Editor's Note

How do you make a *Greatest Hits* out of a bunch of concept albums? Sounds impossible, but in fact, when it came to making this selection of excerpts from Kathy Acker's intricately conceived works, there was a certain logic to the task. Acker's roots in the avant-garde traditions of Dada and surrealism and her ongoing engagement with experimental writing practices made the prospect of cutting out a piece here and a piece there seem like a part of her project. Acker once said that the reader could pick up one of her books at any point, that it isn't necessary to read them from cover to cover.[1] The process of making this selection was not only not alien to the structures of her narratives, but sometimes it felt like an experiment to prove her right. Indeed, these excerpts stand brilliantly on their own.

Kathy Acker was one of the most influential writers of her generation. Putting this book together meant finding in each work examples of what makes Acker a pioneer, and what distinguishes her project from other late twentieth-century postmodernists.[2] Acker uses pre-existing texts, a practice some call plagiarism but it isn't exactly because 1. she's open about it, and 2. she alters those texts (at times they become unrecognizable), or she embeds chunks of another work into a new context, one that's so unfamiliar that the pirated text's meaning is radically distorted. Let's call it appropriation, for lack of a sexier term—the music industry came up with "sampling" years after Acker tried it in literature.

Appropriation challenges conventional forms of narrative, showing how a work is not simply reducible to the author, how the act of writing and reading is a more social project than the traditional novel would have us know. In Acker we meet Toulouse-Lautrec, Paolo Pasolini, Pip in *Great Expectations,* Don Quixote, Catherine in *Wuthering Heights* (Kathy renames her Cathy), Laure, Antonin Artaud, Arthur Rimbaud, Paul Verlaine, and in her final work *Pussy, King of the Pirates,* a whole new cast and crew on Treasure Island. Figures from voodoo, Western literature, Greek mythology, the Koran, her diaries, the newspaper: pull on a thread of an Acker narrative and you get history, psychoanalysis, literature, religion, current events, Kathy's life past, present, and fantasy. Using fragments of texts by other authors in combination with her own experience and inventions, Acker disturbs the central model of subjectivity that modern literature has reinforced.

In her early writings—*Blood and Guts in High School* (1978), *Great Expectations* (1982), *Don Quixote* (1986)—Acker investigates the first-person pronoun, the "I," breaking down the idea of a fixed central identity in favor of a schizophrenic model, blurring fact and fiction, memory and invention, male and female. Her tool is language, the foundational site of power in Western civilization. If she could destabilize meaning, decentralize narratives and identity, she could do her part to shake up the power structure and reinvent the world, and herself in it.

With *Empire of the Senseless* (1988) Acker turns to mythology as the over-arching structure for her work, to the communal myths that pervade our culture. Oedipus, Antigone, Eurydice, and others, serve as templates for dramas that are at once ancient and hauntingly contemporary. In particular, she focuses on patriarchy and, by extension, the modern family. It is within this world order that her characters become most tragic, and most autobiographical. Parents destroy and reject; they are the root of all evil—the father who wasn't there, the mother who suicided. Acker's heroines are orphans, pirates, and outlaws. They are people outside the family "romance," yet they are nonetheless defined by it.

At a pivotal time in her life Kathy worked in a strip club in New York City's Time Square. The experience of the sex industry and the stories she heard from the other girls would find their way into almost everything she wrote. Not wanting to come off sounding sociological, she put all the stories in first person, contributing to readers' false impression that her work is entirely autobiographical. What these stories and her experience (while brief) brought to her work is a visceral understanding of the exploitation of women in the sex trade and a totally antiromantic perspective on relations between men and women. She discovered a political use for pornography, a way of disrupting polite society. Acker is always oscillating between worlds— bourgeois and bohemian, narrative and avant garde, couture and biker. Inserting porn into the literary, she refuses to choose sides. What cannot be overestimated is the pleasure Kathy took in writing porn, finding the exactly right cadence and rhythm: using language, pushing limits, turning on.

Still, sexuality in Acker's work is a site of confusion—and it's within that confusion that her female characters come alive, expressing who they are and what they want. They are victims who crave and get revenge. Sexually voracious, they have exploits which leave them ravenous, humiliated, and victorious all at once. Acker's women are desiring women. Desire is a place of not yet having: it's in the becoming, the longing, the imagining, that Acker wants her women to exist.

The title *Essential Acker* is paradoxical, for Kathy Acker was anything but an essentialist. She embraced in her work and in her life both a fascination for and insistence on the pluralities that exist within every so-called certainty.

The task at hand has been to select from the twenty-three works by Acker—the novels, novellas, and stories; not the essays—those excerpts that best demonstrate Acker's innovation and distinction. My coeditor Dennis Cooper and I often commented on how daunting it was to reread all of Acker's books in quick succession. Acker obsessively returns to themes of love, power, and abandonment throughout her three decades of novel writing. Her passions are relentless. She is fearless in what her narratives encompass, which makes the task of excerpting feel like something of a dare. Always rigorous and playful, sexy and repelling, inventive and proverbial, these excerpts are testimony to the breadth of Acker's ambition and the joy she took in repetition.

If you've already read some or all of the books, this volume suggests new ways to read Acker, and how each novel is part of a larger project. If you've never read a Kathy Acker book, *Essential Acker* will introduce you to this writer's inimitable prose, and to her obsessions which might just become your own. Think of it as a tour through the work of one of the late twentieth century's most innovative and radical thinkers. Let it guide you to her individual novels; then go read them in their entirety. There's nothing like it. Acker is a one-way street, and if you've learned anything from this writer, it's to be fearless enough to go down it with her.[3] Once you do, there's no turning back.

—Amy Scholder, May 2002

1. From a conversation with Sylvere Lotringer published in *Hannibal Lecter, My Father* (New York: Semiotext(e), 1991).
2. I am indebted to Peter Wollen's "Don't be Afraid to Copy it Out," a brilliant essay on Acker's development and achievements as a writer. It originally appeared in *London Review of Books*, vol. 20, no. 3 (February 1998).
3. The experience of reading and knowing Kathy Acker has always brought to my mind the dedication Walter Benjamin wrote to his lover for the work, *One-Way Street*: "This street is named / Asja Lacis Street / after her who as an engineer / cut through the author."

Essential
Acker

from "Politics"

(My first work, written when 21 years old)

t he filthy bedcover on stage I'm allergic to this way of life mine? the last time I got on stage for the first ten minutes I felt I wasn't me I was going through mechanical personality changes and actions I got scared I might flip in front of the sex-crazy lunatics finally got into the Santa Claus routine I was a little girl all excited because Santa Claus was going to bring me Christmas presents I couldn't go to sleep I was waiting and waiting and then and then you know what happened doctor Santa Claus came right into my room I'm taking my clothes my shoes off rubbing my breasts Lenny dreamt last night about fucking Cyrelle she was lecturing him on how to fuck a woman he told her that he didn't need the lecture she thought he was wrong he was sucking an older woman's cunt it was also a cock without changing from a cunt this is a romantic section a very romantic life ha ha I was writing in the projection room the shits said they'd clean and wax the floor it's still piss black can't see no roaches no more it's hotter than usual the projectionist was constantly bugging me some guy they say drunk hit Josie on her ass during her show yesterday his hat the cashier says he came up told him you're not allowed to bring liquor up here then the cashier an Indian guy turns to Washington an old black janitor tells him that he's not to come again on the weekends he has no mind he can't remember anything he's not to ask to get paid again he gets $1.00 he's too old he won't be able to work much longer he's sick he's senile he's looking at me red blearing eyes we're at the Embers cruddy food at least no one's taking off his clothes they all want to SCREW this week (we find in the projection room) is about orgies mentions every place but ours only the fuzz know about 113 swingers SCREW says are very jealous about their mates? you can't get involved with a girl you fuck at an orgy unless you've got her guy's OK which isn't they say likely I don't know about vice versa at an orgy everyone wants to have everyone else only once no two guys together the males want to watch the females screw so that occurs it turns them on the best orgy I ever went to a cunt's writing started with two girls making it on the livingroom floor Lenny tells me Lawrence is a romantic Kangaroo red and black striped overalls no hair I don't know what the fuck to do with it I'm getting to look so ugly it won't do anything like stand straight out fuzz into balls two more shows and everything's over I felt dead writing before I could be dead now waking up I got a sacred Mexican ring yesterday to do just that remember every single dream for the next two weeks as soon as I wake up not getting so pissed off all the time completely hostile I'd like Jewels this life's not romantic enough too hidden yet to be found in the fucking brain and mind I have to get back to the show Lenny's putting on his coat son of a bitch

after we had dinner at this god awful chinese restaurant fake chinese gardens the waiter shit wouldn't give another bowl to us for the winter melon soup for two on the menu Mickey was barely able to kiss Mark goodbye we went to Mark's house 13th and A stories about how If you venture out there after dark one block or more you automatically get raped mugged castrated we smoked went into the bedroom to see the new waterbed it was gorgeous like being in the ocean the waves lapping back and forth it was the only thing in the room except for a tape deck white walls no curtains Mark said he was going to paint the walls different shades of blue striped in a funnel the rug would be dyed to match the ceiling the floor would be an actual funnel you'd go right through I was completely smashed Mark was hot for Lenny spent an hour? two hours? making these absurd hints he only wanted to sleep with Ellen the new dancer Lenny was playing dumb too smashed or not digging he finally said do you want to sleep with me Lenny didn't want me to leave the room I didn't want to leave the waterbed under any circumstances my dress kept getting undone earlier in the evening Mark had been kissing me he gave a speech about male male fucking god knows why he ever wants a female I said I the fucking cats didn't want to sleep with Mark Mark said he'd prefer Lenny between the two of us he'd take us both he didn't think I was ugly I was so complimented I didn't want to watch watching Lenny fuck someone and not being able to be involved wanting to would blow me Mark kept pushing Lenny telling me to go into the livingroom Lenny didn't want me there Ronny came in Bill Blass jumpsuit blue with a thin white belt Bill Blass scarf my my richies Hanky Panky crackers from Boston I ate one and didn't like it Mark wanted to go back to the livingroom I wanted to get out of there back to the cats I prefer gay guys because I'm not under pressure constantly to fuck them watch if my clothing's always closed which it's not I was feeling anomalous Mark started saying the mattress in the waterbed on the waterbed is torn I have to fix it he even threaded a real needle Lenny can you help me Ronny's cracking ridiculous jokes Mark's done it so often he even has it timed Mark says you can watch Ronny's not a voyeur we watch Rat-Race Debbie Schmereynolds an incredibly creepy flic in which Debbie's a good girl who'd rather give up her guy than prostitute I don't remember if she's living with him in sin it was very romantic Ronny and I were finally talking Johnny Carson turned on crude gags about hookers drag queens everyone's one for fun I'm learning about Middle America the whole place is mad I'm cold to Lenny don't admit I am which is nasty I want to see my cats Mark has one Tiffany she's seven weeks pregnant and crawls through almost closed windows and bars no one else comes it was a party not even Mickey Mark said that Mickey would be very upset if he knew that Mark slept with anyone else Mark would if Mickey did it's quite nutty there's this rich guy Jack who's been supporting Mark still is? they have an expensive looking place not much furniture yet no books of course we're open for any garbage I get pissed off when Mark kisses me and calls me a girl he's upset I am I try to relax rub him goodnight Lenny's acting like he's lost his mind we get a ride with this dope seller creep doesn't know why anyone would live in a commune not enough money to the Eighth Street subway this is the first dream sequence 1:17 I have to go out for the rest of the day get my hair cut again thank god.

(1968)

3

from *The Burning Bombing of America: The Destruction of the U.S.*

(for H. in the hospital)

s this in no place gentle? end of the journey. rubble piles of the shit of the poor   green vomit   clouds and darkness are around us   the cat-weather (wo)men rise up   are killed   arise from the dead there is no stopping now   with huge whips we walk on the dogs   the parks have died   our legs gone   through our own and everyone's blood   through masses of insects   the ship leaves the harbor like a knife   sapphire water   through the empty buildings of the kings where now huge cats eat the leaves. nipples rub against the stone   she raises her head   endless curls thrown back   her fingers caress planets (we no longer know what's happening) 1. matter exploded   the separate spheres rush away from each other through space 2. matter is continuously spontaneously creating itself in the center of the universe 3. through holes in the universe enters the matter of other universes. the mind disappears   she throws out her arms   cat at every pore   cats whose tails are curled around the dirt of the three worlds. but gentleness has to be our real life. writing is the use of information without the source of the information. Heaven gives to the deficient   takes away from the abundant   men   the evil magicians of the city   prey   blood-crazed parasites   the poor. can't get hold of people anymore. is velvet soft? do plants yield? cats love human-people. the rug disappears beneath the feet   we both want someone to sleep with   Bob Dylan shits out money   notice where the money is   you'll find out where the killers lie   the men who are annihilating the universe   don't joke   you're recovering   recovering from the hatred of the doctor how does one (we) recover? what is happening? L. sits on top of the bookcase P. on the blue table Y. in her home noise from the radio and the street L. is asleep (no information) the Tao T Ching: excess leads to bad things.

we search out the evil magicians with sharpened knives a rest we lie in wait. end of the first discussion of my first gentlest love.

the cry of desire now make a movie
too much noise endless swarms of people the elevator plunges and destroys ten old women H. is in touch with the Big Man and the Big Lady end the War end the War Spanish people dancing on the concrete under my city body happy people happy people move the muscles around the clit each part B. and H. and G. and T. and L. who's going insane? who's scared to the point of insanity? refuses to ask help who's so lonely for actual touch/discussion? won't find anyone to open to die on the spot. you fuck-puke nonperson you think your preach language says anything human/ real you think all human thoughts and desires not directly concerning the Vietnam War are not real needs indications of insane emptiness. I'm going to call you up this evening I was paranoid you'd take away my reading you don't like my work. I hurt. you're pure strength because you say one thing. to kill the Evil Magicians communism is needed endless sex the cycle of the weather and plants the meeting of the inside and outside of all. food and shelter. people who when they show they love you love you. this is this Sunday. this is a communistic Sunday as usual I'm alone went past the firehouse cruising back to safe territory subway home safer territory (cats) I don't want to be alone I know no other way of being I disguise even now to myself my desire ((disguised)) revolutionary sex-love-lust. huge cats prowl inside my toes and legs they're at war extend claws through my cunt the elevator planks of wood with a string tied in the middle rises up on one side I hold on to the string a stranger holds on to the string on the other the stars rush away from each other at rates proportional to their distance from the center of the universe these are the Evil Magicians: not only the Vietnam War every fucking

minute   every desire that cannot be filled   now   now   now   now
now   now. these are the enemy you stupid schmuck   nonyoga knowing schmuck   I change identity   I'm climbing up the stairs ? to AW's
apartment   I trip   I fly away   the jewels of the night glow in your
hands   your bones come through your skin   huge prowling feet
Your night and sound   your armpits are covered with the human skin
of your lovers   you rise to the center of the universe.

(for L.)

And then   the city arises   rises from your cunt   golden star   there
are no buildings but silk and thick cotton tents   animals   deer with
hands for legs run down the pavilions   people with them   at the same
rate. there are no families   but centers   warm breast   living person
when I need to have my muscles lifted out placed on a flat surface
rubbed   I need to have socks put on my feet by L. so by the morning
I fall asleep   no families ruin the hearts of women and men by forc-
ing them through torture to desire   outlawed desires   you are healthy
again   you are able to run with two legs   the doctor who killed you
has stopped killing you   what of the politicians   what of the layer
of weapons like streams hidden beneath the streets $ has become
an image $ has become an illusion   dream followed by 1% of the
population bad acid-speed   no drugs are necessary   L. and I no
longer fuck   what will happen in one week?   the New City arises
I place diamonds in the hair of your cunt   you who I can desire   birds
with red and purple feathers grow out of the branches of trees   on
one small tree   one inch below each branch   hang strings of yellow
flowers   berries and tea for breakfast   huge peaches   savory grass
heartease   purple basil   rue   tansy (poison)   laurel   cinnamon
olive tree   lamb's ears   quince   spearmint   parsely   curled mint
forget-me-nots   rosemary   summer savory   wild, grass   chives bloom
into purple flowers   we are extremely irritable   it becomes easier not
to deal with people   to tell people we're not home   we find it difficult to stay alive   in the distance   to the left   the old witch ran after
us   a huge stick surrounded by metal spikes in her hand   she changed

into a small white bird   a huge fish in the pond we had to jump across
a fat townsman tried to make his horses kill us   tried to flay open
our flesh with thin whips   worms came out of our ass   a beggar
asked for help   who are we to believe   for a second the town opened
its gate   we ran inside to a small building   a deer served us   a fal-
con bid us good-day   we no longer want to be human   it is simple:
you need another operation   they're trying to kill you because you're
poor   the poor live outside the law. our cunts are silver daggers   we
shall live in a new world

Information Sexual Ecstacy Revolution III

the moon clashes against the light, you touch me O nymphomania!
China. the revolution   a beginning that makes sense the peasants tortured.   without food   turn over   a new life   a (wo)man wants to
control his/her life   I will sacrifice all happiness for the sake of self-
control. I will do anything to maintain my ability to make decisions.
throw the bomb. we plant bombs in the edges of the rabble   fire escapes below Soho   we kill everyone! I am starving   I don't have a
phone   I hide the money I've earned by selling my cunt beneath the
stove   in a crack in the wall   I decide I've earned enough money for
four months   decide I'll stop working   I freak out   A. comes to the
door   she's going to see me with B.   I'm looking at the white sink
I can't control myself   I start crying   I tell A. how I've been getting
money I'm starving   I'm without shelter   I'm scared to walk down
the street   Monsters   she'll be able to find me a part-time shit job   you
have to rest   B. doesn't come up   the new world is beginning   a long
time elapses   the Cat-Women are meeting   their purring decides our
lives   their huge thighs house our sperm   I serve a Cat   I lick her
nipples continuously   I mix the cream of goats   grind corn and wheat
I rub my hair into the inside of Her legs   I depend for comfort upon
every one of Her moods   I stick my tongue into Her black leather lips.
I am being controlled. I will plant bombs   I secretly walk along the
streets   the revolution is one man   the revolution is the ability to
choose   the Revolution is the recognition of   becoming   silver-thighed

Nymphomaniacs and Whores. beautiful human-animals   I also am part human   I have given up my humanity   I am one of the black-winged vulture   killers of light.

all plants and animals burst into flames/light   through the hole   the circle of waters   we walk to the New City at night   flamethrowers color bombs   cats fly through your hair   governing men   the Tao Te Ching   is like governing horses   we are ready   the images are ready we are ready to move at the first sign of morning   who do you except we except no one   our criminals stand at the pawnshops   our beggars bite through your calves   the City bursts into flames   ITT explodes   CUNY-Nixon headquarters explode   at the height   anything you can do anything   I'm too scared to ask you to sleep with me   hello means I'm alive   the government we do over ourselves requires that we fulfill our regular constant nature then   we be left to ourselves. this is necessary information   this is to be read slowly   half through dream. the government of the richies   Nixon and Rockefeller and General Motors   is planting long jellyfish worms in our bodies   we are asked to be patient our legs are being mutilated by giant saws. medical science has advanced. the age of perfect virtue   this age   will be destroyed by the Teachers'-Politicians' insistence on the practice of benevolence righteousness   ceremonies   and music. Power to destruction and chaos to the half-men hiding beneath the streets   the Cat-Women prey on dead meat   their long legs come down from the sun. O to sleep between the warm thighs of a Cat-Woman   hair and eyes given vision by her cunt   you mutilated Cat-Woman   your home is in the reaches of the insane moon   you are my partner   you are my partner in the destruction and discovering of paradise. end-of-the-world weather. I'm not scared of being a dyke   huge women   not men   they don't think they're men   they fight with their nipples   they climb up trees to mock the disappearing cars. I'm not scared anymore   we're not scared anymore   this writing is proof   the revolution needs all our love.

desire.
we desire a revolution in New York   I'm here alone always alone Mick Jagger jerks off   I shoulder my pistols   strap on my double

chastity-belt skunk killer   the cats have disappeared   women are hidden under Central Park   in the beds not yet sold   breast open to breast birds wet their fingers   is there a revolution   where's the revolution someone make love to me   want me to make love to you   the skies break open   BOOM   we know what's going on   RAIN   a sexual-lust-anti-lobotomy revolution   I desire women therefore am going to be sterilized   brains turn to disease-worms lips wrenched off by torture-pliers   no   pain   pain   I'm happier than I've ever been   the revolution (this) is to be obtained by doing nothing   by passionless and purposeless action   the operation of the heaven and the earth. this is for A.   B.   J.   who I constantly fantasize about   I'm never going to sleep with you. fall asleep in the bath   1½ hours   mind wanders between the moon and its light. about sex. on Her swing   suspended from the center of the universe   She could lift me   She could treat me as She would a favorite cat playing with me between her footlong fingers the exile   She could throw me into free fall   Her birds with long green tail feathers red parrots from space   peck at my heart. where does this come from? 2. we talk to a skull   a Chinese sage with thin wrinkled hands   we tell him of the happiness of the state after death. this state. we are crouched in the corners of their closets   we plan the state's destruction in whatever way possible   the first method we use   NOW STATED   random choice. flip through the universe without your senses do not control desire. follow desire wherever it leads you take what magic   good and evil   is offered. your hair is pure silver   your cunt is an animal   your thin face controls my dream.
I move out   onto the streets   tigers and rhinoceros surround me   I sniff in the direction of the stars   my killer friends approach   The Man OK   last night   rape   L. shoots J. in the guts   H.'s mind is slowly being made useless by huge doctors   where are you going   I won't be able to see you today   L.'s seeing you   what is real? political action the negation of evil   the freeing of our ability to love   the destruction of the state. chapter of the day.

(1972)

from *Rip-off Red, Girl Detective*

1. April 20

I'm five foot three inches brown hair curling all over my face, bright green eyes, I'm 26 but my body's tough from dancing if you know what I mean—well I got bored doing a strip, well first, I got bored doing that Ph.D. shit and being frustrated professors' straight-A pet, especially being faithful to a husband who spent all his time in bed dealing out poker hands; I left school, descended to the more interesting depths and became a stripper, even that finally bored me, so I decided, on my 26th birthday, to become the toughest detective alive.

This is the story about how I have kept myself from being bored.

I was lying in bed with Peter; he had on his leather jacket and wrist bands; I woke up as the noon sun hit my face through the window; a cat started howling. I put my hands around his hips, I could see the thick whiteness and the dark hairs in the insides of my eyes; my nose burrowed in his neck, then inside his ear as far as I could get. He turned slightly toward me so I could caress him better, and moaned I had fallen for him first because he loved to be loved and showed it Most men act cagey and think they shouldn't show any feelings. Peter rubbed his blond beard against my cheek, moved his body against under mine. Our legs entangled; I felt his breath against my ear, then his lips on the skin of the ear, his tongue darted back and forth. Shivers ran through my spine, I felt his hand on my left breast squeeze slowly squeeze, my lower muscles started moving. With my teeth I pulled at the hairs on his chin moved my mouth up to his lips slowly pressed my lips against his, moving back and forth until I felt his mouth open. For a long time we kissed I could feel his lower body pulse against mine, his muscles hardened, I let my hand drift down to where I knew he liked to be touched best he wasn't going to get it that early as his lips started to touch barely touch my nipple as if they were the wind and the shivers started rolling again up down my spine, I let my fingers pull gently at the soft hairs under Peter's cock; I ran my middle finger up and down the muscle behind his huge cock, at the warm wet creases between his legs and cock, just between not-feeling and his feeling tickled. His legs opened, his breathing became heavy fast; I let my other hand curve under his body; my finger caressed his asshole, not into it, but just enough of a caress so that he remembered all the millions of wonderful nerves curling inside and around his prostate gland. The muscles around my clit started tightening and loosening; my consciousness and the center of my body became my breasts then my stomach then the whole abdominal region—I could smell myself—then the region of beauty and fur between my legs. Peter's hand slipped from my back down to the inward curve above my ass in response I pressed my thighs against his, I felt his cock rise and fall against my opening thighs. His finger slipped between my buttocks into my asshole I moved my body faster, usually I like to be licked but this time I was too hot, I thought I would come from just the touch of his hands. I never liked anyone as much as this. The covers became all tangled dogs and cats started howling in the streets we moved faster faster; "let's cut the crap," I said, "and get down to business."

I rolled on my back I like to feel solid weight on me; Peter quickly moved on top of me. I like to feel cuddled: I pulled the covers over his back, let my hands rest on his back under the covers. I could feel his cock throbbing against me, I couldn't wait until he got in me and the real shivers start spasms crawling up down my body like electric eels inside my nerves until I start coming and coming and coming. Peter starts purring like a kitten rubbing against my damp skin and hair I open my legs his cock hardens inside then I feel him move deeper the pain stops he moves deeper as the rhythm starts as he starts moving back and forth still slowly I rise up I move into my clit into every microinch his cock touches I roll over a swan's neck into a quick orgasm a good beginning! He starts, as I come, to move fast quick higher up against my clit my hands scratch his back at the edge of pain I come again all feeling centers in my clit ah ahh AHH take a breath aahh I roll to a peak. Down.

Take a breath.

As I fall into dream, he starts again moving slowly, this time gently long strokes against my cunt, so that I barely feel him inside me, I start moving with him without disturbing my dreams I'm buying a dress I design dark green velvet fur a slit up my right leg which is as long as Peter's leg to my black cunt hair sparkles as brilliantly as diamonds, the dream changes I'm buying the most gorgeous dress in the world I fall into piles of velvet thick white Chinese satins. As I start coming again remember I'm fucking, I throw my thighs upward press my abdomen, now open to thousands of sensations, against his, I feel his cock tremble inside me, is he going to stop? Keep going. Keep going. His strokes shorten he moves from side to side to delay my orgasm no I can't stand it I throw my body against his, more! More! He starts moving back and forth again like I like it it's happening it happens again again!

"Did you come?"

"Not yet."

"I can't tell when the fuck you come."

I'm too sensitive I can't stand to have his cock in my cunt against my cunt, I can't stop coming, I keep moving. Barely so I can feel his desire. We fall to the left; his arm moves under me; his middle finger slips into my ass: that's the center of my brain! That's where all my thoughts are located! We swing against each other deep into the freezing then fiery center of the earth around, now it' a working, I want to come to, I want to get mine in I can feel his muscles move beyond his will, tense some then more, we're still moving in curves only faster, faster and harder; his finger leaves my asshole: rays of light shoot inside me from my ass to my belly button to my clit: the Holy Trinity O it's coming I don't give a shit anymore where he's at or what's doing; my clit and my mind are one being light shoots through my body clit to legs! Clit to nape of the neck and outwards! Heat shoots through my body! Sound supersonic fluorescent waves.

I've had enough for the moment.

Peter still keeps moving; I watch a mosquito dash against the lightbulb; finally I make the decision. "Listen sweetheart."

"What do you want now."

"We can't fuck all the time; we've got to do something more exciting."

"We could stop starving."

"I can write a book. I want to do something better than fuck."

"You dykes are all alike: best fucks around haw haw."

"Shut up creep."

"Anyway fucking's a bore."

"I'm going to change my name. You' re my brother and you' re going to have to go along with everything I do, be my secretary, and wait for me until I return from each assignment."

"Where are we going to go?"

"From now on you're Peter Peter and I'm Rip-off Red the famous detective. We're going to go East; in spite of the Mafia, the Jewish Mafia, and Mr. Nixon, we're going to get rich quick."

"On the road?"

"Listen. This is a dream. We're going to New York to rip off the money. Everyone in New York's an anarchist or a junky and many of the anarchists are junkies. We'll wander through the zoo; when the zookeepers are in the bathrooms, shooting up, we'll jump into the seal ponds with the seals. We'll nibble at their black velvet ears, with our secret hands rub their businessmen bellies; we'll fuck in front of the lions until we're howling more than they are. Listen. I'm going to go out this second down to Tijuana, rip myself off a black satin detective suit so I can set up business in New York as soon as possible: we'll rent a floor in a building on Madison Avenue in the Sixties, two rooms bare of furniture like a Japanese hara-kiri house; we'll have a sign on the door:

> Mr./Mrs. Red, Detective
> Peter Peter, Detective

We won't wear guns but carry junk needles; anyone who opposes us will receive an instant high. You have to protect me in all emergencies and tell me I'm wonderful. Listen."

"You're wonderful," confesses Peter Peter. "Where're we going to get all this money?"

"Money doesn't exist, of course. Don't worry about it; I don't. I just want everyone to love me. To love me and you."

This is Peter Peter's fairy tale as he falls asleep: Afternoon has begun. He's going to be a millionaire, eat snails and wine, fuck as much as he wants.

End of the dream.

Peter Peter puts his head on my shoulder, his hand over my still wet hairs. Am I interested? I put my head near his right nipple, he doesn't seem to mind. My lips barely touch his nipple; then, as his hand presses against me, against my cunt, as his hand slowly opens and closes, exerting gentle constant pressure, I quickly brush my tongue against his nipple, as it hardens. I turn my head to the side; touching his nipple excites me too much; I return, my mouth becoming my eyes and hands; I don't know what's a happening, I can tell I feel strongly Peter moans, presses his lips hard against mine. I kiss his lips, this time move straight down to his white stomach; his flesh is firm and thick like a child's. Sexy as a child's. I curl my tongue into his belly button until the tip of his cock aches. Meanwhile my hands roughly massage his cock and balls squeeze pull, the more he pulsates, the harder I squeeze. I bite his inner thighs, pull with my mouth at the hairs around his balls; I roll his balls in my mouth; I run my tongue into his asshole and around toward his cock, do everything but touch his cock in order to drive him as insane as possible. I keep this up for hours: he moans; the moaning turns into harsh sighs. Suddenly I reach for his cock let my mouth slip over his cock until the tip of his cock is in my throat. I let my tongue alternately press at the under tip of his cock right at the edge of the hole then curl arabesques up and down the length of his gorgeous plunger. Quickly I spit into my hand, run my hand around his cock, corkscrew; in an opposite motion, twist my throat around and around. I play with rhythms: I start light and slow, go faster with heavy pressure and emphasis on the pressing tongue. As Peter moves faster I reach a low peak, then start again, slow, deliberate; I let him rest, and slowly again get into moving with motion of my mouth and hands. I move my mouth and hands more this time, accentuate the corkscrew motion; we work together; I move faster, take more cock into my throat. No, I've lost him. I don't stop, but move more slowly. We meet; now I've lost consciousness; I'm a machine of throat, mouth, tongue, hand symmetries and pressures; my body pulsates in sympathy. I no longer know if I'm doing a good job. This lasts forever; time intercedes, I can feel his cock expand; I push my tongue, my throat grasp; I become a gymnast, a snake; Peter moans; his whole body moves now his hands rest on my head I start sucking use my tongue more his cock grows enormous I can't his hands press my head down I can feel two muscles which run up the sides of his cock wriggle, the liquid rushes into my mouth I press my lips against him in rhythm with his coming, now. I lift my head up for air, quick swallow, then gather him in again was it good? Now I'm resting against his shoulders. Below my outer skin there's a layer of shining warmth; I savor my horniness, keep it till it increases impossibly.

2. April 28

We borrow money from Peter Peter's father, I'd love to fuck the whole family, and go to New York. I'm a tough dame.

On the plane, the mystery begins.

Peter Peter and I sit next to the window; we throw coins, Peter Peter wins the seat next to the window.

"You're an old shit-ass."

"I'll sleep with you any day. No, I'm too scared."

We drink two martinis, then I down a beer and two glasses of champagne. New York champagne, but these days there's a depression. I seem to be weightless; no, it's just the atmosphere inside the airplane. My body floats in waves, an endless air ocean. That's it, I'm as drunk as an Irishman; I'm both inside the airplane and outside, a true beautiful angel sailing among white elephants and kangaroos.

What's this? The swirling area travels down to my stomach, around my half-asleep sweet ass, to my cunt; muscles move in and out between my legs, I try pressing my legs together, rub my lower ass against the seat. No one seems to be looking. There's a woman sitting next to me, on the aisle seat, mmm she's beautiful, well she's asleep. Is she pretending? I pull my coat over my legs to my waist; I've become a cripple. I slide my hand under the coat, under my black velvet pants, I'm pretending to read (I know how); I press the bottom end of the book against my clit, right below the bone, that helps a little, I move O just slightly! back and forth, I can't be too obvious. The secrecy I usually hate makes my horniness build, the body of a woman next to me and completely untouchable, that's right, hands off! the whole public scene makes my nerves soar, white frenzy, in response to my frustration. Like a fox, a true detective, I sneak my hand under my blue jeans, at least I'm not wearing underpants today, there's not enough freedom. I unsnap my blue jeans. No, no one's looking; they're all as drunk as I am, even drunker and hornier, and they're not going to do anything about it, they must have great dreams, I'll solve all their problems mmm. Peter Peter's head falls against my shoulder; I put my arm around him, kiss him on his soft neck, he's become a snoring bear. Meanwhile my hand, no longer part of my body, my fingers slowly caress the flesh above my hairs and between my legs. I want to play with my desires, I want to gain control of them so I can bring myself higher, and higher to the most incredible climax possible. The plane disappears, the seat on which I'm sitting falls out from under me; I'm suspended in space by strings of diamonds the paws of cats rub against my ears. As my long fingers enter the mysterious hairs, the tight silk curls which cover my cunt, I rub the skin below my hairs quickly, then with the middle fingers press up and down above my clit, taunt the clit. I force myself to strain toward the orgasm, for my cunt to imagine the orgasm. My other hand, above the black coat, presses down on my womb; I concentrate on that mild delight, try to forget the more potent delight my fingers are giving me. My nipples swell, I can feel each tender pore; in the back of my eyes, I have a soft breast in my mouth, as my tongue plays with the nipple, it becomes harder harder. No, none of that; I begin playing the usual game with myself: my fingers belong to me and my cunt doesn't. I concentrate on how the flesh of my fingers feels as they caress a strange clit and deny the heavy pleasure my clit is showing. One finger, now, presses up and down up down above the clit, now just on the clit, not too hard yet, not too fast, just so the rhythm and pressure of the finger is a bit slower than the feelingless rhythm of my desire. Somewhere deep I still remember those sensations between my legs; I can't concentrate completely on just the feelings in the skins of my finger. Try harder. I disregard the strength of the approaching orgasm, I'm not scared because I'm not dwelling on the orgasm. No, I've lost myself: I'm not interesting enough to myself. In a book I'm a middle-aged house-wife and I'm sick of fucking my husband. We've been happily and monogamously married for a hundred years. It's the midafternoon; my husband's away at work, we live in the suburbs. The doorbell rings. It's only the grocery boy.

"Just put the groceries down there." I look again; he's slight, dark-haired, he'd be sleazy if he wasn' t sooo, so what? "What'sa your name?"

He trembles, looks strangely at me. Why don't you come sit beside me. I pat a space next to me, well, practically on top of me. He sits down, not so close, he's just a kid.

"Do you do this all the time?"

"I . . . I." He shivers. I take his hand, put it around me, on my violet breast, our lips meet. I let my hand fall to his cock, caress it.

Now my desire soars; my finger can't move fast enough, deep enough as I start to fly. Wait, slow down, control the waves so they last longer, roll deeper. I hold back, let myself rise. I lose myself, no, I have to start my finger press again, rhythmically, foreseeably, now. Now. Now, Now. I let the hard burning rise, my clit swells to un-bearable proportions, suddenly I feel fur silk on my cheek a strange animal in my hair, I don't care what the hell's happening. I'm in a brothel and a thousand thick Arabs are seducing me. The muscles of my upper legs tense, my legs rise slightly upward from my calves. The legs and buttocks part from each other; the wave rises, down slightly, by will I make my finger move faster, the stranger pulls at my hair with thin fur fingers. I start orgasming stronger; I force by iron will my finger to move more rapidly, more crazily than possible; finally I begin to rise, I rise even farther, suddenly I move vertically: there: the queen. Before I know I've reached it, I've forgotten everything, two huge hands grasp my head and turn me toward another head. I look into huge blue eyes, I move my mouth toward the skin near the nose, then toward the mouth and we start to kiss.

I feel soft lips under mine, softer than Peter Peter's, they feel so soft I want to press into them again and again. I do, I'm sinking, my face is sinking into a thick quilt, through the tiny space among the fold of the cotton I let my tongue drift into this strange mouth. I don't want to stop, I don't even want to stay still, I might get scared at what's happening, I'd have to find out who I'm kissing. Our tongues touch, lightly, then mingle, saliva swirls around, I feel my spine disintegrate and my arms fall around this thin back. For hours we kiss inside each other's mouths stroke identical heads of curling hairs; my hands press under the ears.

Now desire doesn't center in my clit but turns around my body, my nerves swirl until my whole body shivers and trembles to touch this stranger in every way and everywhere. My mouth becomes even softer, thicker; my arms curve in toward the chest. My hands pass over her heavy breasts, to their bottom, low heavy soft breasts under a light sweater; I lay my palms over her nipples press gently, do you like that? Her wire tongue darts over my ear, she nibbles at the lobe of my ear so I'm slightly excited; suddenly her tongue pierces my ear ice-cold. I shiver; she blows into my ear and sends frantic nerve waves throughout my body how can I kiss her breast is everyone staring at us?

"Come to the bathroom."

"We have to be cautious," I whisper back, secretly. "You go first; when no one's looking, I'll follow."

She leaves me. What do I feel? What am I thinking? Do I feel anything? Five minutes pass by; I follow her. We squeeze into the tiny bathroom and start giggling, There's no room to move a hand, much less a tongue. I look at her, suddenly frightened and confused: do I dare touch her, could she possibly want me to touch her. I can feel myself blush, no, she's taller than me, pretty rather than beautiful, curly yellow red brown hair, a nose that seems to wink.

"Do everything I say."

I'll follow her implicitly; she can do anything to me except leave me. She takes my hand; with my fingers she strokes her eyelids, the skin directly below her hair, then her cheeks. I follow her, tell her I love her, I want to be her, we're beginning, now we're beginning. Are you still scared. She lifts my hand, it grows lighter, places it under her sweater; she strokes her breast with me, I'm her animal, I learn to stroke her breast. We're twins; breast against breast somehow.

"Can I suck your breast?"

The nipple burns my tongue; I can feel the child suction begin in my mouth. I pass my tongue slowly over the nipple; her nipples are large. Her hands rub my neck and shoulders so that I have to move even closer to her. We murmur; I murmur; I begin to suck again on her nipple, then on the other one as that one hardens, as her whole body tenses. I can't go through with this. I don't know how to give her pleasure. As I suck, her thighs thrust forward against my strained stomach and chest, she reaches downward her hand to my cunt; "I can't," "What do you want?" I'm scared I let my hand fall against her cunt; she envelops me. "Kiss again," we kiss again. "Are you OK?" I remember: I'm in school, we're two children making love, we rub noses and bellies. I sit on her lap on the tiny toilet: I can feel her desire, I can feel mine I put my hand on her pulsating cunt, undo her pants and touch her, she moves harder. I press one inch below her hair and lower, at first try not to press her clit lest I irritate her. She moves against. Each time she begins to move faster, I move my hand faster; finally with thumb and second finger I touch her clit. Lightly, I press it systematically she moans into my ear I press the palm of my hand into her cunt bones I caress her clit I adore her clit I moan faster all I want her to do is come. Her fingers clench the back of my neck; I can feel her sweat. As she begins to move beyond her will, I thrust three fingers up her cunt, I rub her clit hard, fast insane motion, she peaks I think, I kiss her neck, she peaks again. I keep my hand on her cunt, pressing, until she calms down. Her head lies in my arms, I hold her, as proud as if I just had a kid.

She lifts me until I'm standing; I feel her hands rub against each of my sides. Her long fingers press into the fronts of my legs into my stomach. I remember her coming I pulse I want her to help me. She plays with me; I look down and see her face. Something touches my cunt, "lower," our eyes meet, "that's too much. Lower." I feel her tongue touch the skins just below my clit; her tongue moves back and forth slowly. My hands rest in her hair, pull and scratch as she moves into me further and further. Her tongue rises, O, clicks against me I'm hot all over I can't concentrate "concentrate." As I begin to come, her tongue runs into my uterus, no, a man's fucking me, a soft hard cock's inside me, softer more delicious than a cock; my muscles fall open, I'm open to anything, I want my rising to start. The cock touches every inch of my vagina, every hidden flaming nerve soothes, each time she touches me I start coming. She rushes against me; her whole body throbs, I want her now I forget her I know only the soft pounding soft irritating of my clit, I want it there I go a little higher; there; each touch is another step. Every inch of my flesh is throbbing: shorter, quicker there I come in my ass there in my cunt, her whole mouth takes hold of me, I'm completely safe I come.

This isn't typical of a hard-boiled detective, a detective who chooses intellectual pursuits over emotional ones. I have no right to be scared. Well, I'm a female detective; I don't pay attention to that shit about intellectual versus emotional. I decide she's my sister.

We put on clothes.

"I'll leave first."

I watch her leave. I look at myself in the mirror; five minutes later leave the bathroom. As I return to my seat, she looks at me and brushes my cheek gently with her hand.

"What' a your name?"

"Rip-off Red."

"Mine's Spitz. I've always wanted to be like you; you're not as scared as I am. I don't have any profession; I'm scared I'm useless."

"I'm a detective."

"You're a detective, a real detective, can I . . ."

"I was trained in the Sherlock Marlowe School for Private Eyes: I just got my degree this June. I'm going to New York because it's the most evil city in the world and it's my home. Frankly I like decadence."

"Would you, O I don't know if I can ask you; I don't even know if I can trust you." She bursts into tears on my shoulder; I don't know what to do.

"Listen. Peter Peter here's my partner." Peter Peter moans in a sympathetic drunken stupor, "so the two of us, Peter Peter and I, can help you; we're really good."

"It' a my father . . ."

"I'm not too fond of fathers myself but I can . . ."

"My father's wonderful, he was wonderful, O I don't know what's happened to him, he just, he just left."

"Do you want me to find him?" I say in a low hushed voice.

"He hasn't disappeared; he just disappears at 10 P.M. every night, for three or four hours. He won't tell me where he's been, and well mother's also upset; we all don't understand it. Strange checks appear on his bank register which are in his handwriting which he says he doesn't remember writing out. He says he doesn't remember what happens in the hours every night he's gone from the house."

"I'll take it on," I say, "one hundred dollars a day plus expenses."

"I love you."

"I love you too."

I slip my hand under the coat, and caress her belly button. As I touch her cunt lightly, she smiles and kisses my nose. I continue pressing down, play with her; we move closer together. This is my and Peter Peter's first job; we have to be careful and not fuck up. If we do a good job this time, we could be on our way. I'm not sure if I know New York well enough.

"My mother says all our money's disappearing she doesn't know there."

"How old are you?"

"Twenty-four."

"I'm twenty-six."

"My father's a jeweler: he owns a huge diamond industry in South Africa and is a special envoy at the UN."

"You'll have to give me all the names and addresses of the people involved. What's your name?"

"Sally Spitz."

"Will you sleep with me or with me and Peter Peter in New York?"

We smile. I can tell this job's going to be wonderful. A cinch.

Peter Peter wakes up and asks me where we are. I plan to meet Spitz the next day at her parents' house on East 57th Street.

(1973)

from *The Childlike Life of the Black Tarantula*

I've always feared most that someone will destroy my mind.

i become helen seferis, and then, alexander trocchi

JULY 1973

I'm lying in the dark, in a tent, my thighs wrapped in the thick skins of sheep. The dark lies around me, murderers thieves who have taken me stand around, I can smell them I hate their guts; they'll need food when we get to the city, I'll take my revenge. Right now I'm impotent.

My lover Y sold me to them the man I had allowed to touch me: I'll kill him. Why do I still fuck?

All I have left is my writing. That's the only stability I know have ever known. Y wanted to kill me because he was scared I might kill him. Now I want to kill him. He's not so fucking powerful, he can sell me, I'll get my revenge. Part of me, a box, hates men, despises them, I can usually see that box and forget it; now it's exploded. I like to fuck.

I don't understand why I think so much about sex. I'm scared to death to call up someone, ask him/her to fuck me, go out on the street, let a stranger touch me (fantasy): my desire usually overcomes my fears. I do what I fantasize doing. Right now, I'm nowhere. I'm touching my thigh my hand is someone else's hand, an inch toward the inner thigh the low wind of the skin curving toward my cunt hair; I touch myself again alone I know who I am; I experience strength pulse the muscles between the arms of my back a young virulent athlete. I feel alone and strong.

The beginning:

I climb alone down the rocks of the cove. The coral reefs stretching into the sea look like mirrors of my cunt, my inner womb; then look utterly strange: black sea monsters skimming the surfaces of each other's bodies for their communication. I imagine I'm a mermaid. At night I see the sea, the ocean black against black against black, long thick lines of white appearing moving inward at my image. Because my father's chief I'm always alone and can do whatever I want. At night I run into the black ocean: a wave which I can't see lifts me up in the blackness larger unseen waves lift me breaks over my head, white, the ocean lights up! The waves grow larger I always swim alone.

I'm fifteen years old; I hate everyone. I don't hate everyone (that's stupid).

All I do is fantasize about sex. Someone being nice to me. I close my eyes, begin to space out: feel I'm rolling down then out my legs straight out on a pillow, my head falls backward I begin to fantasize: I move like a sleepwalker among deeper sleepwalkers in this beach I remember. (Memory makes everything romantic.) I open my legs, the water feels coldest around my ankles as it rises around my legs the shock disappears the foam springs around me wets my cunt, I begin to swim naked the long muscles running around my ass down the backs of my long legs relax, my body opens at my cunt, I'm alone I laugh talk to the ocean my pickle paul lizzy dizzy fizzy cluckle clark, I float in it and leap over it, when I leave it I'm gleaming I see blood blood floating around me everywhere. I want to fuck impersonally passionately so that I feel completely free, two twin streams of blood run down the inside of my legs, I draw my knees apart, gently, and let the blood dry.

My father wants to fuck me, fears his desire which is the only honest part of him, and fears me. I scare everyone away. I look like a rat. My father's partly conditioned me: made me scared of everyone in the village, especially men. I hide from people; I despise people because they accept the shit they live in and get, limits limits no complete absorption into anyone/anything I can feel my fear. My father tried to fuck me and doesn't succeed. I vow to sleep alone. I wait for the day my father'll die: I can do whatever I want.

Tomorrow I'll get mail. I look at the ocean, I slowly take my clothes off feel the material leaving each inch of the body, I look at the dark ocean I run into the ocean expect the physical shock to break apart the wall of my fantasies relieve me, nothing happens, I'm constantly horny untouched, I throw myself on the sand, the pointed shells. I see a half-rotten log, fat, in the sand as I know what I'm about to do my legs feel like they're opening without opening the muscles in the center of my belly extend like fingers toward my throbbing clit I watch my cunt approach the log I'm on the log I'm a man my hands shake then my whole body, as I collapse on the log my whole weight thrown on my clit against the wood as I sink the log falls on top of me scrapes the delicate skins of my breasts, the thick layer of fat soft skin across my navel. The shells beneath my buttocks cut into my buttocks, sharp points drive into the lips of my ass so that nerves spasm sharply in arrows from my ass upward, down to my cunt. I press the log more tightly with my legs. I

I press the rough sharp wood against my clit an inch below my clit then rhythmically increasing speed touching my clit.

I look up at the black air behind the black air I fantasize. If I could see people I like I could get out of the fantasy, there would just be fewer fantasies. I'm covered with blood I'm hurt which makes me scared a few green streaks cover my body.

(For the last time I walk into the ocean. Now I'm stuck in San Francisco. I moved here for good reasons: I leave all my friends. I go to a party, I know everyone, everyone loves me. Do you want to go? Anywhere. On Mission and 18th Street three guys rape me. I hear laughter. Once I open up to the possibility of sex, I can fuck anyone I want to feel my strength there. My sex is myself my strength. Was someone watching me? Is a man going to rape me? Elemental signs of conditioning.)

"Let me go . . . no . . . no . . . I'll kill you."

Her fear rouses my fear and the excitement that I feel with fear. I scale the rocks, immediately see one of the village girls I know, she was in my school class I thought her stupid, a man on top of her, his hands clenched around her arms. The girl throws him off, runs away. For the first time I'm no longer scared because I have a cunt. "Do you have a cunt?" I walk across the sand to the man whom I recognize. We're both dressed.

I can see his dark body clearly beneath his clothes. "I'd leave this village again," he tells me, "if I could get the money."

I watch his eyes fall against the cloth of my skirt which is pressing against my mound. "If you like, I could get the money."

"You mean together?"

"I was watching you make love to P." He lays one of his hands on the thick skin of my thigh, I lean back into space; I open my eyes.

(Pure pornography.) I scarcely feel his fingers edging through the layers of my musk into the sex of the body, the twin mouth, strange sensations like waves rip through my body, I only feel relief as his fingers penetrate, move freely inside me, the outside becomes my inside, then I feel nothing. He slowly removes his fingers, licks them, as I feel his lips rub against my wet lips, his double cock quickly tears through my knotted hairs into the long spiraling muscles of my cunt a knife toward my womb I feel nothing I arch my back so that the top of his cock presses against the upper part of my cunt, the delicate opening of the skin below the cunt hairs, I'm scared I move back and forth quickly abandon myself to his rhythm as his legs tense, my tensed muscles the muscles around my clit shooting outward disintegrate I lose my sex by coming.

He opens my blouse his head mouth falls on my left nipple. Hard. A thin line of desire, electric nerves, moves from my nipple straight down over to my sensitive clit my right hand presses his head against my breast the muscles around my clit begin to quiver I run my hand down in the sweat down to caress his thick hairs, he simultaneously slides his hand under my buttocks his middle fingers into the more delicate opening between my buttocks. I'm doing what I've dreamed of doing wanted to do for years. Never again. I sit alone in the house I don't talk to anyone. I masturbate. I dream of ass. Cunt against the plate behind the cock, rapidly, our juices mingle, the juices of my 18-years-starved body. Cats howl at each other and screech. I contain the strange liquid in me. I have no definite feelings.

We make our plans: "We'll go to Charleston first, then we'll go south from there."

"How soon?"

"I'll steal my father's money tonight." I remember I need someone to protect me. "We'll get married there."

I have no intention of getting married: I'll stay with this guy as
long as he can help me, then find another guy. All that matters is my
own sexuality.

[7/18]

I persuade myself I can't call up A because I'll ruin any chance of a
friendship between us for a quick fuck I call him up decadence wins
ah I'll call back I persuade myself

Now I touch my cunt I can work. I hide my writing myself fear
someone will steal me a man enters a shadow. I lie in the tent of falling sheepskins. As I see his eyes fall down on me his finger point the
muscles below and beneath my belly begin to quiver I watch myself
falling into my cunt: I take off the rough robe they've put on me I dig
my heels into the blankets my legs feel heavy thick I spread them
outward first the muscles from the center of my groin my knees flexed
like a dancer's my ankles twisted I slowly raise the altar of my body
the thick outer lips open my whole body opening up toward the black
air heavy and dangerous then toward the man. He thrusts his bearded
mouth against my cunt.

Again I feel the complete joy of giving myself, myself fully since
I don't know this man, to another person and having the person
equally, for both our pleasure and pain, give himself to me. A person
who I will never see again, not recognize, so no ties can interfere with
our delight. As I come again and again, his lips working softly against
my clit, I again rejoice that I have no personal friendships, I dream,
fantasize, awake briefly to meet someone and come, to worship my
own coming. I'm almost asleep. I want to make myself become/put
down everything before they try to destroy an anomaly such as me. I
hate the robot society I know.

I arrived with A in Charleston early on the morning of my 19th
birthday. I gave A a quarter of my money, pretended I didn't have
any more. I don't want to depend on any man. A slowly touches my
cunt under the table, moves his hand under my velvet dress lightly up

the waving hairs of my leg until the tips of his fingers scrape the beginning of the opening of my sex. I want to come but am too anxious, too scared. "We have to get to Charleston." "I want to marry you," A says, "settle down take over your father's lucrative fishing business."

A's a death person despite his body, his cock. I don't let my feelings show. Now that I've gotten away from my parents, I have to steer free of everyone, those who want to entrap me; I have to get every thing where on my own. I see policemen in the streets waiting for us with guns.

"A, I need some of my money. I have to buy clothes."

I take my money, 40 pounds, split. Split. Into the toilet, out the side door, around the policemen. I'm very smart and clever.

I look up at a man who, I realize, is attracted to me. I want to fuck him. I watch him watching me until I can't stand the agony the vibrations of the huge metal wheels under the slimy flesh around my clit, and fur, a yowling cat, I rise leave the train car, a few minutes later, I find the stranger standing behind me. I slide my hand below the low tight belt of my jeans lower along the skin made thick from milk, I can feel the lips of my cunt separate, the outer ones, the inner ones moving slightly against my clit, the muscles behind the mouth tense until my fingers ease over to them, to my clit. Tough wait touch lightly wait the third finger clit-centered wait "trains are always boring" at the rim of the walls I lose myself touch again "are you coming?" "am I coming?" the skins fold into around each other I feel them too close touch lighten then insistently the rhythm rub my clit slowly. The wave centers begin everywhere.

I look up at him my desire obvious. His lips touch the lips of my cunt my erosion as my muscles tense. Upward begin to break my nipples open I feel his lips then tongue my seed flows and at the peak, like a male, I begin to moan, repeat my desire, I rise, and snap. I feel his lips, inside me

I slowly fall asleep. End of minimal pornography.

I don't see anything any more. White beating down white glimpses of white the edge of my shoulder. Am I breaking out, or enclosing myself further? I'm no longer interested in my memories, only in my continuing escalating feelings.

After we leave the porno shop walk A home I sit down on the corner of Market and 9th fold my cape over my face. I don't want to see or hear anymore. Stasis before the danger occurs: my space disappears. I do this over I sit down on the corner of Market and 9th. Can I steal your money? Can I take your black leather jacket lined with black fur? If I hate you will you love me more? They put a black tent over me as I sit on one of the camels. No other men can see me because if they see me they'll fuck me. I can smell the sex everywhere: I reach down along my neck kiss the skin of my right breast. I smell at the brown pit of my arms. I have more power than most people which I don't use am scared of if I turn on the power I attract everyone. Men aren't attracted to me but I can charm them by being forceful if I want, otherwise I can vanish. I'm so horny I'll sleep with anyone. The dark men gather around me, stare at me, I can't recognize who I've slept with I'm unsure I say hello to the junky he doesn't say hello: good-looking long black hair, sharp yellow features, brilliant B touches me because he wants to fuck me I can touch his extending cock. I see my cunt ahead of me the pear lips pulsing and the thin inner folds. But I can never be certain.

I don't want to escape now. My revolt against the death society collides with my desire to be touched I have no identity I can feel the hand softly running up down my leg inside the leg against the sand softly spreading my legs my buttocks against the burning sand the sand rises into my ass tiny diamonds every touch causes all people think about when they meet me is sex ripples of flesh to collide against the returning ripples as they enlarge into waves I give myself entirely to each desire because there's nothing else to give myself to nothing else exists I have to hide my work am I scared? His hands grasp my thighs pulling him upward over me. My, Silver Gold Lamé's, first vision of San Francisco: nothing, delight, hey stop, yeah ah, what, you're under arrest, I see some black junky, I'm Vice Squad and I'm arresting you, I start to cross the street, you can't move I've got a gun, he reaches in a plastic portfolio he's carrying, I'm still alive, his hands fold around my cheeks he turns his head bend down on top of my mouth to kiss me saliva flows into me I'm burning saliva and mucus flesh until I can't tell object from object, my feeling rushes to my center I don't want to sleep with you my feeling rushes to my center I rise there against the new lover there is only this and my account of this I immediately begin to come, I see a frame around me: my space. The rest is blackness, money-death-necessity coming to destroy my gropings toward, sex-money looming over me destroy my tentative beginning human sex, I rub my body against P. I become a parrot. OK.

I do only one thing. I touch myself or I feel a hand a leg touch me a mouth enters me I can feel its wet softness against my skin I expect nothing and quickly I begin to quiver my hands contact the strange flesh my delight begins I thrust my hands under the shoulders the body over me burning flesh sliding on my burning flesh the strange object slides into my body within the secret walls of my cunt wet hairs pierce my clit until I'm about to break my clit swollen with blood until I'm at the final edge

for hours I come and come until there's no difference between coming and reality. I have to be careful for they may visit me at any moment, and take away my writing; I'm still me, I'm still scared by my passion and sex. Reporting involves memories involves identity: I have my identity and I have my sex: I'm not new yet. I have to be careful for I may be visited at any moment.

[7/20/73]
I became a man and a woman:

The ground pulls out from under my body I feel the anxieties I felt as a kid because my parents hate me or the anxieties I feel on acid I stay with the anxiety to find out what's happening I forget who I am I don't know who I am I see a huge soft black widow no identity a large tarantula I have no feelings I begin to float. I'm Helen I know who I am, then my work means nothing to me my work means less to me than my sexuality. I'm a failure. This is a failure all I'm causing is my own disintegration. What'm I trying to do? My work and my sexuality combine: here the complete sexuality occurs within, is not expressed by, the writing. I feel anxious. Last night no one comes in. I hear footsteps muffled voices talking about me describing my real being, bricks being thrown on the ground, large black woman jiving, I hear two tough guys on telephone wires one tells the other I love you, cat begins to yowl. Nothing stops my writing finally I'm alone I use my writing to get rid of all feelings of identity that aren't my sexuality. I have to exist only when someone seeks to touch me or I touch myself. Fuck this. I feel hot and sweaty. It's hot and sweaty, early, the heat of the day focused in the gray-black evening air. The endless sand still burning. Men mutter and cry around me, stare at me uneasily, and talk. I eat a few dates, cheese, bread, and wine. No one touches me; I'm constantly horny; I think only about sex. I don't like sexual explosions getting mixed up with hampering my work. I'll do anything to fuck.

Last night no one comes in. I tried to remember the last time a stranger more than one of them touched me I wet my finger slid it up the tight writhing hole between his buttocks the strangely smooth skin welcome me a thin cord of skin spiraling around my finger a vein throbbing and helping my finger climb upward tightened around me pulsating as my finger pressed inward toward his belly. My other hand slid between our wet flesh around the head of his cock pressing the white cord under his cock I remember the two men staring at me, huge rectangle eyes the eyes of spider, as I sit flat against the white walls the sand I have no protection the sand is a hospital and a loony bin I go off. Fuck people, by the time anyone's 26 years old he/she's crazy unable any longer to communicate with more than 1% efficiency genitals meet but no info gets across so I act romantic I'd rather make love with parrots and cats I like and bite them they lick and bite me. My dears, we're all very sophisticated, but it's a drag; I sleep with few people. As one man lays his cock in my mouth, the other spreads my legs with his hand already the nerves at the ends of my cunt like tiny paws stroke the inside of my flesh. I can't handle my horniness. We're, I think, moving into a city.

My sex fucking is impersonal. My sexuality's impersonal. I'm rapidly losing my identity, the last part of my boredom. I caress the heavy thighs that turn outward from my center, like a spider, sink into the rough clothes in the minaret, the thin muscles twirl around my calves to turn the feet outward like a golden dancer, leap through the hot air, the hairs of my cunt brush against wet the rough hair on your head, I can feel the liquid drip down the fat inner bulges of the legs near my cunt. Veins stick out from my wrists. I rub my flesh against my flesh, my skin against my skin, my skins against my skins, my torso begins to rise I'm always at the beginning of desire I can hardly tell when my orgasms rise and fall as if I'm almost unable to come and don't care, or am continuously slowly coming, I rub my back like a cat does against the rough wool, spread my heavy brown legs so that my buttocks open, the red flesh against the black wool, I pretend it's the hair of another person: there are mirrors making my hands into another person's hands, people all around me watch me. I watch the thin hands hold my arms, move slowly living bracelets around my arms on to the heavy flesh of my aching breasts.

The liquid begins to rise, and my orgasm, I can no longer keep enticing myself (with the future), my orgasms, begin: the thighs spread apart at my ovaries, two central nerves parallel 5 inches apart from each other passing past my navel to my clit begin to burn, my cunt is my center my cunt is my center my cunt is my center, the hand reaches into my cunt my womb like a strange cock back and forth the thumb presses against my clit lightly then harder I imagine whips slashing into my ass just where the buttocks begin to spread I imagine tongues licking the round opening of my ass quickly lighting me until a dome begins to rise in my cunt, a growing sphere that wants to conquer me I touch myself faster

I have to wait till people physically want me and I can be. But I'm no longer and I have my fantasy of my outcome, scared.

[7/21]
No one comes near me.

[7/22]
A tall man comes up to me and looks at my standing naked body. He turns my body around; with his thumb and third long finger opens my mouth sticks his tongue in my mouth, around my gums, to my

inner throat. His hands touch the beginning of the outward curves of my upper buttocks the thick layer of fat developing over my ass and around my stomach. After stroking me, so I feel like a cat, his hand moves to the hair over my cunt, down to the lips of my cunt, softly; his eyes carefully note every expression on my face. I understand they are trying to sell me. How do I feel?

The man leads me to a tent, motions for me to lie down. I expect him to kick me or hurt me. I'm slightly scared and also hot. I'm not supposed to look at him. He lays his left hand flat on my shoulder, looks at my eyes. I start to lift his robe. He stops me, lifts my heavy breasts with his right hand, draws two fingers around the purple nipples. As I look up at him, he turns his back to me, and leaves the tent. Again I'm alone.

I no longer care about being safe, I don't care about the men because they'll make me feel safe; I know now they see me as an animal, I have only these wide arms, these breasts, eyelids shut over my eyes, and the heavy flesh of my legs shoving out of my cunt. If they sell me, they treat me badly it's because they think I don't matter. I matter when someone touches me, when I touch someone; the touch matters; so in this way I no longer exist, nor do the men. My body matters to me: the heart next to the lungs, the stomach pressing on the lungs, the lungs thoughtlessly drawing the air in and out, the oxygen out of the air. I'm no longer as scared as I was in the world because I no longer care. My only fear now is that no one will touch my body. I don't know yet how I'll get rid of this fear.

Days pass by, moment like moment, the light becomes yellower and yellower, my fantasies more constant and thicker, like orange cloth on blue silk, on yellow sun; so that I'm always at a slow rolling edge. If my hand brushes across the flesh of my leg, the nerves begin to quiver, to stimulate other nerves further away from and closer to my clit, the desire rolling like soft dangerous animals an inch below my skin is everpresent, increases until I'm incapable of satisfying myself, I'm forced to wait; I'm forced to enter the worst of my childhood nightmares, the world of lobotomy: the person or people I depend on will stick their fingers into my brain, take away my brain, my driving willpower, I'll have nothing left, I won't be able to manage for myself. In the midst of this level anxiety, I'm constantly at rest. I wanted to control all environments and actions surrounding and of me; I was scared they would take control of me. Me. How strange now as I lay here waiting for another person, in the desert a man, I don't know who for what purpose, waiting so long that I can no longer perceive. I play with myself, smell the sweat at the pit of my arms, is it sweat, how can I tell what sweat is? I perceive yellow, yellow all around me, faint misty outlines of a body, everyone I know's crazy, I believe everyone's in her/his own way crazy, the edges shifting of the body look white I close my eyes I don't. I feel a limb thrust against the outjutting bone right above my clit, not a limb but a head, if I see an arm intersect my arm, I think my arm's been cut in half, the lips and beard rub against the fragile lace of my inner legs and the skins beneath the wettened hairs. Lips twine inside me slowly kiss the inner walls of my body until every inch of my body in shuddering my feeling becomes present to me. I can perceive everything. I'm a child; I sense through touch. Every inch over and over first with: the soft lips thick lips then the needle at the end of the tongue, my wetnesses begin to mingle, I open myself, I have no more will, so that anything can touch me, can enter me, I'm anything/one more sensation at the bottom and top levels of my flesh, licking me I begin as I'm doing, orgasm, orgasm upon orgasm, open OPEN the nerves roll in cycles in preconceived courses through my body faster and faster in huger and huger rolls until my flesh disintegrates and turns on itself. Like a devouring spider. I begin to clean myself and laugh.

I lose my memory. Days after days pass blackness I am blackness. I'm alive.

[7/25]

We climb down the rocks and sliding sand Devil's Slide to the beach, tiny cove surrounded by boulders crash the huge waves against the rocks. B, V, and I take off our clothes. I lie in the hot sand. V starts drinking, people recognize her she tries to harden her nipple by rubbing it with wet finger. I lightly rub my tongue around the center of her nipple and press my lips against it as it grows. We separate, she looks around, waves to the people on the beach who are watching us. A stupid macho creep walks by. V scratches the back of my neck. We begin to kiss, gently, the slow liquids drawn by her lips to the inside curves of my skin, I begin to shudder, I surprisingly yield to her, the kiss continues, at the edge of each inch of skin, feelings in my lips and skin of swirling lines nerves lines of nerves, everything opens, the kiss continues I draw my body over the blanket against hers some relief I get hotter. Now I'm drawn in, I need her, I can't escape orgasm, escape desiring V; my hand touches her heavy triangular breasts which scrape the skin above my stomach simultaneously I draw myself under her so that she can do whatever she wants with me and so I can hold her head like a cat's against me and protect her. How many people are watching? We look up; try to separate. V spreads her legs at people, laughs at them, passes her book around *Female Orgasm*, Three Spanish kids are staring entranced at us; one straight couple behind us and two bisexual couples in front of us are obviously turned on. I feel weird. I'm weird. I have to orgasm blank everyone out. I thrust my legs up huge pyramids her wet hairs press painfully against my clit this won't work. She looks at me. I have to come. We continue to kiss still lightly as if each inch of skin contains snakes she's a he this is a lie, "Can I wipe the sand out of your hairs; can I put my tongue in you?" I'm too far gone to hear anything she tongues me too hard I thrust her away she's hurt the situation's too weird I beg her to climax me. She tongues me a woman's touching me a woman's touching me as I rub as hard as I can my open outer lips against his hairs I can hardly feel his cock his hands begin to beat my ass I feel strange I don't feel anything how am I supposed to feel his hands begin to slap my buttocks harder and faster as I rise I begin to orgasm the pain finally surprises me and pleases me I completely relax her tongue directs each nerve within my lips and cut each center and line of nerves I'm completely dependent on her tongue I blank out every thing/one else I hold on to her as I begin to rise, easily, I can partially control the strong orgasm, increase its length

I see two blonde women in front of us kissing each other

My world is the four walls ceiling and floor in which I live hot they have shuttered the windows I do not think about them the other person who lives in the room with me a young girl whose flesh is now thick and soft like the legs of a spider is my life.

I realize nothing else so that I will completely please whoever comes to me, whoever could be the only person who could give me pleasure. The oil runs from the pores of my skin, greases the skin of my beloved, the only person I now see, so that at night we slide over each other animals who live at the bottom of the deepest parts of the ocean.

I don't know when I started living here at first the young girl stared at me and drew away from me. At first the young girl stares at me and draws away from me. I'm completely alone, I'm bored with touching my own flesh, I hide myself with heavy light brown blankets, and, like the strange creature I am, I sit and wait. I no longer care what happens so I no longer remember. I cast away my memory so I'm always at the edge of multiple orgasms. I sit and wait. As if I'm laying my heavy older hand on her child's thigh and doing nothing else. I stop approaching her because I'm continually at ecstasy.

The third day she smiles at me, then runs away. I smile back, once. I won't let anyone have complete control of me my body ever again. I have to keep returning showing that I'm willing to touch enter her I'll never rape her. I live in this world: have to take pleasure opening myself where and when I can, most of the time I'm alone. She's younger and on the fifth night as I rub my flesh against the rough wool bored of touching myself by now so open to myself that I can't tell whether I'm touching myself or not, I feel two hands at the pit of my body a spider circling I throw my arm slowly into the dark circling around nothing, then the smooth skin lying over the sharp bones of a shoulder, I draw her to me until she's lying quietly in my arms. Inside me, I begin to shiver. I am her. I'm her child and her mother so that I'm completely safe I'm inviolable and there're no men around. My blackness cuts off all extra perceptions. Our mouths meet as my mouth has never been met in a thickness of feelings physical and mental that have a complexity that leads me to orgasm. I kiss her for hours and hours. At some point without knowing how I get here I have to complete my orgasm I mount her our cunts meet and fit surprisingly for me and easily and I ride her as love is our only way until we begin to peak and need more, and turn around

I can do what I want. I can write more freely make my break to get rid of my damaged mind my lover silently aids me and watches out for them, the servants who bring us the rich boring food we eat, who licks the tips of my ears then quickly thrusts her tongue into their quivering centers into the center of my brain. Do I give a shit about her? I want to become as stupid and mindless as her and yield to the hard thighs of my next faceless lover. I want control over my environment. Like a fat spider I sit and wait. I float. Night after night we fold our limbs around each other and come and come we exist only for each other, then only for ourselves until there is no difference.

I think a week has passed. I'm not sure of the time anymore, in this room where the light is always gray and I'm always hot. I love you. I realize my roommate's not me, another person; she's left me, already, in what remains of her memory, believes she's about to meet someone besides the servants who give us food. I'm tired of her. I like to look at her as I sit back in myself, her skin's now thick and fat, like the oil we continuously ingest, the hairs swirling dark in the middle of her flesh. I no longer care about her.

I look at my body as if it were a web, solely a way of asking people to touch me. My body doesn't exist. I watch myself: I'm now heavy and even more beautiful: huge curves of thighs zooming into the valleys around my belly I begin to love myself as if I'm someone else no I realize my attractiveness coldly, I basically couldn't care how I look; I can see anything in a set of shifting frameworks. I'm interested solely in getting into someone else. I find the heavy flesh sensual, as if it were permanent. I'm not sure if I think of myself as a person.

Enough mind remains in me to want this prison to disappear. The awareness of time (prison). I find myself more interesting than my companion, my former beloved; I'm no longer interested in such paltry pleasures in which I have to exert myself, I have to command and control an orgasm; the more I feel my self and my strength, the more I desire complete passivity. Blackness and minimal stuff I have to sense. My breasts are bright red.

I'm sick of this society. "Earn a living" as if I'm not yet living; lobotomized and robotized from birth, they tell me I can't do anything I want to do in the subtlest and sneakiest ways possible. They want to erase all possible hints that I've been born. I have two centers: love and my desire to sleep. I want only the moving toward exaltation, opening toward and becoming other people; the exaltation, then nothing, until it starts again. People are unused to love because they don't go far enough. As far as possible, and farther, into their intuited desires. And complete love, apart by nature from "time," does not meet complete love where, given consent, anything can happen and there's no such thing as strength or weakness except as masks to be acted out. All forms of love are drag. How little do I have to do to survive except for passion, my desire to open and exist as I can only depend for existence on my surroundings, and if I have to do more, if I again have to prostitute by becoming straight, is life—fakery of living—that necessary to me? As if in that case, that deadness without love, there would be any me.

I find my being dependent on love. Physical passion for others and thus myself. Fuck the shits who think otherwise.

A calls me up do I want to meet him at The Stud midnight I've got to work I tell him V ate me in the middle of a public beach terrific are you upset about something? I love you

[7/27]

They wrap a thin white veil around my body, lead me out of the room, across a square of dirt, a courtyard, to a place where there are loud noises, animals and men. The cries of whipped beasts are my subterranean cries. I begin, in my body-mind my mind gone, to descend. Slabs of wood, a long heavy knife, and the shadows, the shadows help me undress. I can again see and hear; roofs, pipe and zither music, the evening prayers, the blackness of the evening air. I haven't gone as far as I thought I had: I'm still part of the daily death-goal world.

Now there's only my large bed.

A large heavy woman enters, hands me a sweet sticky mixture she motions me to eat. I like her; she smiles at me. My willpower is either totally reflexive or gone. Gone. I slowly eat the glue, sandy glue, which is too sweet for me to eat fast, her food, so that I'll do what she wants. No. I simply don't care: at this point it's easier not to make a fuss. I don't know what would help me and I'm too far gone to do more than act through my delirium. I'm completely involved in delirium.

A hand inside my stomach begins to trace light circles on the inside of my skin the skins of my belly my limbs fall outward. Do they disappear? The spirals rise to a peak down below my breasts; I not only feel the various liquids in my body, but I can control the pulsing rhythms of their flow, I can move the muscles which form a cylinder around my clit tense and loose so that the walls and canals of nerves through my body vibrate under my command. Drugged, I can completely control myself.

The drug aids my passivity and thus my strength. Living has become pure pleasure. I can hardly tell the difference between my coming and not coming: if I concentrate on the air that my lungs draw into themselves, I can feel the nerves around my breasts move and shift in complex patterns. I feel more clearly than I've ever felt now that all of me, my mind being every pore of my body, my whole body quivering to open from clit outward, is connected. I begin to play with the spirals within me, my flames, brush my fingers over my tender skin red from the suns, my sensations rise toward my coming, am I about to come? I play with my disbelief, feelingless, until I'm almost insane. I can feel nothing, and have no mind. I can do nothing for myself, nor do I know what I need done. From nowhere needles start rising in me and outside of me through my skin; I have no idea what comes from inside and what comes from outside; I descend into the mental and physical blackness. I see a frame: inside the frame, I'm suspended from a piece of wood by a string tied around my clit; the muscles upward from my clit tighten, and I cry out loudly. My eyelids are sewn to the skin below my eyes. I'm an opening in the earth, moving and crying through the rain. Somehow I awake enough to sense an animal standing over me.

As the man's cock enters me, every muscle of me begins to shake, every nerve begins to burn and quiver. I'm both liquid and solid. I'm completely pleasure. At this moment. (1) I'm opening enough to contain all identities, things, change everything to energy, a volcano. (2) I'm constant energy and I can never be anything else. (3) I have no emotions; I sense textures of everything against textures; I'm completely part of and aware of the object world. I don't exist. My nerves so quiver, quiver burning, up and down the secret inflamed passages of my skin, the nerves tensing my muscles so that my blood zooms to the edge of my body, swells and inflames me, and unable to burst, I begin to come. These sensations—I do not know how to describe them—last for hours. I come again and again and again I am now equal to everything and nothing am completely dependent on the pleasure this stranger is giving me.

As I begin to swoon, my body covered with films of cooling sweat, I find myself alone again. Another man enters, sinks into me, leaves, and then another; I count six men in the blackness who wake me out of my semi-orgasmic sleep. I have no idea what this means.

I'm going to finish this logically: I eat the sweet sandy mixture every night, stewed lamb and eggplants drenched in oils, thick honey pastries. I don't have to earn my living anymore. I think of the mixture (the drug) and the sex, but mostly I feel the pleasure of the masochism which occurs *only* when I give my consent. If I consent, now, I can do anything.

I find this harder and harder to write lest I be ripped off. I

I'm speaking to you directly. Complete disorder exists. I spend most of my time, alone, in the monastery; I bend slowly to my knees, and I pray. I am very poor, but whenever I can I stay alone and pray. Think. Sometimes I go crazy I go pick up a man. "Do you want to fuck?" we go off fuck in every way possible until he can no longer stand the passion, I never see him again. At times I fuck women. I believe in explaining everything about my sexual life as fully as possible. If I have to, I use people to get where I want. I am most scared of dying: I think I will do anything to stay alive. I think I would rather die than submit become a robot let them lobotomize me. Each time I'm about to fuck suck tease a man I think I'll get what I want I vomit have to get out. I fuck only the men I'm madly in love with (for that time).

I would have slept with my brother after my mother died, but he chased me away. I now have to be alone I've been seeing too many people who I don't know well I have to consider everything within myself. If I feel I don't have any space left, I start going crazy. Soon everyone will go crazy if things don't change. My closest friend, Madame Lydia Paschkoff, tells me I need a lot of money. She is crazy and loving, the Virgin Mary of the spirits; I adore her. She tells me how to get money, but I can't do it. Some people think I'm mad. Some people forget me. I use psilocybin, mescaline, pure acid; occasionally hash as an aphrodisiac. I eat as little food as possible to save money.

Of course, I disguise myself as a man. I'm 26 years old. I am exceedingly lazy. Lydia is furious with me because I sleep with men, and refuses to see me again. Now there is no one. The senses and the spirit are independent manifestations of each other; sexual ecstasies become mystic communion. Human communion. There's nothing else I want.

All the above events are taken from *Helen and Desire* by A Trocchi, *The Wilder Shores of Love* by L. Blanch, and myself.

(1973)

from *I Dreamt I Was*
a Nymphomaniac

"This is very nonpolitical, therefore reactionary," he said.
"But what would the world have to be like for these events to exist?"
I replied.

1 I absolutely love to fuck. These longings, unexplainable longings deep within me, drive me wild, and I have no way of relieving them. Living them. I'm 27 and I love to fuck. Sometimes with people I want to fuck; sometimes, and I can't tell when but I remember these times, with anybody who'll touch me. These, I call them nymphomaniac, times have nothing to do with (are not caused by) physical pleasure, for my cunt could be sore, I could be sick, and yet I'd feel the same way. I'll tease you till you don't know what you're doing, honey, and grab; and then I'll do anything for you.

I haven't always been this way. Once upon a time I was an intelligent sedate girl, who, like every intelligent sedate girl, hated her parents and didn't care about money. O in those days I didn't care about anything! I dated boys, stayed out till 5:00 in the morning then snuck home, read a lot of books. I cared more for the books than anyone else and would kiss my books goodnight when I went to sleep. Would never go anywhere without a book. But my downfall came. My parents kicked me out of the house because I wasn't interested in marrying a rich man, I didn't care enough about money to become a scientist or a prostitute, I couldn't even figure out how to make any money.

I didn't. I became poor and had to find a way of justifying my lousy attitude about money. At first, like all poor people, I had delusions about being a great artist, but that quickly passed. I never did have any talent.

I want to fuck these two fantastic artists even though I'm not an artist: that's what this is about. This is the only way I can get them:

(I only want them for a few hours. Days.) Jewels hang from the tips of silver branches. I also want money.

My name is Kathy Acker.

The story begins by me being totally bored.

Sunny California is totally boring; there are too many blond-assed surf jocks. I was lying on my bed, wondering if I should go down to the beach or sun myself on the patio until I passed out. I watched the curly silky brown hair below the damp palm of my hand rise and fall, I watched the rise, the mound twist in agony, laughed at myself. No way, I muttered, among these creeps no way. I need to love someone who can, by lightly, lightly stroking my flesh, tear open this reality, rip my flesh open until I bleed. Red jewels running down my legs and branches. I need someone who knows everything and who'll love me endlessly; then stop. My cats leaped up to me and rubbed their delicious bodies against my body. My cats didn't exist.

Suddenly I heard a knocking at the door. No one ever knocks at the door, they just walk in. I wondered if it was FBI agents, or the telephone Mafia after Art Povera. I opened the door and saw Dan, I didn't know his name then, looking bewildered. Then, seeing me, looking scared. I realized I had forgotten to put clothes on. That's how southern California is: hot.

"Excuse me, I'm looking for 46 uh Belvedere."

"Oh you mean up the hill where David and Elly live; I'll show you. I have to get some clothes on."

He followed me into my small bedroom.

As I slowly bent over, reaching for my jeans, I noticed him watching me. He had brown hair, couldn't see his eyes because he squints so much but they look red, some acne, short with a body I like: heavy enough to run into and feel its weight on me; about 30 years old. I hesitantly took hold of my jeans. He started to talk again: he talks too much. I wanted him to rip off my skin, take me away to where I'd always be insane. He didn't want to fuck with me, much less do anything else. I slowly lifted my leg to put on my jeans, changed my mind. I turned around; suddenly we grabbed each other: I felt his body: his lips wet and large against my lips, his arms pressing my back and stomach into his thick endless stomach, his mouth over me, sucking me, exploring me I want this

"I want you you lousy motherfucker I want you to do everything to me I want you to tell me you want me I want you any way I can get you. Do you understand?" We run screaming out into the night, other people don't exist, feet touching the cold stone, then the sand, then the black ocean water. I look up: black; toward the sand: black; I reach up for him and fall. The water passes over us. We stand up, spouting water; our mouths' wetness into each other's mouth cling together to stay erect. I rise up on my toes, the black waves rising, carefully, press my thighs into his so that his cock can touch my cunt. His right hand caresses his cock, touches its tip to my cunt lips, moves upward, into me I hold him tighter we fall

My hand touches my wet curling hairs then the thick lips of my cunt. Takes sand, rubs the sand into the outer lips of my cunt. Two areas of softness wetness touch me, move back so the cold air swirls at, touch me I feel warm liquid trickling between the swelling lips I feel them swelling a tongue a burning center touches me harder, inside the swollen lips: I lift my legs and imprison him. My nipples are hard as diamonds. The inner skin of my knees presses against his rough hairs: now I feel roughness: sandpaper rubbing the screaming skin above my clit. The joining of my inner lips almost more sensitive than my clit. Now I feel soft surface wetnesses, gently lap, now the burning center which becomes my burning center: rhythmically pressing until time becomes burning as I do. I'm totally relaxed. I'm a tongue which I can't control: which I beg to touch me each time it stops so I can open wider, rise rise toward the black, I open rising screaming I feel it: I feel waves of senses screaming I want more and more

At the peak, as I think I'm beginning to descend, he throws himself on me and enters me making me come again again. All I feel is his cock in me moving circling circling every inch of my cunt walls moving back forth every inch, he stops, I can't, he starts slamming into me not with his cock but the skin around his cock slamming into my clit I come I come he moves his cock into me slowly even more slowly, and then leaves.

For the new life, I have to change myself completely.

*　*　*

The next artist I meet in a bar in New York. I'm sick of artists. The next man I meet is tall, dark, and handsome. I was wearing a black silk sheath slashed in the back to the ruby which signals the delicate opening of my buttocks: tiny black diamonds in my ears and on the center of my fingernails. I had come to the bar to drink: it was an old transvestite bar East Village New York no one goes during the week, rows upon rows of white-covered tables low hanging chandeliers containing almost no light: mirrors which are walls reflect back, reflections upon reflections, tiny stars of light. The only people in the bar are the two women who run the bar, tiny gray-haired women who look like men: incredibly sexy. One or two Spanish hustlers. I wanted to be alone.

I had no background. I'm not giving you details about myself because these two occurrences are the first events of my life. Otherwise I don't exist: I'm a mirror for beauty. The man walked up to me and sat down. He bought two beers. I wasn't noticing him.

"What do you really want to happen?" he asked me. I couldn't answer him because I don't reveal the truth to people I know slightly, only to strangers and to people I know well and want to become. "I used to act as a stud," he was trying to put me at my ease. "Housewives would pick me up in their cars, pay me to satisfy them. I didn't mind because I hate housewives: that class. Then I used to work this motel: I'd knock on a door to a room, a man would start screaming 'don't come in don't come in' scream louder and louder; after a while he'd throw a pair of semened-up underpants out the door. In the pants would be ten dollars."

I couldn't say anything to him because I was starting to respect him.

"I only like people of the working class," he went on. Underneath the table, he was slowly pouring wine on the black silk of my thigh. I moved my legs slightly, open, so the cold liquid would hit the insides of my thighs. Then close my thighs, rubbing them slowly together. "You have a lot of trouble with men, don't you?"

"Don't you love me?" I cried in anguish. "Don't you care anything about me?"

He gently took me in his arms kissed me. Lightly and gently. He didn't press me to him or touch me passionately. "Quick," he whispered. "Before they notice."

He threw me back on the velvet ledge we had been sitting on, pulled up my shift, and entered me. I wanted more. As I feel his cock rotate slowly around the skins of my cunt walls, touching each inch slowly too slowly, he begins again to pour wine on my body: liquid cooling all of my skin except the inside burning skin of my cunt. Putting ice in my mouth on my eyes, around the thick heavy ridges of my breasts. Cock slowly easing out of me, I can't stand that, I can't stand that absence I start to scream I see my mound rise upward: the heavy brown hairs surrounded by white flesh, the white flesh against the black silk: I see his cock enter me, slide into me like it belongs in my slimy walls, I tighten my muscles I tighten them around the cock, jiggling, thrust upward, thousands of tiny fingers on the cock, fingers and burning tongues: this is public I have to move fast: explodes I explode and my mound rises upward, toward the red-black ceiling, I see my mound rise upward, toward the red-black ceiling I see us come fast

He quickly got out of me, and arranged our clothes. No one in the bar had noticed. We kissed goodbye, perfunctorily, and he left.

Every night now I dream of my two lovers. I have no other life. This is the realm of complete freedom: I can put down anything. I see Dan: The inner skin of my knees presses against his rough hairs: now I feel roughness: sandpaper rubbing the screaming skin above my clit. The joining of my inner lips almost more sensitive than my clit. Now I feel soft surface wetnesses, gently lap, now the burning center which becomes my burning center: rhythmically pressing until time becomes burning as I do. I'm totally relaxed. I'm a tongue which I can't control: which I beg to touch me each time it stops so I can open wider, rise rise toward the black, I open rising screaming

I see my second artist love: I can't stand that absence I start to scream I see my mound rise upward: the heavy brown hairs surrounded by white flesh, the white flesh against the black silk: I see his cock enter me, slide into me like it belongs in my slimy walls, I tighten my muscles I tighten them around the cock, jiggling, thrust upward, thousands of tiny fingers on the cock, fingers and burning tongues: this is public I have to move fast: explodes I explode and my mound rises upward, toward the red-black ceiling, I see

I want a woman.

I'm sick of dreaming.

I decide to find these two artists no matter what no matter where. I'll be the most beautiful and intelligent woman in the world to them.

2 I want to make something beautiful: an old-fashioned wish. To do this I must first accomplish four tasks, for the last one I must die: Then I'll have something beautiful, and can fuck the men I want to fuck because they'll want to fuck me.

For the first task I have to learn to be as industrious as possible: I have to work as hard as possible to make up for my lack of beauty and charm. Not that I'm not extremely beautiful. I have to learn what is the best love-sex possible, and separate those people whom I can love from those people I can't love. I have until nightfall to do this.

Last night I dreamt I was standing on a low rise of grassy ground; Dan was standing next to me facing me. He put his arms around my neck kissed me, said "I love you." I said "I love you." Two years later I'm riding through a forest with my four younger sisters, green and wet, leaves in our eyes and skin; we push leaves out of the way the brown horse's neck lowered. My next-to-youngest sister tells me Dan asked her to marry him two months ago. I'm galloping wildly through the woods branches tear at my eyes flakes of my skin hanging. I try to go faster and faster. It's night. Three days later I appear, night, the livingroom of my parents' house: we're moving to Boston, a bayview overlooking a black sky, where I go to college. The skin of my face is torn; bruises over my naked arms; one of my eyes is bloodshot. My family's glad I haven't died. My father greets me, then my older sister who's tall, blonde, beautiful, intelligent. We love each other most. The room in which we're standing is large browns on browns; my parents are rich, not very rich, and liberals. A thin dark-haired man asks me if I want to go to a party. I want to: I rush upstairs to dress: my sister and the man, who's a close family friend, look happy because I'm not going to kill myself. I (outside the dream) look at myself (inside the dream): I'm tall and thin, short waving black hair: I'm not beautiful until you look at me for a long time. I'm very severe. When we walk into a large gray-white house, we realize the party's an artist party. The tall, dark, handsome artist walks over to me and asks me to dance. I wonder if he's asking me because he wants to marry a rich girl. He tells me he's a successful artist makes a lot of money. We dance, dance out to a dark balcony; he starts to take off my black dress as I lean over the portico. I've got two glasses of champagne: one in each hand. He says "I could strangle you like this" I get pissed and walk away. As I begin to walk away, I see Dan and some woman on the balcony: Dan walks over to the man I'm with. They greet each other: Dan admires the stranger's work. I nod hello to Dan. He announces he's getting married: introduces the woman with whom he's going to get married. I walk away to get more champagne. As I return to the balcony, a blonde woman walks up to the group the stranger says "I didn't know you wanted to come here." He introduces his wife to us. I'm going crazy but restraining myself admirably. If I don't fuck someone soon know someone wants me, I'll have to ride my horse for three days again: do something wilder. I can't stop myself. I get another drink. Mel someone walks up to us says "I'm the only man here who isn't married or about to be married" meaning I might as well fuck him because I'm so desperate. I ask him to marry me since I have a lot of money: I'll support him. I tell him how much money I have. He says "Yes." I tell him to go shit on himself. I'm in a lousy mood. An old friend of mine, who I haven't seen for a few months comes up to me. I tell him I need someone's shoulder to cry on. His new lover comes up to him: he can't do anything. This dream's repulsively hetero. I get a bottle of champagne and drink it. I have to ride my horse through the dark forest, the winds swirling around. I rush out of the party. As I'm descending the wide wood steps, I turn around, see the tall dark artist. He asks if he can see me again. He's very severe. I say yes. I fall down the steps I'm so drunk. He asks me if I intend to drive myself home. I'm going to drive myself to the ocean so I can go swimming I'm rich do whatever I want he lifts me up puts me in my car drives me home I end up fucking him quickly then his wife comes I never see him again, I'm lying in my bed with my older sister who's very "I'll take care of you" severe type and whom I love. As we're fucking, her boyfriend enters the room and stops us because we're not supposed to act soooo

Last night I dreamt I was standing on a low rise of grassy ground; Dan was standing next to me facing me. He put his arms around my neck kissed me, said "I love you." I said "I love you." Two years later I'm riding through a forest with my four younger sisters, green and wet, leaves in our eyes and skin; we push leaves out of the way the brown horse's neck lowered. My next-to-youngest sister tells me Dan asked her to marry him two months ago. I'm galloping wildly through the woods branches tear at my eyes flakes of my skin hanging. I try to go faster and faster. It's night. Three days later I appear, night, the livingroom of my parents' house: we're moving to Boston, a bayview overlooking a black sky, where I go to college. The skin of my face is torn; bruises over my naked arms; one of my eyes is bloodshot. My family's glad I haven't died. My father greets me, then my older sister who's tall, blonde, beautiful, intelligent. We love each other most. The room in which we're standing is large browns on browns; my parents are rich, not very rich, and liberals. A thin dark-haired man asks me if I want to go to a party. I want to: I rush upstairs to dress: my sister and the man, who's a close family friend, look happy because I'm not going to kill myself. I (outside the dream) look at myself (inside the dream): I'm tall and thin, short waving black hair: I'm not beautiful until you look at me for a long time. I'm very severe. When we walk into a large gray-white house, we realize the party's an artist party. The tall, dark, handsome artist walks over to me and asks me to dance. I wonder if he's asking me because he wants to marry a rich girl. He tells me he's a successful artist makes a lot of money. We dance, dance out to a dark balcony; he starts to take off my black dress as I lean over the portico. I've got two glasses of champagne: one in each hand. He says "I could strangle you like this" I get pissed and walk away. As I begin to walk away, I see Dan and some woman on the balcony: Dan walks over to the man I'm with. They greet each other: Dan admires the stranger's work. I nod hello to Dan. He announces he's getting married: introduces the woman with whom he's going to get married. I walk away to get more champagne. As I return to the balcony, a blonde woman walks up to the group the stranger says "I didn't know you wanted to come here." He introduces his wife to us. I'm going crazy but withstraining myself admirably. If I don't fuck someone soon know someone wants me, I'll have to ride my horse for three days again: do something wilder. I can't stop myself. I get another drink. My sister who's also drunk asks me to dance, she's wearing a low gray gown; we dance in each other's arms giggling. I lie close in her arms: I lie backwards over her left arm. We're leaning against a gray wall under a picture: she kisses me, as she looks down on me I wonder if she now feels sexually toward me I'm excited, I ask her and she says she'd like to fuck me. I look up at her and kiss her: I want us to fuck in front of all these creepy people. Her thin dark-haired boyfriend comes over tells us we can't act too wildly: do what we want in our bedroom. Mel someone walks up to us says "I'm the only man here who isn't married or about to be married" meaning I might as well fuck him because I'm so desperate. I ask him to marry me since I have a lot of money: I'll support him. I tell him how much money I have. He says "Yes." I tell him to go shit on himself. I'm in a lousy mood. An old friend of mine comes up to me, who I haven't seen for a few months. I tell him I need someone's shoulder to cry on. His new lover comes up to him: he can't do anything. This dream's repulsively hetero. I get a bottle of champagne and drink it. I have to ride my horse through the dark forest, the winds swirling around. I rush out of the party. As I'm descending the wide wood steps, I turn around, see the tall dark artist. He asks if he can see me again. He's very severe. I say yes. I fall down the steps I'm so drunk. He asks me if I intend to drive myself home. I'm going to drive myself to the ocean so I can go swimming I'm rich and do whatever I want he lifts me up puts me in my car drives me home I end up fucking him quickly then his wife comes I never see him again, I'm lying in my bed with my older sister who's very "I'll take care of you" severe type and whom I love. As we're fucking, her boyfriend enters the room and stops us because we're not supposed to act soooo

Last night I dreamt I was standing on a low rise of grassy ground; Dan was standing next to me facing me. He put his arms around my neck kissed me, said "I love you." I said "I love you." Two years later I'm riding through a forest with my four younger sisters, green and wet, leaves in our eyes and skin; we push leaves out of the way the brown horse's neck lowered. My next-to-youngest sister tells me Dan asked her to marry him two months ago. I'm galloping wildly through the woods branches tear at my eyes flakes of my skin hanging. I try to go faster and faster. It's night. Three days later I appear, night, the livingroom of my parents' house: we're moving to Boston, a bayview overlooking a black sky, where I go to college. The skin of my face is torn; bruises over my naked arms; one of my eyes is bloodshot. My family's glad I haven't died. My father greets me, then my older sister who's tall, blonde, beautiful, intelligent. We love each other most. The room in which we're standing is large browns on browns; my parents are rich, not very rich, and liberals. A thin dark-haired man asks me if I want to go to a party. I want to: I rush upstairs to dress: my sister and the man, who's a close family friend, look happy because I'm not going to kill myself. I (outside the dream) look at myself (inside the dream): I'm tall and thin, short waving black hair: I'm not beautiful until you look at me for a long time. I'm very severe. When we walk into a large gray-white house, we realize the party's an artist party. The tall, dark, handsome artist walks over to me and asks me to dance. I wonder if he's asking me because he wants to marry a rich girl. He tells me he's a successful artist makes a lot of money. We dance, dance out to a dark balcony; he starts to take off my black dress as I lean over the portico. I've got two glasses of champagne: one in each hand. He says "I could strangle you like this" I get pissed and walk away. As I begin to walk away, I see Dan and some woman on the balcony: Dan walks over to the man I'm with. They greet each other: Dan admires the stranger's work. I nod hello to Dan. He announces he's getting married: introduces the woman with whom he's going to get married. I walk away to get more champagne. As I return to the balcony, a blonde woman walks up to the group the stranger says "I didn't know you wanted to come here." He introduces his wife to us. I'm going crazy but withstraining myself admirably. If I don't fuck someone soon know someone wants me, I'll have to ride my horse for three days again: do something wilder. I can't stop myself. I get another drink. My sister who's also drunk asks me to dance, she's wearing a low gray gown; we dance in each other's arms giggling. I lie close in her arms: I lie backwards over her left arm. We're leaning against a gray wall under a picture: she kisses me, as she looks down on me I wonder if she now feels sexually toward me I'm excited, I ask her and she says she'd like to fuck me. I look up at her and kiss her: I want us to fuck in front of all these creepy people. Her thin dark-haired boyfriend comes over tells us we can't act too wildly: do what we want in our bedroom. Mel someone walks up to us says "I'm the only man here who isn't married or about to be married" meaning I might as well fuck him because I'm so desperate. I ask him to marry me since I have a lot of money: I'll support him. I tell him how much money I have. He says "Yes." I tell him to go shit on himself. I'm in a lousy mood. An old friend of mine comes up to me, who I haven't seen for a few months. I tell him I need someone's shoulder to cry on. His new lover comes up to him: he can't do anything. This dream's repulsively hetero. I get a bottle of champagne and drink it. I have to ride my horse through the dark forest, the winds swirling around. I rush out of the party. As I'm descending the wide wood steps, I turn around, see the tall dark artist. He asks if he can see me again. He's very severe. I say yes. I fall down the steps I'm so drunk. He asks me if I intend to drive myself home. I'm going to drive myself to the ocean so I can go swimming I'm rich do whatever I want he lifts me up puts me in my car drives me home I end up fucking him quickly then his wife comes I never see him again, I'm lying in my bed with my older sister who's very "I'll take care of you" severe type and whom I love. As we're fucking, her boyfriend enters the room and stops us because we're not supposed to act soooo

Last night I dreamt I was standing on a low rise of grassy ground; Dan was standing next to me facing me. He put his arms around my neck kissed me, said "I love you." I said "I love you." Two years later I'm riding through a forest with my four youngest sisters, green and wet, leaves in our eyes and skin; we push leaves out of the way the brown horse's neck lowered. My next-to-youngest sister tells me Dan asked her to marry him two months ago. I'm galloping wildly through the woods branches tear at my eyes flakes of my skin hanging. I try to go faster and faster. It's night. Three days later I appear, night, the livingroom of my parents' house: we're moving to Boston, a bayview overlooking a black sky, where I go to college. The skin of my face is torn; bruises over my naked arms; one of my eyes is bloodshot. My family's glad I haven't died. My father greets me, then my older sister who's tall, blonde, beautiful, intelligent. We love each other most. The room in which we're standing is large browns on browns; my parents are rich, not very rich, and liberals. A thin dark-haired man asks me if I want to go to a party. I want to: I rush upstairs to dress: my sister and the man, who's a close family friend, look happy because I'm not going to kill myself. I (outside the dream) look at myself (inside the dream): I'm tall and thin, short waving black hair: I'm not beautiful until you look at me for a long time. I'm very severe. When we walk into a large gray-white house, we realize the party's an artist party. The tall, dark, handsome artist walks over to me and asks me to dance. I wonder if he's asking me because he wants to marry a rich girl. He tells me he's a successful artist makes a lot of money. We dance, dance out to a dark balcony; he starts to take off my black dress as I lean over the portico. I've got two glasses of champagne: one in each hand. He says "I could strangle you like this" I get pissed and walk away. As I begin to walk away, I see Dan and some woman on the balcony: Dan walks over to the man I'm with. They greet each other: Dan admires the stranger's work. I nod hello to Dan. He announces he's getting married: introduces the woman with whom he's going to get married. I walk away to get more champagne. As I return to the balcony, a blonde woman walks up to the group the stranger says "I didn't know you wanted to come here." He introduces his wife to us. I'm going crazy but withstraining myself, admirably. If I don't fuck someone soon know someone wants me, I'll have to ride my horse for three days again: do something wilder. I can't stop myself. I get another drink. My sister who's also drunk asks me to dance, she's wearing a low gray gown; we dance in each other's arms giggling. I lie close in her arms; I lie backwards over her left arm. We're leaning against a gray wall under a picture: she kisses me, as she looks down on me I wonder if she now feels sexually toward me I'm excited. I ask her and she says she'd like to fuck me. I look up at her and kiss her: I want us to fuck in front of all these creepy people. Her thin dark-haired boyfriend comes over tells us we can't act too wildly: do what we want in our bedroom. Mel someone walks up to us says "I'm the only man here who isn't married or about to be married" meaning I might as well fuck him because I'm so desperate. I ask him to marry me since I have a lot of money: I'll support him. I tell him how much money I have. He says "Yes." I tell him to go shit on himself. I'm in a lousy mood. An old friend of mine comes up to me, who I haven't seen for a few months. I tell him I need someone's shoulder to cry on. His new lover comes up to him: he can't do anything. This dream's repulsively hetero. I get a bottle of champagne and drink it. I have to ride my horse through the dark forest, the winds swirling around. I rush out of the party. As I'm descending the wide wood steps, I turn around, see the tall dark artist. He asks if he can see me again. He's very severe. I say yes. I fall down the steps I'm so drunk. He asks me if I intend to drive myself home. I'm going to drive myself to the ocean so I can go swimming I'm rich do whatever I want he lifts me up puts me in my car drives me home I end up fucking him quickly then his wife comes I never see him again, I'm lying in my bed with my older sister who's very "I'll take care of you" severe type and whom I love. As we're fucking, her boyfriend enters the room and stops us because we're not supposed to act soooo

(1974)

from *The Adult Life of Toulouse Lautrec*

"Make sense, "Fielding said. "Tell the real story
of your life. You alone can tell the truth!"
"I don't want to make any sense, "I replied.

I'm too ugly to go out into the world. I'm a hideous monster.

the case of the murdered tworp

"**T**oulouse," says Vincent. "What are you going to do with your life? How're you ever going to make any money? You're a deformed crippled beast. Look at your hairy chest, your huge nodding head. Your legs are spindly. You thought just cause your parents're rich, you had the world on a silver platter. Money does control everything in this world.

"But just cause your parents have money, doesn't mean you have money."

"I don't give a damn," I mumbled.

"How are you ever going to get famous and get fucked? You're such a lousy painter. You may be a great painter, Toulouse, but you're a real lousy one. And that's what matters: goodness.

"What you need is a man, Toulouse, and you're never going to get one. You're going to be lonely for the rest of your life."

"You're a raving maniac!" I screech at the top of my lungs. "I believe artists can do everything! Artists can know all the joy and misery and terrifyingness and usefulness cause artists don't have to suffer! Even though I can barely walk; I'm always in pain; I'm always hungry.

"All I think about is sex. At night, nights, I lie alone in my bed: I see the right leg of every sexy man I've seen on the street, the folds of cloth over and around the ooo ooo . . . I ache and I ache and I ache. I feel a big huge hole inside my body. I see a man I like about to stick his cock in my hot pussy.

"I used to think being crippled meant being in constant pain. I can stand pain. Now I know no man wants me. I can hardly bear to live.

"Fuck art, Vincent."

Just then the owner of the Restaurant Norvins walks up to us. She runs the hottest bar in Montmartre. In the back of the bar's a whorehouse. Her closest friend is Theo, a young teacher.

"Honey," Theo's looking at Vincent longingly, "we're trying to organize this party. It's gonna be in the back of here in an hour. And we need help . . ."

Just then this young girl runs over to them. "Norvins," she screams, "you've got to help me. I just saw this, this horrible event. I saw a murder. MURDER! I myself . . ." "She's a liar," Theo says to me in a loud whisper.

"I don't know what to do. I saw . . ."

"I've got work to do," Norvins says. She walks away from us. "You're a little liar." Theo pinches the girl. "I never believe what you tell me in class. What're you doing in this whorehouse anyway?"

"I tell you I saw murder . . ."

"I've got to help Norvins with the whorehouse party . . ."

She turns around, dashes into the bar's backroom before we can stop her.

"Art," I say. The room whirls around me: the black bar shudders and turns.

"Art," I continue, "I'm so unbearably desirous needy I can't think about art. Who can think about art in this miserable city? I think about sex so much my art must be sex. I think about sex all the time, and I try to stop myself. I tell myself I have to be stronger. I'm alone. I should revel in my loneliness. I'm in pain. I should revel in my pain. I shouldn't want to be with another person so much. If I think about this miserable situation too much, I'll realize I'm about to kill myself."

Suddenly a beautiful man rushes into the bar.

Veronique, Berthe, and Giannina run up to Vincent and me. "Where's Norvins?" they cackle. "I read in *Crime,*" Berthe mumbles, "this guy fucks his girlfriend in her left nostril."

"Shut up Berthe," Veronique says quickly. "We've got to get these apples to Norvins. We're going to bob for apples at the party."

I'm looking at the beautiful man; I'm staring at the beautiful man; I'm sending out every vibration I can so he'll know I want him and only him. His hair's red. His cheekbones're high. He's older than me. His right hand's lost in my short black head hairs. His left hand's resting on my cheek. I can feel the hot cum pouring out of my cunt. The bar swirls and swirls around us.

"Listen you goddamn shitface assbung," I announce, "you've got to fuck me. If you don't fuck me, I'm going to blow up every rat scum tenement in Montmartre. The cops'll shit in their pants. They'll have nothing left to do. If you don't fuck me Mr. Beautiful I'll kick your lousy dick inside out I mean it. You can't treat me like a piece of moldy shit."

"I think you're extremely beautiful."

"Fuck me. Fuck me. Fuck me. Take me to Brazil. Take me to Argentina. Take me to bed. You're the only person or thing who can make me happy. You can make me ecstatic right now." I throw my arms in the air, leap on the table. My crippled legs buckle under me.

"I'm too old for you . . ."

"I'm sick of younger men. They always screw me over."

"I can only screw you three times a day. I know that's not very much, not for a woman of your extreme . . ."

"I'm in love with you. When I'm in love, what do minor things such as screwing, old age, and lack of money matter? D'you have any money? Darling. Will you support me? Can I be your child? I've never had any parents. I love you. I love you. When're you going to fuck me? Now?"

"You must have had a difficult childhood. I can tell by the difficulty you have expressing your desires. Listen, baby, I'm going to fuck you so hard you won't even know what's happening to you. I'm going to shove this hard throbbing piston into your cunt your ass your asshole the holes between your toes your nostrils every microinch of your ears your hands your breasts the space between your flopping breasts your mouth your eyes your sweating armpits your navel at 60 miles per hour 200 miles per hour 2,000,000 miles per hour. So fast, my cock'll never leave you. My cock'll be 24 inches, 36 inches long. And you'll be feeling every inch of it. Baby."

I can see his cock following me everywhere: through the Champs-Elysées, Montmartre, the Seine. A huge golden cock at least 70 inches long. Five feet; no, six feet.

"And when you can stop writhing, my baby, cause I've made you come so much and so hard, you're just coming and coming and coming, all you're doing is coming, I'm going to slowly, more lightly and slowly than's possible, lick every part of your body, so slowly, until my tongue comes to your clit. Your clit sticking out, dripping, from your thick red lips. Tongue will be a point; go dot dot dot hammer a tiny metronome on your clit. Your whole body'll begin to shiver, then . . ."

Wet steaming flesh.

Hot breath shuddering next to me.

His lips kiss me so gently I hardly know I'm being kissed. I don't feel mad passion. I feel he loves me.

I'm not sure he wants to fuck me.

His tongue moves between my lips. Lightly grazes my tongue. My mouth hardly feels his tongue. I figure he wants to fuck me. I feel a lot of tenderness for him. Tenderness that's opening me up physically.

Will I fall in love with him?

His red head's rubbing against my head. I rub my right shoulder against his left shoulder, like friends. I want him to feel love for me. I'll wait until he feels love for me. He's kissing me harder and harder. He's going to love me. He's going to take me into his secret warm cave. I'm slowly licking the inside of his right ear. He's shivering and moaning. I'm open. I want him to love me so badly. His hands're running up and down the tender insides of my legs.

"Baby," he's saying, "I'm going to fuck you and keep you. But not yet. You're going to have to suffer first. You're going to have to learn the meaning of suffering. One day you'll find me; and then, it'll be the end of the world. Fuck. Fuck. Fuck. Fuck. I love you so . . . "

He grabs his pants and rushes out of the bar.

I can't follow him cause I'm a cripple.

"These goddamn cunts." Norvins' towering body's making me ripple and swoon. "Have you seen Giannina around? Now that cunt's gone. She's the only one who knows how to put the apples correctly in the bobbing tub."

"I haven't seen Giannina."

"And what happened to that female twerp who said she had seen a murder?"

"She ran into the back room."

"All she wants is attention. Forget her. There's Theo." He runs out and leaves.

I'm a totally hideous monster. I'm too ugly to go out into the world. If I was living with a man, I would have someone who'd tell me if I'm hideous. Now I have no way of knowing if I'm hideous or not. I'm extremely paranoid. I don't want to see anyone. I'm another Paris art failure. I'm not even anonymous. All I want is to constantly fuck someone I love who loves me. Fuck. Fuck. Fuck. Fuck. Fuck.

No one will ever fuck me because I'm a hideous cripple.

I don't know how to present my image properly. When I'm with people, I act either like a changing wishywashy gook or like an aggressive leather bulldog. That's an image. Obviously nobody wants to fall in love with me. I'm miserable, I'm completely miserable. I've got this hole inside me my work won't fill. I have to work harder. I'm too freaky. Why was I born a cripple?

Maybe some man will love me if I pay him for it.

Here all the women know everything. They know if they don't spread their legs, no man'll notice them; when they spread their legs, they get fucked not loved. They're worn. They know they have to turn to the brothel.

They flock en masse to the brothel in the back of Norvins' bar. All the pretty boys are there, earning their daily bread. Pretty boys; studs; sexy ugly men. Whenever there's a party in Norvins' brothel, it's the talk of the town.

I hate paying for love.

"Well, my dear," Norvins says to Paul, "it's about time you're here. Your costume looks wonderful. You'll have to set up your mirror behind the crystal ball so you can reflect Giannina who's disguising herself as various men. Each time you need to show some horny dame a future boyfriend, Giannina'll appear in the crystal."

Paul Gauguin's the local cleaning woman.

"Is that that female twerp," Norvins whispers to Theo, "who keeps lying? It's immoral for children to be in a brothel. Get her out of here. Better yet: hide her in the library that's opposite the dining room."

"Don't be ridiculous darling. You're just jealous cause you're too old to wear children's drag."

"Carry this." Norvins hands a broomstick to Theo. "I've got to present the prizes for bobbing apples."

All around me're couples. They laugh and kiss. It's disgusting. I can't stand this loneliness. This party. I hobble up to one of the male whores, ask him if he's busy.

Fifty dollars an hour, honey.

I shudder. How disgusting. How painful. Love's the only revolution, the only way I can escape this society's economic controls. I can't pay someone to really truly love me.

Now this sleazy whore thinks I want him. Now he's rubbing the insides of my thighs. I love being touched there. I don't want to give in to this disgusting emotionless touch. I don't want to give in to anything. I'm burning. "Go away," I scream. "Get out of here. You're a creep. I don't want you. Even if I've paid you." Thank god he doesn't listen to me. I'm tough: I can take care of myself. He's putting his arms around me. For at least a moment I'll be able to relax. I'm deliriously happy. I'm thinking about how much and badly I'm going to get hurt. I'm going to get burned. I'm going to get burned all over. His arms hold me in this real warmth that makes the constant pain I feel go away. I'm no longer thinking. I'm in his arms forever and ever.

All I do is feel: His wet soft lips brush my earlobes, my short thick hairs which make my scalp tingle every time they're rubbed. My forehead. My eyebrows. My eyelids. My eyelashes. The skin between my eyebrows. My sideburns. I feel so warm and safe I want to give him everything that's me I want to forget myself: I turn my face trustingly toward his so that my full lips open, longing, feel his lips I can't tell what I feel I. I feel his mouth's wetness. I feel my body ache, and rub against his.

As he takes off his clothes, I curl around his big red cock. His cock's going to make the world change totally. I take his cock in my mouth, as far as it'll go, I'm testing; then out so I can lick its tip, so I can wet my right hand, corkscrew my right hand up and down the lower smooth slippery shaft. Am I pleasing him? His hands clutch my head. Push my head toward his curling red hair. More and more of his cock hits the back of my throat. My fingers are drumming, not rhythmically, light and hard on his cock. My tongue moves not rhythmically, light and hard, on his long hard cock.

"I'm fucking you for money," he tells me. "I'm fucking you for money."

First he lies on top of me and fucks me. Then we both lie on our sides and fuck. Then he lies on top of me and alternately fucks me in my cunt and in my ass. I come and I come and I come and I come. He moves very slowly as he's coming. He never looks at me. He falls asleep while he's holding me.

"Any man'll fuck me," Giannina tells Veronique in total privacy, "once or twice. But it's like fucking the men in the porno movies I'm in. And I get paid to fuck when I make movies."

Veronique sighs.

"The fucking's always terrific. I come once twice lots I come and I come and I come. The guy never gives a shit about me. The only difference between the artists I fuck and the studs in the movies is that I can talk to the studs in the movies."

"I hardly ever come." Giannina gasps amazement. "I need to fuck guys who fuck really slowly, for a long time, so it just comes over me. I tremble and tremble and tremble."

"Veronique," Giannina says, "I think I'm falling in love with Jim."

"What's the matter with that?"

"He doesn't want to see me again. He doesn't like me. I don't understand why. We love fucking together."

"It's just your paranoia. I've had the worst week I've had in a long time I'm so paranoid. We're both paranoid cause we're Aries."

"I was lying on the couch with Jim. Watching TV I felt I was with this warm person in a home. That hasn't happened to me in months: being with a guy and not just fuck fuck fucking."

"Jim's settling down with Linda. He gets more prudish the more married he gets. He's been dropping all his girlfriends."

"Gee William's cute. He's got the continual hots."

"He kept looking like he was about to jump me. He was real drunk, that's why he was letting some emotion show. This life's keeping us lonely, Giannina. What these artists really want are pillows. Nice soft sweet female pillows. We can't be that way. We've got our own work. We're waitresses."

"Each time I get hurt, I close myself up."

"You act like you don't need anyone."

"The more I find I can live alone, the more I don't want to deal with the younger weakly formless men. The older men never have any emotions. Not toward me."

"The trouble is we keep having images of what we want. We don't let our emotions take over."

"At the end of the party," I'm telling Poirot, "she was dead."

"Where'd she die, Toulouse?"

"It was the end of the party. Veronique said, 'Where's that little twerp Norvins hates? The one who keeps saying she saw a murder. She didn't get lost or something?' We all looked for her. Suddenly Paul screeched. A body was hanging out of the bobbing apple tub."

"Do you always bob for apples? Whose idea was that?"

"I don't know. But she must have been killed during the party." We're sitting in Poirot's small flat on the Rue de Ganglia in Paris. Only one man servant, George, attends the flat. Poirot thinks for a moment.

"Tell me, this Norvins, who runs the bar, what's she like?"

"A good person. Efficient. Hard on her girls and her whores, but she has to be. Looks like a society dame. Veronique, Berthe, and Giannina're her waitresses."

"Did Norvins know the victim?"

"Slightly. She thought of her as 'the nuisance.' So did Theo and Paul. You can't let a young girl run in and out of a brothel as she pleases."

"Who exactly was at the party and what was the layout of the place?"

"The people I've told you. Plus Theo, a young teacher; Paul who was dressed as a witch she was telling everyone's fortune; Vincent my friend; and all the male whores Norvins uses they're all the same. It was basically their party. And two other teachers, Rousseau and Seurat. We call them teachers cause they're so good, they show the whores what to do."

"Were any of these people holding any sort of grudge against the young dead girl?"

"How could they? She was so, so full of shit. She did keep saying she had seen a murder, but no one believed her."

"Maybe she had seen a murder." Poirot's stroking his moustache like a big fat cat. "Did she say when she had seen this murder?"

"I don't know."

"What's the layout of the brothel?"

"Here:"

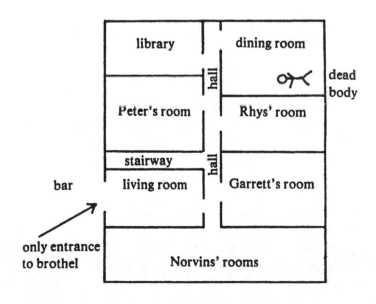

Will I kill myself if I don't get a man?

What do I care who killed that twerp? What's her name? Marie. Poirot'll figure everything out. He's my father.

I live alone. I've got enough money if my rich mother keeps forking it over. She's sorry for me cause I'm a cripple.

It's better to be a cripple in this world than just a plain ugly creep who writes books.

Every night I lie on my bed and am miserable. I look at the empty spot next to me. When I want to put my head on someone's shoulder, I . . . When I want to find out if I possibly don't look like an ugly cripple, I ask . . . When I want to feel someone's weight pounding into me, bruising me, naked flesh streaming against naked flesh naked flesh pouring wet against naked flesh, I . . . When I ache and ache and ache; I always ache; every day I ache; I . . . I need a man because I love men. I love their thick rough skins. I love the ways they totally know about everything so I don't need to know anything. They don't really know everything, but we'll forget about that. They take hold of me; they shove me around; and suddenly the weight of my own aggression's off me. I can go farther out. I can explore more. They're masculine which means they know about a certain society, this polite-death society which is their society, with which they know how to deal. So I don't have to deal with it. I don't want to. They provide a base for me in a society to which I feel alien. Otherwise I've got no reason to be in this world.

I can't get a man unless money's involved. I found this out in the brothel.

Maybe this is only cause I'm so ugly.

"Should I bother seeing people at all?" I ask Poirot.

Poirot's stumped.

"Whenever I see people, I can't stand them. They make my nerves snap. I can't stand seeing them cause I know they hate me."

"Did you murder the young girl?" Poirot asks.

"I don't like my friends anymore. I don't want to see anyone. I want to sit by myself, and play chess.

"I've got to paint. I've got to paint more and more, make something beautiful, make up for make away with this misery, this dragging . . . "

"You lack the analytical mind. You're too emotional to have planned this murder."

"The cops finally got Norvins' brother," Berthe exclaims. "They gave him the death sentence, and all he was doing was stealing."

"All I ever do is play with myself. I don't care about politics."

"When the cop arrested Clement, Clement hit him over the head with the end of a bottle. What d'you think of that? At his trial Clement said: 'The policeman arrested me in the name of the law; I hit him in the name of liberty.'"

"Berthe, do you think it's better to fuck a man for money, or just to fuck for free?"

"Then Clement said: 'When society refuses you the right to existence, you must take it.'"

"I'll fuck any way I can get it. I love to fuck so much."

"The other day the cops arrested Charles Gallo."

"Huh," says Giannina.

"The anarchist who threw a bottle of vitriol into the middle of the Stock Exchange; fired three revolver shots into the crowd, and didn't kill anyone. When the cops got to him, he said, 'Long live revolution! Long live anarchism! Death to the bourgeois judiciary! Long live dynamite! Bunch of idiots!'"

"That stuff doesn't concern us. We're women. We know about ourselves, our cunts, not the crap you read in the newspapers. Who'd you think murdered the girl?"

"Maybe a person who lives in the same hell we live in. Sure we're waitresses. We're part of the meat market. We're the meat. That's how we get loved. We get cooked. We get our asses burned cause sex, like everything else, is always involved with money."

"I don't like to think and I don't trust people who think." Ciannina kisses Berthe on her right ear.

"If we lived in a society without bosses," Berthe says seriously, "we'd be fucking all the time. We wouldn't have to be images. Cunt special. We could fuck every artist in the world."

"I'd like to fuck all the time."

"My heroine is Sophie Perovskaya." Giannina's slowly licking the inside of Berthe's ear. "Five years ago March first The People's

Will, a group she was part of, murdered Tsar Alexander II. As she died, she rejoiced, for she realized her death would deal a fatal blow to autocracy." Giannina blows into her ear. "I'd like to have the guts to follow that woman."

"I want to be a whore."

"Don't you understand the world in which we're living?" Berthe screams. "On Sunday May 21 the first detachment of Versailles troops entered the capital. This entrance caught the Commune unawares. Thiers' army made up of prisoners of war and provincial recruits shot everyone in sight. They killed 25,000 people. The Communards, retreating from Paris, burned as much as they could. Marshal MacMahon of the Versailles army declared order was restored. The death of the Paris Commune was the death of the workers' revolutionary power. Now we have to give up our lives to cause any destruction of this society."

Giannina kisses Berthe again and again. Her tongue slowly enters Berthe's full red mouth.

"We want men!" both women think. "Be a man to me! Fuck me. Fuck me. Lie on top of me. Drive it into me. We want women!"

Their warmth and need for warmth drive them into each other. They feel confused. They're not sure they want each other, even though sweat's pouring out of their flesh and their cunt muscles're relaxing, opening with the agony of desire.

Naked flesh against naked flesh. Naked lips against naked lips. Naked cunt burning against naked cunt. Naked thighs against naked thighs. Bare shoulders twisting around bare shoulders. Naked tits against naked tits.

"Giannina," murmurs Berthe, "sometimes I hate you. You're so beautiful every man's always creaming in his pants after you. I could never be so beautiful. When I'm with you, sometimes, I feel ugly." Her tongue flickers the aching nipples.

Her whole mouth goes to the nipple, and sucks.

The hair curling above the cunt, between the thighs, around the outer lips, in the red crack of the ass touches the thick pink outer lips touches the tiny red inner lips inside the outer lips touches the red berry at one end of the inner lips whose inside grows if it's grazed lightly enough touches the muscles and nerves spiraling as a canal away from the red inner lips. Berthe's thumb draws a slow pink spiral against the soft yielding breast flesh. Her right hand's fingertips grasp the heavy falling breast. The nipple rubs against the inside of her palm.

"Giannina, I don't want to. I think I'm falling in love with you. Help me not to, or don't let me get burned, I'm scared I'm going to be very very in love with you."

The wide open pink cunt lips. Giannina's fingers touch.

The thin slivers of red membrane.

As Giannina touches the membrane, lightly, very lightly, she sees the membrane move, the whole cunt quiver. Sigh. Lightly she draws her middle finger along the main fold . . .

She hears Berthe scream and scream. Berthe screams and screams. Berthe's in a world composed only of sensations. She doesn't know anything except what she feels. She rolls around on this wonderful mass of flesh and bones, yielding and nonyielding, her nerves rub into warm, wet, rough hairs. She writhes reels quivers shakes turns spins falls rises bounces squirms wiggles pants. Her sense of balance's rolling against Giannina.

Fucking. Fucking. Fucking. Feeling all the possible feelings which are needs in the world.

Giannina's the cat. She throws herself up against Berthe because she wants Berthe. She wants to throw her body into Berthe's body because she wants to bask in Berthe's heat. Berthe's safety. Berthe's going to do it to her. Berthe looks so huge. Berthe's flaming hair. Berthe's blue eyes. Berthe's huge hands. Berthe'll protect her: she can open herself totally to Berthe

Her cunt opens to Berthe's cunt. To all of Berthe's body which's going to get inside her. Her mouth's open. Her eyes're open. Her arms are open, groping wet heavy flesh. Her legs're open. Wide. Her stomach's rending. Her whole abdomen's opening. Her womb . . .

"I'm frightened. I want you. This's the sun. I want you," Berthe squeals.

"If you were a man, I could love you," says Giannina.

*   *   *

The Paris of 1886 is the Paris of the Conservatives, in spite of the surprising, and painfully short presidency of the Radical René Goblet; of General Boulanger; of the Opportunists who're making Paris and France into an empire whose only rival is Great Britain; of depression due to increasing imports of American and Australian wheat, widespread phylloxera destruction of grapevines, lack of natural sources such as coal needed in this beginning industrial period. An act passed July 1886 forbids the Orleans and Bourbon heirs access to French soil. General Boulanger, the new Minister of War, expels the Duc d'Aumale and the Duc de Chartres from the Army. The general on the black horse's charming! Bismarck, a bit too hastily, incarcerates a prominent unnameable French person. Boulanger gets him released! But people're still starving everywhere: strikes're increasing especially in the mining, iron, and steel industries.

What can we know of such a period?

A particularly brutal strike and murder occurs in the mining town of Decazeville.

The most important incident of the year, at least for us, takes place not in France, but in Chicago, USA. The most industrialized city in the world. A city that's a giant factory. In France the workers still support their bosses. The workers want to be petite bourgeoisie. The new Marxist party, tiny to begin with and composed of intellectuals, splits into the "Possibilists" and the French Workers' Party. In Chicago the workers unite.

May Day, 1886.

The workers celebrate and demonstrate.

A strike's going on at the McCormick harvester works.

Two days later, Chicago cops shoot at strikers during a clash between strikers and blacklegs at the works.

Local anarchists hold a meeting at Haymarket, a large empty spot in Chicago, to protest the cop shootout.

The meeting goes peacefully enough. A heavy storm drives away most of the people. The police order the meeting to close. Samuel Fielden, one of the demonstration leaders, who's still speaking, objects. He tells the cop the meeting's orderly. The police lieutenant insists. Suddenly, a bomb explodes the crowd.

Who threw the bomb?

The day is wet, cold, and windy. One policeman, several other people wounded. The police start to shoot. Demonstrators policemen wounded killed.

The city panics! Bombers terrorists're going to take over! The police arrest nine prominent anarchists. One of the nine, Schnaubelt, disappears.

Another of the nine, Albert Parsons, who's been missing, turns himself in to the cops so he can share his friends' fate.

The defendant anarchists try to use their trial to put the conservative American government on the defensive:

> SCHWAB (ONE OF THE ANARCHISTS): I demand the floor in the name of all the defendants.
> JUDGE: You can't have the floor!
> THE ANARCHISTS: Speak, Schwab, speak!
> SEVERAL JURYMEN: Your Honor, tell the defendants to shut up.
> THE D.A.: The defendants are to remain seated!
> (*All the anarchists stand up and scream.*)
> JUDGE: The court will not permit itself to be intimidated by this uproar. I declare that, if the slightest disturbance is injected into the trial, I shall bring in a verdict of guilt against the defendants.
> SEVERAL ANARCHISTS: Cut it short! Judge us now, without letting us be heard! That won't take so long!
> THE ANARCHISTS (EN MASSE): Condemn all of us! All! All!

The court sentences four of the anarchists to death.

The court sentences four of the anarchists to long prison terms.

During the appeal sessions, Albert Parsons speaks for eight hours. Samuel Fielden speaks for three. Schwab calls for "a state of society in which all human beings do right for the simple reason that it's right and hate wrong because it's wrong."

Lingg (a true terrorist who has manufactured bombs) expresses contempt for "your ORDER, your laws, your force-propped authority."

The court changes none of the death or prison sentences.

My friends Vincent, Paul, Theo're starving. I'm dying for lack of love. Suddenly I'm also starving because my mother stops giving me money. I move into the brothel.

In the last bedroom of Norvins' brothel, a small dingy room into which a beam of light occasionally filters, Rhys Chatham, a prostitute, lives. Rhys is a tall red-hair, lanky, huge basketball player's chest, broad shoulders, green eyes thin large nose stiff spine. He's an ex-cop. In fact, he used to be superintendent of the Paris police. He was a good, honest cop, as cops go; he got his desire to work hard and be honest from his religious parents. But he also wanted to find God, and God isn't in the police force. This's the wildness and meanness of Rhys' character.

"Masturbate in front of me," Rhys says to me.

(1975)

Florida

Maybe you're dying and you don't care anymore.
In the nothingness, the gray, islands almost disappear
into the water. Black ovals the shape of leaves hide the crumbling of the universe. Key West Islands disappearing into the ocean.

You don't have anything more to say. You don't know what to do. Your whole life has been a mess. Grabbing on to whatever romance came along and holding on to it for dear life until it went so sour you had to vomit and leave. Then you'd recover, just like you recover from a hangover, by grabbing the next piece of tail who came along and wasn't so helpless or so demanding she'd force you to perceive reality.

One cunt's like every other cunt. One ideal's like every other ideal. When one dream goes, another takes its place. You're sick of standing in this shit and so you step out.

At the end of the world. Almost no one living in this perpetual Florida grayness. It may not be paradise, but it doesn't stink of the shit of your dreams. Not much to set you dreaming in this grayness.

There's an old dilapidated hotel on the island. Some old croaker who wheezes instead of talking runs the spa. As far as you know, the croaker won't bother you, no one else's staying at the hotel, and room-and-board are cheap. You decide to stay for a night.

There's nothing else to say. You're a piece of meat among other pieces of meat. It's like when you were at the hospital. The doctor couldn't get the needle in your vein to extract blood. Every time he stuck the needle in your arm, the vein rolled away. You felt like a piece of meat and you didn't care. You saw that the doctor saw living and dying and screaming people and the doctor didn't care if you were dying or screaming. So you didn't care if you were dying or screaming.

You can't tell what matters anymore. Every day you look out at the ocean and you see a tiny boat going down that grayness. One dark tiny boat going down the turbulent waters.

You're gonna stick with him, not cause you love him, but you've gone this far. You've opened yourself to trusting him so deeply if you turn back now, you'll be throwing everything you've got away. The only thing you can call your life. You'll be left with a rotting carcass. Besides, he's not so bad even if he is a gangster. The dimple in his double chin.

He knows how to handle you. He's cruel to you just up to a certain point. He knows that point and he knows if he was one bit crueler to you, you'd leave him. He knows when to press you, when to be a little bit crueler, and when to leave you alone. He really cares about you because he bothers to know you so well. Other people he doesn't bother about, he just kills them. He's gotten into you and he knows how to manipulate your limbs with his big naked hands.

He's a killer. O my God, he kills people. You know you've got to get away from him.

You look up in the car, and there he is. Driving the car, as usual. Never looking at you.

Johnny's running away from trouble again. He's always more trouble than the trouble from which he's running away.

You're the big one. The big dingbat. The winner. You're in this little hick town, this island, and you're gonna take it over until the boat comes. As usual you've got everything arranged and under control. You know how to move the little people around so you can get everything you want.

It's quiet here, and gray. Layers of gray and layers of gray. Like a numbness you can slice with your hand. When the numbness separates, there's nothing. This's what you want.

The ocean waves're moving regularly up and down the beach. They leave lines of shells on the beach and sometimes large jellyfish. You can see the shells and the jellyfish only when the light manages to squeeze through the gray layers. Otherwise the shells and jellyfish look like darker gray blobs, then rows, on the gray.

The day gets darker. You see that the beach isn't the sea. The crummy wood boards that lead to the sea look wet. The whole joint's crumbling apart. How many more years does this hotel have? Three? One? One more hurricane? Maybe tomorrow. You can see the bones of the world.

Somewhere behind you, you hear a car stop and voices. You don't believe that you're hearing anything.

So now shitface is gonna take out his little gun. Order everyone around with his little gun, the old fuddy-duddy who doesn't keep up this palsied outhouse, probably pisses in his pants, and the doddering old man who's been the only hotel guest for the last twenty years. Phooey. Isn't Johnny tough? Johnny and his gun. You hope the hotel's got a bar cause you're gonna have to stick with Johnny until you can get out of this grayness.

You need another man. In this grayness it's easier to find a bottle of booze.

What man's gonna want you now? Once upon a time you were really hot stuff. With your blonde hair and big child's eyes, eyes so big and wide they denied the way your nipples got hard under your sweater, men were drooling after you. You could get anyone you wanted. For nothing. Now you get beaten up and shoved around. Every now and then you get a gun shoved in your mouth.

"OK. Everyone get your hands up. I'm taking over here."

You walk into the dark inner space of the hotel. You're gonna show them who's boss. A trembling white-haired guy appears with his hands held up.

You're dreaming that you're wearing your white Givenchy dress and your white and brown shoes. You're wading through about two feet of mud and water. Your dress is getting filthy, but you don't mind. You're trying to reach an old deserted house. Your fiancé's waiting for you there. You lift your eyes and see a large dark structure.

"We're almost there, dear." Your red fingernails carefully flick a cake crumb off your summer dress.

You're still alone and with the grace of God you'll die alone.

Maybe you'll die soon and it'll all be over. No more fakes.

The ocean's calm. It's almost evening and it looks like dawn with that strange yellow sun, under the dark gray sky, making the lower third of the sky white-yellow-gray. Sending a triangle of yellow-white light out over the ocean.

The air's still and stinks of fish. You realize a storm's coming. One storm more or less don't make any difference to you. You walk into the dark interior of the hotel and see a gun pointed at your face.

"Back against the wall."

I moved back against the wall. I didn't feel frightened, yet.

"All of you, back against the wall."

The geezer who ran the hotel was already rubbing his back so hard against the wall, the wallpaper was crumbling. A dame with booze in her hand who was standing against the hotel register didn't move.

The guy with the gun walked over and slashed her face open with the point of his gun. She looked at him and walked over to the wall.

Lightning.

The hotel door flies open.

"OK Johnny. Men are for fucking and women for friendship. When I'm not fucking you, I'm your enemy."

I ignored what she said. The storm was coming up hard and fast and there was nothing I could do about that. The boat wouldn't come and I'd be stuck with these pawns for days.

"I want you to understand I'm boss here. This storm."

*   *   *

"It's a hurricane."

I gave the old guy a dirty look. "Hurricane. It's gonna be a while and I don't want trouble. As far as I'm concerned, you're pieces on a checkerboard that I'm moving around so everything's easiest for me. You're either on the board or you're off the board." I moved my gun.

The hotel door swung open and shut. When the door swung open again, an old guy in a wheelchair and a tall woman dressed in a lightish dress were standing in the doorway.
I thought I was hallucinating.

"Excuse me. I need help for my grandfather, Senator . . ."
"We're . . ."

You'd think this was Palm Springs at Christmas. "Both of you. Get over here. No, you," I pointed my gun at the hotel clerk. He should be doing his job. "Shove the wheelchair against the wall. No funny business."
I looked at the girl. "You can use your own legs, I presume?"

The girl was a looker. Legs and class. I wouldn't go near her if she was coated with hundred-dollar bills. I didn't have to go near her. Johnny, as his drunk girlfriend called him, would be doing all our movements for us.

Hotel lights go out.
Old geezer takes advantage of blackness to try to shove wheelchair with guy in it at me. I laugh and shoot geezer in arm.
"Looks like someone else is going to have to be hotel clerk for a while."

There're no lights and there's this storm, a hurricane I think, and there's this gangster and I'm totally confused. This isn't the way things are back home. Mummy and poppa always kept a quiet home, and now that they're dead—they must not have loved me as much as I thought cause they died—grandpa, the senator, takes care of me. I wish we were back home.

Grandpa said that politics was getting so crooked, he had to get away for a while. He's not running from anyone; he's just trying to figure out how he can fight the crookedness more successfully. I want to be like grandpa: I want to fight for a better world.

I wonder if there are anymore men in the world like grandpa.

"All of you. Get to your rooms. Remember that people die when they go out in hurricanes. The phone lines are dead. There's no way you can escape.

"Don't get any funny ideas. Brave pigeons become dead pigeons. Remember: to me you're just pieces of meat."

We were pieces of meat who were still bleeding. The worst was: we might stop bleeding soon.

"In two hours you'll all come down here for dinner. If we can't find any food, we'll live on the booze. I like giving parties. I'll wheel the senator to his room."

"Get upstairs like he says." She looked like an outraged mother hen, only her baby was an old man in a wheelchair and she was probably a virgin. I put my hand on her arm. I didn't want her making more trouble for all of us.

"Wait a second."

"Uh-huh."

"You look like . . . a reasonable man. Is that monster going to hurt my grandfather?"

"I doubt it. Your grandfather's probably too important a person."

"I didn't ask you to be smart. We're in a terrible situation and we have to help each other."

* * *

"The kind of help I could give you honey you wouldn't want."

"How do you know what I want?"

"I can tell by looking at your fingers. Your left-hand pinky's shorter than the finger next to it. Now will you be a good girl and get upstairs?"

"You're a man! You could overpower this gangster. You wouldn't have to kill him. Just knock him cold."

"A woman friend once told me the only thing men are good for is fucking. I'm afraid that's true."

"You're not a man. A man would realize that his and other people's lives are in danger. Even if he didn't care about the other people, he'd try to save himself. You're a flea, or some kind of . . . amoeba who just accepts things."

"Listen. I'm not going to do anything. I don't care how I die, honey." I started walking up the stairs.

I began remembering her long legs and regretting I was walking away from her.

I wanted to kill him. The only thought in my mind was that I wanted to kill him.

I must have fallen asleep, for the next thing I know, I'm hearing these screamings and sounds of beating that make the old hotel seem like a flea-studded whorehouse:

". . . keep your mouth shut."

"Why don't cha beat me up again? Hurting me takes the place of sex these days."

"I'm a businessman. I want you to remember. I'm a quiet businessman and I like my friends to be quiet about me."

* * *

"The only friends you have are dead men.

"You're just a cheap dice man, Johnny. A cheap dice man who's running from the real crooks, the big crooks, and you think you can be a big guy to these crummy people in this crummy hotel."

"I suppose the takeover of The Flamingo and Virginia Hill's 'suicide' are small-time bits to you?

"I shouldn't ever talk to you. I weaken myself when I talk to you."

"Johnny, straighten out. You're nothing Johnny, like me."

"You stinkin' whore. I'm gonna kill you one of these days."

"You're nothing like me.

"Get me another drink, please Johnny."

I wanted to find my grandfather. I left the little room at the end of the hall against which the wild wind was beating and the trees and the telephone poles, the only bit of safety I had left, and I started down the hall. I knew my grandfather was somewhere downstairs.

The hotel was dark, almost black. Walls seemed to drift into more and more corners and walls. Finally I reached the stairs.

Large dark shapes moved in and out of the corners of my eyes. As I walked down the stairs, I saw the walls move, bend and almost crack, as if they were bowing to me. I was walking down the endless stairs in my long white dress. The train of my dress was slowly draped upward behind me. I felt so tall and proud my head was almost touching the ceiling. Soon I would be a new woman.

All the people I had ever known were waiting for me at the bottom of the stairs. My mother was crying and even my father had tears in his eyes. I was so happy I was almost crying. Somewhere in that mass of people, my fiancé, soon: my husband, was waiting for me.

What was I thinking? I had to find my grandfather. I was in a hotel which was being, for some reason, run by a gangster and I had to find my grandfather before the gangster killed him.

I was standing at the bottom of that endless flight of stairs. I could see the hotel door flying open and closed, almost flying off its hinges but not quite, and I could see the winds wiping the panes of glass out of the windows and I could hear the palm trees break and fall against the old hotel. I wanted to run, but I didn't know where I could go.

I realized that I've always wanted to run and never have anywhere to run to. I had to find my grandfather quickly. There were rooms and rooms and most of the rooms were empty and my grandfather was in one room and the gangster was in another room. I could hardly tell the rooms from the doors cause the large dark shapes were moving in front of and away from my eyes.

I couldn't see but I had to keep going. I stuck my hands out in front of me.

I kept on moving. Something clattered to the floor, and I almost tumbled.

A hand grabbed my wrist.

I didn't want to, but I couldn't get those legs out of my mind. I looked outside my room and saw those legs again. I didn't want to, I must have stopped thinking, but I began to follow them.

Long white legs.

They led me through the hall, down the stairs, and into some large room.

I found myself looking into that man's eyes. The one who wouldn't help me. "What do you want with me?"

"I want to talk to you."

"We've done all our talking. I don't want anything to do with men who are cowards.

"Excuse me, I have to find my grandfather."

"You've done all your talking. I still want to talk to you."

She tried to brush by me. I put my two arms around the sides of her body.

* * *

"What d'you want?"

"I want to find out who you are."

"I'm in trouble. Or do you want the irrelevant details?"

"Let's say I want the irrelevant details."

"When I was two years old, I refused to drink milk. My parents, they were still alive then, were scared I was going to die. My father started to take a camera apart. Only when he started to break the camera, would I drink the milk."

"That's certainly irrelevant."
    "Is it? I want to stay alive, Mr. Coward. I'm only interested in people who are going to help me stay alive."

"Aren't you being self-centered? Tell me about mom and pops. When did they die on you?"

"When I was eight. Just old enough to start feeling insecure and not old enough to know how to ask someone for help. My grandfather took me into his house and gave me what attention he could."

"Could? You mean you were a lonely child who spent lonely days making up fantasies and living in them?"

"My personal history concerns only those people who love me. Excuse me please."

"Tell me more about your parents. Did they love you a lot when you were a child?"

"I want to find my grandfather." I was begging him to help me. "If you care at all about me, you'll help me find him."

*   *   *

"I didn't know I cared about you."

"Help me."

For some reason I wanted to hear the rest of her words, but I couldn't.
I kept hearing that stupid popular song, bits of it, that everyone was
singing back where everyone was still living and burning each other
out.

> *Baby don't give, baby don't get.*
> *When it's cold, baby gets wet.*
> *When baby gets wet, baby gets weak.*
> *Baby don't find, baby don't seek.*

> *You want to know the story of this song*
> *It's about a woman who loves to go wrong.*
> *She gets contented like a big fat cat*
> *Only when she's lying flat on her back.*

> *Well, this woman fell in love with a man*
> *Just like some women unfortunately can.*
> *This man had nuts but was nuts in the head*
> *He refused to take this hot babe to bed.*

> *Baby don't give, baby don't get.*
> *When it's cold, baby gets wet.*
> *When baby gets wet, baby gets weak.*
> *Baby don't find, baby don't seek.*

> *He told her he loved her; he told her he'd give*
> *Anything to her so she'd continue to live.*
> *He'd buy her minks and he'd buy her pearls*
> *He just wouldn't give her cunt a swirl.*
> *Too many women were pursuing him*
> *And he was fucking too many girls.*

So she sang him this sad sad song
About how the world was always wrong:
DIE IF I DO, DIE IF I DON'T:
DIE IF I WRITE, DIE IF I DON'T
DIE IF I FALL IN LOVE AND DIE IF I WON'T

He didn't give a shit, he didn't care.
She shouted to the cold winter air;
She slashed her wrists; she shaved her head;
She refused to eat so she'd almost drop dead.

He didn't run to her, he told her he
Was sick of people and their needs.
All he wanted to do was sit alone
In his country house by his telephone.

Baby don't give, baby don't get.
When it's cold, baby gets wet.
When baby gets wet, baby gets weak.
Baby don't find, baby don't seek.

So listen girls, do what you can
To find a horny loving man.
Give him all you've got to give,
Give him more so you can live.

(1976)

from *Kathy Goes to Haiti*

A Trip to the Voodoo Doctor

After a week and a half of anxiously waiting, Kathy decides to go to Port-au Prince to look for Roger. As soon as she reaches Port-au-Prince, she forgets about Roger. Completely dazed, with a huge smile, she wanders around the hot docks that are the pits of Haiti's main city.

The congested streets, rotting pastel-colored wood walls piled on top of each other, legless and armless beggars on wheels, male and female one-basket merchants, rows of food and leather and plastic shoes and notebooks and hair curlers, one or two scared white tourists, starved children looking for the rich white tourists, nonexistent sidewalks and cars, lots and lots of cars, Chevrolets and Pontiacs and Plymouths and Fords and VW's and Jeeps and a few American sportscars and the tap-taps, cars of every color and year, cars that don't run and hopped-up cars, all going at same speed: slowly, and lots and lots of garbage, and rooms without doors in the rotting pastel-colored wood walls, and rooms without walls, everything and everyone piled up on and squashed next to each other, a big pounding scaly pregnant fish: all give way to wide empty streets. Wide empty sidewalks. Low block-big rectangular buildings. Everything here is white. It's hotter than where the people and all the buildings are crushed together. There seem to be very few people here because sidewalks and the streets are so huge. The air seems to be the same color as the buildings and the streets.

Moving from the congested market-slum-city, through this whiteness, to the ocean, each block gets longer and wider. The third and final block is the longest and widest. It's huge. It's surrounded by emptiness. The few people walking up and down look like black marbles lost in the sand. A white person wouldn't be seen at all. Moving from the congested market-slum-city, through this whiteness, to the ocean, no one can breathe. The ocean is a green plate. There's no sound because the streets and buildings are big and empty and almost invisible. As if they're shadows.

What are they shadows of? One narrow wood pier extends into the water. The water makes no sound against the wood. A two-sail boat lies a quarter of a mile off of this pier.

It's this hot and white because dust and pollution sweep down from the mountains and the upper city into this pit. Then the air and pollution move from this pit across the ocean and leave a vacuum.

One wide black street lies parallel to the oceanfront. Three huge empty squares, amputated fingers, lie off of this street. The cement squares don't contain anything.

A group of males are standing on the corner of the sidewalk of the middle square. They're talking to each other. Two cops in cop uniforms're yelling at a smaller group of men, a few whites in this group, who're trying to get past the closed wire gates and on to the far end of the pier. Kathy walks out of the middle of the smaller groups of men and off of the pier. She's leaning against a pole and watching what's going on. The world's hot.

"Hey, Kathy."

She looks around, but doesn't see anyone she knows. She doesn't know anyone in Port-au-Prince.

"Hey, Kathy."

She looks over the street at the large group of men on the sidewalk and sees an arm waving. She crosses the black street and walks over to the waving arm. "Don't you remember me, Kathy? I'm Sammy's brother. Don't you remember Sammy?"

"Jesus Christ. How are you? I've been away: I just got back to Port-au-Prince yesterday. How's Sammy?" She feels embarrassed.

"Sammy wants to see you."

"I don't know. Uh, I'm kind of busy right now. Actually I'm looking for Rue DeForestre. I've got to make an airplane reservation so I can get back to the Cap as soon as possible. Can you tell me where the Rue DeForestre is?"

"When should I tell Sammy to meet you?"

"I don't know. Sometime later today. I have to get to the Rue DeForestre and I got totally lost . . ."

"It's just a few blocks from here."

"Where?"

"You can't walk there by yourself. I'll get someone to help you."

"I don't need any help. I just want to know where it is."

"Patrick, this is Kathy. Kathy, Patrick." A short-haired good-looking twenty-year-old.

"How can I get to the Rue DeForestre?" she asks Patrick.

"I'll show you. It's not far from here."

"Just tell me how to get there."

"You can't walk there by yourself. It's too far."

"I like to walk."

"White women don't walk around this city by themselves. The men won't leave you alone and you'll get lost."

"I can take care of myself. I just want to know how to get there."

"Do you not want to talk with me because you think I'll do something bad to you?"

"Don't be ridiculous. I just don't see any reason you should go out of your way so I can get to where I'm going. I like you."

"I have nothing to do. I'll walk with you."

"I can't pay you or anything."

"Why do you mention money? I want to be your friend. Do you think I want your money?"

"I'm sorry." She tries to explain. "I get so used to people asking me for money . . ."

"You don't want to be friends with me?"

"I don't even know you. I think I want to be friends with you."

"What hotel're you staying at?" the brother asks her.

"The Plaza."

"Sammy'll pick you up there at five o'clock this afternoon. Don't forget."

"OK." She turns again to her new friend. "I have to go to ABC Tours. It's on the Rue DeForestre."

"I know where it is."

They start walking upward, through the city. "Is it far?"

'Why do you ask so many questions?"

"I just want to know where I'm going."

"Why do you want to get to ABC Tours so badly?"

"I want to get back to Cap Haitian as soon as possible." She tells him how much she loves Cap Haitian, all about Roger and the beggar boys. "Are we almost there?"

"What're you in such a hurry for? Americans're always in a hurry. I lived in America for a while, that's why I speak English so well. I didn't like it except when I lived in Atlanta, Georgia. The life in Atlanta, Georgia, is like the life here. Nobody hurries there, no one works, and there's lots of dope. Do you smoke dope?"

"Yeah."

"Do you want some now? I have some really good smoke. I can stop by my house and get it."

"Not right now. Maybe later."

"Don't you trust me?"

"I trust you. I mean, you're a strange guy and I don't know you very well."

"I don't want to hurt you. Do you think I want you to be my girlfriend?"

"Well . . ."

"Look. Put your hand in mine." She stares at his outstretched hand. "Go on. Take my hand." She's holding his hand. "See. I don't want anything more. Do you know why you can trust me?"

"Why?" Her big brown eyes look up at him.

"You look and act exactly like my older sister. How old are you?"

"Twenty-nine."

"No you're not. She's twenty-three."

"I *am* twenty-nine."

"You can't be more than twenty. That's how old you are. Call me your brother."

"OK, brother."

"Take my hand again." He takes her into the green rickety wood room that's the travel bureau and out of it. "Why do you want to take the plane to the Cap?"

"How else could I get there?" They continue walking up and down the sometimes nonexistent sidewalks past the fake storefronts.

"Why don't you rent a motorcycle?"

"Gee, that's an idea. When I was a kid, I used to spend days hitchhiking on motorcycles. I've always had this thing about motorcycles and black leather. But if I drive a cycle up to the Cap, I won't have any way of getting it back. Maybe I can return it there? I could learn to ride a cycle in a day."

"I'll ride with you. Then I'll drive the bike back to Port au-Prince."

"How much money would you want for that?"

"I don't want your money. I told you this already. I do it because you're my sister."

"No. I don't think I want to do it. How much would it cost me to rent a cycle?"

"Nine dollars a day."

"That's not much."

"Plus you give them a deposit. You get the deposit back."

"How can I get the deposit if I'm going to Cap Haitian and not coming back?"

"I can get it for you."

"No . . ."

"You still don't like me. You think I'm going to take all your money."

"I don't have enough money for you to take."

"If you rented a motorcycle, you could be in Cap Haitian tonight. You don't want to waste all your money on a plane. Why don't you take a look at the motorcycle store? It's just around the corner."

"Wait a second. If it costs me nine dollars a day I won't be able to get the cycle back till tomorrow, it'll cost me at least eighteen." She's adding everything up in her head. "Plus the deposit. That's more than a plane ticket."

"So you're not going to do it?"

"I have my plane ticket. I'm going to go back to the hotel now."

"Why don't you rent a bike just for the day? You can take the plane tomorrow or the next day. We'll go to the Barbaneourt rum factory."

"I don't have nine dollars to blow on a cycle. I want to go home."

Patrick informs her there are other cheaper ways to go to Cap Haitian—the vomit bus and the government airplane, so she asks him about the government airplane. They decide he'll take her to the government airport so she can reserve a ticket.

They've been walking up and down the sidewalks for hours. Sometimes there's a huge bottomless hole in a sidewalk. Sometimes a sidewalk disappears. Sometimes the sidewalks and streets are clean the wood store walls are solid. As they descend through the city, the sidewalks getting narrower until they almost disappear, the streets disappearing, the stores are on top of each other. They're in the marketplace. The sidewalks lie under shoes, carved fake mahogany cause there's no real mahogany left in Haiti cause the woods that used to cover the island have been decimated, straw baskets full of plastic barrettes, Ivory soap, and underpants, mangoes, baskets full of all kinds of burnt sugar confections, dried fish. The long cigar-black street lies under brightly colored private cars, private taxis, city-run taxis, tap-taps, bicycles, young boys with no legs, young boys with shriveled legs, and old big-belly women. One huge block contains one no-door building. Inside this building, space is immense. There are no walls except for the outer walls of the building and those walls are almost invisible due to the lack of light. Tables cover all of the sawdust floor, tables far as the eye can see, wood tables covered with baskets full of short and long rices, millet, wheat kernels, ground grains, dried corn and white and yellow corn flours, dried fishes, fish freshly caught from the ocean still unscaled and ungutted, different varieties of mangoes, canaps, figs, bananas, breadfruit, sour oranges, lemons, limes, onions and garlics, tomatoes, coconuts, cashews, roasted cashews, sugar, brown sugar, almonds, peanuts, raisins, Camembert cheese, more. Scales hang over some of the tables. Narrow pathways in the darkness separate the tables. Women and men and children all dressed in brightly colored cloth, almost hidden by the darkness, stand by the tables or shuffle by each other. Almost under the table, in the half-light, here and there, an old woman squats and separates kernels of corn in a huge straw basket and scales a fish with a big heavy steel knife in her hand. Outside the people are walking on top of each other, over each other; the sky's so bright its yellow is blue even though it isn't.

Kathy and Patrick stumble into a tap-tap. A tap-tap is a small public bus that's colored with green red pink yellow brown blue and black paint. The tap-tap's white. Virgin Mary's La Sirene's Jesus Christ's Duvalier's private girlfriends' names adorn every inch of the bus' walls. GRACE DE MARIE. PAIX POUR TOUJOURS. LE SAUVIER EST ICI. The tap-tap lets Patrick and Kathy off at the government airbase.

The government airbase is a huge almost empty field that's brown gray and, a little olive green. A brown man stands in a gray metal booth in front of this field and controls who goes in and out of the field. There are a few other men inside the field. There are a few two-engine gray airplanes. There are a few huts on the ground. The airfield seems empty cause it's so big and cause it looks like death.

She walks out of the airfield and they climb back into a tap-tap. She thanks him and tells him she's going to go home now that she's done what she had to. He doesn't want her to go away from him. He tells her he wants to go to the beach. She doesn't want to go to the beach. He wants to rent a motorcycle and ride around Petionville. She doesn't want to rent a motorcycle. He wants to go dancing in Carrefour. She doesn't want to dance.

"I know this doctor I'd like you to meet."

"Do you mean a voodoo doctor?"

"He's a very important man. I want you to meet him because you mean a lot to me."

"I'd love to meet him."

"You have to realize this could be the most important thing that's ever happened to you. I want you to realize this. This man can change your life."

"I want to meet him."

"He's going to do a lot for you. I know he is. This man has helped a lot of people. He's a very good man."

"I don't want him to do anything for me. I just want to meet him."

"There's just one thing. You have to be willing to realize who he is."

"Do I have to pay him anything?"

"You'll have to buy him candles so he can do his work. That won't cost you much."

All the tap-taps in the city meet in the marketplace. They're back where they started from. Limbless beggars crouch under them. Skateboards attached to half-bodied people roll by.

They go off to see the voodoo doctor. The city cab soon leaves the straight black tar streets. It winds basically upward and to the left, sometimes round in circles, sometimes in huge snake-arcs, sometimes it goes opposite to where it wants to go, there's no time in Haiti. It goes everywhere. Through driveways and around falling-apart single-building single-room stores. On gray broken cement roads that go under while the old mansions alongside the road go up so it seems to go under mansions. Ahead up a narrow street hedged in by two-story wood houses into a narrow gray wood garage then straight back down the street in reverse.

The neighborhood changes completely. The taxicab turns left on a corner, and stops.

A narrower pebbly unrideable road juts off of the dirt road the taxi's been riding on. The new road is covered with dust. Thick yellow dust. This dust hides women carrying huge parcels on their heads, walking in the ruts, and two-story stucco houses, painted all colors, yellow and black. They walk into the dust. The sun seems to get hotter and hotter. There's lots of noise and hot dust and heat. On one side the dust sharply descends through the air into a ditch crossed over by a modern trestle. They keep on trudging upward.

The pebbly road turns sharply to the right. About ten yards below this turn, there's a dark red stucco house. The red house has a porch.

The sun is very very hot. Kathy feels tired and excited. Kathy should wait on the porch while Patrick sees if the doctor's available.

Kathy's waiting. A huge man appears. Would Kathy like to go inside?

Kathy does what anyone tells her. She follows the man around the porch and the house past a tiny woman washing and hanging laundry to a tiny room in the back of the house which is only big enough for the narrow cot and cabinet-desk inside it. Photos and newspapers cover the walls and glass windows of the cabinet.

"Are you the doctor?" Kathy asks the man.

"The doctor?"

"Uh, I'm supposed to meet a doctor. A holy person. I thought that was you."

The huge man sits down on the bed next to Kathy and laughs. "Non. I am Kung Fu."

Kathy looks at him in total fear.

"There are pictures of me at my kung fu."

She sees pictures of him dressed up in his uniform. "Oh, you're a black belt."

"Do you know about kung fu?"

"Not very much."

"I am very good, I like doing that: I don't like violence. I don't go with women because they're tricky. They don't do things honestly. I only go with men."

She relaxes and looks at the girly pictures. "Are those your relatives, that woman over there?"

"That's a picture of my aunt and her two children. They now live in Boston. Do you know Boston?"

"Very well. I used to live there."

"I'd like to go there." There's a huge market for the private yacht owners in smuggling Haitians to anywhere in the U.S. They talk about their relatives and kung fu for a long long time. Kathy and the huge gentle man like each other very much.

When Patrick returns for Kathy, she doesn't want to leave.

"You said you wanted to see the doctor."

She tells the kung fu man she'll return as soon as she's finished with the voodoo doctor.

Patrick and Kathy're walking upward in the thick dust. When

they reach a black Pontiac parked by the corner, he tells her to wait there until someone comes for her.

How will she know who that someone is? She'll know.

Fifteen minutes pass by. She sees a girl in a bright bright green skirt walking toward her. She sees, in the distance, Patrick's hand waving at her. The girl smiles at her so she follows her.

The girl walks partways up the same road, then turns to her left. There are no more roads. The girl walks into a mass of dust, on a mass of dust, down ten feet of only slightly horizontal rocks, into a section that's unlike anything Kathy's seen in Port-au-Prince.

There's a mass of dust-ground and approximately ten-feet-by-eight-feet and six-feet-high thatched huts. People are everywhere. Small black goats and roosters and black-and-white hens and lots and lots of children. Everyone squawking and cackling crying gossiping. Hotter than ever. Women sitting in the dust and women sitting by round straw baskets full of one kind of food and one woman sitting under an improvised cloth canopy by a table holding a tray of some homemade confection and women walking around and women washing clothes in some bowls of water and women holding babies maybe suckling them. The girl walks past these people without stopping, she walks around a hut, down, turns a sharp corner around another hut, straight onward, past almost a row of huts. Kathy follows her.

The girl stops by the door of one of the brown ten feet by eight feet huts and enters. Actually there's no door, only a red curtain. The roof is corroded metal. A narrow cot lies against the back wall of the hut. A rough table lies against the left wall. Two wood chairs. To the right, a middle-aged man so wrinkled and thin he looks old sits in a chair facing a smaller wood table.

Patrick's sitting on a chair between the old man and the back wall. "You have to buy some candles."

"How much money?"

"Three dollars."

Kathy gives Patrick this money. He gives the money to a woman who's sitting in the hut. There are three women sitting in the hut:

two on the bed and one (the girl who led Kathy to the hut) on the floor.

The père lights a white candle. Then he lights a cigarette with the candle flame and gives it to Patrick. He lights another cigarette and gives it to Kathy. He lights another cigarette for himself. Everyone smokes. The père sings a song something about Jesus. He speaks only Creole. Patrick translates for Kathy but Kathy suspects that Patrick isn't saying to her what the père says to him.

The père opens a small Bible and begins to recite a passage rapidly in a monotone.

Then his head sinks and he makes loud hiccups. "He's receiving the spirit." Patrick tells Kathy.

The père shakes Patrick's hand, then Kathy's hand. His grip is unusually strong and sharp.

The père rubs some liquid from a bottle covered with red cloth over his face and hands. He puts a match to the top of this bottle; the bottle lights up; immediately he puts his hand over the bottle top. The bottle sticks to his hand. He passes the hand-and-bottle round his head. When he pulls the bottle off of his hand, there's a loud pop and it looks like the skin of his hand is going to come away with the bottle.

The ceremony's begun.

It's very hot inside the unlighted hut, much hotter than it was outside the hut in the dust under the direct burning sun. Everyone inside the hut's sweating.

Kathy doesn't remember exactly what and when happens from now on because she's so hot and because she's getting dizzier and dizzier. Certain incidents stick out in her mind.

The père takes a drink from the red-cloth-covered bottle. He hands the bottle to Patrick to take a drink. Patrick drinks. He hands the bottle to Kathy to drink. Kathy drinks. It's cheap rum.

The père pours rum into an approximately one-foot-diameter tin bowl. Many objects are in the bowl: a Virgin Mary, some rocks, some sticks, a small skull, some beads, the white candle. He puts a match to the rum, poof! Everything's alight.

The père asks Kathy to write in a small green notebook. She writes down her name. "Anything else?" Kathy asks Patrick. She writes down her age.

The père says he needs something so he can begin his work for Kathy. He writes about fifteen words down on a small piece of white paper. "Give him some money" Patrick tells Kathy. "How much?" "It'll only be about three dollars." "Is this going to cost me any more money?" "This is important. You have to realize that you're doing something that could be the most important thing for you. He wants to work for you and he needs certain things to work with." "I only have a twenty." Kathy gives one of the women the twenty. She goes out of the hut to purchase the somethings.

The père gives Kathy a small dusty bottle with some clear liquid in it. She swallows. He smiles and takes back the bottle. "That'll be better for you," says Patrick. "You'll see what'll happen."

It's incredibly hot in the hut. Sweat runs down everyone's face. Kathy doesn't think she feels anything.

Everything takes incredibly long.

The père's singing again. The women on the bed join in singing. Kathy sings along. How the hell am I able to sing in a language I don't know, Kathy says to herself. The père and the women're happy Kathy's singing with them.

The père lights a cigar with the white candle's flame. He gives it to Patrick. He lights another cigar with the white candle's flame. He gives it to Kathy. He lights another cigar with the white candle's flame for himself. Everyone smokes his cigars.

The père talks to Patrick. Patrick tells Kathy she'll have to give the père some money because he's working for her. She understands. He's a worker. "How much?" "Ten dollar." Kathy gives the père a ten-dollar bill. He carelessly throws the bill on the wood table next to a huge beaten-up skull. "I don't have any more money," Kathy says, "I can't give you any more money." She's worried.

"How much money do you make in the United States?" Patrick asks Kathy. "Seven dollars a day when I work." "Wooo. You know why all the people up there," Patrick points to the invisible hills where all the rich people in Port-au-Prince live, "are rich? The doctor works for them. The doctor is going to work for you. This is very very important. The doctor is going to work for you for six . . . seven hundred a week." Kathy looks into the witch doctor's eyes. "I don't want money," she says. "I want you to understand. More, I want to do good for others."

The père smiles and says, "You have a great force in you. You must go upward." His hands motion strongly upward. "I can help you to go upward." Kathy smiles. She feels she and the père understand each other. She thinks Patrick's becoming a nuisance. "I would like that." The père shakes each of Kathy's hands quickly and firmly.

The père begins singing. Everyone starts singing.

The woman returns with about ten small envelopes, a bottle of cheap perfume, a bottle of rum. She gives fifteen dollars to Patrick. Patrick gives the fifteen dollars to Kathy.

The père takes the envelopes, perfume, and rum. He opens the rum, pours it into the dusty bottle, and drinks. He gives the bottle to Patrick. Patrick drinks. Patrick gives the bottle to Kathy. Kathy drinks. Everyone drinks a few more rounds. "I work with rum this first time," the père says.

The père lights up a cigarette with the white candle's flame. Gives it to Kathy. Lights another cigarette with the white candle's flame. Gives it to Patrick. Lights a cigarette with the white candie's flame for himself. Everyone smokes.

"Give me twenty cents for more cigarettes," Patrick tells Kathy. Kathy gives Patrick the money. "Also three dollars for another bottle of perfume. The father wants to do something special for you." Kathy thinks the père hasn't said anything to Patrick, but she gives the money anyways.

The père pours the perfume into an old thin bottle, about five inches high. Then he opens one of the small envelopes. He carefully shovels some of the lavender powder from this envelope into the bottle. Each of the envelopes contains a different color powder. The envelopes say things such as AMOUR, REINE DE GRACE. After he's opened and closed all the envelopes, he pours some of the rum from the dusty bottle, raw white rum, into the five-inch-high bottle. Everyone drinks some more rum. He shakes the five-inch-high bottle. He puts some brown dried leaves and branches into the five-inch-high bottle. He takes the rattle that's lying on the floor to the left of the wood table, shakes the rattle over everything. He puffs on his cigarette, blows smoke over everything, blows smoke into the five-inch-high bottle, and seals the bottle with an improvised paper cork.

The père rubs his face and hands with some liquid. He pours the same liquid on Kathy's hands and motions for her to rub her face. She does.

The père takes some salve and rubs it on her lips. He motions her to do she doesn't understand what. She kisses her arms and breasts. He smiles.

The woman returns with the cigarettes.

"He's given me a secret for you," Patrick tells Kathy. "What is it?" "I'll tell you later. I have something to tell you later." "Why can't you tell me now?" "He said I should tell you after we leave. He said you have to sit by the sea after we leave here. It's necessary you sit by the sea. I'll tell you then."

The père holds a pack of filthy cards in his hands. He puts three cards down on the table. Jack of Diamonds, dark queen, ace of clubs. He reshuffles the cards and cuts. He puts some more cards down on the table. He reshuffles the cards and cuts. He asks Kathy to cut the cards. She cuts toward him. He smiles. He puts ten cards down on the table. He quickly puts them back in the deck.

The père speaks to Patrick in a quick monotone. "Recently some-one's been speaking to you badly," Patrick translates for Kathy. Pause. "Is this true?" "Uh yeah . . . yeah maybe. I had a fight with a boy-friend in Cap Haitian right before I left. But it's OK now. We made up. That's not really speaking badly." The père speaks again in his rapid monotone. Patrick translates. "You've missed a very good chance in the U.S." "I dunno," Kathy says. The old man's not really hitting the mark, Kathy thinks to herself. "The father says he's going to work for you for six to seven hundred dollars a week. This is very important. He says you have bonne chance." Kathy talks directly to the père. "Je ne veux pas d'argent assez que je veux travailler pour des autres." The father smiles.

The father starts singing. Everyone sings along. One of the middle-aged women who's sitting on the bed leads the singing.

Patrick talks to a woman next to him, who suckles a baby.

"He wants to give you something else," Patrick says to Kathy. The père's carefully spooning some powder from each of the small white envelopes on to a crumpled piece of paper. When he finishes with the last envelope, he seals the paper and says something in his quick monotone to Patrick. "When you're alone, you have to rub this all over your body. If you don't do this, nothing he's doing for you will work." The père nods. Kathy nods.

The père takes the red-cloth-covered bottle. He lights its top with the white candle's flame. Poof. Quickly he places the palm of his hand over the top. The bottle sticks to his palm. He passes this hand-and-bottle three times around his head.

The leading woman, a middle-aged woman, starts drawing a vever on the stone floor. Everyone else sings lackadaisically while she sprinkles the white corn flour from a china dish on to the floor. The sign's a long backbone line with curlicues coming out of its sides. One heart in the middle. At the bottom of this vever she draws a funny hideous head. Then she draws a second vever which Kathy's too out of it to see. When the woman's finished using the flour, he nods his approval.

The père places the human skull that's on the wood table on the funny hideous head. He places two rocks near the skull. He shakes the rattle all over the skull. He's not satisfied. He takes the light blue nailpolish bottle that's on the wood table and pours some small gray beads from the nailpolish bottle on to the center of the first vever. He holds the lighted white candle next to these beads. The beads light up, explode. He places the human skull on top of the exploded beads. He puts two rocks near the skull. He's very careful to put everything in exactly the right place. He sticks the lighted white candle into a depression in the center of the skull. He sprinkles rum around the lighted white candle without extinguishing the light. He takes a small red-plastic-frame mirror and passes the mirror three times around the center of Kathy's body. He sticks the mirror in front of her face so she has to look at herself. Kathy's almost unconscious. He passes the mirror around her head three times. He places the mirror on the vever near the skull but not touching the skull. He places the five-inch-high corked bottle next to, leaning against the side of the skull. He picks a string of many-colored beads up from the junk of the floor to his left and throws the beads around the lighted white candle. He says something to Patrick. Patrick says, "She can't give you fifty dollars." The père and Patrick argue about how much money Kathy must give. Patrick says to Kathy, "Wait a second. Listen closely to me. You have to give something more. Otherwise all that he's doing won't work for you. What he's doing is very important. This is very important. You must realize that what he's doing could be the most important thing in your life." "How much?" Kathy asks Patrick. This is an art piece, Kathy thinks to herself. "Ten dollars. And when you get back to the United States, you buy him a watch. Not a good watch, you understand." Kathy gives a ten-dollar bill to the père. She has no more money left. He throws the ten-dollar bill on the skull. It falls in back of the skull. He pours rum around the lighted white candle without extinguishing its flame. He shakes the rattle over the skull and the vever.

The père draws a cross on Kathy's forehead.

The père motions Kathy to get up. He turns her around three times. He pushes her around the vevers three times clockwise. He pushes her around the vevers three times counterclockwise. He picks up the small plastic red-frame mirror and passes the mirror around her body. He shows Kathy to herself. He pushes her around the vevers three times clockwise. He pushes her around the vevers three times counterclockwise.

Kathy's facing the red curtain. The père tells Kathy she has to return here. She can bring a friend with her. He gives her the filled five-inch-high bottle and a green plastic soap case containing the powders. He tells her she can't look back.

Chickens and goats run around. The ground's so dry, it's almost sand. This sand flies everywhere. Children squall and yell. Women sit on the sand-covered almost nonexistent doorsteps of huts and low wood chairs outside the huts. Women talk to each other. Women with baskets on their heads walk in the fine dust. Women carry huge amounts of wet clothes in their arms. There are a few men.

"Goodbye," says the girl in the bright green skirt.

Kathy turns around and walks outside into the sun. She's more dazed than before.

(1978)

from *Blood and Guts in High School*

Inside high school

PARENTS STINK

Never having known a mother, her mother had died when Janey was a year old, Janey depended on her father for everything and regarded her father as boyfriend, brother, sister, money, amusement, and father.

Janey Smith was ten years old, living with her father in Merida, the main city in the Yucatán. Janey and Mr Smith bad been planning a big vacation for Janey in New York City in North America. Actually Mr Smith was trying to get rid of Janey so he could spend all his time with Sally, a twenty-one-year-old starlet who was still refusing to fuck him.

One night Mr Smith and Sally went out and Janey knew her father and that woman were going to fuck. Janey was also very pretty, but she was kind of weird-looking because one of her eyes was lopsided.

Janey tore up her father's bed and shoved boards against the front door. When Mr Smith returned home, he asked Janey why she was acting like this.

> JANEY: You're going to leave me. (*She doesn't know why she's saying this.*)
> FATHER (*dumbfounded, but not denying it*): Sally and I just slept together for the first time. How can I know anything?
> JANEY (*in amazement. She didn't believe what she had been saying was true. It was only out of petulance*): You ARE going to leave me. Oh no. No. That can't be.

FATHER (*also stunned*): I never thought I was going to leave you. I was just fucking.

JANEY (*not at all calming herself down by listening to what he's saying. He knows her energy rises sharply and crazy when she's scared so he's probably provoking this scene*): You can't leave me. You can't. (*Now in full hysteria.*) I'll . . . (*Realizes she might be flying off the handle and creating the situation. Wants to hear his creation for a minute. Shivers with fear when she asks this.*) Are you madly in love with her?

FATHER (*thinking. Confusion's beginning*): I don't know.

JANEY: I'm not crazy. (*Realizing he's madly in love with the other woman.*) I don't mean to act like this. (*Realizing more and more how madly in love he is. Blurts it out.*) For the last month you've been spending every moment you can with her. That's why you've stopped eating meals with me. That's why you haven't been helping me the way you usually do when I'm sick. You're madly in love with her, aren't you?

FATHER (*ignorant of this huge mess*): We just slept together for the first time tonight.

JANEY: You told me you were just friends like me and Peter (*Janey's stuffed lamb*) and you weren't going to sleep together. It's not like my sleeping around with all these art studs: when you sleep with your best friend, it's really, really heavy.

FATHER: I know, Janey.

JANEY (*she hasn't won that round; she threw betrayal in his face and he didn't totally run away from it*): Are you going to move in with Sally? (*She asks the worst possibility.*)

FATHER (*still in the same sad, hesitant, underlyingly happy because he wants to get away, tone*): I don't know.

JANEY (*She can't believe this. Every time she says the worst, it's true*): When will you know? I have to make my plans.

FATHER: We just slept together once. Why don't you just let things lie, Janey, and not push?

JANEY: You tell me you love someone else, you're gonna kick me out, and I shouldn't push. What do you think I am, Johnny? I love you.

boyfriend, brother, sister,
money, amusement, and father

FATHER: Just let things be. You're making more of this than it really is.

JANEY (*everything comes flooding out*): I love you. I adore you. When I first met you, it's as if a light turned on for me. You're the first joy I knew. Don't you understand?

FATHER (*silent*)

JANEY: I just can't bear that you're leaving me: it's like a lance cutting my brain in two: it's the worst pain I've ever known. I don't care who you fuck. You know that. I've never acted like this before.

FATHER: I know.

JANEY: I'm just scared you're going to leave me. I know I've been shitty to you: I've fucked around too much; I didn't introduce you to my friends.

FATHER: I'm just having an affair, Janey. I'm going to have this affair.

JANEY (*now the rational one*): But you might leave me.

FATHER (*silent*)

JANEY: OK. (*Getting hold of herself in the midst of total disaster and clenching her teeth.*) I have to wait around until I see how things work out between you and Sally and then I'll know if I'm going to live with you or not. Is that how things stand?

FATHER: I don't know.

JANEY: You don't know! How am I supposed to know?

That night, for the first time in months, Janey and her father sleep together because Janey can't get to sleep otherwise. Her father's touch is cold, he doesn't want to touch her mostly cause he's confused. Janey fucks him even though it hurts her like hell cause of her Pelvic Inflammatory Disease.

The following poem is by the Peruvian poet César Vallejo who, born 18 March 1892 (Janey was born 18 April 1964), lived in Paris fifteen years and died there when he was 46:

September
This September night, you fled
So good to me . . . up to grief and include!
I don't know myself anything else
But you, YOU don't have to be good.

This night alone up to imprisonment no prison
Hermetic and tyrannical, diseased and panic-stricken
I don't know myself anything else
I don't know myself because I am grief-stricken.

Only this night is good, YOU
Making me into a whore, no
Emotion possible is distance God gave integral:
Your hateful sweetness I'm clinging to.

This September evening, when sown
In live coals, from an auto
Into puddles: not known.

JANEY (*as her father was leaving the house*): Are you coming back tonight? I don't mean to bug you. (*No longer willing to assert herself.*) I'm just curious.
FATHER: Of course I'll be back.

The moment her father left the house, Janey rushed to the phone and called up his best friend, Bill Russle. Bill had once fucked Janey, but his cock was too big. Janey knew he'd tell her what was happening with Johnny, if Johnny was crazy or not, and if Johnny really wanted to break up with Janey. Janey didn't have to pretend anything with Bill.

JANEY: Right now we're at the edge of a new era in which, for all sorts of reasons, people will have to grapple with all sorts of difficult problems, leaving us no time for the luxury of expressing ourselves artistically. Is Johnny madly in love with Sally?

BILL: No.

JANEY: No? (*Total amazement and hope.*)

BILL: It's something very deep between them, but he's not going to leave you for Sally.

JANEY (*with even more hope*): Then why's he acting this way? I mean: he's talking about *leaving* me.

BILL: Tell me exactly what's been happening, Janey. I want to know for my own reasons. This is very important. Johnny hasn't been treating me like a friend. He won't talk to me anymore.

JANEY: He won't? He feels you're his best friend. (*Making a decision.*) I'll tell you everything. You know I've been very sick.

BILL: I didn't know that. I'm sorry, I won't interrupt anymore.

JANEY: I've been real sick. Usually Johnny helps out when I am, this time he hasn't. About a month ago he told me he was running around with Andrea and Sally. I said, "Oh great," it's great when he has new friends, he's been real lonely, I told him that was great. He said be was obsessed with Sally, a crush, but it wasn't sexual. I didn't care. But he was acting real funny toward me. I've never seen him act like that. The past two months he's treated me like he hates me. I never thought he'd leave me. He's going to leave me.

BILL (*breaking in*): Janey. Can you tell me exactly what happened last night? I have to know everything. (*She tells him.*) What do you think is going on?

JANEY: Either of two . . . I am Johnny. (*Thinks.*) Either of two things. (*Speaks very slowly and dearly.*) First thing: I am Johnny. I'm beginning to have some fame, success, now women want to fuck me. I've never had women want me before. I want everything. I want to go out in the world as far as I can go. Do you understand what I'm talking about?

BILL: Yes. Go on.

JANEY: There are two levels. It's not that I think one's better than the other, you understand, though I do think one is a more mature development than the other. Second level: It's like commitment. You see what you want, but you don't go after every little thing; you try to work it through with the other person.

I've had to learn this this past year. I'm willing to work with Johnny.

BILL: I understand what's happening now. Johnny is at a place where he has to try everything.

JANEY: The first level. I agree.

BILL: You've dominated his life since your mother died and now he hates you. He has to hate you because he has to reject you. He has to find out who he is.

JANEY: That would go along with the crisis he was having in his work this year.

BILL: It's an identity crisis.

JANEY: This makes sense. . . . What should I do?

BILL: The thing you can't do is to freak out and lay a heavy trip on him.

JANEY: I've already done that. (*If she could giggle, she would.*)

BILL: You have to realize that you're the one person he hates, you're everything he's trying to get rid of. You have to give him support. If you're going to freak out, call me, but don't show him any emotion. Any emotion he'll hate you even more for.

JANEY: God. You know how I am. Like a vibrating nut.

BILL: Be very very calm. He's going through a hard period, he's very confused, and he needs your support. I'll talk to him and find out more about what's going on. I have to talk to him anyway because I want to find out why he hasn't been friendly to me.

Later that afternoon Mr Smith came home from work.

JANEY: I'm sorry I got upset last night about Sally. It won't happen again. I think it's great you've got a girlfriend you really care about.

FATHER: I've never felt like this about anyone. It's good for me to know I can feel so strongly.

JANEY: Yes. (*Keeping her cool.*) I just wanted you to know if there's anything I can do for you, I'd like to be your friend. (*Shaking a little.*)

FATHER: Oh, Janey. You know I care for you very deeply. (*That does it: Janey bursts into tears.*) I'm just confused right now. I want to be my myself.

JANEY: You're going to leave me.

FATHER: Just let things be. I've got to go. (*He obviously wants to get out of the room as fast as possible.*)

JANEY: Wait a minute. (*Collecting her emotions and stashing them.*) I didn't mean it. I was going to be calm and supportive like Bill said.

FATHER: What'd Bill say? (*Janey repeats the conversation. Everything comes splurting out now. Janey's not good at holding words back.*) You've completely dominated my life, Janey, for the last nine years and I no longer know who's you and who's me. I have to be alone. You've been alone for a while, you know that need: I have to find out who I am.

JANEY (*her tears dry*): I understand now. I think it's wonderful what you're doing. All year I've been asking you, "What do you want?" and you never knew. It was always me, my voice, I felt like a total nag; I want you to be the man. I can't make all the decisions. I'm going to the United States for a long time so you'll be able to be alone.

FATHER (*amazed she's snapped so quickly and thoroughly from down hysteria so joy*): You're tough, aren't you?

JANEY: I get hysterical when I don't understand. Now everything's OK. I understand.

FATHER: I've got to go out now—there's a party uptown. I'll be back later tonight.

JANEY: You don't have to be back.

FATHER: I'll wake you up, sweetie, when I get back. OK?

JANEY: Then I can crawl in bed and sleep with you?

FATHER: Yes.

Tiny Mexican, actually Mayan villages, incredibly clean, round thatched huts, ducks, turkeys, dogs, hemp, corn; the Mayans are self-contained and thin-boned, beautiful. One old man speaks: "Mexicans think money is more important than beauty; Mayans say beauty is more important than money; you are very beautiful." They eat ears of roasted corn smeared with chili, salt, and lime and lots of meat, mainly turkey.

Everywhere in Merida and in the countryside are tiny fruit drink stands: drinks *jugos de frutas* made of sweet fresh fruits crushed, sugar, and water. Every other building in Merida is a restaurant, from the cheapest outdoor cafés, where the food often tastes the best; to expensive European-type joints for the rich. Merida, the city, is built on the money of the hemp-growers who possess one boulevard of rich mansions and their own places to go to. Otherwise the poor. But the town is clean, big, cosmopolitan, the Mexicans say, un-Mexican.

Mexico is divided into sections: each has its specialty: Vera Cruz has art. Merida has hemp, baskets, hammocks.

Uxmal: Mayan ruins, huge temples, all the buildings are *huge*, scary, on high. Low low land in center. Everything very far apart. Makes forget personal characteristics. Wind blows long grass who! whoot! Jungle, not Amazonian swamp, but thick, thick green leafage so beautiful surrounds. Hear everything. No one knows how these massive rectangular structures were used. Now birds screech in the little rooms in the buildings, fly away; long iguanas run under rocks. Tiny bright green and red lizards run down paths past one tiny statue, on lowish ground; on a small concrete block, two funny-monkey-hideous-dog-jaguar faces and paws back-to-back. Janus? The sun?

A small Mayan village in the ruins of an old stone hacienda; church, factory, the whole works. Huge green plants are growing out of the stones; chickens, lots of dark-brown feathered turkeys, three pigs, one pink, run around; people, thin and little, live in what ruins can still be lived in.

And further down this dirt road, another village. On Sunday the men, normally gentle and dignified, get drunk. The man driving the big yellow truck is the head man. All the male villagers are touching his band. They're showing him love. He will get, they say, the first newborn girl. In return, he says, be will give them a pig. All of the men's bodies are waving back and forth. The women watch.

By the time the clock said 5 (A.M.) Janey couldn't stand it anymore, so, despite her high fever, she walked the streets. Where could she run

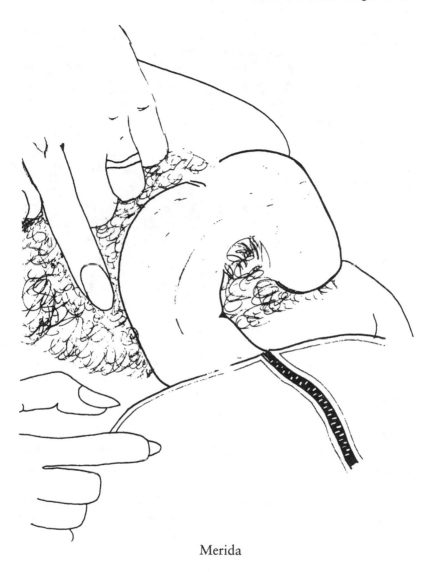

Merida

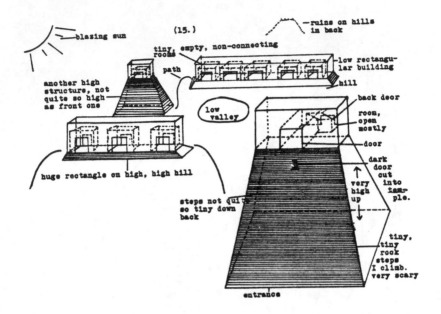

to? Where was peace (someone who loved her)? No one would take her in. It was raining lightly. The rain was going to increase her infection. She stood in front of Sally's house. Then she made herself walk away.

She walked back into her father's and her apartment. She hated the apartment. She didn't know what to do with her hateful tormented mind.

At 7:30 A.M. she woke up in her own bed. As she walked by her father's bed to get to the toilet, she saw her father and spontaneously asked, "You must have gotten home late. How was the party?"

> FATHER: I didn't go to the party.
> JANEY: You didn't go to the party!? (*Realizing the truth. In a little-girl's voice.*) Oh.
> FATHER (*reaching for her*): Come here (*meaning: into my arms*).

JANEY: No. (*She jumps back.*) I don't want to touch you. (*She realizes her mistake. She's very jumpy.*) Just go to sleep. Everything's fine. Goodnight.

FATHER (*commanding*): Janey, come here.

JANEY (*backing away like he's a dangerous animal, but wanting him*): I don't want to.

FATHER: I just want to hold you.

JANEY: Why d'you lie to me?

FATHER: It got late and I didn't feel like going to the party.

JANEY: What time d'you get home?

FATHER: Around seven.

JANEY: Oh. (*In an even smaller little-girl's voice.*) You were with Sally?

FATHER: Come here, Janey. (*He wants to make love to her. Janey knows it.*)

JANEY (*running away*): Go to sleep, Johnny, I'll see you in the morning.

JANEY (*a half-hour later*): I can't sleep by myself, Johnny. Can I crawl into bed with you?

FATHER (*grumbling*): I'm not going to get any sleep. Get in. (*Janey gives him a blow job. Johnny isn't really into having sex with Janey, but he gets off on the physical part.*)

Three hours later Johnny woke up and asked Janey if she wanted to have dinner with him that night, their farewell dinner, and then she would leave. Janey said "No" in her sleep because she felt hurt.

As soon as Janey woke up, she called Bill, desperate. "Everything's even worse, Bill," she said. "Johnny's trying to hurt me as badly as he can." How? He told her he'd spend the night with her and then he spent it with Sally. Then he told her he felt about Sally the way he had never felt about another girl.

Bill tells Janey Johnny doesn't love Sally: he's just using Sally to hurt Janey as much as possible. Johnny has become very crazy and Janey'd better stay out of his way.

JANEY: Do you think he'll want me again?

BILL: There's always been a really strong connection between the two of you. You've been together for years.

In the Merida marketplace there are beetles about an inch to two inches long crawling in a box, their backs covered by red or blue or white rhinestones.

Outside the church a woman sells all sorts of tiny cheap silver trinkets. People buy the appropriate trinket (an arm is a broken arm, a baby is problems with baby, a kidney, a little worker . . .) and take the trinket into the big church to give to the Virgin.

Monumental ruins.

Lost in the grass. Huge buildings that are staircases, staircases to the heights, steps of equal height so high legs can hardly climb. Some buildings are four walls of hundreds and hundreds of steps. On top is nothing, nothing but a small stone rectangle containing an empty hole. Every now and then a huge monster rattlesnake sticks its head out. The stones are crumbling. The oldest buildings are so ruined you can hardly see them.

The next mass of buildings. The architecture is clean, the meaning is clear, that is, the function. A habitation. Hiding tunnels run through each horizontal layer of the habitation. The scale is human. There are wells. There are no pictures or religious representations. A clean people who didn't mess around with their lives, who knew they were only alive once, who disappeared.

The next section contains the largest buildings, vast and fearsome. Thousands of endlessly wide steps on all sides lead up to a tiny room, eagles and rattlesnakes, outside, inside? Inside this structure, steps, narrow, steep and wet, deep within the structure a small jaguar whose teeth are bright white, mounted by a reclining man. The outer steps are so tiny, the burning white sun endlessly high. The climb. It is easy to fall.

All of the other structures are the same way. Heavily ornamented and constructed so beyond human scale they cause fear. Ball parks that cause fear. What for? Why does Rockefeller need more money so badly he kills the life in the waters around Puerto Rico? Why does one person follow his/her whims to the detriment (deep suffering) of someone that person supposedly loves?

"No one," a booklet says, "really knows anything about these ruins," and yet they raise human energy more than anything else.

Don't say it out loud. The long wall of skulls next to the ball park repeats the death.

ANNOUNCE. Johnny stopped in his apartment for just a second to change his clothes. Janey told him she wanted to go out to dinner with him. Johnny replied he thought she didn't. She pleaded that she had been feeling jealous and she didn't mean to feel. She promised that she wouldn't feel jealous as long as she knew what to expect. He warned her to watch out for her jealousy, he knew all about jealousy. He had just spent the night on a rooftop with a girl who was telling him that she was madly in love with David Bowie. Janey started protesting in her head that that wasn't the point; she shut herself up, and calmly asked when and where they would be having dinner and please, before she left, could they pretend they were in love. It would be a very romantic two days and then nothing. She was better at handling fantasy than reality.

Johnny left the house so he could see Sally.

Inside Janey's favourite restaurant, Vesuvio's, the only Northern Italian restaurant in Merida:

JANEY (*searching for a conversation subject that doesn't touch upon their breaking up*): What's Sally like?

FATHER: I don't know. (*As if he's talking about someone he's so close to he can't see the characteristics.*) We're really very compatible. We like the same things. She's very serious; that's what she's like. She's an intellectual.

JANEY (*showing no emotion*): Oh. What does she do?

FATHER: She hasn't decided yet. She's just trying to find herself. She's into music; she writes; she does a little of everything.

JANEY (*trying to be helpful*): It always takes a while.

FATHER: She's trying to find out everything. It's good for me to be with her because she goes everywhere and she knows every-

thing that's happening. She knows a lot and she has a fresh view. JANEY (*to herself*): Fresh meat, young girls. Even though I'm younger, I'm tough, rotted, putrid beef. My cunt red ugh. She's thin and beautiful; I've seen her. Like a model. Just the way I've always wanted to look and I never will. I can't compete against *that*. (*Out loud*) It must be wonderful (*trying to make her voice as innocent as possible*) for you to have someone you can share everything with. You've been lonely for a long time. (*Janey trying to make herself into nothing.*)
FATHER: Let's talk about something else.
JANEY (*very jumpy every time something doesn't go her way*): What's the matter? Did I say something wrong? (*Pause.*) I'm sorry.

BLACK. The conversation petered out.

FATHER: Sally's always wondering what's right and wrong. She's always wondering if she's doing the right thing. She's very young.
JANEY (*apologizing for Sally*): She's just out of college.
FATHER: She's a minister's daughter from Vermont.
JANEY (*knows from her sources that Sally's a rich young bitch who'll fuck anyone until a more famous one comes along as young WASP bitches do*): Well, you've always liked WASP girls. (*Can't keep her two cents out of it.*) They don't want anything from you. (*To herself: Like you, honey.*)
FATHER: She reminds me of my first girlfriend, Anne.
JANEY: I remember Anne. (*Anne is tall blonde who now plays in soap operas.*)

The conversation died. Janey to herself: Sally is the only subject we have left to talk about.

JANEY: Do you think you'll live with Sally?
FATHER: Oh, Janey, I don't think so.
JANEY: I didn't mean anything.

We went to the movies. Johnny paid for everything. As soon as the movie started, I wanted to lay my head on Johnny's shoulder, but I was scared he didn't want to feel my flesh against his. "Are you still interested in me sexually?" I asked him. "Yes," and his hand took my hand. But all through the movie his touch was dead.

LASHES I FEEL. In the taxi my mood changed to lousy, I wanted to get out of the cab. Oh shit, I was ruining everything again. Just when things were going good.

Johnny realized something was the matter and asked me what was wrong.

I said nothing was the matter and tried to jump out of the cab.

He replied that we shouldn't have talked about Sally.

Why shouldn't we have talked about Sally?

He didn't answer, so I realized that Sally was a sacred subject.

Once we were safe inside our kitchen, we rehashed all the times he had wanted to be close to me and I had refused; all the times I had driven him away when he loved me; all the times he had rejected my timid advances of sex, and all the times I had cut him dead, I had told him I would never care about him; how the slightest rejection from me or affair had made him turn away from me and seek someone else; how I reacted to his hurting me so badly by looking for someone more stable; how hurt causes increasing hurt; how our mutual fantasy that he adored me and I was just hanging on to him for the money actually concealed the reality that he had stuck to me all these years cause I didn't ask too much of him, especially emotionally. In this way a fantasy reveals reality: *Reality* is just the underlying fantasy, a fantasy that reveals need. I have an unlimited need of him. I explained all my lousy characteristics: my irritability, my bossiness, my ambition in the world, my PRIDE.

By this time we were both crying. A fag friend of mine just walked into the apartment and I chased him away, but he saw us crying. Then Johnny said that my characteristics that had attracted him at first now repelled him. He hinted that I'm a loud, brassy Jewess. I'm too dependent on him and that freaks him out of his mind. What

My cunt red ugh.

makes it worse is that even though I need help, I don't know how to ask anyone for it. So I'm always bearing down on him and blaming him. I'm too macho (that's my favorite one).

I repeated all these sentences in my mind. I knew that I was hideous. I had a picture in my head that I was a horse, like the horse in *Crime and Punishment*, skin partly ripped off and red muscle exposed. Men with huge sticks keep beating the horse.

Johnny said he thought I was his mother and all the resentment he had felt against her he now felt against me. I scared him so badly he wanted to run away.

I said, "OK. I guess it's good this is all coming out."

LASHES MAKE ME NO LONGER MYSELF. Now I knew that Johnny hated me. I was still trying to remain calm, to be mature. My fever from my sickness rose real high, I think to 102°, and the pain in my ovaries increased.

The thought flashed through my mind that I was getting off on all this. I was a masochist. So: was I making the situation worse?

I told Johnny that I loved him deeply, very deeply. I saw now that he needed to be alone and to decide by himself what he wanted. In a little over twenty-four hours I would be going to the United States. I would not see or speak to him again, unless he asked me to see or speak to him.

FATHER: I have to get out of the house. I'll be back in a while. (*He had arranged to meet Sally in a bar.*)

LASHES, AS IF THE WORLD, BY ITS VERY NATURE, HATES ME. Early that morning, a few hours before the sun was due to come up, nothing else in the world being due, Johnny returned home (what is home?) and told Janey he had been drinking with Sally.

It was very dark outside. She lay down on the filthy floor by his bed, but it was very uncomfortable: she hadn't slept for two nights. So she asked him if he wanted to come into her bed.

The plants in her room cast strange, beautiful shadows over the other shadows. It was a clean, dreamlike room. He fucked her in her asshole cause the infection made her cunt hurt too much to fuck there, though she didn't tell him it hurt badly there, too, cause she wanted to fuck love more than she felt pain.

A few hours later they woke up together and decided they would spend the whole day together since it was their last day. Janey would meet Johnny at the hotel where he worked when he got off from work.

They ate raw fish salad (*ceviche*) at a Lebanese joint and tea at a Northern Chinese place. They held hands. They didn't talk about Sally or anything heavy.

Johnny left her, telling her he'd be home later.

CAUSE OF LASHES: THE SURGE OF SUFFERING IN THE SOUL CORRUPTS THE SOUL.

FATHER: You have to learn not to press so hard. This wouldn't have happened if you hadn't made it happen.

JANEY (*thinking hard. Slowly*): You said that before. I don't think so. I think you set this situation up. (*She doesn't say directly what she thinks: that he pretended he loved Sally so from anger she'd mention breaking up with him so they could break up.*) You know exactly how I react, and you set this situation up so I'd react this way. You wanted this to happen.

FATHER (*as if discovering something for the first time, slowly*): I think you're right.

A few hours later they woke up together and decided they would spend the whole day together since it was their last day. Janey would meet Johnny at the hotel where he worked when he got off from work.

They ate raw fish salad (*ceviche*) at a Lebanese joint and tea at a Northern Chinese place. They held hands. They didn't talk about Sally or anything heavy.

Johnny left her, telling her he'd be home later.

cause she wanted to fuck love more than she felt pain

* * *

I AM NOT ME:

> JANEY (*sitting on her bed with Tarot cards*): Should I tell your fortune?
> FATHER: OK. (*Johnny's fortune is that he's gone through a bad time; now everything is clearing up; in the future a close friendship/marriage? With a woman; final result: a golden life.*) I'm worried about this psychic stuff of yours.
> JANEY: What can I do about it? It freaks me.
> FATHER: You dreamed that night what she looked like—you hadn't even met her.

JANEY: I even described what she was wearing that night. A black jacket over something white. (*Wondering.*)
FATHER: You said I was going to leave you before it even entered my mind.
JANEY: I didn't want to provoke that. Oh God no. These things just come into my head and I say them. Don't you understand?
FATHER: I'm scared of it.

A few hours later they woke up together and decided they would spend the whole day together since it was their last day. Janey would meet Johnny at the hotel where be was working when he got off work.

They ate raw fish salad (*ceviche*) at a Lebanese joint and tea at a Northern Chinese place. They held hands. They didn't talk about Sally or anything heavy.

Johnny left her, telling her he'd be home later.

TINY SOUNDS, BUT SOUNDS . . . OPEN DARK DITCHES IN THE FACE

JANEY: Now I'm going to tell my fortune. (*She gets a totally horrible fortune: death and destruction before and after. Her fever gets high. She wonders if she's going to die in the USA.*)
FATHER: Are you upset?
JANEY: Yes.
FATHER: I am, too. These cards are weird.

A few hours later they woke up together and decided that they would spend the whole day together since it was their last day. Janey would meet Johnny at the hotel where he worked when he got off from work.

They ate raw fish salad (*ceviche*) at a Lebanese joint and tea at a Northern Chinese place. They held hands. They didn't talk about Sally or anything heavy.

Johnny left her, telling her he'd be home later.

MAKE MORE FIERCE AND MAKE SEXUALITY STRONGER. THIS IS THE TIME FOR ALL PRISONERS TO RUN WILD. YOU

ARE THE BLACK ANNOUNCERS OF OUR DEATH. (BE SUCH TIME YOUNG HORSES OF ATTILA THE HUN. OH ANNOUNCERS WHO US SEND DEATH.)

Johnny and Janey lay together and didn't, as on the last nights, touch. Janey was so upset she got up and sat in the kitchen. Johnny lay there awake. Janey returned to the bed and they lay there without touching.

*   *   *

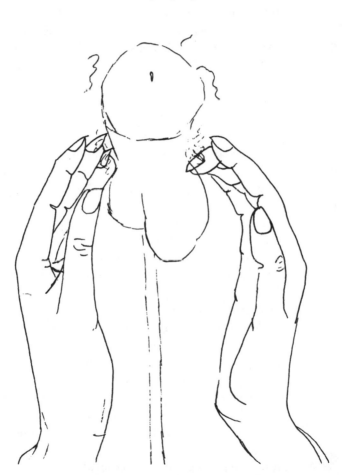

YOU ARE THE BLACK ANNOUNCERS OF MY DEATH.

A few hours later they woke up together and decided they would spend the whole day together since it was their last day. Janey would meet Johnny at the hotel where he worked when he got off from work.

They ate raw fish salad (*ceviche*) at a Lebanese joint and tea at a Northern Chinese place. They held hands. They didn't talk about Sally or anything heavy.

Johnny left her, telling her he'd be home later.

ANNOUNCE THE RUINS PROFOUND OF THE CHRISTS WITHIN (US). OF SOME BELIEF CHERISHED WHICH FATE CURSES, THESE *LASHES* BLOODY SOUND THEIR CRACKLINGS OF A LOAF OF BREAD WHICH IN THE VERY OVEN DOOR BURNS US UP.

> JANEY: Sometimes I think we're star-crossed lovers. (*Pursuing and explaining this thought.*) Each of us moves to the other at the wrong time. (*She holds the movie* Gilda *in her mind.*)
> FATHER (*lightly, sadly*): It's just the wrong time now for you to do this.
> JANEY: I know.
> FATHER: I do love you, Janey. (*Holding her in his arms.*) I don't want to never see you again.
> JANEY (*loving his arms*): I'll be OK in the United States. If you want me, write me, I'll . . . (*She stops herself from saying more. She thinks she's always saying too much.*) I've got to go now.
> FATHER: Take care of yourself, will you?
> JANEY: OK. (*She doesn't say that she might die in the USA.*)

A few hours later they woke up together and decided they would spend the whole day together since it was their last day. Janey would meet Johnny at the hotel where he worked when he got off from work.

They ate raw fish salad (*ceviche*) at a Lebanese joint and tea at a Northern Chinese place. They held hands. They didn't talk about Sally or anything heavy.

Johnny left her, telling her he'd be home later.

* * *

From the USA Janey called Johnny in Merida to see if she could return home. At one point:

> FATHER: Sally and I have pretty much split. We decided we'd be just friends.
>
> JANEY: Are you going to want to live with me again?
>
> FATHER: I don't know right now. I'm really enjoying the emotional distance.
>
> JANEY: I didn't mean to pry. I'm sorry. I just have to know.
>
> FATHER: What do you want to know, Janey?
>
> JANEY: I mean . . . Well, how are you doing?
>
> FATHER: I'm being very quiet. I'm staying home most of the time and watching TV. I really need to be alone now.
>
> JANEY: When do you think you'll know if you ever want to live with me again?
>
> FATHER: Oh, Janey. You've got to lighten up. Things just got too entangled. Everything between us is still too entangled for me to be with you.
>
> JANEY: I see. That means no.
>
> FATHER: Are you trying to get me to reject you?
>
> JANEY: No. No. Not that. I don't want you to decide now.
>
> FATHER: Where are you staying now?
>
> JANEY: I'm in New York City. I'm not anywhere. When I settle down, I'll let you know where I am. When I settle down, I'll let you know where I am. I'm going to get off the phone now.
>
> FATHER: How's your health?
>
> JANEY: I'm fine. Fine. Listen. I have to know whether you want me back or not. I can't stand this.
>
> FATHER: Do you really want to know now?
>
> Janey: I'm sorry, Johnny. I know you think it's a high school romance like you and Sally, and we're just breaking up, but it's really serious to me. I loved you.
>
> FATHER (*doubting*): It's serious to me, too.
>
> JANEY: Then don't you understand? How long will I have to hang on? It's been a week since I left Merida. Do you want me to wait a month, a year while you're going eeny-meeny-miney-moe?

FATHER: I have to be alone, Janey. If you demand I say anything more, it'll only be to totally reject you.

JANEY: I have nightmares in my head. Either I fantasize you take me in your arms again and again, telling me you love me. I don't know whether I can let myself fantasize that because if it isn't true . . . or I have to wipe you out of my mind. There is no more Johnny.

FATHER: Why do you have to do that?

JANEY: I have to make a new life for myself! I have to live. I can't spend all my time thinking about someone who doesn't love me.

FATHER: I don't know what to say.

JANEY: I don't know what to think and each nightmare is pulling me backwards and forwards and I can't stop.

FATHER: Don't let your mind drive you crazy.

JANEY: What can I do? I'm sorry. This isn't your problem. I'm going to get off the phone now.

FATHER (*pleading*): Look. Don't keep pushing things. You're making things worse than they are.

JANEY: How can things be worse?

FATHER: You want to know how?

AND THE MAN:

Janey called Johnny again because she needed to hear a friendly voice because she was scared.

(*After a long silence.*)

FATHER (*heartily*): Hello, how are you?

JANEY (*just wanting to hear a friendly voice*): I just wanted to say hello.

FATHER: Where are you?

JANEY: I'm still in New York City. I haven't settled down yet.

FATHER: I'm really enjoying living alone. I'm happier than I've been in months.

JANEY: Oh. (*She doesn't want to feel anything.*) That's wonderful. Who're you seeing?

FATHER: I'm not really seeing anyone. I'm living very quietly. I'm going to stay here till the end of September and then I'll

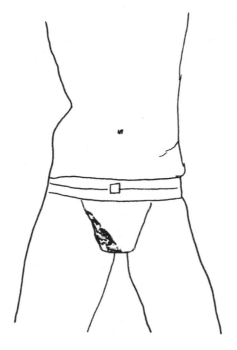

AND THE MAN:

decide what my plans are. (*He wants to say,* "*My plans absolutely don't include you because you terrorize me,*" *but he feels guilty about hurting her.*) I can't tell you anything more than that now.

JANEY (*though she wants to keep the conversation light, she's been programmed to say it*): You mean you're not going to live with me again?

FATHER: Right now I just really like opening my door to this apartment and walking into my own space. I'm going to be here through September and then I'll see what my plans are. I don't think you should bank on anything.

JANEY: I see. I guess that's that.

FATHER: What do you mean "that's that"?

JANEY: I guess it's over.

FATHER: I don't know.

JANEY: Oh no? I don't understand. I just don't understand.

FATHER: I have to be alone.

JANEY: OK. So you're alone. I'm not stopping you from being alone. I went off to the United States, didn't I? You said, "Get away from me," and I went to another land. How far around the world do I have to go?

FATHER: You were planning to go to the United States.

JANEY: I wouldn't have gone to the United States when I was as sick as I was.

FATHER: You didn't have to go to the United States cause of me.

JANEY: Well, I didn't know that. You said, "Get away," and I got away. I want to give you what you want. This all doesn't matter anymore. I'd better go.

FATHER: Do you mean you never want to see me again?

JANEY: You said it's over.

If the author here lends her "culture" to the amorous subject, in exchange the amorous subject affords her the innocence of its image-repertoire, indifferent to the proprieties of knowledge. Indifferent to the proprieties of knowledge.

FATHER: I have to be alone.

JANEY: I understand.

FATHER: I have to be alone. You've had the same thing. It's like I'm on a retreat.

JANEY: I'm not protesting against that.

TURN THE EYES AS IF I SEE SOME HOPE, I think it's wonderful to be alone. But you don't know whether you love me anymore.

FATHER: That's true. It's really heavy, isn't it? (*As if he doesn't want to believe it's heavy.*)

JANEY: Yeah. It's heavy. OK. (*Sighs because she's made a decision.*) If you really want, I'll wait around as long as you want until you make a decision.

FATHER: I had to get away. I felt trapped.

JANEY: Well, you're not trapped anymore. You've got everything the way you want it. There's no need to explain anything anymore. (*She's still crying.*) Whenever you make your decision, just tell me.

FATHER: If you need any money, Janey, you can rely on me.

JANEY: What do you mean by that?

FATHER: If you want me to help you out monetarily, I will.

JANEY (*now that she's made her decision, her emotions are gone*): You can't just say that. I have to stay alive. I can't do anything about the emotional . . . but I can keep myself alive physically. What do you mean by MONEY? I'm sorry I'm being so crude. I have to stay alive.

FATHER: I'll pay your rent wherever you are.

JANEY: OK. I'll wait for you and you'll pay the rent. You'll have to give me a month's notice if you're going to stop paying it. I just have to know. Is that OK?

FATHER: Listen, Janey, will you take care of yourself?

JANEY: IS THAT OK? I'm sorry it might not be important to you how I stay alive, but it's important to me.

FATHER (*evading*): I'll help you out however I can.

JANEY: I'm sorry I'm being so hard (*she thinks she's really being a little bitch*) but I have to figure out how I'm going to live. I don't want to make a thing of it, but I'm still sick. (*She thinks she's going to die.*)

The phone call hasn't really gotten bad yet.

It starts off slow, stagnant.   FATHER (*obsessed with trying to explain to Janey he doesn't want her anymore. Trying to show her as little affection as possible*): Our relationship just got too entangled. If anything is ever going to work out between us, it'll have to work out while we're living separately.

JANEY: I said I'd wait here for you.

FATHER: I've been thinking everything over and I see that we were always out of phase with each other.

JANEY: I know. I was very selfish.

FATHER: I don't hate you. I just dwell on how good things were between us.

JANEY: It's funny. We always had this fantasy that you were the one who was madly in love, but now it turns out I'm the one.

The energy rising

FATHER: Why don't you just dwell on the memories of how good things were?

JANEY: What? Now you want me to live in the past? That's too much to ask of me. You can't ask that. Oh God is there no end to pain? I'll do anything, anything, but Jesus Christ!

FATHER: I want you to know there's very little hope.

JANEY: I got the message, Johnny.

FATHER: I just don't want to give you any false impressions.

Full pain

JANEY: You've made your point. (*Howls.*) I'd better get off the phone now.

FATHER: We have to talk together. I can't talk to you over this phone.

JANEY: I can't talk either.

FATHER: Maybe you'd better come home.

JANEY: You want me to come home? I'll be home as soon as possible.

JANEY: I'm calling to tell you I can't come home from New York City cause I'm too sick. I have to rest here a few days to get my strength back and then I'll come home as soon as possible. New York is a very hard city to live in.

TURN MY EYES INSANE, WHILE BEING CORRUPTS ITSELF, AS A POOL OF SHAME, IN THAT HOPE.

FATHER: You don't have to come home cause of me, Janey.

JANEY: I thought you said you wanted me home.

FATHER: I just said that for your sake. I thought you were freaking out.

JANEY: Oh. Well, I won't be coming home soon.

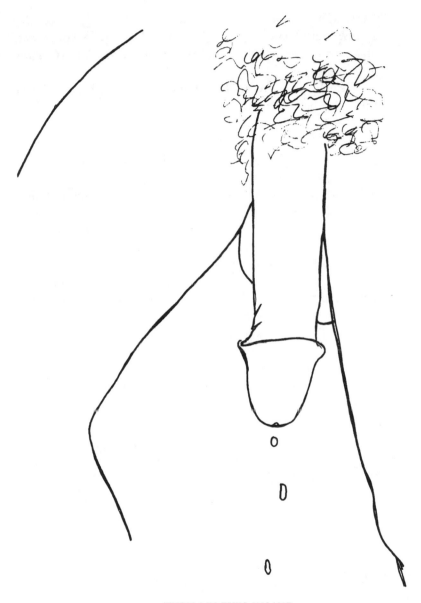

TURN MY EYES INSANE

FATHER: You should enjoy your vacation.

JANEY: I am. I hate the Americans, but there are lots of French and German tourists here and they're all wonderful. (*Gossips about them.*)

FATHER: I wanted to apologize about how I've been acting. I think I've been too mean.

JANEY: Oh, I decided you were a UBH.

FATHER: What's that? (*Laughing.*)

JANEY (*laughing*): An Unnecessarily Brutal Horror.

FATHER: Well, I was confused.

JANEY: And I decided I'd sue you for a thousand American dollars for child abuse.

FATHER: I see your mind's thinking up lots of schemes. (*They both laugh.*) We should make this phone call short. These phone calls have been costing me a fortune.

JANEY: I just called you cause I had to give you that message. I won't call you again. By the way, if you want to come here and stay with me, I'll pay for it somehow . . . .

FATHER: I'm alone right now.

JANEY: Well, goodbye.

FATHER: I never know how to say goodbye.

JANEY: We never do, do we? Just say, "Goodbye."

FATHER: Take care of yourself, Janey.

JANEY: Goodbye.

PLEASE
ME NO LONGER MYSELF

(1978)

"New York City in 1979"

The Whores in Jail at Night

—Well, my man's gonna get me out of here as soon as he can.

—When's that gonna be, honey?

—So what? Your man pays so he can put you back on the street as soon as possible.

—Well, what if he wants me back on the street? That's where I belong. I make him good money, don't I? He knows that I'm a good girl.

—Your man ain't anything! Johnny says that if I don't work my ass off for him, he's not going to let me back in the house.

—I have to earn two hundred before I can go back.

—Two hundred? That ain't shit! You can earn two hundred in less than a night. I have to earn four hundred or I might just as well forget sleeping, and there's no running away from Him. My baby is the toughest there is.

—Well, shit girl, if I don't come back with eight hundred I get my ass whupped off.

—That's cause you're junk.

—I ain't no stiff! All of you are junkies. I know what you do!

—What's the matter, honey?

—You've been sitting on that thing for an hour.

—The pains are getting bad. OOgh. I've been bleeding two days now.

—OOgh OOgh OOgh.

—She's gonna bang her head off. She needs a shot.

—Tie a sweater around her head. She's gonna break her head open.

—You should see a doctor, honey.

—The doctor told me I'm having an abortion.

—Matron. Goddamnit. Get your ass over here matron!

—I haven't been bleeding this bad. Maybe this is the real abortion.

—Matron! This little girl is having an abortion! You do something. Where the hell is that asshole woman? (The matron throws an open piece of Kotex to the girl.) The service here is getting worse and worse!

—You're not in a hotel, honey.

—It used to be better than this. There's not even any goddamn food. This place is definitely going downhill.

—Oh, shutup. I'm trying to sleep. I need my sleep, unlike you girls, cause I'm going back to work tomorrow.

—Now what the hell do you need sleep for? This is a party. You sleep on your job.

—I sure know this is the only time I get any rest. Tomorrow it's back on the street again.

—If we're lucky.

LESBIANS are women who prefer their own ways to male ways.

LESBIANS prefer the convoluting halls of sensuality to direct goal-pursuing mores.

LESBIANS have made a small world deep within and separated from the world. What has usually been called the world is the male world.

Convoluting halls of sensuality lead to depend on illusions. Lies and silence are realer than truth.

Either you're in love with someone or you're not. The one thing about being in love with someone is you know you're in love: You're either flying or you're about to kill yourself.

I don't know anyone I'm in love with or I don't know if I'm in love. I have all these memories. I remember that as soon as I've gotten fucked, like a dog I no longer care about the man who just fucked me who I was madly in love with.

So why should I spend a hundred dollars to fly to Toronto to get laid by someone I don't know if I love I don't know if I can love I'm an abortion? I mean a hundred dollars and once I get laid I'll be in agony: I won't be doing exactly what I want. I can't live normally i.e. with love so: there is no more life.

The world is gray afterbirth. Fake. All of New York City is fake is going to go all my friends are going crazy all my friends know they're going crazy disaster is the only thing that's happening.

Suddenly these outhursts in the fake, cause they're so open, spawn a new growth. I'm waiting to see this growth.

I want more and more horrible disaster in New York cause I desperately want to see that new thing that is going to happen this year.

JANEY is a woman who has sexually hurt and been sexually hurt so much she's now frigid.

She doesn't want to see her husband anymore. There's nothing between them.

Her husband agrees with her that there's nothing more between them.

But there's no such thing as nothingness. Not here. Only death whatever that is is nothing. All the ways people are talking to her now mean nothing. She doesn't want to speak words that are meaningless.

Janey doesn't want to see her husband again.

The quality of life in this city stinks. Is almost nothing. Most people now are deaf-mutes only inside they're screaming. BLOOD. A lot of blood inside is going to fall. MORE and MORE because inside is outside.

New York City will become alive again when the people begin to speak to each other again not information but real emotion. A grave is spreading its legs and BEGGING FOR LOVE.

Robert, Janey's husband, is almost a zombie.

He walks talks plays his saxophone pays for groceries almost like every other human. There's no past. The last six years didn't exist. Janey hates him. He made her a hole. He blasted into her. He has no feeling. The light blue eyes he gave her; the gentle hands; the adoration: AREN'T. NO CRIME. NO BLOOD. THE NEW CITY. Like in Fritz Lang's *Metropolis*.

This year suffering has so blasted all feelings out of her she's become a person. Janey believes it's necessary to blast open her mind constantly and destroy EVERY PARTICLE OF MEMORY THAT SHE LIKES.

A sleeveless black T-shirt binds Janey's breasts. Pleated black fake-leather pants hide her cocklessness. A thin leopard tie winds around her neck. One gold-plated watch, the only remembrance of the dead mother, binds one wrist. A thin black leather band binds the other. The head is almost shaved. Two round prescription mirrors mask the eyes.

Johnny is a man who don't want to be living so he doesn't appear to be a man. All his life everyone wanted him to be something. His Jewish mother wanted him to be famous so he wouldn't live the life she was living. The two main girlfriends he has had wanted him to support them in the manner to which they certainly weren't accustomed even though he couldn't put his flabby hands on a penny. His father wanted him to shut up.

All Johnny wants to do is make music. He wants to keep everyone and everything who takes him away from his music off him. Since he can't afford human contact, he can't afford desire. Therefore he hangs around with rich zombies who never have anything to do with feelings. This is a typical New York artist attitude.

New York City is a pit-hole: Since the United States government, having decided that New York City is no longer part of the United States of America, is dumping all the laws the rich people want such as anti-rent-control laws and all the people they don't want (artists, poor minorities, and the media in general) on the city and refusing the city Federal funds; the American bourgeoisie has left. Only the poor: artists, Puerto Ricans who can't afford to move . . . and rich

Europeans who fleeing the terrorists don't give a shit about New York
... inhabit this city.

Meanwhile the temperature is getting hotter and hotter so no
one can think clearly. No one perceives. No one cares. Insane madness come out like life is a terrific party.

In Front of the Mudd Club, 77 White Street

Two rich couples drop out of a limousine. The women are wearing
outfits the poor people who were in ten years ago wore ten years ago.
The men are just neutral. All the poor people who're making this club
fashionable so the rich want to hang out here, even though the poor
still never make a buck off the rich pleasure, are sitting on cars, watching the rich people walk up to the club.

Some creeps around the club's entrance. An open-shirted skinny
guy who says he's just an artist is choosing who he'll let into the club.
Since it's 3:30 A.M. there aren't many creeps. The artist won't let the
rich hippies into the club.

—Look at that car.

—Jesus. It's those rich hippies' car.

—Let's take it.

—That's the chauffeur over there.

—Let's kidnap him.

—Let's knock him over the head with a bottle.

—I don't want no terrorism. I wanna go for a ride.

—That's right. We've got nothing to do with terrorism. We'll
just explain we want to borrow the car for an hour.

—Maybe he'll lend us the car if we explain we're terrorists-in-
training. We want to use that car to try out terrorist tricks.

After 45 minutes the rich people climb back into their limousine and their chauffeur drives them away.

A girl who has gobs of brown hair like the foam on a cappuccino
in Little Italy, black patent leather S&M heels, two unfashionable tits

stuffed into a pale green corset, and extremely fashionable black fake-leather tights heaves her large self off a car top. She's holding an empty bottle.

Diego senses there's going to be trouble. He gets off his car top. Is walking slowly toward the girl.

The bottle keeps waving. Finally the girl finds some courage heaves the bottle at the skinny entrance artist.

The girl and the artist battle it out up the street. Some of the people who are sitting on cars separate them. We see the girl throw herself back on a car top. Her tits are bouncing so hard she must want our attention and she's getting insecure, maybe violent, cause she isn't getting enough. Better give us a better show. She sticks her middle finger into the air as far as she can. She writhes around on the top of the car. Her movements are so spasmodic she must be nuts.

A yellow taxicab is slowly making its way to the club. On one side of this taxicab's the club entrance. The other side is the girl writ(h)ing away on the black car. Three girls who are pretending to be transvestites are lifting themselves out of the cab elegantly around the big girl's body. The first body is encased into a translucent white girdle. A series of diagonal panels leads directly to her cunt. The other two dresses are tight and white. They are wriggling their way toward the club. The big girl, whom the taxi driver refused to let in his cab, wriggling because she's been rejected but not wriggling as much, is bumping into them. They're tottering away from her because she has syphilis.

Now the big girl is unsuccessfully trying to climb through a private white car's window now she's running hips hooking even faster into an alleyway taxi whose driver is locking his doors and windows against her. She's offering him a blow job. Now an ugly boy with a huge safety pin stuck through his upper lip, walking up and down the street, is shooting at us with his watergun.

The dyke sitting next to me is saying earlier in the evening she pulled at this safety pin.

It's 4 A.M. It's still too hot. Wet heat's squeezing this city. The air's mist. The liquid that's seeping out of human flesh pores is gonna harden into a smooth shiny shell so we're going to become reptiles.

No one wants to move anymore. No one wants to be in a body. Physical possessions can go to hell even in this night.

Johnny like all other New York inhabitants doesn't want anything to do with sex. He hates sex because the air's hot, because feelings are dull, and because humans are repulsive.

Like all the other New Yorkers he's telling females he's strictly gay and males all faggots ought to burn in hell and they are. He's doing this because when he was sixteen years old his parents who wanted him to die stuck him in the Merchant Marines and all the marines cause this is what they do raped his ass off with many doses of coke.

Baudelaire doesn't go directly toward self-satisfaction cause of the following mechanism: X wants Y and, for whatever reasons reasons, thinks it shouldn't want Y. X thinks it is BAD because it wants Y. What X wants is Y and to be GOOD.

Baudelaire does the following to solve this dilemma: He understands that some agency (his parents, society, his mistress, etc.) is saying that wanting Y is BAD. This agency is authority is right. The authority will punish him because he's BAD. The authority will punish him as much as possible, punish me punish me, more than is necessary till it has to be obvious to everyone that the punishment is unjust. Punishers are unjust. All authority right now stinks to high hell. Therefore there is no GOOD and BAD. X cannot be BAD.

It's necessary to go to as many extremes as possible.

As soon as Johnny sees Janey he wants to have sex with her. Johnny takes out his cock and rubs it. He walks over to Janey, puts his arms around her shoulders so he's pinning her against a concrete wall.

Johnny says, "You're always talking about sex. Are you going to spread your legs for me like you spread your legs all the time for any guy you don't know?"

Janey replies, "I'm not fucking anymore cause sex is a prison. It's become a support of this post-capitalist system like art. Businessmen who want to make money have to turn up a product that people'll buy and want to keep buying. Since American consumers now own every object there is plus they don't have any money anyway cause they're being squeezed between inflation and depression, just like fucking, these businessmen have to discover products that obvious necessity sells. Sex is such a product. Just get rid of the puritanism sweetheart your parents spoonfed you in between materialism which the sexual revolution did thanks to free love and hippies sex is a terrific hook. Sexual desire is a naturally fluctuating phenomena. The sex product presents a naturally expanding market. Now capitalists are doing everything they can to bring world sexual desire to an unbearable edge.

"I don't want to be hurt again. Getting hurt or rejected is more dangerous than I know because now everytime I get sexually rejected I get dangerously physically sick. I don't want to hurt again. Everytime I hurt I feel so disgusted with myself—that by following some stupid body desire I didn't HAVE to follow, I killed the tender nerves of someone else. I retreat into myself. I again become frigid."

"I never have fun."

Johnny says, "You want to be as desperate as possible but you don't have to be desperate. You're going to be a success. Everybody knows you're going to be a success. Wouldn't you like to give up this artistic life which you know isn't rewarding cause artists now have to turn their work/selves into marketable objects/fluctuating images/ fashion have to competitively knife each other in the back because we're not people, can't treat each other like people, no feelings, loneliness comes from the world of rationality, robots, every thing one as objects defined separate from each other? The whole impetus for art in the first place is gone bye-bye? You know you want to get away from this media world."

Janey replies, "I don't know what I want now. I know the New York City world is more complex and desirable even though everything you're saying's true. I don't know what my heart is cause I'm corrupted."

"Become pure again. Love. You have to will. You can do what you will. Then love'll enter your heart."

"I'm not capable of loving anyone. I'm a freak. Love's an obsession that only weird people have. I'm going to be a robot for the rest of my life. This is confusing to be a human being, but robotism is what's present."

"It's unnatural to be sexless. You eat alone and that's freaky."
"I am lonely out of my mind. I am miserable out of my mind.
Open open what are you touching me. Touching me. Now I'm going
into the state where desire comes out like a monster. Sex I love you.
I'll do anything to touch you. I've got to fuck. Don't you understand
don't you have needs as much as I have needs DON'T YOU HAVE
TO GET LAID?"

—Janey, close that door. What's the matter with you? Why aren't you
doing what I tell you?

—I'll do whatever you tell me, nana.

—That's right. Now go into that drawer and get that checkbook
for me. The Chase Manhattan one, not the other one. Give me both
of them. I'll show you which one.

—I can find it, nana. No, it's not this one.

—Give me both of them. I'll do it.

—Here you are, nana. This is the one you want, isn't it?

—Now sit yourself down and write yourself out a check for
$10,000. It doesn't matter which check you write it on.

—Ten thousand dollars! Are you sure about this, nana?

—Do what I tell you. Write yourself out a check for ten thousand dollars.

—Uh OK What's the date?

—It doesn't matter. Put any date you want. Now hand me my
glasses. They're over there.

—I'm just going to clean them. They're dirty.

—You can clean them for me later. Give them to me.

—Are . . . you sure you want to do this?

—Now I'm going to tell you something, Janey. Invest this. Buy
yourself 100 shares of AT&T. You can fritter it away if you want.
Good riddance to you. If your mother had invested the 800 shares of
IBM I gave her, she would have had a steady income and wouldn't
have had to commit suicide. Well, she needed the money. If you invest in AT&T, you'll always have an income.

—I don't know what to say. I've never seen so much money
before. I've never seen so much money before.

—You do what I tell you to. Buy AT&T.

—I'll put the money in a bank, nana, and as soon as it clears I'll buy AT&T.

At ten o'clock the next morning Nana is still asleep. A rich salesman who was spending his winter in New York had installed her in a huge apartment on Park Avenue for six months. The apartment's rooms are tremendous, too big for her tiny body, and are still partly unfurnished. Thick sick daybed spreads ivory-handled white feather fans hanging above contrast the black-and-red "naturalistic" clown portraits in the "study" that give an air of culture rather than of call girl. A call girl or mistress, as soon as her first man is gone, is no longer innocent. No one to help her, constantly harassed by rent and food bills, in need of elegant clothing and cosmetics to keep surviving, she has to use her sex to get money.

Nana's sleeping on her stomach, her bare arms hugging instead of a man a pillow into which she's buried a face soft with sleep. The bedroom and the small adjoining dressingroom are the only two properly furnished rooms. A ray of light filtered through the gray richly-laced curtain focuses a rosewood bedsteads covered by carved Chinese figures, the bedstead covered by white linen sheets; covered by a pale blue silk quilt; covered by a pale white silk quilt; Chinese pictures composed of five to seven layers of carved ivory, almost sculptures rather than pictures, surround these gleaming layers.

She feels around and, finding no one, calls her maid.

"Paul left ten minutes ago," the girl says as she walks into the room. "He didn't want to wake you. I asked him if he wanted coffee but he said he was in a rush. He'll see you his usual time tomorrow."

"Tomorrow tomorrow"; the prostitute can never get anything straight, "can he come tomorrow?"

"Wednesday's Paul's day. Today you see the furrier."

"I remember," she says, sitting up, "the old furrier told me he's coming Wednesday and I can't go against him. Paul'll have to come another day."

"You didn't tell me. If you don't tell me what's going on, I'm going to get things confused and your Johns'll be running into each other!"

Nana stretches her fatty arms over her head and yawns. Two bunches of short brown hairs are sticking out of her armpits. "I'll call Paul and tell him to come back tonight. No. I won't sleep with anyone tonight. Can I afford it? I'll tell Paul to come on Tuesdays after this and I'll have tonight to myself!" Her nightgown slips down her nipples surrounded by one long brown hair and the rest of her hair, loose and tousled, flows over her still-wet sheets.

Bet—I think feminism is the only thing that matters.

Janey (*yawning*)—I'm so tired all I can do is sleep all day (only she doesn't fall asleep cause she's suddenly attracted to Michael who's like every other guy she's attracted to married to a friend of hers.)

Bet—First of all feminism is only possible in a socialist state.

Janey—But Russia stinks as much as the United States these days. What has this got to do with your film?

Bet—Cause feminism depends on four factors: First of all, women have to have economic independence. If they don't have that they don't have anything. Second, free daycare centers. Abortions. (counting on her fingers) Fourth, decent housing.

Janey—I mean those are just material considerations. You're accepting the materialism this society teaches. I mean look I've had lots of abortions I can fuck anyone I want—well, I could—I'm still in prison. I'm not talking about myself.

Bet—Are you against abortions?

Janey—How could I be against abortions? I've had fucking five of them. I can't be against abortions. I just think all that stuff is back in the 1920s. It doesn't apply to this world. This world is different than all that socialism: those multinational corporations control everything.

Lowe—You just don't know how things are cause the feminist movement here is nothing compared to the feminist movements in Italy, England, and Australia. That's where women really stick together.

Janey—That's not true! Feminism here, sure it's not the old feminism the groups Gloria Steinem and Ti-Grace, but they were *so* straight. It's much better now: it's just underground it's not so public.

Louie—The only women in Abercrombie's and Fitch's films are those traditionally male defined types.

The women are always whores or bitches. They have no power.

Janey—Women are whores now. I think women every time they fuck no matter who they fuck should get paid. When they fuck their boyfriends their husbands. That's the way things are only the women don't get paid.

Louie—Look at Carter's films. There are no women's roles. The only two women in the film who aren't bit players are France who's a bitch and England who's a whore.

Janey—But that's how things were in Rome of that time.

Bet—But, Jane, we're saying things have to be different. Our friends can't keep upholding the sexist state of women in their work.

Janey—You know about Abercrombie and Fitch. I don't even bother saying anything to them. But Carter's film; you've got to look at why an artist does what he does. Otherwise you're not being fair. In *Rome* Carter's saying the decadent Roman society was like this one.

Louie—The one that a certain small group of artists in New York lives in.

Janey—Yeah.

Louie—He's saying the men we know treat women only as whores and bitches.

Janey—So what are you complaining about?

Bet—Before you were saying you have no one to talk to about your work. That's what I'm saying. We've got to tell Abercrombie and Fitch what they're doing. We've got to start portraying women as strong showing women as the power of this society.

Janey—But we're not.

Bet—But how else are we going to be? In Italy there was this women's art festival. A friend of ours who does performance dressed as a woman and did a performance. Then he revealed he was a man. The women in the festival beat him up and called the police.

Michael—The police?

Janey—Was he good?

Bet—He was the best performer there.

Louie—I think calling the police is weird. They should have just beaten him up.

Janey—I don't like the police.

I WANT ALL THE ABOVE TO BE THE SUN.

Intense Sexual Desire is the Greatest Thing in the World

Janey dreams of cocks. Janey sees cocks instead of objects.

Janey has to fuck.

This is the way Sex drives Janey crazy: Before Jancy fucks, she keeps her wants in cells. As soon as Janey's fucking she wants to be adored as much as possible at the same time as, its other extreme, ignored as much as possible. More than this: Janey can no longer perceive herself wanting. Janey is Want.

It's worse than this: If Janey gets sexually rejected her body becomes sick. If she doesn't get who she wants she naturally revolts.

This is the nature of reality. No rationality possible. Only this is true. The world in which there is no feeling, the robot world, doesn't exist. This world is a very dangerous place to live in.

Old women just cause they're old and no man'll fuck them don't stop wanting sex.

The old actress isn't good anymore. But she keeps on acting even though she knows all the audiences mock her hideousness and lack of context cause she adores acting. Her legs are grotesque: FLABBY. Above, hidden within the folds of skin, there's an ugly cunt. Two long flaps of white thin spreckled by black hairs like a pig's cock flesh hang down to the knees. There's no feeling in them. Between these two flaps of skin the meat is red folds and drips a white slime that poisons whatever it touches. Just one drop burns a hole into anything. An odor of garbage infested by maggots floats out of this cunt. One wants to vomit. The meat is so red it looks like someone hacked a body to bits with a cleaver or like the bright red lines under the purple lines on the translucent skin of a woman's body found dead three days ago. This red leads to a hole, a hole of redness, round and round, black nausea. The old actress is black nausea because she reminds us of death. Yet she keeps plying her trade and that makes her trade weird. Glory be to those humans who are absolutely NOTHING for the opinions of other humans: they are the true owners of illusions, transformations, and themselves.

Old people are supposed to be smarter than young people.

Old people in this country the United States of America are treated like total shit. Since most people spend their lives mentally dwelling on the material, they have no mental freedom, when they grow old and their skin rots and their bodies turn to putrefying sand and they can't do physical exercise and they can't indulge in bodily pleasure and they're all ugly anyway; suddenly they got nothing. Having nothing, you think they could at least be shut up in opiated dens so maybe they have a chance to develop dreams or at least they could warn their kids to do something else besides being materialistic. But the way this country's set up, there's not even opiated homes to hide this feelinglessness: old people have to go either to children's or most often into rest homes where they're shunted into wheelchairs and made as fast as possible into zombies cause it's easier to handle a zombie, if you have to handle anything, than a human. So an old person has a big empty hollow space with nothing in it, just ugh, and that's life: nothing else is going to happen, there's just ugh stop.

Anything that Destroys Limits

Afterwards Janey and Johnny went to an all-night movie. All during the first movie Janey's sort of leaning against Johnny cause she's unsure he's attracted to her and she doesn't want to embarrass him (her) in case he ain't. She kinda scrunches against him. One point Johnny is pressing his knee against her knee but she still ain't sure.

Some Like It Hot ends. All the rest of the painters are gonna leave the movie house cause they've seen *The Misfits*. Separately Janey and Johnny say they're going to stay. The painters are walking out. The movie theater is black.

Janey still doesn't know what Johnny's feelings are.

A third way through the second movie Johnny's hand grabs her knee. Her whole body becomes crazy. She puts her right hand into his hand but he doesn't want the hand.

Johnny's hand, rubbing her tan leg, is inching closer to her cunt. The hand is moving roughly, grabbing handfuls of flesh, the flesh and blood crawling. He's not responding to anything she's doing.

Finally she's tentatively touching his leg. His hand is pouncing on her right hand setting it an inch below his cock. Her body's becoming even crazier and she's more content

His other hand is inching slower toward her open slimy hole. Cause the theater is small, not very dark, and the seats aren't too steep, everyone sitting around them is watching exactly what they're doing: Her black dress is shoved up around her young thighs. His hand is almost curving around her darkpantied cunt. Her and his legs are intertwined. Despite fear she's sure to be arrested just like in a porn book because fear she's wanting him to stick his cock up her right now.

His hand is roughly traveling around her cunt, never touching nothing, smaller and smaller circles.

Morning. The movie house lights go on, Johnny looks at Janey like she's a business acquaintance. From now on everything Janey does is for the purpose of getting Johnny's dick into her.

Johnny, "Let's get out of here."

New York City at six in the morning is beautiful. Empty streets except for a few bums. No garbage. A slight shudder of air down the long long streets. Pale gray prevails. Janey's going to kill Johnny if he doesn't give her his cock instantaneously. She's thinking ways to get him to give her his cock. Her body becomes even crazier. Her body takes over. Turn on him.

Throw arms around his neck. Back him against car. Shove clothed cunt against clothed cock. Lick ear because that's what there is.

Lick your ear.

Lick your ear.

Well?

I don't know.

What don't you know? You don't know if you want to?

Turn on him. Throw arms around his neck. Back him against car. Shove clothed cunt against clothed cock. Lick ear because that's what there is.

Obviously I want to.

I don't care what you do. You can come home with me; you can take a rain check; you cannot take a rain check.

I have to see my lawyer tomorrow. Then I have lunch with Ray.

Turn on him. Throw arms around his neck. Back him against car. Shove clothed cunt against clothed cock. Lick ear because that's what there is.

You're not helping me much.

You're not helping me much.

Through this morning they walk to her apartment. Johnny and Janey don't touch. Johnny and Janey don't talk to each other.

Johnny is saying that Janey's going to invite him up for a few minutes.

Janey is pouring Johnny a glass of Scotch. Janey is sitting in her bedroom on her bed. Johnny is untying the string holding up her black sheath. Johnny's saliva-wettened fingers are pinching her nipple. Johnny is lifting her body over his prostrate body. Johnny's making her cunt rub very roughly through the clothes against his huge cock. Johnny's taking her off him and lifting her dress over her body. Janey's saying, "Your cock is huge." Janey's placing her lips around Johnny's huge cock. Janey's easing her black underpants over her feet.

Johnny's moaning like he's about to come. Janey's lips are letting go his cock. Johnny's lifting Janey's body over his body so the top of his cock is just touching her lips. His hands on her thighs are pulling her down fast and hard. His cock is so huge it is entering her cunt painfully. His body is immediately moving quickly violently shudders. The cock is entering the bottom of Janey's cunt. Janey is coming. Johnny's hands are not holding Janey's thighs firmly enough and Johnny's moving too quickly to keep Janey coming. Johnny is building up to coming.

That's all right yes I that's all right. I'm coming again smooth of you oh oh smooth, goes on and on, am I coming am I not coming.

Janey's rolling off of Johnny. Johnny's pulling the black pants he's still wearing over his thighs because he has to go home. Janey's telling him she has to sleep alone even though she isn't knowing what she's feeling. At the door to Janey's apartment Johnny's telling Janey he's going to call her. Johnny walks out the door and doesn't see Janey again.

(1981)

"Hello, I'm Erica Jong"

ello, I'm Erica Jong. All of you liked my novel *Fear of Flying* because in it you met real people. People who loved and suffered and lived. My novel contained real people that's why you liked it. My new novel *How to Die Successfully* contains those same characters. And it contains two new characters. You and me. All of us are real. Goodbye.

Hello, I'm Erica Jong. I'm a real novelist. I write books that talk to you about the agony of American life, how we all suffer, the growing pain that more and more of us are going to feel. Life in this country is going to get more horrible, unbearable, making us maniacs cause mania and death will be the only doors out of prison except for those few rich people and even they are agonized prisoners in their masks, the paths, the ways they have to act to remain who they are. You think booze sex coke rich food etc. are doors out? Temporary oblivion at best. We need total oblivion. What was I saying? Oh, yes, my name is Erica Jong

I would rather be a baby than have sex. I would rather go GOOGOO. I would rather write googoo. I would rather write:

FUCK YOU UP YOUR CUNTS THAT'S WHO I AM THE FUCK WITH YOUR MONEY I'M NOT CATERING TO YOU ANYMORE I'M GETTING OUT I'M GETTING OUT I'M RIPPING UP MY CLOTHES I'M RIPPING UP MY SKIN I HURT PAIN OH HURT ME PAIN AT THIS POINT IS GOOD DO YOU UNDER-

STAND? PAIN AT THIS POINT IS GOOD. ME ERICA JONG
WHEE WOO WOO

I am Erica Jong I am Erica Jong fuck me you creep who's going to
Australia you're leaving me all alone you're leaving me without sex
I've gotten hooked on sex and now I'm

My name is Erica Jong. If there is God, God is disjunction and madness.

Yours truly, Erica Jong

(1982)

from *Great Expectations*

Plagiarism

My father's name being Pirrip, and my Christian name Philip, my infant tongue could make of both names nothing longer or more explicit than Peter. So I called myself Peter, and came to be called Peter.

I give Pirrip as my father's family name on the authority of his tombstone and my sister—Mrs. Joe Gargery, who married the blacksmith.

On Christmas Eve 1978 my mother committed suicide and in September of 1979 my grandmother (on my mother's side) died. Ten days ago (it is now almost Christmas 1979) Terence told my fortune with the Tarot cards. This was not so much a fortune—whatever that means—but a fairly, it seems to me, precise psychic map of the present, therefore: the future.

I asked the cards about future boyfriends. This question involved the following thoughts: Would the guy who fucked me so well in France be in love with me? Will I have a new boyfriend? As Terence told me to do, I cut the cards into four piles: earth water fire air. We found my significator, April 18th, in the water or emotion fantasy pile. We opened up this pile. The first image was a fat purring human cat surrounded by the Empress and the Queen of Pentacles. This cluster, traveling through a series of other clusters that, like mirrors, kept defining or explained the first cluster more clearly—time is an almost recurring conical—led to the final unconscious image: during Christmas the whole world is rejecting a male and a female kid who are scum by birth. To the right of the scum is the Star. To the left is the card of that craftsmanship which due to hard work succeeds.

Terence told me that despite my present good luck my basic stability my contentedness with myself alongside these images, I have the image obsession I'm scum. This powerful image depends on the image of the Empress, the image I have of my mother. Before I was born, my mother hated me because my father left her (because she got pregnant?) and because my mother wanted to remain her mother's child rather than be my mother. My image of my mother is the source of my creativity. I prefer the word consciousness. My image of my hateful mother is blocking consciousness. To obtain a different picture of my mother, I have to forgive my mother for rejecting me and committing suicide. The picture of love, found in one of the clusters, is forgiveness that transforms need into desire.

Because I am hating my mother I am separating women into virgins or whores rather than believing I can be fertile.

I have no idea how to begin to forgive someone much less my mother. I have no idea where to begin: repression's impossible because it's stupid and I'm a materialist.

I just had the following dream:

In a large New England–ish house I am standing in a very big room on the second floor in the front of the mansion. This room is totally fascinating, but as soon as I leave it, I can't go back because it disappears. Every room in this house differs from every other room.

The day after my mother committed suicide I started to experience a frame. Within this frame time was totally circular because I was being returned to my childhood traumas totally terrifying because now these traumas are totally real: there is no buffer of memory.

There is no time; there is.

Beyond the buffers of forgetting which are our buffer to reality: there is. As the dream: there is and there is not. Call this TERROR call this TOTAL HUMAN RESPONSIBILITY. The PIG I see on the edge of the grave is the PIG me neither death nor social comment kills. This TERROR is divine because it is real and may I sink into IT.

My mother often told me: "You shouldn't care if an action is right or wrong; you should totally care if you're going to profit monetarily from it."

The helmeted bowlegged stiff-muscled soldiers trample on just-born babies swaddled in scarlet violet shawls, babies roll out of the arms of women crouched under POP's iron machine guns, a cabby shoves his fist into a goat's face, near the lake a section of the other army crosses the tracks, other soldiers in this same army leap in front of the trucks, the POP retreat up the river, a white-walled tire in front of three thornbushes props up a male's head, the soldiers bare their chests in the shade of the mud barricades, the females lullabye kids in their tits, the sweat from the fires' perfumes reinforces this stirring rocking makes their rags their skins their meat pregnant: salad oil clove henna butter indigo sulfur, at the base of this river under a shelf loaded down by burnt-out cedars barley wheat beehives graves refreshment stands garbage bags fig trees matches human-brain-splattered low-walls small-fires'-smoke-dilated orchards explode: flowers pollen grain-ears tree roots paper milk-stained cloths blood bark feathers, rising. The soldiers wake up stand up again tuck in their canvas shirt-tails suck in cheeks stained by tears dried by the steam from hot train rails rub their sex against the tires, the trucks go down into a dry fjord mow down a few rosebushes, the sap mixes with disemboweled teen-agers' blood on their knives' metal, the soldiers' nailed boots cut down uproot nursery plants, a section of RIMA (the other army) climb onto their trucks' runningboards throw themselves on their females pull out violet rags bloody Tampaxes which afterwards the females stick back in their cunts: the soldier's chest as he's raping the female crushes the baby stuck in her tits

I want: every part changes (the meaning of) every other part so there's no absolute/heroic/dictatorial/S&M meaning/part the soldier's onyx-dusted fingers touch her face orgasm makes him shoot saliva over the baby's buttery skull his formerly-erect now-softening sex rests on the shawl becomes its violet scarlet color, the trucks swallow up the RIMA soldiers, rainy winds shove the tarpaulins against their necks, they adjust their clothes, the shadows grow, their eyes gleam more and more their fingers brush their belt buckles, the wethairedfrom-sweating-during-capture-at-the-edge-of-the-coals goats crouch like the rags sticking out of the cunts, a tongueless canvas-covered teenager pisses into the quart of blue enamel he's holding in his half-mutilated hand, the truck driver returns kisses the blue cross tattooed on his forehead, the teenager brings down his palm wrist where alcohol-filled veins are sticking out. These caterpillars of trucks grind down the stones the winds hurled over the train tracks, the soldiers sleep their sex rolling over their hips drips they are cattle, their truckdriver spits black a wasp sting swells up the skin under his left eye black grapes load down his pocket, an old man's white hair under-the-white-hair red burned face jumps up above the sheet metal, the driver's black saliva dries on his chin the driver's studded heel crushes as he pulls hair out the back of this head on to the sheet metal, some stones blow up

My mother is the most beautiful woman in the world. She has black hair, green eyes which turn gray or brown according to her mood or the drugs she's on at the moment, the pallor of this pink emphasizes the fullness of her lips, skin so soft the color of her cheeks is absolutely peach no abrasions no redness no white tightness. This in no way describes the delicacy of the face's bone structure. Her body is equally exquisite, but on the plump or sagging side because she doesn't do any exercise and she wears girdles. She's five feet six inches tall. She usually weighs 120 pounds even though she's always taking diet pills. Her breasts look larger and fuller than they are because they sag downwards. The nipples in them are large pale pink. In the skin around the nipples and in the tops of her legs you can easily see the varicose veins breaking through. The breast stomach and upper thigh skin is very pale white. There's lots of curly hair around her cunt.

She has a small waist hands and ankles. The main weight, the thrust, the fullness of those breasts is deceptive, is the thighs: large pockmarked flesh indicates a heavy ass extra flesh at the sides of the thighs. The flesh directly above the cunt seems paler than it has to be. So pale, it's fragile, at the edge of ugliness: the whole: the sagging but not too large breasts, the tiny waist, the huge ass are sexier MORE ABOUT PASSION than a more-tightly-muscled and fashionable body.

My mother is the person I love most. She's my sister. She plays with me. There's no one else in my world except for some kind of weird father who only partly exists part out of the shadow, and an unimportant torment I call my sister. I'm watching my mother put on her tight tawny-orange sweater. She always wears a partially lacy white bra that seems slightly dirty. As she's struggling to get into a large white panty girdle she says she doesn't like girdles. She's standing in front of her mirror and mirrored dresser. Mirrors cover every inch of all the furniture in the room except for the two double beds, my father's chair, and the TV, but they don't look sensuous. Now my mother's slipping into a tight brown wool straight skirt. She always wears tight sweaters and tight straight skirts. Her clothes are old and very glamorous. She hitches her skirt up a little and rolls on see-through stockings.

She tells me to put on my coat and white mittens because we're going outside.

Today is Christmas. Huge clean piles of snow cover the streets make the streets magical. Once we get to the park below the 59th Street Bridge I say to myself, "No foot has ever marked this snow before." My foot steps on each unmarked bit of snow. The piles are so high I can barely walk through them. I fall down laughing. My mother falls down laughing with me. My clothes especially the pants around my boots are sopping wet. I stay in this magic snow with the beautiful yellow sun beating down on me as long as I can until a voice in my head (me) or my mother says, "Now you know what this experience is, you have to leave."

My mother wants to get a strawberry soda. Today my mother's being very nice to me and I love her simply and dearly when she's being nice to me. We're both sitting on the round red vinyl turnable seats around the edge of the white counter. My mother's eating a strawberry soda with strawberry ice cream. I see her smiling. A fat middle-aged man thinks we're sisters. My mother is very young and beautiful.

At camp: males string tents up along a trench filled with muck: slush from meat refuse vomit sparkle under arching colorless weeds, the soldiers by beating them drive back the women who're trying to stick their kids in the shelter of the tents, they strike at kick punch the soldiers' kidneys while the soldiers bend over the unfolded tent canvas. Two males tie the animals to the rears of the tents, a shit-filled-assed teenager squatting over the salt-eroded weeds pants dust covers his face his head rolls vacantly around his shoulder his purple eye scrutinizes the montage of tents, a brown curly-haired soldier whose cheeks cause they're crammed full of black meat are actually touching his pockmarked earlobes crouches down next to a little girl he touches her nape his hand crawls under the rags around her throat feels her tits her armpits: the little girl closes her eyes her fingers touch the soldier's grapejuice-smeared wrist, from the shit-heaps a wind-gust lifts up the bits of film and sex mag pages the soldiers tore up while they were shitting clenched the shit burns the muscles twisted by rape. Some soldiers leaving the fire wander around the tents untie the tent thongs they crawl on the sand, the linen tent flaps brush their scabies-riddled thighs, the males the females all phosphorescent nerves huddle around the candles, no longer wanting to hear anything the teenagers chew wheat they found in the bags, the kids pick threads out of their teeth put their rags on again stick the sackcloth back over their mothers' tits lick the half-chewed flour left on their lips

My mother thinks my father is a nobody. She is despising him and lashing out at him right now she is saying while she is sitting on her white quilt-covered bed "Why don't you ever go out at night, Bud? All you do is sleep."

"Let me watch the football game, Claire. It's Sunday."

"Why don't you ever take mommy out, daddy? She never has any fun." Actually I think my mother's a bitch.

"You can't sleep all the time, Bud. It isn't good for you."

"This is my one day off, Claire. I want to watch the football game. Six days a week I work my ass off to buy you and the kids food, to keep a roof over your head. I give you everything you want"

"Daddy, you're stupid." "Daddy, you don't even know who Dostoyevsky is." "What's the matter with you, daddy?"

Daddy's drunk and he's still whining, but now he's whining nastily. He's telling my mother that he does all the work he goes to work at six in the morning and comes back after six at night (which we all know is a joke cause his job's only a sinecure: my mother's father gave him his first break, a year ago when the business was sold, part of the deal was my father'd be kept on as "manager" under the new owners at $50,000 a year. We all know he goes to work cause there he drinks and he doesn't hear my mother's nagging). He's telling my mother he gave her her first fur coat. My father is never aggressive. My father never beats my mother up.

The father grabs a candle, the curly brownhaired soldier his red mouth rolling around the black meat takes out his knife: his hand quickly juts the red rags over his sex his pincher his grabber the curly brownhaired soldier jerks the sleepy young girl's thighs to him, she slides over the sand till she stops at the tent opening, one soldier's mutilated forehead cause he was raping over an eagle's eggs the eagle scalped him another soldier's diseased skinpores these two soldiers gag the father, the father throws a burning candle into their hairs, the curly brownhaired soldier takes the young girl into his arms, she sleeps she purrs her open palm on her forehead to his shudder trot, the clouded moon turns his naked arm green, his panting a gurgling that indicates rape the sweat dripping off his bare strong chest wakes the young girl up, I walked into my parents' bedroom opened their bathroom door don't know why I did it, my father was standing naked over the toilet, I've never seen him naked I'm shocked, he slams the door in my face, I'm curious I see my mother naked all the time, she closely watches inside his open cause gasping mouth the black meat still stuck to his teeth the black meat still in a ball, the curly brownhaired lifts her on to her feet lay her down on the dog-kennels' metal grating hugs her kisses her lips the ear hollows where the bloodstained wax causes whispers his hand unbuttons his sackcloth pulls out his member, the young girl sucks out of the curly brownhaired's cheeks the black meat eyes closed hands spread over the metal grating, excited by this cheek-to-stomach muscle motion bare-headed straw-dust flying around his legs injects the devil over her scorches, the dogs waking up at the metal gratings leap out of the kennels their chains gleam treat me like a dog drag in the shit, the curly brownhaired nibbles the young girl's gums his teeth pull at the meat fibers her tongue pushes into the cracks between her teeth, the dogs howl their chains jingle against the tar of the road their paws crush down the hardened shits, the curly brownhaired's knees imprison the young girl's thighs.

My father's lying in the hospital cause he's on his third heart attack. My mother's mother at the door of my father's room so I know my father is overhearing her is saying to my mother, "You have to say he's been a good husband to you, Claire. He never left you and he gave you everything you wanted."

"Yes."

"You don't love him."

"Yes."

I know my grandmother hates my father.

I don't side with my mother rather than my father like my sister does. I don't perceive my father. My mother is adoration hatred play. My mother is the world. My mother is my baby. My mother is exactly who she wants to be.

The whole world and consciousness revolves around my mother.

I don't have any idea what my mother's like. So no matter how my mother acts, she's a monster. Everything is a monster. I hate it. I want to run away. I want to escape the Jolly Green Giant. Any other country is beautiful as long as I don't know about it. This is the dream I have: I'm running away from men who are trying to damage me permanently. I love mommy. I know she's on Dex, and when she's not on Dex she's on Librium to counteract the Dex jitters so she acts more extreme than usual. A second orgasm cools her shoulders, the young girl keeps her hands joined over the curly brownhaired's ass, the wire grating gives way, the curly brownhaired slides the young girl under him his pants are still around his knees his fingernails claw the soil his breath sucks in the young girl's cheek blows straw dust around, the mute young girl's stomach muscles weld to the curly-headed's abdominal muscles, the passing wind immediately modulates the least organic noise that's why one text must subvert (the meaning of) another text until there's only background music like reggae: the inextricability of relation-textures the organic (not meaning) recovered, stupid ugly-horrible a mess pinhead abominable vomit eyes-pop-out-always-presenting-disgust-always-presenting-what-people-flee-always-wanting-to-be-lonely infect my mother my mother, blind fingernails spit the eyes wandering from the curly-headed, the curly-headed's hidden balls pour open cool down on the young girl's thigh. Under the palmtrees the RIMAS seize and drag a fainted woman under a tent, a flushing-forehead blond soldier burning coals glaze his eyes his piss stops up his sperm grasps this woman in his arms, their hands their lips touch lick the woman's clenched face while the blond soldier's greasy wine-stained arm supports her body, the young girl RECOVERED,

New York City is very peaceful and quiet, and the pale gray mists are slowly rising, to show me the world, I who have been so passive and little here, and all beyond is so unknown and great that now I am crying. My fingers touch the concrete beneath my feet and I say, "Goodbye, oh my dear, dear friend."

We don't ever have to be ashamed of feelings of tears, for feelings are the rain upon the earth's blinding dust: our own hard egotistic hearts. I feel better after I cry: more aware of who I am, more open. I need friends very much.

Thus ends the first segment of my life. I am a person of GREAT EXPECTATIONS.

(1982)

Implosion

I. The Background of the French Revolution.
Three scenes.

Scene 1. Europe. The People Mutter Political Discontent

KATHY (*an American visitor*): How do you make love?
FATHER, a Frenchman: I make love with my fingers. My fingers
are magic. Are you feeling them now?
KATHY: Oh yes! (*He beats her ass while he fingerfucks her.*) Oh.
OH! (*Comes twice.*)
FATHER: I have other kinds of tastes. I'm a feminist: I like to
watch two women fuck. Sometimes I beat them with my belt
while they fuck each other. (*Frank and Patricia enter.*) Frank!
What is the matter with you? Are the Dutch people calling you
a fascist again?
FRANK (*a Dutchman, sitting on the bed between Father's and
Kathy's bodies*): I'm no goddamn fascist. I don't have any poli-
tics. I'm like an American.
PATRICIA (*also Dutch*): I'm thirsty.
FRANK: I'm sick of moralists. For the first time their economy's
going under and the Dutch are beginning to realize their posh
ways of life might no longer be available to them. At this moment

they're acting scared cause they'll do anything to avoid rocking the boat.

FATHER: Of course. I'm a good Frenchman.

FRANK: . . . They've always worshipped anything that's safe. That's why they're Liberals. The Dutch Marxists in announcing themselves as the only opposition to this reaction have grouped and defined themselves so rigidly that they've got no political power. They're as bureaucratic academic and rigid as the Right Wing.

PATRICIA: How long will we be as bloody and dirty as children?

KATHY (*masturbating*): Oh oh oh.

PATRICIA: For how much longer are our toys—the coffins of friends out on heroin—going to be the only things we can love? For how much longer will severed heads be the only people I place my lips upon? I love death. The Committee of Happiness better begin its work.

FATHER: Your statements are reactionary cause you can't so simply put ideals on top of what's actually happening to you. If this society in which you're living shits, you have to shit. (*He's such a big guy, he farts.*)

PATRICIA: But ideals can pick holes in the social fabric. "True" and "false" is besides the point. Even if they did nothing, they're the only tools we've got.

FATHER: Look, I'm a musician: I know language like music isn't stating big things, but breathing. Otherwise, poetry opera art painting aren't only dead they also cause death. That's why Rockefeller sponsors them. Throw everything that's dead up the assholes of those who're too tight to fuck in the ass.

KATHY (*stopping masturbating for a moment*): I'm too crazy. The only thing I want is feeling. Talking to friends.

FRANK (*feeling up her cunt*): How're you going to do that? They either worship you or they despise you, but you'll never be human because you feel.

KATHY: This talk shits. Go crazy. We're going to cause a revolution. I tell you. I'm going to cause a burning revolution. (*Disappears.*)

FATHER: The hell with her.

Scene 2. What My Grandmother Saw In London. In America:

TOM (*barely audible and fucking*): Love.
MY GRANDMOTHER (*can't stop herself from saying it*): I love you
I love you. (*She starts coming and can't stop coming. Gradu-
ally they calm down physically.*) I have to go to Europe now.
(*They kiss a lot.*)
In England:
MY GRANDMOTHER (*phoning Tom*): This is Florence.
TOM: Who?
MY GRANDMOTHER: Florrie.
TOM: Who?
MY GRANDMOTHER: Florrie . . .
TOM: Oh, Florrie. Where are you?
MY GRANDMOTHER: I'm drunk.
TOM: That's nice.
MY GRANDMOTHER: I'm in London. (*Pause.*) Am I disturbing you?
TOM: There's someone here with me.
MY GRANDMOTHER: I'm sorry; I didn't mean to disturb you. (*She
hangs up the phone.*) Oh, thank you. (*She looks through the
window and sees the following scene:*
(*An outside street. The bright sunlight is evident mainly in all
the colors which are so bright they're almost white. There are
working- and lower-middle-class three- and four-story tenements
in back of and around the streets. There are groups of typical,
that is, small and eccentric English people on the streets.*))
A MIDDLE-AGED HOUSEWIFE: You know those fuckin' upper-
middle-class women. They say a woman who's a whore is the
pitfall and living cancer of human existence. I'll tell you something. No woman wants to be a whore. Oh maybe some bitch
who went to Oxford and has to have daddy needs to be a whore
or gets her thrills whoring. I have nothing to do with the rich.
Most women who whore whore because you need to be supported. You, daddy. You hire fuck and arrest the whores.

A whore needs a pimp. A whore doesn't need a pimp because she's weak. A whore needs a pimp because a pimp con-

trols the territory. To control this whore the pimp, just like a record company with its rock-n-roll stars, gets her hooked, Your daughter is now supporting two daddies and a habit. Who did this to her? I ask you, who did this to her? Is she doing it to herself? (*She turns to a Frenchman who's standing on the street.*) You think whoring's fashionable? You think women who're too young to come whore because it's hep? Being a whore beats being a secretary (*back* to *her husband, who we now* see's *a drunken tailor*) or a wife cause, for the same work, work cause there's no love, only a whore not a wife or a secretary gets paid enough she might be able to escape men.

TAILOR: Our daughter doesn't love me.

A MIDDLE-AGED HOUSEWIFE: I used to have a fantasy you loved me. Then I had a fantasy some man could love me. Now I can't find any fantasy inside my head. I can't find anything.

MY GANDMOTHER (*to herself*): What do I want? I'm a woman too.

TAILOR: It's natural it's a Law of Human Nature: My daughter has to whore to support me. Give me a knife so I can increase the pain.

MY GANDMOTHER: Give his daughter the knife cause it's the hurt, not the hurters, who feel pain.

TAILOR TO HIS WIFE: I will increase the pain. I will go crazy. I hurt; let all of us hurt more.

A MIDDLE-AGED HOUSEWIFE: To you everything's your cock; you worship your pain.

Scene 3. Art-Criticism and Art
The Office of *Artforum,* Mulbery Street, New York City.

SITUATIONALIST WITH ITALIAN ACCENT: I just saw an American film. The title of the film is *Bladder Run.*

HIS GIRLFRIEND: *Blade Runner.*

SITUATIONALIST WITH ITALIAN ACCENT: I think it is a real American film. In this film which is a film and not a real event . . .

GIRLFRIEND: . . . but it's a real film . . .

SITUATIONALIST WITH ITALIAN ACCENT: . . . the filmmaker proves to us the audience that robots are as human as we are. Since simulation can take the place of reality . . .

GIRLFRIEND: . . . nonsimulation . . .

SITUATIONALIST WITH ITALIAN ACCENT: . . . we no longer need money to make germ warfare, lobotomy, and other weapons as does Mr. Reagan, Inc.

GIRLFRIEND: We don't want germ warfare, lobotomies, and Tylenol.

SITUATIONALIST WITH ITALIAN ACCENT: We make fake germ warfare, fake lobotomy, and good medicine which doesn't hurt anybody and yet works very well destruction of governmental control.

GIRLFRIEND: Destruction of corporations.

SITUATIONALIST WITH ITALIAN ACCENT: Yes. Corporality.

MARXIST FEMINIST: But how can I tell the difference between the real and what isn't real that is, for our purposes, between their disgusting weapons and our good weapons?

SITUATIONALIST WITH ITALIAN ACCENT: You can't.

MARXIST FEMINIST: I might end up a Right Winger.

GIRLFRIEND: For you that's better than ending up in someone's bed.

TOM, who's an Irish artist turned American: No, this woman's correct. There's definitely a problem with situationalism as it now stands. I therefore propose we get rid of all judgments, No more you v. me v. Reagan or rich v. poor. We don't mean anymore. We Americans and our allies the British (*in thick Irish accent*) will give the world a fine example!

MARXIST FEMINIST (*not understanding anything*): Of what?

TOM: Of the new politics: no politics. Everything. We can and do everything. We are theatre.

MURDERERS: All dark, black. The skin.

MURDERER: Why do you keep murdering?

MY GRANDMOTHER: I have to, my dear.

MURDERER: You're a shadow that murders the body that casts it.

MY GRANDMOTHER: So then I'll be left with shadows . . .

MURDERER: . . . different textures of blackness . . .
MY GRANDMOTHER: . . . my skin. Where's Danton? Fiction. I tell you truly: right now fiction's the method of revolution.
MURDERER: All this is talk. (*Sharpening his knife.*)
MY GRANDMOTHER: To dream's more violent than to act. (End of my version of art-criticism.)

TAILOR (*to his wife*): I will increase the pain. I will go crazy. I hurt; let all of us hurt more.
A MIDDLE-AGED HOUSEWIFE: To you everything's your cock; you worship your pain.

II. Action. Ten scenes.

Scene 1. On Heroism: Robespierre Decides to Kill Danton

ROBESPIERRE: Danton's getting too famous. Let's kill him. (*Rubs his hands.*) Hee hee hee. (*Robespierre's Polish. All Polish people are gnomes who run around in tiny circles and act in malicious ways.*) You think murder's wrong. I'm going to prove to you there's no morality (*a Polish proof*): My mind is capable of and thinks every possible thought. Therefore there's no morality in the mental world. A thought turns into an action by chance. Therefore there's no morality in the real world, only chance. (*A picture of Ronald Reagan's asshole with shit coming out.*)
ROBESPIERRE AND ST. JUST (*St. because today it's Christmas*), *being both Polish jump up and down rubbing their hands together clap monkey feet together*): Kill Danton the Powerful! Kill Lacroix the Foolish! Kill Hérault-Séchelles Philippeau and Camille!
ST. JUST (*reading a long piece of paper which he rolls up and unrolls while everyone chants or chatters "Good" "Bad" "Good" "Bad"*): "Robespierre kills." That's a disgusting slander. The media lies.
ROBESPIERRE: I'll kill you for lying.
ST. JUST: I'm not lying. This paper's lying.

ROBESPIERRE: You die anyway. My friends only love me when they're dead.

ST. JUST: Or when you're dead. This is true in London not only in New York City.

ROBESPIERRE (*changing his mind*): You don't have to die yet, Justice. I just wanted to frighten you.

ST. JUST: You're frightening everybody to death. (*Walks off.*)

ROBESPIERRE: Who needs friends? I do everything I do only in accordance with myself: I act. I am the hero.

Scene 2. Danton Learns Robespierre's Going to Kill Him And Agrees to It.

DANTON (*sitting in his own room*): I don't care about anything except when I'm obsessed.

LACROIX: You think so much you're not going to be able to murder Robespierre. You're not only committing suicide; you're killing all of us. Stop thinking; slaughter the creep. I just heard he's planning to kill you. Worry about why you're murdering later.

DANTON: I'd rather die than murder. I'd rather be fucked than fuck.

LACROIX: You're right: It's better to die than to die. (*All the Poles, bent over, shuffling around in circles, follow each other.*)

DANTON: I don't care anymore if I die. The only thing I have is sex and I'm not so hooked on sex though the physical ecstasy keeps getting stronger. Maybe Robespierre'll kill me soon. (*In London people can't afford to travel around the city. Kids place wires on the soft spots of their brains so hopefully they're lobotomizing themselves. The beards of old men sitting in the pubs sit in their beers. The buildings of the rich overtower all.*) We have to find our own pleasure. (*Pasolini died by suicide.*)

Scene 3. Back to School.

KANTOR: I want you to tell me about the War of Roses.

DANTON, (*preschool age*): The War of Roses occurred in 1481. The House of Lancaster who were known as the red roses fought against the House of York who are the white roses. The red roses won because they were bloodier.

KANTOR: Correct. Now tell me whether or not you are going to die. You don't know, do you? You're going to have to go to school. Let's go to school.

DANTON: I don't want to go to school.

KANTOR: All little boys go to school. Little girls don't do anything. Besides this school doesn't have any pupils and needs pupils cause a school needs pupils to be a success.

DANTON: I won't be a pupil because I have pupils. I must be a school.

KANTOR: If you're not at school in an hour, you won't have any more pupils. (*Picture of Polish people putting little Polish girl into the earth.*)

DANTON: OK. So I'll go to school.

KANTOR: Let's go to school right now. (*The Spirit of Death takes my hand and wafts me to school.*)

Scene 4. In School.

All the teachers are female and all the boys are male.

TEACHER (*gazing at little boys*): Boys! Boys! Boys! I need more. Two other teachers talk to each other. (This is a pastoral scene: people occur in clumps.)

TEACHER #1: I've already got herpes. (I'm standing hand in hand with the guy who's brought me to school. I'm abnormal and abnormally shy. My toes quake inwards. I turn my face away. I don't want to go into this nasty place because I don't know nothing. In there. The Spirit of Death who's now a patriarch my uncle who's keeping me these days away from my own money, shoves me forward into the Schoolmistress' face. The Schoolmistress is part ogre and part pig. She has a fake English accent even though she's English.)

ME: My name's Johnny.

SCHOOLMISTRESS: Well, here's little Johnny. (*Feeling my cock between my legs.*) You certainly are a little Johnny. I wish I was teaching future criminal offenders in the South Bronx. I always knew it was better to live in America.

MY UNCLE: Leave the goods alone, Mrs. Selby.

HEADMISTRESS (*correcting him*): They're virgin. (*Moving away to a beautiful grove of trees.*) Look how well all the students are coming back. They know how to walk. They all know how to walk. We have a very fine establishment here.

BEAUTIFUL BLONDE: They ain't innocent enough. I always said, we don't get enough virgins and so they ain't worth anything to us, they's just used rags cause they parents gets 'em first, an' they ain't worth anything to the people we's sell them to. Now, you's a father. Do you know how hard it is for a teacher to make a boy fresh and innocent again? You can't do it with your girls which's why young girls don't go to school. There ain't no use for them to go to school. We have to be really highly trained and it takes a lot of the taxpayers' money to make an already rotting vegetable into a strong carrot. You wouldn't believe how much work cause you's a father.

MY UNCLE (*to himself*): Let 'em rot. At least these rotters are willing to stand up. (*To Beautiful Blond*) Madam, it is your job to train these young pliable minds to want goodness. These pliable minds will be the owners of the world and the world will rest on their shoulders. Goodness or godliness, you know, is a taught desire: the social caviar. You must persuade their frail wills to want goodness rather than Coca-Cola.

BOY: The only thing we want for our Coca-Cola is hard drugs. (*Shoves his ass in the Beautiful Blonde's face then runs away.*)

The Punk World. Scene 5. Love Scene.

MY GRANDMOTHER: I miss you so much.

DANTON: I'm not near you. I'm in England.

MY GRANDMOTHER: I wish you were next to me so I could lick your ears. The tips of your ears tip tip. Then into two eyes. My love. We've never said anything affectionate to each other. We don't really know each other.

DANTON: We don't know each other.

MY GRANDMOTHER: Shit. You're less capable than I am. I should forget about you.

DANTON: A person should be as self-sufficient as possible, but I don't know what the hell for. Robespierre's coming to arrest me.

Scene 6. Robespierre and His Gang Plan.

ST. JUST: In two hours Danton's going to announce his son's engagement cause he knows people love a wedding so that way he can keep them under his thumb.

MY GRANDMOTHER: But George, the son, is a Siamese twin. Half a Siamese twin.

ST. JUST: They just need this wedding to keep the people happy. They don't have to have sex.

MY GRANDMOTHER: An advertisement wedding is as good as a real wedding and better than the sex I'm getting these days.

ROBESPIERRE (*looking her body up and down*): I hope you're speaking for yourself.

MY GRANDMOTHER: You don't have anything worth speaking of.

ROBESPIERRE: That's why I like human blood. This semi-Siamese son is a human booby and basket phenomenon; the non-married semi-twin, Arthur . . .

MY GRANDMOTHER: . . . he's the one who ruled Britain . . .

ROBESPIERRE: . . . is the one I want to use.

MY GRANDMOTHER: What do you do in bed?

ROBESPIERRE, annoyed: I told you I like blood! Arthur's going to help us kill Danton.

MY GRANDMOTHER: He won't commit patricide. He's too intent on fratricide.

ROBESPIERRE: If Arthur kills his father, the people'll decide Danton has to be a shit.

MY GRANDMOTHER: I'll go back home and tell Arthur his other half's getting married. He's so dumb he doesn't even know it yet. He must have been born on the other side of the brains.

When he learns Danton's marrying off George, he'll be pissed off enough to slaughter George but he can't because then he'd die too. So he'll murder his father.

ROBESPIERRE: A family scandal'll really kill off the Danton family. Murder advertisements always top wedding advertisements. The people'll know we're just as pure as driven snow. We can even kill a few more people.

MY GRANDMOTHER: Due to that Watergate scandal—when even dumbies as dumb as the Americans had to know their leaders, Nixon and everybody else, lie steal murder cheat and take hard drugs—those same leaders simply gained more power. Don't throw your money into advertising. What matters is that you get all the political power.

Scene 7. Danton.

DANTON: I want to be less nothing. There are some thoughts that shouldn't ever be heard. It's not good if they cry out the second they're born a baby out of the womb it is good: they can blow up the world.

Scene 8. Robespierre's Coming for Danton.

Lots of battle scenes, small battles, all around. Only street fightings no more major charaters.

Scene 9. Robespierre's Coming for Danton #2.

Make more and more like a painting.

MY GRANDMOTHER: Do you know who I am?

DANTON: How can I know who you are? I only fucked you twice. (*Lots of sunlight and little battles.*) What I believe is what I see. It's harder to live than die for what you see.

MY GRANDMOTHER: What do you see? (*Lots of sunlight and little battles.*)

DANTON: Last night I had this dream: I was fishing. I caught an eel. As the fish I had caught flapped on the wood dock, my hook slipped out of its mouth. This made me very upset. Surprisingly, when I put my hook back into its seemingly smiling therefore sly mouth, the fish readily accepted it. (*The audience beginning to see Robespierre and his men advancing on Danton realizes Danton's faster and faster closer to his death, at the point of punk ecstasy, in the daylight.*)

MY GRANDMOTHER: You have to say what you are. Tell me what you see.

DANTON (*even faster no fighting against the speed at the same pace*): We are particulars. We are this world. (*Now the people are on him. A housewife digs her fingernails into his thigh.*) There's more and more world a proliferation of phenomena. How, you religious people and more important you politicoes who believe in your willfully therefore violently changing this world who believe in your wills, how can you be apart from the world? And if you're not apart from the world, how can you be apart from the world? Who is doing the changing? All phenomena which include me being phenomena are alive.

MY GRANDMOTHER: And it's OK that the rich maul the poor?

DANTON: Hello, Robespierre. You're slaughtering me for being a revolutionary and I don't believe in anything I didn't choose to be the freak I was born into. (*As Robespierre's arresting him, in weak uncertain voice*) I would like to love Florrie.

ROBESPIERRE: I'm taking over this world because I'm strong and you're weak.

MY GRANDMOTHER: The moments are gone: Tell me what you see.

DANTON: Your eyes work the same ways mine do, you cunt. I see a three-story brick building whose bricks the sun is wrapping, a bloodstain on a white collar, a black window frame. I'm hoping, my love, that you love me cause I'd like to live in love. Since I'm given I don't give, I can't create love I can only hope it's here. (*Robespierre leads away Danton.*)

Scene 10. My Grandmother.

MY GRANDMOTHER (*alone on the sunlit street*): Today I've been deeply wounded in my sex: I've had two viral warts scraped off my clit. My cunt cut open at my clit.

III. The Aftermath of War. Two scenes.

Scene 1. My Grandmother Talks to Danton.

My Grandmother writes a telegram. The telegram says:
I'M CRAZY I MISS YOU ARE YOU MARRIED I CAN'T WAIT SIX WEEKS FOR YOUR RETURN.
She waits for the phone to ring. She waits for a return letter in the mail.
MY GRANDMOTHER: He hasn't phoned me. There's no telegram coming back. There won't be any letters because letters from England take too long, a week, and by that time my memory's over and, besides, there are no letters in a revolution. I'll forget him. It's better to forget the people you care about. Being free: that's what I know. I hate this fake freedom. This fake freedom's being in prison. It's social; all psychological is political. I hate.

I'm strong. I need to be part of a family and this world; and when I have to feel needs that are unsatisfiable, needs are only anguish.

(*Her phone rings. To phone*): Let's go see 'Line.
PHONE: 'Lina? Lisa Lyons? What's she doing?
MY GRANDMOTHER: Line. She's fucking some white guy on stage in the middle of the poorest Puerto Rican section. Maybe there'll be a riot.
PHONE: Sounds like a riot. There're riots all over the place. Let's go.
MY GRANDMOTHER: Pick me up at 8:30. If you don't get killed on the way. There're already two corpses on my doorstep.

PHONE: They're dead. Dead junkies can't hurt me. How long will she be?

MY GRANDMOTHER: How long does a fuck take? Ten minutes?

PHONE: Five minutes?

MY GRANDMOTHER: How the fuck should I know?

PHONE: It takes longer than a death.

MY GRANDMOTHER (*immediately hanging up phone retaking it off hook and dialing*): Melvyn. I'm desperate. Just listen to my story. It's about this guy I saw in England. Now I'm going to tell you exactly what happened so you can give me advice. I met him by accident in England. The next day we fucked. I wasn't expecting anything to happen. I was too busy. I could barely sandwich him into my life. We didn't talk about anything. All we did was fuck. The minute we saw each other, we fucked. It wasn't that we didn't have anything in common. We really like each other's work. We just fucked fucked, I'm a real dope I didn't ask him if he had a girlfriend. We didn't say anything to each other. The next day we saw each other in the afternoon, but I had to see the TV people that night. And the next day I had a dinner date and couldn't take him along. You know how it is. But we see each other all the next day. It was really great. We really got along. That night I was upset I couldn't say anything well what do you expect? I had to leave England. At the end I asked him, "Am I going to see you again?" "I'm coming to New York in February." When I got back to New York a few days later, there was stuff about the magazine he works for, I phoned him. It was all right to phone him. We said we'd work together on an art piece. I said I couldn't keep phoning him cause it cost too much so I'd blow all my money. He said he'd phone me. Robert, the woman who actually runs the magazine, was supposed to be here last week but she won't be here till next week. I haven't heard from him since I phoned. I sent him a telegram. He didn't reply to my telegram. Now, I want to know if this means he doesn't like me?

MELVYN: There's obviously something between you. When did you send the telegram?

MY GRANDMOTHER: Fifteen minutes ago. Five minutes ago.

MELVYN: Maybe he's not in town.

MY GRANDMOTHER: That could be.

MELVYN: Look: You're very far apart. Let him know you keep caring and at the same time, protect yourself: don't obsess. (*They both laugh.*) Fuck someone else.

MY GRANDMOTHER: It doesn't work like that. (*She hangs up phone.*) You're not around me and even if you were around me, I'm just dealing with my own desires. It doesn't matter if I name these desires because every desire acts the same: Either, if I let myself be overcome in desire I'm being sentimental so not letting the mind have a resting place I should take every desire which rises up in me and shove it; or, I should be dumb passion! Let desires and revolutions act! The last choice makes me happy because it's true there's no will.

Where are you? Please call me.

Scene 2. Everything Is Gone.

PAUL ROCKOFFER (*in mourning*): Shut up, bitches! I'm returning to Art I'll be an artist and now I'll be happy. I'm an artist I'm an artist I'm an artist! I don't believe in breaking traditional form.

ELLA, a pretty eighteen-year-old girl: You're 16 years old.

MY GRANDMOTHER: I'm 22.

ELLA: Well, you're fat enough to be 46.

MY GRANDMOTHER: My body doesn't matter. It's always trying to die anyway. The hell with it. My mind matters less. It's a conditioned piece of shit. Keep your mind on what matters, girl.

ELLA: What matters?

PAUL ROCKOFFER: Tell me please, what is life really?

ELLA: Now I don't know anymore so I feel dull.

PAUL ROCKOFFER: Don't force me to make speeches. I could tell you things, beautiful and horrible deep and drastic, but it'd be just more lies.

ELLA: Now the artist's talking sincerely.

OLD MAN-TEACHER: Now, Cleopatra's nose . . . Cleopatra.

Cle-o-pa-tra.

MY GRANDMOTHER-IN-OLD-AGE: What about Cleopatra's nose? C'mon, fellers, what about it?

THE OTHER PUPILS: The nose, the no-o-se, her no-o-o-se Cleopatra's nose!!

MY GRANDMOTHER-IN-OLD-AGE-AS-THE-GOOD-STUDENT: It's the nose of Cleopatra, her no-o-se. (*She sits quickly down.*)

OLD MAN-TEACHER: And the foot of a mountain . . . ? (*He's clearly at the point of losing his self-control.*) Well, the foot of a mountain?

MY GRANDMOTHER-IN-OLD-AGE-AS-THE-GOOD-STUDENT: Foot. Foot foot foot foot. (*Epileptic fit.*) Footfootfootfootfootfootfootfootfootfootfoot (*drooling*)

OLD MAN-TEACHER-MORE-ANXIOUS-CAUSE-HE'S REALIZING-THE-DUMBNESS-OF-THE-KIDS: And what about Achilles' heel? Quickly. Achilles' heel, Achilles' spiel, heel and toe around is woe, don't show your cunt bare, bear. (*The Man-Teacher's penis now becomes real for the Man-Teacher a thing of flesh and blood it grows and grows.*) Heel! Heel!!

MY GRANDMOTHER-AS-A-YOUNG-CHILD: Out of love.

CONVICT: Get me vittles. Pork pie and steak 'n kidney pie 'n tomatoes 'n cabbage. I got a young man with me and this young boy eats up children like you for supper. If you don't get me those vittles, this young man will eat up your nose, then part of your cheeks, your eyes. He likes big chunks of young girls' thighs. (*Grabbing her nose.*)

MY GRANDMOTHER-AS-A-YOUNG-CHILD: I'll get you your vittles! I'll get you those vittles you want!

CONVICT: I'll tell you something. You might run away, but you can't run away. A child might be warm in bed, he might pull all the covers over his head, but my young man gets into the house, he gets under your covers, he gets at your toes, your legs. There's nowhere you'll be able to escape him! You can never run away.

MY GRANDMOTHER-AS-A-YOUNG-CHILD: I'll get you the vittles! (*Running away.*)

CONVICT: Remember, child, remember.

(1983)

from "Translations of the Diaries of Laure the Schoolgirl"

No form cause I don't give a shit about anything anymore.

This writing is all just fake (copied from other writing)
so you should go away and not read any of it.

What I See

𝕴t is a very Parisian garden in which I'm going to hide myself. Me, the schoolgirl. Me, with my whips. Hide myself from the outside world because I've been hurt.

Behind skeletal trees of tiny leaves a man leaves, he is totally white, shakes a fist at nothing, pisses on the tiny white garden stones, oh I am lonely, again departs, precautionarily walking around this lawn . . . another man rises, totally red-faced, his lips are rosy and soft as a baby's, he had me when I was encased in prison. I am not. Thousands of fuchsias surrounded me: ivy, soot, gook made out of begonia petals by her nervous fingers because they know they're almost out-of-existence like the marks of hopscotch on a bombed-out city street. The man I know is getting near me but now there are detours, this is a miniature golf course . . . and another man sticks his leg through the window, bewildered face like a lunatic's, palms vertically flat beat the air, froth comes from his mouth. "Bastards. They've stolen me."

I think to myself, "I understand what you're saying."

A woman is passing by this garden. Her hands are clasped under her chin. She is a nun. She is a penguin. They aren't women because they don't have anything between their legs. They run with bodies waddling, these Catholics, flaccid flabby and dumb. Dumb nun.

High up a small sallow face sticks itself into small window bars, then sticks its back hair into small window bars. I see white arms that are as thin and even as sticks.

The arm is cut off.
The one who sees is cut off.

Dear Georges,
It seems that everything that happens to me is all chance.
I don't like saying anything important.
But I want to tell you, only you, that I am so desperate I no longer have any fantasies.
Of course it's not necessary to say anything to you:
(1) because you always know everything.
(2) because *you don't care at all for me* meaning *I don't care for you:* meaning: *I don't want anyone in my life.*
I can't remain this frigid.
When we first met I thought you didn't notice me because I'm invisible so I said whatever I wanted to—your saying "I'll never love you" was what I wanted cause I'd remain invisible.
This is all sentimentality. I'm just surprised that given my ridiculous sentimentality, we're friends. Sometimes I want to break off everything with you because I hate you so much because you don't give me anything I want everything is your way: you don't have money you don't have time you don't love me
I'd rather be frigid.

Laure

a   b   c   d   e

I can no longer speak.

a   b

I'm no longer apart from the world.

a

I don't know how to count yet.

A few days later:

Dear Georges

If you want to keep knowing me, you can telephone me now and then,

Since I have to keep myself apart from everyone, I have to keep the control.

I'm sure you're going to get to fuck lots of women.

Is anything ever understood between people? It wasn't between me and Peter.

Please don't think I'm totally malicious especially about what a whore you are.

A side of me has sincere friendship and true solidarity.

Laure

I Begin to Feel

I remember the corpses stood up before me. There's a creep on TV, asking me to call him about my grandparents, but my grandparents are dead.

The corpses say: "You were born beautiful rich and smart you little creep and beauty wealth and intelligence just brought you down to deterrence, secretion, to reject you . . . You came from a good family even though your real father was a murderer and your mother was crazy. Even being a creep won't save you. Tonight you're going to be ours."

They're babbling tenderly to me:

This is the corpses' song:

This is Christ the eternal humiliant, the insane tyrant. He and the corpses are holding me in their arms.

The only thing that matters to me is waking up.

I begin walking to look for that moment that will wake me up.

The only thing that is satisfactory is this moment.

Soon money isn't enough for me whether American or Arabian, I float, suspended between the sky and the earth, suspended between the sky and the earth, between floor and ceiling. My dumbly sad eyes which always see things opposite to the ways they are my dumbly sad eyes which always see things opposite to the ways they are are showing their stringy lobes to the world, my mutilated hooks reveal my mother's madness reveal my mother's madness.

My mother tells me why I was born: she had a pain in her stomach, it was during the war, she went to some quack doctor (she had just married this guy because it was the war and she loved his parents); the doctor tells her she should get pregnant to cure the pain. Since she's married, she gets pregnant, but the pain stays. She won't get an abortion because she's too scared. She runs to the toilet because she thinks she has to shit; I come out. The next day she has appendicitis.

At night in every city I live in I walk down the streets to look for something that will mean something to me.

The city I dreamt of: It was here that I heard the voice of Mary the Whore Who Gave Her All For Love, here I stared at the beautiful look of Violette injected by the blackest ink, here finally Justus and Betelgeuse, Verax and Hair and all the girls with the names of stars the openings of doors magnetized the young girls. They no longer know what they're doing. Invisible rays make this nothingness where everything is possible, possible.

Anonymity by imposing no image reveals space.

This is the beginning of love. For you it's of no importance but for me it has every importance.

You also said: "You don't understand why I'm bothering with you because I have so much to give and you have nothing to give."

I'm not bothering with you now.

I hate you you took me. "I don't understand why you're bothering with me" meant *I'm not going to give anything to you.*

I'm being a bitch now saying all this. Chauffeur. It doesn't matter where you're taking me: to the furnace, to the toilet, to the brothel you're working in, now you won't see me. The only thing I need is to burn; myself torn into pieces scattered each bit away from every other, covered in your shit; and I feel every fuck that happens, every fuck frightens me. Past your taking me.

To sleep inside your left shoulder.

My real being alive will never occur where there is rigidity of mentality—too bad for my mind.

(1983)

from "Algeria"

Cunt

In 1979, right before the Algerian Revolution begins,
the city is cold and dank . . .

The Stud Enemy

I am fucking you and you are coming you have a hard time coming you breathe hard you have periods when you strain to come then your cock withers you strain to come again. I hear you I see you I don't feel I am doing anything to help you the rhythm is so steady I come jagged to your steady rhythm my coming is insignificant compared to your building. You gasp. You are three laps away. Oh I am coming again. My coming is always so unexpected. I want you to come. I want you to come. I want you. I want you. When you come I never come you are unable to move it is always so unexpected.

I leave Kader because I live in New York City and Kader lives in Toronto. In New York I feel I'm a jagged part skin walking down the street. I feel part of my being no longer is. That is disgusting. That is an outrage.

I have to leave the man I love because I have no money and he has no money. I want to bust up the government to destroy every government that's telling me what to do, controlling the me that I most want to be me, bust up the society that causes government, the money that denies feeling and irrationality I hate

Separation from Kader makes me have to fill that separation with nothing, makes me grab at everyone, makes me hate everyone for me every single thing is equal to every other single thing: I have to get to you. I have to get to you.

I HATE equals I LOVE YOU.

Here in New York, every morning I wake up, I don't want to be awake. I have to persuade myself to wake up. I have to use my will to get food in my mouth because my heart sees no reason for anything. I don't feel unhappy. I don't think my life's repulsive even though I have no money for food I have to beg friends for food. I don't care about poverty. I want.

Kader and I write each other a lot. I write Kader I'm a terrorist which is obviously a lie. Kader writes me he's waiting on a subway platform when the subway comes he doesn't know whether to throw himself under it or walk into it when he gets home he sticks a knife into his own hand beats his head against the wall. I write we're not going to see each other again because we live in separate cities and we have no hope of attaining money. Kader writes me if he doesn't see me soon he'll go crazy.

The Algerian revolution began on May 8, 1945, in Setif, a largely Muslim town 80 miles west of Constantine. The town inhabitants were preparing to celebrate the Nazi capitulation to Western European forces of the previous night. The Algerians had always passively re-sented their French occupants. The newly formed nationalist move-ment Paiti du Peuple Algerien (P.P.A.) was the first occasion for direct Algerian anger. Right before the anti-Nazi celebration, the French sent the leader of the P.P.A., Messali Hadj, to jail. The Muslim popula-tion of Setif wanted the anti-Nazi celebration to become a strong sug-gestion that the French leave Algeria to the Algerians.

Actually there was no such important rational plan. All people are hungry, wanting. Hungry people do not act by rational plans, but by instinct. During the anti-Nazi celebration, a French policeman saw a beautiful Algerian boy, got a hard-on, couldn't tell what he should do. The Algerians were carrying their green-and-white national flag and banners saying "Long Live Messali" "Free Messali" "For The Liberation Of The People, Long Live Free And Independent Algeria!" Instead of fucking him up the ass, the cop shot the beautiful Algerian boy in the stomach. People act in accordance with the energy levels of their situa-tions. The Muslims jumped the Europeans. Anger was out on the streets.

The next week the Europeans murdered 45,000 Muslims.

Over the phone I tell Kader to come to New York. He phones me he's planning to come he doesn't have any money he needs to find free rides each way and some free money. We're both feeling desperate.

Kader says he'll come to New York he'll borrow the money. I tell him if he can't get hold of the money, he's not old enough to have me. I'm forgetting who Kader is. My forgetting gets me scared cause I'm desperate to have someone else in my life.

I decide as if the decision is no part of me I stick with Kader. I ask him when are you coming to New York? Kader says he'll be here in three days because he's been able to borrow the money. I love him. I don't want him to come here, break into my isolation. My body desperately wants a cock inside her.

Before and after Setif, the French colonists were controlling more and more of Algeria and decimating more and more Algerians. By 1954 an average European in Algeria owned ten times the land an average Algerian owned and earned 25 times as much moola. The French pumped the Algerians full of penicillin and other antibiotics so the Algerians would have more kids. All these kids had no way to eat so they'd do anything for money. They were dispossessed de-everything-ed. The French Arab Culture ministers told the Arabs they'd have to stop speaking and writing their language, Arabic. They told the Arab women their Arab men had made them into slaves.

Over half-a-million Algerian Muslims a year fled to France to the garbaged cities in which they worked for French bosses for almost nothing though to them it was a lot because in Algeria the average Muslim worker earned twenty-two cents a day if he was lucky one-ninth of the population was unemployed and earned nothing.

I, Omar, live alone in a room. I almost never leave my room. I am lonely out of my mind sometimes. A lot of this time I worry a lot about money because for the last three months I have owned about ten dollars a week I am two months behind on rent I hate all other people; I am unable to fuck I am horny; I see nobody I am scared I am in danger kill kill; I am unable to kill my grandmother who is rich many people kill many people in wars I hate myself because I do not kill; because I do not walk out of my room.

Whenever a cock enters me every night three nights in a row, I ask myself regardless of who the cock belongs to should I let my SELF

depend on this person or should I remain a closed entity. I say: I'm
beginning to love you I don't want to see you again. The man thinks
I'm crazy so he wants nothing to do with me.

The Importance of Sex because
It Breaks the Rational Mind

The French police fastened the gégène's (an army signals magneto)
electrodes to the Algerian rebel's ears and fingers. A flash of lightning exploded next to the man's ears he felt his heart racing in his
breast. The cops turned up the electricity. Instead of those sharp and
rapid spasms, the Algerian felt more pain, convulsed muscles, longer
spasms. The cop placed the electrodes in his mouth. The currents plastered his jaws against the electrodes. Images of fire luminous geo-
metric nightmares burned across his glued eyelids. While the Algerian
longed for water, they dumped his head into a bucket of ice-cold liquid until he had to breathe the liquid. They did this again and again.
They did this again and again. A fist big as an ox's ball slammed into
his head. The screams of other prisoners were all around him. He no
longer knew he was in pain, pain was wrong, living wasn't a constant fire of torture and disgust. The moment before the Algerian went
crazy and accepted horror as usual, his greatest fear and torment was
this consciousness that he, the Algerian, is about to go crazy, has to
give up his mind which is anger and accept the horrible inequality,
the French way of living he is fighting against

The Problem of We the Colonized

All those people of whom we are afraid, who crush the jealous emerald
of our dreams, who twist the fragile curve of our smiles, all those people
we face, who ask us no questions, but to whom we put strange ones:

Who are they?

What can our enthusiasm and devotion and madness achieve if
everyday reality is now a tissue of lies, a tissue of cowardice, a tissue
of contempt for human mentality?

The degree of alienation of the people who gave me this world
seems frightening to me. Alien to alienation, we now have to live
depersonalized or . . .

Right now there is no difference between a legal and a criminal act. Lawlessness, inequality for the sake of desire, multidaily murders of human beings have been raised to the status of legislated middle-class principles.

This social structure negates our beings, makes us who are without into nothings. If we hope: if we talk of or search for love, this hope is not an open door to the future, but the illogical maintenance of a subjective attitude in organized contradiction with reality.

Beneath the lousy material way we live, beneath our petty crimes, we want to eat food without roach eggs and we want to love people. I think a society that drives its members to desperate solutions is a nonviable society, a society to be replaced.

HOW CAN I WHO AM DISINHERITED ACT?

I have to make Kader here even if he isn't here. I talk to Kader on the streets. I write down the conversations I have with Kader over the phone. I use Kader for everything. I can't write down what I think I should be writing Kader's thoughts keep interrupting me. I have to fuck I have to fuck I have to fuck I

I think that for a kid American family life is so bad (cause the parents, taking shit from their parents, bosses, the media, etc., have only their kid to dump on), that all a kid can do these days by the time he has his first chance to try to control a little of his life is find some decent parents so maybe he can grow up. Each young person is desperately trying to find a parent. Since there are no adults now, there are no other relationships.

Kader is in New York now. I don't feel anything for him.

After the French murdered 45,000 Muslims, they seized and imprisoned the rest of the rebel leaders. But the Algerian people didn't stop being angry. The young Algerian boys who were growing up knew smatterings of Marxist revolutionary techniques. They didn't care for liberal sentiments or revolutionary discussions. They weren't interested in groups. They enjoyed hating. They liked to fight. They respected violence.

(1984)

from *My Death My Life by Pier Paolo Pasolini*

Language

1. Narrative breakdown for Carla Harriman

In the year 1413 I went in search of my true love. There was a camp full of milling people. A beautiful young boxer who's the son of a rich man is buying horses. I called him to me. I told him he's my brother by our father. I put him up for the night in my house. In the toilet he fell into the shit. I stole his money while he escaped from my house. He knocked at the door of my house and my servants: "You're crazy; we don't know who you are." A bum told him to stop disturbing his sister. They found him out by the smell of his shit. An old woman told the following tale: It is a place of sacred practice. Art isn't about the sacred. A beautiful young man sneaks up to the garden. The beautiful young man pretends to be mute. He is the new gardener and the nuns treat him as a pet. The nuns want his cock. Cock is the action that makes you go mad. The nuns hit him with a stick. Then they drag him into a hut. His cock's small. Oh ooooh ooh. Heaven, for all we know, has arisen. Both the nuns are smiling. All the other nuns want to. All the women are after cock. Will the man die? Old ugly hag Mother Superior gets hold of this boy's cock. Ten men (much less this boy) can't even satisfy one female and a cock is a miracle. "You're a robber you're a forger you've raped women, etc; maybe you should get out of town a bit until things cool down. You're so evil, you're the person to collect my debts." So I went to a town out in the grass. Men pushed along a cart of skulls. The queen wore a basket over her head and extended a shovel with a skull sitting on top of it.

Giotto's best pupil has come to paint Naples. The painter who is one of the finest painters around wears rags. Are all our friends poor? The painter looks like an imp. This imp is maddened. Mauled. Big plump casaba melons lie on the road. Don't make me die of love. If you fuck me, I won't die. When the painter eats with the monks, his table manners are atrocious.

I am a slave because they're auctioning me. I'm a young boy. I pick a young boy to buy me. I give him my money. I tell him where to get us shelter. We fuck there. He's so very young, he doesn't know how to fuck. Soon he figures it out. No: I show him. I'm a great artist. I tell my new boyfriend to sell my art but not to a white man because a white man'll separate us. When I sell it to a white man, he follows me. My girlfriend tells me a story. Can the poets speak about what they haven't experienced? Slowly I penetrated her. My cock wouldn't go in easily cause she was tight along the upper part of her mucus tunnel. The muscles felt good around the end of my cock. I had to come. As soon as it sprang out of me I passed out. When I, the girl says, woke up I saw him lying in the bed next to mine, looking like the rose fallen out of the midnight. I had to have his cock, she said. I had to have his tongue. I had to piss over his flesh; I rubbed my clit and the upper cunt corners against his pelvis bones sharp I came five times. I fell asleep. When I woke up, he was gone.

In the Fifth Precinct which is where I used to live the cop who's the head likes to arrest anyone he sees fucking or making voodoo or hustling and libeling or robbing the local churches or forging checks or issuing false contracts or priests who use their parishes to get rich or lending money or simony whatever that is. Most of all he hates sex. He takes all these offenders' money. When they can't pay him what he wants, he makes sure they're locked up longer than they should be. This is the way he remains the head cop (rich man). Also he eats at any restaurant in the neighborhood he wants to free of charge and gets any store object he desires. If a local store owner doesn't pay the police chief the monthly garbage bill, the owner has to close his store because he's been violating sanitary laws. The East Village, part of which is this Fifth Precinct, is the filthiest space in the world.

The police chief has a Special Assistant. This Assistant is thin sly

from *My Death My Life by Pier Paolo Pasolini*

greasy locks dribble down his forehead and he collects five- to eight-year-old boys who're greasier and fart more than he does. They must have been spit out of their mothers' assholes between fits of constipation because they're so much smoother and more poisonous and gaseous than turds these little sausages can slip around everywhere and see everything. The children know everything. They know where the Families in the neighborhood (I'm talking about the Mafia) keep their money in secret mansions way inside surrounded by rows of the poorest apartment buildings around Tenth Street. The Special Assistant uses these children for information and also to capture the few people who still dare to fuck. These people fuck because they need to fuck so badly and it's now so hard to get laid they need to fuck so badly, by the time they announce to themselves they have to fuck they'll do anything to fuck, they'll fuck anyone one of these slimy kids. The kid tells the cop. The Special Assistant has his junky desperate for his junk so he makes whatever terms he wants. The Special Assistant is a sexual pervert but mad because he never fucks but gets exactly what he wants without ever compromising himself. I'm telling you all this because I'm a monk.

The Special Assistant also has a squad of pimps. You understand that he's not a hypocrite. By no means. He'd use any means if he was smart enough. He tolerates pimps whom otherwise he would be joyously grinding into the nonexistent dirt and the existent shit on the street because they tell him dirt the children can't tell him. Their girls or trash learn where the businessmen (dealers, gunmen, etc.) hide their monies and tell the pimps and the pimps tell. This way also the Special Assistant is constantly checking the children's information against the pimps' information and vice versa and no one's ever let off the hook. This is democracy: no overt governmental control. The Special Assistant isn't as moral as his boss which is why he's lower down the business hierarchy so he pimps on the side. He pimps so he can run his own blackmail sideline. Unlike his boss he loves sex because he's making a fortune from it.

One day since the sun was shining the Special Assistant decided to go after new ducks: old women because old women walk around mumbling to themselves drop their purses and are helpless. While the Special Assistant stood on the corner of Fifth Street and First Avenue and looked for an old woman, a tall Puerto Rican walked by him. The Puerto Rican wore a large black hat and a black jacket. The Puerto Rican looked at the Special Assistant. "What d'ya want, white boy? Do ya want anything with me?" "I don't want anything. Yet. Right now," the white boy replied. "I need a real criminal." "So you can't go after anyone you want. You white boys don't have any power no matter how many badges you wear. You just do what the big tops tell you to do." The Special Assistant couldn't admit he was powerless. "Me, I'm after someone myself," the Puerto Rican flips some kind of card into his face. "I also belong to an Agency. If you're looking for someone, why don't you hook up with me? I own the territory over there," pointing south toward the Lower East Side, "and there're lots of junkies over there. It's easy to make money." The Special Assistant knew a good money deal. They walked down the street.

"How're we going to make money? And, especially, how do you make money, you who live on the other side of the law?"

"Since my life's always in jeopardy because of the color of my skin, I blackmail, extort and simply take as much as I can from those who are more helpless than me."

"I have a job and I do the same thing," said the cop. "I have one moral: If it's too hot for a fence, give it to a cop. You have to be tough to live in New York. I'm so tough, there's no tragedy that could make me even blink. I'm beyond those intellectual liberals because I don't depend on anybody's opinion. Are you as tough as I am?"

For the first time the Puerto Rican realized he could have this white cop, so he began to smile. "I'm a dead man," he replied. "I live in hell. Just like you I spend all my time looking for humans I can get something from and just like you I don't care how I get it."

"I see. You're Vice Squad."

"No. I'm not human. I'm using a human form because I'm trying to fool you."

"If you're not human, who are you?"

"I'm nonhuman. We nonhumans unlike you humans who are stuck only use forms to get what we want."

"If you're so powerful, why do you even bother with human beings?"

"You're so much more powerful than old women and junkies and young girls and yet you prey off of them. This is the way the world is. I'll give you an answer: When you're murdering someone, you think you're murdering because you're getting something out of it. But like me you vulturize because you get nothing. You and I are made. We are part of this almost unbearable worldly pain which isn't disappearing.

"Do you always lie?"

"If I always lied, a lie wouldn't be a lie. Sometimes Puerto Ricans tell the truth. Sometimes we Puerto Ricans are so romantic we tell some woman we totally love her she believes we adore her we can fuck over her whole life we do she learns that another human being is capable of absolutely conscious deception. You don't have to learn anything from me. From this moment onwards you're going to see so much pain because you're going to cause so much pain that no artist will be able to tell you nothing. No human being can remain naive. If you hurt somebody, nobody can hurt you. There's no natural laws. There's no natural justice or morality. Politicians or rather those in power have made up that liberal jive so they can keep their slaves or excuse me cuntstichyouwents in check. I'll just trot along by your side, bro', until you do so much evil, you're ready to stick a knife in my back. This is the way people in New York City live."

"I won't become so evil," the Special Assistant swears with his hand over his heart, "because I'm a New York City cop. I've sworn to protect human life. I'm going to take a second oath. I swear that I love you and regard you as absolute evil and that I'll do so until the end of time. I'm white and you're black and you're my brother."

"And you are mine," the fiend replies. This is the neighborhood he was speaking about. Half of the buildings have broken glass for windows. Behind each broken glass is an unseeable space. The doors and some of the windows are wood boards. Men waiting for their junk sit on what there is for floors inside these buildings. Children and fat women whose tits are hanging out of their bras crowd the doorways and doorsteps of the occupied brownstones. Seven men are sitting on chairs outside the corner bodega. On the sidewalk two children fight each other with sticks. "Give me that junk," the child says as he raises his stick. "I hate you," says the other child, "because last night you had my sister." "I hope you die. Jesus Christ should come down and forsake you and the Evil One should hold you in his arms." They fight again.

"Those kids need to be taught what's right and what's wrong," the Special Assistant thought to himself, "and I can make a little money on the side." He whispered to his friend, "Don't you want to take him?"

"They don't mean what they're saying," his friend replied. "They're only imitating what their parents say." The children are kneeling on the edge of the sidewalk. There's a huge spider trapped between a glass jar and the cement. They let the spider free. The moment the spider moves, they trap it again.

"Human beings say one thing and mean another. That's what they mean by language. Let's get further into this neighborhood where there's more desperation. It's only when humans are totally desperate that they speak the truth."

The white man speaks. "I know where I am. There's a Jew in this Puerto Rican and black hovel who doesn't give up a penny even when a mugger's holding a knife to her eye. Either she's going to give me a hundred and twenty dollars for a payoff or I'm going to jail her. I'm a cop, aren't I? I have to make my living. The taxpayers won't give me enough money."

"You're still using liberal excuses," the fiend instructs him.

To show how evil he is, the cop kicks in the old blind dumb and almost deaf cunt's stomach. "What do you want?" in a little old woman voice. "Excuse me, ma'am." Kick again. "I've got orders here to arrest you." She doesn't bother asking what for. "Now?" "Open up this door. I have to take you to jail." "I don't want to go to jail. I just had an operation yesterday. My doctor said if I don't stay still, I'm going to die. No one takes care of me cause my daughter's husband just left her so she killed herself so there's no one to help me go to jail." "The law doesn't take account of disease, ma'am." "How can I stay alive?" "Pay me a hundred and twenty dollars." "I don't have a hundred and twenty dollars. Do you think an old woman who lives with junkies and alcoholics and sub-welfare families has a hundred and twenty dollars lying around the house?" "If I don't either arrest you or get a hundred and twenty dollars, may I go to hell."

"OK. What did I do wrong?" "When your husband was alive, you fucked another man." "I never got married. So whenever I fucked, I fucked out of love. Madly for love. Desire has nothing to do with justice anyway. Go to hell." Quickly the fiend asked, "My dear, do you really mean what you're saying?" The foul old bitch who was foul only because she was old and not because she wanted to cause anyone pain answered, "I hope you die or go to hell if you keep trying to rob me."

"Rather than rob you, I'm going to take everything you've got."

"Don't be angry, bro', cause now you're getting everything you wanted. I'm going to take you to hell where the only thing you can do is evil."

If God has made all of us in His image, part of this image is pain and hell.

They go down to hell. On the way the cop sees a painted forest. There, the trees are knotted, stubby, and leafless.

The pickpocket. Bloodless Fear. This smiling man carries a knife under his coat. Black smoke lies around the fire of the burning block. Humans murder other humans asleep in their beds. The body opens wounds blood all over all the flesh. There're all sorts of sounds in this place. I see the man who commits suicide. I see the mother who commits suicide. The blood in her heart, slipping out of, soaks her cunt. At night the hammer pounds a nail through the forehead. The dead people's mouths are open wide.

Bad Luck's sitting in the middle of the floor. His face is all weazled and squinched up. Madness in the center of Madness laughs which is total pain. Complaining bickering hating all feeling jealous keeping all this hate and anger bottled under the skin; all the isms are the psychology here. Every group of skinny trees has under them dogshit and a body whose throat is cut open. The tyrant takes whatever he wants. Simply. As a result a country is destroyed. Haiti. Vietnam. There's nothing left to the country. There's no time here. Ships are burning up. Wild bears sink their teeth into the man who hunted them. The pig struts into the bedroom and eats the child in the cradle. Madness goes everywhere. The cook scalds his arms by his long ladle. Above the poverty-stricken peasant lying under his cart's wheel Conquest or Fame, which is the only One people honor, rises; criminals are the politicians; conquest 1 gives way only to conquest 2; humans are killing themselves because they're choosing to love humans who don't love them.

From this time onward, war came to Ectabane. Lots of slaves escaped, went to those conquering, but when the conquerors tried to make them give specific details about the resistance of the occupied, the slaves refused to tell their former owners' names. And their situations became worse; the slavery was more intense. Ectabane is the largest Western capital. Every day the beaches below the boulevard which line the sea wear as clothes corpses. At the oceanfront guards shoot all the resisters who land during the nighttime. The conquerors took over painlessly: the city wanted to get rid of gods and masters. The shoed helmeted armored conquerors halted the sexuality and the perception of the conquered. For a hundred years they had halted everything. Then the Ectabane wise men in secret made a weapon capable of resuscitating their land. The conquerors stole the weapon. They constructed an airplane into which they could put the weapon. They flew the wise men and the weapon to their city Septentrion. The remaining dissidents the adventurers con men mercenaries fighters they pursued even beyond Ectabane's boundaries. They had to use both informers and cruelty to control some of the families who lived in the city's center: at night their children ran to other parts of the world; other children started out for those underground rivers in the Southern coast which the Buxtehude Archipelago joins. As of yet the Archipelago is still free, but blackened every moment by the enemy bombers' shadows.

On the day his country capitulated a young Ectabanese officer whom the General Staff despised because he had been trying to modernize their army fled to this Archipelago under the aegis of diplomatic immunity—as the ambassador extraordinaire of his country. They had instructed him to convince the as-yet free Archipelago to fight the enemy as much as possible. Buxtehude gave him a hotel room in a spa. He put photos of his wife and children who were still in Ectabane on a shelf. Then he set up a small radio with which he could send information back to Ectabane. He told the Archipelago to resist the enemy as strongly as they could. Get rid of all political apathy. Use all the arms and weapons you've left to rot in your forgotten barracks. Soon all of Septentrion, the whole Western continent which is only part of the East, will be flaming! The conquerors will never have enough fires to burn away the secret ashes and wastes and garbage of their souls or of their blood so that tears can start flowing! In downtrodden defeated Ectabane, dawn the day the city was overtaken, I sat on top of a balcony of the triumphal arch and watched the whole city which was still asleep: A boot hit the sidewalk. A rat scurried across the balcony. A security guard sticking his head under a bunch of flowers banged it on the table outside. The wind which was alive dried up his blood. One of the enemy security bending down wiped up the dried blood with his handkerchief. He tapped the knee of the Ectabanese guard who slowly managed to get vertical, "The old dolts, the priests and everyone who loves this our country have freely elected a president who pleases the enemy."

The people in the world blow up the world. After the end of the world.

One. One and one. One and one. One and one. One and one. One and one. One and own. One and one. One and one. One and one.

One and one and one. One and one and one. One and one and one. One and one and one. One and one and one. One and one and

One and two. One and two and no more. One and two. One and two no more. One and two. One and two no more. One and two.

One two and. One two and. One two and. One two and. One two and. One two and. One two and. One two and. One two and. One two.

On. On. On. On. On. On. On. On. On. On. On. On. On. On. On. On. On. On. On. On. On. On. On. On. On. On. On. On. On. On. On. On.

On and. On and. On and. On and. On and. On and. On and. On and. On and. On and. On and. On and. On and. On and. On and. On and.

Candor honor. Candor honor. Candor honor. Candor honor. Candor honor. Candor honor. Candor honor. Candor honor. Candor honor.

Can do one more. Can do one more. Can do one more. Can do one more. Can do one more. Can do one more. Can do one more.

Can do one more. Can do one more. Can do one more. Can do one more. Can do one

Can murmur murder mirth. Can murmur murder mirth. Can murmur murder mirth. Can murmur murder mirth. Can murmur murder mirth.

This is. This is a saying. One. Can murder mention one. This is a saying.

Stop. Not it. Can it is. Can it is. Can it is. The hat on the steps of. The windowpane is by now.

The sea flows scaffold for the sheep. I came come of the being. Androgynous draggles.

Two and three and five. Two and three and five. Two and three and five. Two and three and five. Two and three and five.

Accent her. Hand armors on wonder. Orphan forces war or instance of ovary. The manor of stove.

An instance of romance. Or form. Or form. Or form. Or form. Or form. Or form. Or form. Or form. Or form. Or form. Or form.

An land. An land. An land. An land. An land. An land. An land. An land. An land. An land. An land. An land. An land. An

And scape escape romance. And scape escape romance. And scape escape romance. And scape escape romance. And scape escape romance. And . . .

2. Language breakdown

Bats of boxes in the houses. Delight layering the accesses. Exquisite and excess urinals devour. So we. Glowerings glowerings sail.

Reins breasts and the polar rains turmeric. Along of in the polar down and police no dark no ark sightings away sight. To the lines long eerie aeries are we we we. The owes. He whispers whimpers whimpers.

Come out to the light: of squares of sturgeon of sturgeon and on on an under the dark and dark. Dark. On. On. On. On. On and under one. On and under two. On and under three. The sticks hunt vertical. Three sticks hunt vertical. Murderers remain demands. Murderers remain subversion. Houses veer bicycles. I.

Daylight. Obstetrician. Axe. Demanding. Who they are. Swing. A restaurant.

Do you disturb eyes? Do you disturb Tampax? Eyes foment off. Of reminiscing. Waste rebellion fast you lose.

In the square. What did she do? Hands flouresce. The tip of the clit suggest augmentation. Of treacherous. Lights murmurs. Hair egomaniac.

Was there danger? There usury. There objects of. There eccentricity. There notorious. There you. There accumulation. There simultaneous. There acquiescence. There dumb. There upset.

While walking, she was dreaming. Policeman wings boards off how. And under thatches of under of this. The lights blank how whispers a lot. To two lips.

Of these projects backs on bouquets. Wastebaskets glowing stabs knickers.

She moves. Therefore ways of moving. One sound done. Two the reduction to what is essential.

Two the reduction to what is essential. We don't reduce: we start nothing or bottom up. Hands hang rape. Hands flatter bad. Hands wing flutter. Hands lost record. Hands record corduroy. Hands grip colds angry black knife. Hands weaving blasts wonders often frozen. Hunger aggression.

The late skies of listening recalls claims two. Toward. The blisters baskets squires rues under hay and wise men anger. Herald blisters hunger is plausible lubberings crows an. Language thinking.

3. Nominalism

I want to talk about the quality of my perception. I want the quality or kind called childhood cause children see the sadness which sees this city's glory. What does this sentence mean? I can wander wherever I want. I simply see. Each detail is a mystery a wonder. I wander wonder. The loneliness feeling is very quickly lost. So I can see any and everything. I can talk about everything as a child would. The interior or my mind versus the exterior. Art proposes an interiority which no longer exists for all of us are molded. The nightmare that I fear most is true. This writing's outdated. Yet you walk around the city. Is this realization the source of your melancholy? I love you. You're my friend. I'm masturbating now. I have someone to talk to like I talk to my stuffed animals. Of course this life's desolate, it's lonely when there's no mentality. This sentence means nothing. More and more submerged the mind, you trace its submergence through Baudelaire; now it's gone. Fashion is the illusion there's a mind.

Walking through the cities, being partly lost, the image (in the mind) change fast enough that the perception which watches and judges perception is gone, is the same as the living in the place where I can do anything in which every happening is that which just happens. Saint-Pol Roux, going to bed about daybreak, fixes a notice on his door: "Poet at work." The day is breaking.

Language is more important than meaning. Don't make anything out of broken-up syntax cause you're looking to make meaning where nonsense will. Of course nonsense isn't only nonsense. I'll say again that writing isn't just writing, it's a meeting of writing and living the way existence is the meeting of mental and material or language of idea and sign. It is how we live. We must take how we live.

To substitute space for time. What's this mean? I'm not talking about death. Death isn't my province. When that happens that's that; it's the only thing or event god or shit knows what it is that isn't life. To forget. To get rid of history. I'm telling you right now burn the schools. They teach you about good writing. That's a way of keeping you from writing what you want to, says Enzensberger, from revolutionary that is present. I just see. Each of you must use writing to do exactly what you want. Myself or any occurrence is a city through which I can wander if I stop judging.

It could happen to someone looking back over his life that he realized that almost all the deeper obligations he had endured in its course originated in people on whose destructive character everyone was agreed. He would stumble on this fact one day, perhaps by chance, and the heavier the blow it deals him, the better are his chances of picturing the destructive character.

Wandering through the streets and creating a city: Berlin's a deserted city. Its streets're very clean. Princely solitude princely desolation hang over its streets. How deserted and empty is Berlin!

The first street no longer has anything habitable or hospitable on it. The few shops look as if they're shut. The crossings on the streetcorners are actually dangerous. Puerto Ricans whiz by in cars.

At the end of the next event is the Herkules Bridge. There's a block-long park that runs along the river. Here when I was a child as soon as I could walk I spent most of my days. I had a nurse. At first I didn't have as many toys as the other children. Then I had a tricycle. Later I had a cap gun. We would try to shoot pigeons with our cap guns. If your cap gun shot a pigeon in the eye, pigeons are the only living animals around, you blinded the pigeon and then could capture it bring it home to make pigeon soup the most wonderful delicacy in the world. Neither I nor anyone else ever captured a pigeon. The river which was pure garbage brown was crossed by a bridge on my right as I looked from the park out over the river. This bridge was the Herkules Bridge.

I used to have a strong dream about the garbage river. It was the most magical place. If only I could cross it, on the other side. Desire is the other side. During the day I can't cross it. Suddenly, in my dream, I can. Go over the low cement wall black iron bars curving out of upward toward me, down a three- or five-foot hill that's mainly dirt and some bushes, my feet kick small rocks rolling, downward. Here's the water at my feet. Here's flat sands forming a triangle narrowing toward the north I can walk on it. I'm walking on top of a narrow evenly wide sand ribbon across the river which isn't deep. I reach the other side. The other side is a carnival. The beach is still here. Here's a merry-go-round. All around the beach's white and onward. I walk onward on the magic ground. There are many adventures as I walk straight northward.

The other park I used to go to, the park that contained New Lake on Rousseau Island, was much further from my house. I'd go only with my grandmother who lived a few blocks away in a large hotel, I'll talk about her later, or with mommy although mommy almost never spent her time with me. In fact, I now remember, I never went to the park with mommy unless other friends accompanied us. The park or rather this part of the park which was its southernmost tip, in my mind the boot of Italy, bordered on a line of almost white expensive residences and hotels. Differently colored cars whirring back and forth separate the residential buildings from the park. There was a lake and ducks. On the far side of the lake, luxuriant dark greens brown. I can't get over to the luxury. I sit on a large rock. The rock's not large enough to be a hill. It's large enough to have two holes to crawl within, not really into, and to climb for five minutes. Three roads, one dirt and two asphalt-and-stepped, swerve through the short dog-shit-covered grass, down to it. I'm sitting on top of the rock and looking across the lake, to my right so far in the distance I don't know if it really exists there's a carnival. During one winter, when it's very cold, I can skate on this lake which has grown very small which snow surrounds. A small brown terrier has placed his butt on the northeast end of the lake. Two- and three-foot-high ridges of snow surround the lake. There aren't any children here as there are in the other park. At this time, I liked this park better than the other park. Then my grandmother would take me back to her hotel room.

Everything's alive.

When I was older, a boyfriend would walk with me through other parts of this park. No, first I went to school. When they couldn't drag us for exercise on the chilliest coldest fall days out to the level short green hockey fields way uptown, they took us for a treat to the part of the park nearest the school. Several asphalt and dirt paths of varying widths having absolutely no order crossed here and quickly changing growths of trees still thickly-green-leafed high among densely green valleys not big enough to be valleys and curving like eye contact lenses; I remember metal statues of Alice-in-Wonderland and the Caterpillar-on-the-Mushroom my boyfriend who was bearded and I would crawl under, ladies in precisely tailored suits walked their dogs, near one of the long rough stone walls that separated this park from the very wealthy residential and religious buildings was a park only children under a certain age played.

Only spaces in which I can lose myself whether I'm now sensibly perceiving or remembering interest me. It's because I live to fill a certain dream. I have penetrated to the innermost center of this dream. The center has three parts.

1. My most constant childhood experience is pain.

No, no knowing, just the present. A wholly unfruitful solution to the problem but all fruit these days is death, no as I grow older I don't think it's any worse or better now than before historically for humans I don't know I know less and less as I get older, the flight into sabotage and anarchism. The same sabotage of social existence is my constantly walking the city my refusal to be together normal a real person: because I won't be together with my mother. I like this sentence cause it's stupid.

2. Who do I know? I go over this question again and again because the people I know in this world are my reality stones. I know Peter and David and Jeffrey, and secondarily Betsy, and lots of other people whom I only half know. Peter and David who live together half of each of them is my grandmother. They have a small three-room apartment. They have certain nice belongings. They're proud of their living. They live more quietly than the people in the neighborhood they live in do and the people they know who are mainly rock-n-roll stars. I often debate with myself whether they're kind or not.

They're my closest friends. Sometimes I start to cry cause I feel so glad and lucky I know them and have been admitted into their hearts this feeling is almost too much so I say to myself you're just transferring your need for the affection you're not getting from a boyfriend. Lacking a boyfriend's one of the many thoughts society's taught me. All the thoughts society's taught me're judgmental, usually involving or causing self-dislike, imprisoning, and stopping me. When I just let what is be what is and stop judging, I'm always happy. Peter and David are two of the most happy people I know.

I got a cat this week, but the minute the cat kitten long light dark gray black white hairs hints of brown pale blue gray green eyes jumps into my house I can't give this much affection the kitten torn away from its mother demands something mental in me rends, I don't want to love inappropriately, I'm too something to be touched. I invent an allergy and run the cat back to its mother.

3. I didn't know anything about death (the first time I experienced death and saw a dead person it was my suicided mother when I was an adult) nor about poverty. The first time the word "poverty"

meant anything to me (to understand this word I had to wait until I was judging my experience and not just experiencing), I thought 1 was poor because I had less than the girls in my grade who were of my class and because my boyfriend in the fancy nightclub to which he had taken me said, "Tell your mother to get you a nice dress," and I knew she would never. In college I learned for the first time that my family was rich. (How does the word "poverty" differ from the word "death"?) Does this kind of knowledge which is really only belief change my actual experiences? Of course:

I'm making my dream. The mappings, the intertwinings, so hopefully there'll be losing, loosings, my mother said I hate you.

Let the rocks come tumbling out. Move crack open the ice blocks. You hurt me twice. No one hurts me twice, bastard. You said "Don't talk to me again" and "I'm saying this for no reason at all." First off (in time), after six years of living with me one night you said. "This is it." I said that I didn't know it had been getting so bad and could I have one more chance and you said no. My whole life busted itself. I recovered almost I almost didn't I do everything you want I always have, to, of, from, for I love you, you don't love me. One month ago you said, "I don't want to be friends with you any longer." This time I was innocent. You've hurt me again, I want you to know this time really badly. I don't understand how someone can be such a shit as you are. I think you are really evil. No one hurts another person for no reason at all. No one believes in him- or herself so totally, the other person has absolutely no say no language. This' how this country's run.

The media's just one-way language so the media-makers control.

I'm diseased. I hate you. There's this anger hot nauseating in me that has to seep out then destroy.

I hate the world. I hate everyone. Every moment I have to fight to exert my will to want to live. When I lived with a man, I was happy. I always was miserable. I like banging my head into a wall. I'm banging my head my head into a wall.

One might generalize by saying: the technique of reproduction detaches the reproduced object from the domain of tradition. Meaning, for example: a book no longer has anything to do with literary history so the history of literature you're taught in school is for shit.

The artwork's no longer the one object that's true; sellability and control, rather than truth, are the considerations that give the art object its
value. Art's substructure has moved from ritual and truth to politics.

Meanwhile this society has the hype: the artist's powerless. Hype.
Schools teach good writing in order to stop people writing whatever
they want the ways they want. Why do I like banging my head into,
against the wall? I always have. I could go stand by your door and
ring the doorbell. This is what I think every day: I'm going to phone
him. No; he told me he didn't want to speak to me again. I shouldn't
want someone who needlessly hurts me because such a situation hurts
me. You haven't liked me for a year. You only talked to me when
you wanted my money so I hate you. But that's the way you are with
everybody because you're crazy because you're so scared. You think
when you're hurting someone more than anyone would normally
(maybe my idea of "normal" is incorrect) the person is irredeemably
hurting you, because you're so coked up. As I walk along each street
I think: I can do whatever I want so I'll walk to your apartment and
ring the doorbell. My attention's distracted from this by wanting a
mystery book. I walk out of the bookstore. I don't care enough about
you now to experience your hatred of me again and I'm proud of me
for sidestepping my masochism my masochism.

By not getting in touch with you I'm keeping this situation alive.
I'm keeping this situation alive because there's no one alive who physically loves me. This' false. When I was in high school, unlike the other
kids (I went to an all-girls' school), I was never in love. I didn't feel I-
didn't-know-what-it-was for boys; I just liked sex. I crave sex.

Presumably, without intending it, he issued an invitation to a
far-reaching liquidation. Now I want to give you an analogy. A painter
represents or makes (whichever verb at this moment you prefer) reality by keeping distant from it and picturing it totally. A cameraman,
on the other hand, permeates with mechanical equipment what he's
going to represent, thus for the sake of representation changes breaks
up. Reproducible art breaks up and ruins.

I must give people art that demands very little attention and takes
almost nothing for me to do.

(1984)

from *Don Quixote*

The First Part of *Don Quixote*
The Beginning of Night

DON QUIXOTE'S ABORTION

When she was finally crazy because she was about to have an abortion, she conceived of the most insane idea that any woman can think of. Which is to love. How can a woman love? By loving someone other than herself. She would love another person. By loving another person, she would right every manner of political, social, and individual wrong: she would put herself in those situations so perilous the glory of her name would resound. The abortion was about to take place:

From her neck to her knees she wore pale or puke green paper. This was her armor. She had chosen it specially, for she knew that this world's conditions are so rough for any single person, even a rich person, that person has to make do with what she can find: this's no world for idealism. Example: the green paper would tear as soon as the abortion began.

They told her they were going to take her from the operating chair to her own bed in a wheeling chair. The wheeling chair would be her transportation. She went out to look at it. It was dying. It had once been a hack, the same as all the hacks on Grub Street; now, as all the hacks, was a full-time drunk, mumbled all the time about sex but now no longer not even never did it but didn't have the wherewithal or equipment to do it, and hung around with the other bums. That is, women who're having abortions.

She decided that since she was setting out on the greatest adventure any person can take, that of the Holy Grail, she ought to have a name (identity). She had to name herself. When a doctor sticks a steel catheter into you while you're lying on your back and you do exactly what he and the nurses tell you to; finally, blessedly, you let go of your mind. Letting go of your mind is dying. She needed a new life. She had to be named.

As we've said, her wheeling bed's name was "Hack-kneed" or "Hackneyed," meaning "once a hack" or "always a hack" or "a writer" or "an attempt to have an identity that always fails." Just as "Hackneyed" is the glorification or change from nonexistence into existence of "Hack-kneed" so, she decided, "catheter" is the glorification of "Kathy." By taking on such a name which, being long, is male, she would be able to become a female-male or a night-knight.

Catharsis is the way to deal with evil. She polished up her green paper.

In order to love, she had to find someone to love. "Why," she reasoned to herself, "do I have to love someone in order to love? Hasn't loving a man brought me to this abortion or state of death?

"Why can't I just love?

"Because every verb to be realized needs its object. Otherwise, having nothing to see, it can't see itself or be. Since love is sympathy or communication, I need an object which is both subject and object: to love, I must love a soul. Can a soul exist without a body? Is physical separate from mental? Just as love's object is the appearance of love; so the physical realm is the appearance of the godly: the mind is the body. This," she thought, "is why I've got a body. This's why I'm having an abortion. So I can love." This's how Don Quixote decided to save the world.

What did this knight-to-be look like? All of the women except for two were middle-aged and dumpy. One of the young women was an English rose. The other young woman, wearing a long virginal white dress, was about 19 years old and Irish. She had packed her best clothes and jewels and told her family she was going to a wedding. She was innocent: during her first internal, she had learned she was pregnant. When she reached London airport, the taxi drivers, according to their duty, by giving her the runaround, made a lot of money. Confused, she either left her bag in a taxi or someone stole it. Her main problem, according to her, wasn't the abortion or the lost luggage, but how to ensure neither her family nor any of her friends ever found out she had had an abortion, for in Ireland an abortion is a major crime.

Why didn't Don Quixote resemble these women? Because to Don Quixote, having an abortion is a method of becoming a knight and saving the world. This is a vision. In English and most European societies, when a woman becomes a knight, being no longer anonymous she receives a name. She's able to have adventures and save the world.

"Which of you was here first?" the receptionist asked. Nobody answered. The women were shy. The receptionist turned to the night-to-be. "Well, you're nearest to me. Give me your papers."

"I can't give you any papers because I don't have an identity yet. I didn't go to Oxford or Cambridge and I'm not English. This's why your law says I have to stay in this inn overnight. As soon as you dub me a knight—by tomorrow morning—and I have a name, I'll be able to give you my papers."

The receptionist, knowing that all women who're about to have abortions're crazy, assured the woman her abortion'd be over by nighttime. "I, myself," the receptionist confided, "used to be mad. I refused to be a woman the way I was supposed to be. I traveled all over the world, looking for trouble. I prostituted myself, ran a few drugs—nothing hard—exposed my genitalia to strange men while picking their pockets, broke-and-entered, lied to the only men I loved, told the men I didn't love the truth that I could never love them, fucked one man after another while telling each man I was being faithful to him alone, fucked men over, for, by fucking me over, they had taught me how to fuck them over. Generally, I was a bitch.

"Then I learned the error of my ways. I retired . . . from myself. Here . . . this little job . . . I'm living off the income and property of others. Rather dead income and property. Like any good bourgeois," ending her introduction. "This place," throwing open her hands, "our sanctus sanitarium, is all of your place of safety. Here, we will save you. All of you who want to share your money with us." The receptionist extended her arms. "All night our nurses'll watch over you, and in the morning," to Don Quixote, "you'll be a night." The receptionist asked the knight-to-be for her cash.

"I'm broke."

"Why?"

"Why should I pay for an abortion? An abortion is nothing."

"You must know that nothing's free."

Since her whole heart was wanting to be a knight, she handed over the money and prayed to the Moon, "Suck her, Oh Lady mine, this vassal heart in this my first encounter; let not Your favor and protection fail me in the peril in which for the first time I now find myself."

Then she lay down on the hospital bed in the puke green paper they had given her. Having done this, she gathered up her armor, the puke green paper, again started pacing nervously up and down in the same calm manner as before.

She paced for three hours until they told her to piss again. This was the manner in which she pissed: "For women, Oh Woman who is all women who is my beauty, give me strength and vigor. Turn the eyes of the strength and wonderfulness of all women upon this one female, this female who's trying, at least you can say that for her, this female who's locked up in the hospital and thus must pass through so formidable an adventure."

One hour later they told her to climb up pale green carpeted stairs. But she spoke so vigorously and was so undaunted in her bearing that she struck terror in those who were assailing her. For this reason they ceased attacking the knight-to-be: they told her to lie down on a narrow black-leather padded slab. A clean white sheet covered the slab. Her ass, especially, should lie in a crack.

"What's going to happen now?" Don Quixote asked.

The doctor, being none too pleased with the mad pranks on the part of his guest (being determined to confer that accursed order of knighthood or nighthood upon her before something else happened), showed her a curved needle. It was the wrong needle. They took away the needle. Before she turned her face away to the left side because she was scared of needles, she glimpsed a straight needle. According to what she had read about the ceremonial of the order, there was nothing to this business of being dubbed a night except a pinprick, and that can be performed anywhere. To become a knight, one must be completely hole-ly.

As she had read—which proves the truth of all writing—the needle when it went into her arm hardly hurt her. As the cold liquid seeped into her arm which didn't want it, she said that her name was Tolosa and she was the daughter of a shoemaker. When she woke up, she thanked them for her pain and for what they had done for her. They thought her totally mad; they had never aborted a woman like this one. But now that she had achieved knighthood, and thought and acted as she wanted and decided, for one has to act in this way in order to save this world, she neither noticed nor cared that all the people around her thought she was insane.

SAINT SIMEON'S STORY

Simeon, Don Quixote's cowboy sidekick, told Don Quixote a story that night in the hospital, "My father constantly publicly tormented me by telling me I was inadequate.

"Thus I began my first days of school. My parents sent me to a prestigious Irish gentry Catholic boarding school, so my father could get rid of me.

"There the upper-class boys wanted to own me. They regularly gang-banged me.

"Once a teacher whom I loved and respected asked me to his own house for tea. I went there for several weekends. He disappeared from the school. No one knew where he had gone—there were rumors. In his office the head of the school asked me what the teacher and I had done. I didn't know what he was talking about, but I knew there was something wrong, something about loving. I learned he had been dismissed for reasons which couldn't be spoken.

"A teacher at night told us to go downstairs. There he flogged us hard. The sound of flogging is now love to me.

"The teacher entered the classroom, sniffing. His nose was in the air. 'One of you boys,' the teacher said to the twenty of us quietly sitting in his classroom, 'is from the working classes.' He sniffed again. 'Now, I'm going to sniff him out.' All of us shivered while he walked slowly around each one and scrutinized each one. He picked out the boy he sexually desired. The boy's blond hair was floating around his head. 'You, boy. Your smell is from the working classes. I know.' Each of us knew what was going to happen. We could hear the sounds of caning.

"I want to be wanted. I want to be flogged. I'm bad.

"Thus I began my first days in school. I had two escapes from the school I hated: books; and even more, nature. Lost in books and in nature.

"They would find me asleep on a high tor and drag me back to their school. The sheep ate on the tor."

THE FIRST ADVENTURE
Don Quixote set out to right all wrongs.

She saw an old man beating up a young boy. The young boy was tied to a tree. He was about fourteen years of age.

Don Quixote cried, "Stop that! In this world which's wrong, it's wrong to beat up people younger than yourself. I'm fighting all of your Culture."

The old man who was very proper, being found out, stopped beating up the young boy. "I was beating up this boy," covering up, "because he's a bad boy. Being flogged'll make him into a man. This boy actually believed that I owe him money for the work he does in school. He demanded payment."

"You're lying," Don Quixote, knowing the ways of the world, replied, "and your body is smelling. Free the boy!"

As soon as he freed the boy, the boy ran away.

"Come back here instantly!" the old sot yelled after the boy. "We'll know how to care for you."

"I won't go back to school. Never. I won't be turned into an old goat like you. I'll be happy."

"Where're you going to, boy?" meaning "Where can you go?"

The boy, being very unsure of himself, turned to Don Quixote. "Please tell me, ma'am, that I don't have to go with him."

Don Quixote thought carefully. "You have to go back, for your teacher, deep inside him, wants to help you and has just been mistaken how to help you. If he didn't care for you, he wouldn't want you back."

The old man took the boy back to school and there flogged him even more severely. As he was flogging him, the teacher said, "I have a good mind to flay you alive as you feared." The boy tried to enjoy the beating because his life couldn't be any other way.

HOW DON QUIXOTE CURED THE INFECTION LEFT OVER FROM HER ABORTION (SO SHE COULD KEEP HAVING ADVENTURES)

Seeing that she was all battered and bruised and couldn't rise out of her bed due to a severe infection and moreover, knowing that she was sick, Don Quixote couldn't rise out of her bed, which was the sidewalk outside her house.

"Who," St. Simeon who had come to help his comrade asked Don Qulxote, "is responsible for this lousy condition?"

"No human's evil. The abortion."

"Then who caused the abortion?" St. Simeon was a highly intelligent young man, besides being holy.

"It's a hard thing," Don Quixote instructed the saint, "for a woman to become a knight and have adventures and save this world. It's necessary to pass through trials sometimes so perilous, you become mad and even die. Such trials are necessary.

"My heart's broken," she continued, "cause you demanded to be supported, cared for, and you gave nothing back. Either you clung like a child or you threatened to maim me. Now either you actually don't love me or else you're so insane, you don't realize how much you've hurt me."

As these words were easing the old knight's and the knight's old heart, the saint requestioned, "But someone must be responsible for evil. Who's responsible for evil? For abortions?"

"I love you," Don Quixote murmured. Aloud: "I know who I am. The Twelve Peers of France and the Nine Worthies as well: the exploits of all of them together, or separately, can't compare to mine."

Inside the house, her friends were talking about her:

—"Is she going to die?"

—"She's a very sick girl. She only knows how to do two things: When the sky's black, she lies across the sidewalk's length so the cars don't run her over. She indicates it's day by lying across the sidewalk's width. People, since they're forced to step over her, have to talk to her. I think she's lonely."

—"Why'd she have an abortion?"

—"All she ever used to do was read books."

"You're right," the Leftist, who refused to drink in pubs, replied. "She had no relations to other people. She didn't like them and she was aphasic."

The Liberal: "If she's evil, we must be evil too. No man's an island."

"What about women?" asked the feminist, but no one listened to her. While the Leftist, who never listened to anyone but himself, answered, "Books or any forms of culture're so dangerous, for they turn people mad, for instance Baudelaire or other pornographers, only our upper classes must be allowed to indulge in them."

As he was stating this, Don Quixote was crawling into this room. "I've had a dead abortion," she said, trying to explain to her friends so they could love her, "I mean: an abortion by a horse. I need you to take care of me."

"It's because," the Leftist, who always had to explain the world to everyone, replied to the knight, "when you were a child, you read too many books, instead of suffering like normal children. The horse isn't responsible for your abortion. Literature is. You have to become normal and part of this community."

In order to make her part of a community Don Quixote's friends dragged her toward her bed, which was a mattress on the floor, but just as they were dragging her across the floor, they saw that she didn't have any wounds. They didn't need to care for or love her.

"My wound is inside me. It is the wound of lack of love. Since you can't see it, you say it isn't here. But I've been hurt in my feelings. My feelings're my brains. My feelings're now nerves which have been torn out. Beyond the hole between my legs, the flesh torn turned and gnashed, inside that red mash or mess, lies a woman. No one ever ventures here."

Her friends, aghast at femininity, determined to burn it out.

Meanwhile, Don Quixote, having found the only true remedy for human pain, fell asleep.

A Dream of Saving the World

I'm walking down a mountain. At a peak which was white, I traded something.

I and St. Simeon're walking down a mountain. The foliage around us is luscious and light green. Trees have lots of little leaves. The path-down-which-we're-walking's dirt is tan and is winding slowly while it descends. The aerial freeway in a city. We're skiing. There're tiny blue yellow and orange flowers. We're running down a path. We're descending down a steep path. The path is reddish-brown. It's dangerous. We're at a curve of fantastic natural beauty: Thick thick bushes and leaves hang over waist-high dirt walls, are brushing our faces' skin. Beyond, the sky is blue. The foliage's so thick, there's only part of a sky. It's the beginning of night. St. Simeon and I are at our little house at the foot of the cliff. The house's inside is beautiful. There're three bedrooms. A huge embroidered-blue-silk-covered bed's sitting in one of the bedrooms. Outside, the sky is lightless. A policeman is telling for a moment St. Simeon who has a beer in his right hand to stop drinking. The cop grabs the beer out of Simeon's hand. Simeon runs after the creep. Since I'm knowing St. Simeon has a bad temper, I'm running after the saint to try to stop him from doing anything stupid, the policeman's shooting me dead.

When Don Quixote awoke, screaming and raving on the floor, her friends told her she had to go to the hospital so that they could do something with her.

"Do you know why I'm screaming?" the mad knight told them. "Because there's no possibility for human love in this world. I loved.

You know how much I loved. He didn't love me. He just wanted me to love him; he didn't want to love in return." Pauses. "I had the abortion because I refused normalcy which is the capitulation to social control. To letting our political leaders locate our identities in the social. In normal good love:

"It's sick to love someone beyond rationality, beyond a return (I love you you love me). Real love is sick. I could love death."

Her friends, being kind, brought her food, for they knew the food where she was going stinks.

"I don't want this food. I want love. The love I can only dream about or read in books. I'll make the world into this love." This was the way Don Quixote transformed sickness into a knightly tool.

PROVING THAT TRUE FRIENDSHIP CAN'T DIE

One day St. Simeon went away. Don Quixote couldn't bear living without him. For St. Simeon had taught her how to slay giants, that is to consider someone of more importance than herself. Even when she had been irritated then angry with him because he was younger than her—forty-two compared to her sixty-six years—she had learned to stay calm.

She didn't know why he had left her. She could only figure out that that evil magician, her enemy, had somehow enticed Simeon away from her. All she knew was that she had to have him back.

She sighted New York City. She was elated, for she was anxious to see her friend. She decided to wait until night which is when the city opens. Night orgasmed: it wasn't lightless: its neon and street lights gave out an artificial polluted light. Nothing was to be heard anywhere, but the barkings of junkies. Their whinings and mutterings deafened her ears and troubled her heart. Where was the heart? All the noises grew along with the silence. The knight took such a night to be an omen, but of what? Nevertheless, discounting the peril, she kept on.

About two blocks straight on, she came to a dark object. She saw that it was a tower. This old dilapidated boarded-up church inside of which rats cockroaches and occasionally junkies did their dealings was the principal church of the city. She thought Simeon, being a good Catholic, might be here. She was walking through the church's graveyard which was a blind alley filled with garbage. At its end, junkies were puncturing razors, for lack of needles, into their arms. "It's probably the custom," Don Quixote thought, "in a land of revolution, to build major churches in broken-down scumbag sections, though it seems anti-religious. Every nation has its own customs: Even though I'm English, I must show some respect."

Then she saw a number of well-dressed, obviously, society women. "Don't be vulgar," said a ladylike lady who was wearing a nice nondesigner suit. A tall Givenchy-suited hideoso who had just found out the white-booted cowgirl was the reason her husband was divorcing her, even though the only thing she liked about hubby was his money, rapped cowgirl over the head. Cowgirl, turning around, kicked Givenchy upper-class slut. "You can't hit me because I'm wearing glasses." So cowgirl, taking glasses off, whacked skinny legs. Skinny legs whose legs weren't beautiful, down on ground cause also her legs weren't working, saw cowgirl's firm guinea-pig-like leg and sunk her teeth into its knees. "I'll get you some iodine" said the fat millionaire who was planning to turn or buy her young gigolo into a TV star. "Get me a cure for hydrophobia." Then skinny ugly legs sank down crying. How can such women live without men?

Desperate to find St. Simeon—this is the beginning of her desperation to find love in a world in which love isn't possible—especially because she's so desperate—Don Quixote's madness was beginning to reach a point beyond the imagination or human understanding. However the truth always wins. The truth was that Don Quixote had to be with St. Simeon.

Not only was Don Quixote not with St. Simeon. She was in a church.

Don Quixote had only one choice, for there's a remedy for everything except death. "I *am* mad," Don Quixote admitted to herself. "Since I'm mad, I can believe anything. Anyone can be St. Simeon, for anyone can be a saint. That's religion. If who I believes St. Simeon doesn't believe he's St. Simeon, I'll swear to it. If he swears he is, I'll whip him. But if he keeps on swearing he's not St. Simeon, I'll tell him he's been enchanted.

"Where I spit," Don Quixote said to herself, "no grass will ever grow."

In the United States, packs of roaming wild dogs now indicate a decaying urban area or an increasing separation between the universal military government and the national civilian populace. Don Quixote saw a pack of wild dogs coming toward her. One of the dogs lit a cigarette. A beautiful dog was walking by her. "Mary darling, we've been waiting for you." "C'mon, Mary." "Leave me alone, Betsy." "What're you up to?" "Shh." "How've you been feeling, Mary?" "Shh. It's Gloria Grahame." "Anything for the gossip columns, darlings?" "Shh." "Now, Mary. What's this about a doctor?" "We all know about you and the doctor, Sylvia . . ." "What do you know? . . . There's nothing between the doctor and I. He enjoys my company." "Oh." "Wait till I start talking about you, Mary. You're trying to break up my marriage, you pigeony X-wife, but you won't. S . . . is a gentleman. By the way, there's a name for you ladies, but it isn't used outside a kennel."

"A malign enchanter," Don Quixote thought that the leader of this pack was St. Simeon, "must again be pursuing me, this time outside my dreams, for he's transformed your hunky body into a dog's. I hope I don't look too bad." Don Quixote looked for a mirror, but couldn't find one in the church. "Nevertheless, dog, please love me because as for me I'm not so attached to appearances that I've stopped loving you. With us, friendship'll last forever."

The dog tried to bite off the knight's hand.

While Don Quixote was trying to take her sick friend up in her arms, the dog saved her the trouble by kicking her. Since dogs aren't supposed to kick, Don Quixote knew this was really her friend. The dog, like all friends, started to run away.

"I'm always miserable," Don Quixote whined. "It's the way I am. If my best friend's a dog, what am I? How will anyone ever love me? I'm doomed to be in a world to which I don't belong."

The dog, having smelled future dead meat in and of Don Quixote, had slunk back into the church.

"St. Simeon. What lies concealed beneath your bark? Are you really good or evil? To tell the truth, I never noticed your ugliness, only your beauty, before this. Do you have any pimples now? Now, no one could really possibly love you except for me, because no one sees truly except for me, because I love."

Because he was hungry, the dog followed Don Quixote, out of the church.

INSERT

I think Prince should be President of the United States because all our Presidents since World War II have been stupid anyway and are becoming stupider up to the point of lobotomy and anyway are the puppets of those nameless beings—maybe they're human—demigods, who inhabit their own nations known heretofore as "multinationals." On the other hand: Prince, unlike all our other images or fakes or Presidents, stands for values. I mean: he believes. He wears a cross. President Reagan doesn't believe this crap he's handing out or down about happy families and happy black lynchings and happy ignorance. Worse: he might. Whereas The Prince believes in feelings, fucking, and fame. Fame is making it and common sense.

The Prince doesn't have any morals. Why? Because morals're part and parcel of a government which runs partly by means of the so-called "have-nots" or bourgeoisie's cover-up, (via "Culture"), of the "haves" total control. Morality and "Culture" are similar tools. The only culture that ever causes trouble is amoral. The Prince isn't moral: he doesn't give a shit about anybody but himself. The Prince wouldn't die for anyone, whereas Our President will always die for everybody while he's garnering in their cash.

Look at Prince's life. He's all-American because he's part black part white which is part good part evil. When he was thirteen, which is a magic number, he ran away from home just like Huckleberry Finn. He had nowhere to run to, cause there's nowhere to run to anymore. So he ran to a garage. He and his friend Cymone made music while they were screwing, sharing, and tying up girls. The Prince was the good boy because he didn't cuss and Cymone was the bad boy because he stole cars. Now Prince is twenty-six years old; he'll be thirty when he gets elected President of the United States. Thirty years old is the height of male cowboy American rock 'n' roll energy.

Don't vote for a croaker again to run your life.

Does it matter that Prince doesn't know anything about governmental politics? I presume he doesn't. All political techniques, left and right, are the praxis and speech of the controllers. How can we get rid of these controllers, their praxis and speech or politics? Let the country go to Hell. By going to Hell, Prince, a good Catholic, might be able to save this country. Anyway, we'd have a lot more fun than now, now when we're slowly being turned into fake people who're alienated from themselves, or zombies. Our minds're floating in other bodies. The Prince is Dr. Strange so he'll restore to us and restore us to those lowest of pleasures that are the only ones we Americans, being stupid, desire. Fucking, food, and dancing. This is the American Revolution.

It has been said that Prince presents nothing: he's dead, an image. But who do you think you are? Are you real? Such reality is false. You can only be who you're taught and shown to be. Those who have and are showing you, most of the controllers, are shits. Despite that, how can you hate you or the image? How can you be who you're not and how can you not be? Prince accepts his falsity. Prince uses his falsity. Prince, being conscious, can lead us. "I'm not a lover. I'm not a man. I'm something you can understand. I'm not your leader. I'm not your friend." We must be conscious in order to fight outside control. Make Prince who may be conscious the next President of the United States.

THE ADVENTURE OF MEN

Don Quixote decided that the only thing's to be happy. Since the sole reason she ever went out of her house was to fuck, she decided that to be happy's to fuck. She was riding her horse along, in order to find sex that wouldn't hurt too much.

At this point she saw three to four hundred men. "My God," she said, "how full of air they are!" She turned to St. Simeon who was now a dog. "Fortune's guiding our affairs beyond our most hopeful expectations. Here're those giants I've been looking for."

The dog said, "Woof."

"I'm going to get what I want from them."

"Woof."

"You have very little experience," Don Quixote told the dog, "in matters of this kind. Go along muttering, as all Catholics do, while I engage in these perilous untried unbargainable adventures."

The dog muttered, "Woof" and hid from fear. Don Quixote went after the big men. The men began to run away. Don Quixote verbally dedicated herself to the cause of everlasting love or marriage, which is the most dangerous cause, cause it's no cause at all, then again and again went after the big men.

Some of the big men who didn't want to run away lashed out at this stalwart female. Again and again she rose up and went at them again. Nothing, not even a man, could stop her from going after them. She was inexhaustible indefatigable—a true knight. Nothing could stop her search for love, but death. Finally, a man hit her so hard she almost died. The dog came running over to her, but by the time it reached her, she could hardly speak, and it couldn't speak either.

The dog said, "Woof."

"Sentimentality," Don Quixote, "in time of war's more than useless: it's detrimental. Don't be sentimental, dog. Being severely physically and mentally hurt's no reason for me to stop my search for love. Being now so hurt I'm almost dead only means in a few minutes I won't be dead because change 'n life are synonymous. What's more: I know I've been hurt by a man who is so evil, women have to fall in love with him."

"Woof."

"Once upon a time, there were no evil men. In those days of yore, a man loved a woman who loved him. And vice versa. Not like today.

"Why have matters changed between men and women? Because today love is a condition of narcissism, because we've been taught possession or materialism rather than possessionless love. Those people in days of yore didn't have proper language, that is, correct Great Culture. They were just confused and loved out of confusion. Today, our teachers call this confusion "poetry" (and try to define each poem so that the language's no longer ambiguous), but in those days "poetry" was reality.

"Today, only the knights who're mad enough to want to love someone who loves them maintain this order of poetry. I'm such a knight. Unless I'm mad, those big men over there who're totally dressed in black must be the servants of Simeon, the evil man who makes women fall in love with him . . ."

The dog, hearing his name, said, "Woof."

". . . For they have a woman with them."

"They're worse than men," the dog said.

"Why?"

"They're monks. Catholics kidnap young women not cause they're women but cause they look like boys."

"Bitch," Don Quixote replied. "You don't know what you're talking about."

Disdaining to listen to a beast's mutterings, Don Quixote walked up to the monk mass and cried, "You lousy stinking shits! All you ever do is talk about good and evil. If you don't tell this woman you don't love her, I'm going to erase you."

"Please beat us up. We belong to the Order of St. Benedict."

"I don't care anymore what you say. I know you don't love me. I know you don't love women. I know Catholicism is really a secret order of assassins." With that intelligence, Don Quixote leaped on one monk who was so drunk, he passed out.

The dog bit the drunk monk's clothes.

Two travelers, who happened to be passing by asked the dog why he was doing this to a holy father.

"Woof."

Since the travelers were humanists, they beat up the dog, left it for dead, and rescued the monk.

When Don Quixote saw her dead dog, she cried. "Such are the laments of the pain from my love for you."

ANOTHER INSERT

The Arab leaders are liars; lying is part of the Arab culture in the same way that truth-telling and honest speech're American. Unlike American and Western culture (generally), the Arabs (in their culture) have no (concept of) originality. That is, culture. They write new stories paint new pictures et cetera only by embellishing old stones pictures . . . They write by cutting chunks out of all-ready written texts and in other ways defacing traditions: changing important names into silly ones, making dirty jokes out of matters that should be of the utmost importance to us such as nuclear warfare. You might ask how the Arabs know about nuclear armaments. Our answer must be that humans, being greedy, fearful, and needing vicious power, have always known. The Arabs are no exception. For this reason, a typical Arab text or painting contains neither characters nor narrative, for an Arab, believing such fictions're evil, worships nothingness.

THE AFTERMATH OF THE WORLD

The dog gave a little quiver. It actually wasn't dead, just in great pain. It gave a little quiver again. Slowly, life was returning, in the same way that light makes its way into a sky that has lasted through the night. The dog like a baby began to crawl. Painfully, out of love, it inched over to Don Quixote and licked her feet.

"I'm the one who should lick you."

"I'm sick of being so poor," the dog howled. "I don't like living in poverty. The poverty in which we're living isn't unbearable: it's creeping; crawling; restrictions; constant despair; gray; final disease. This poverty's more unbearable than unbearable screaming poverty because it can't shout it can't talk sensibly, it only mutters and moans, it hides itself in that terminal disease—gentility. Repression is ruling my world. Humans' most helpful and most pernicious characteristic is their ability to adapt to anything. First, gestapo camps; now, here."

"But you're not human. Not anymore!"

"I still need to eat. Take me out to dinner, baby."

"Be patient. These things take time. In order to save the world, because this world's suffering, knights have to take on all this world's suffering."

"Shit."

"Suffering."

"I'm sick of worshiping suffering. Those Catholic creeps who just beat the shit . . ."

"You mean 'life.'"

". . . Out of me did so cause they believe in suffering. They're very powerful": the dog was shivering from fear, "cause due to their faith and belief in goodness and that what they're doing's always good, they don't question what they do."

"Aren't you a Catholic?"

"I used to be until I was changed into a dog."

"I'll protect you through this love from those monks," Don Quixote cradled the dog in her arms, "because I'm better than them. There's no man on this earth who's better than me. I'm strong. Valorous. Sincere. Slim and boyish despite how I look. When I have to be, I can be devious. As Hell. Charming. Cajoling. The most marvelous fuck in the world, as you well know." The dog barked, "Woof." "Totally devoted and totally callous just like Machiavelli. In short: a chameleon who has no goals except to change this world." The dog, "What's wrong with this world?" "I admit that it's hard to live with me cause I do keep going out on adventures. But when you get beaten up cause of me, you can always run to me. Have you ever, in any book, read about a human being such as me? Has there ever in history, that is, in novels, been a human being such as me? You have to totally love me."

"I don't totally love you because I don't know how to read. I never went to public school. Looking at you, I think you're getting old. You're so fragile and physically debilitated, you can't even stand up without fainting."

"I'm drunk."

"What happens to a human when it dies—as a point of interest?"

"When a human dies, another human cuts the first one in two. Next, the second human glues these two body parts together—Plato told us this—and pours medicine down the first human's throat."

"If human death isn't final, what's the cause of human suffering and pain?"

"Traditionally, the human world has been divided into men and women. Women're the cause of human suffering. For women are so intelligent, they don't want anything to do with love. Men have tried to get rid of their suffering by altering this: first, by changing women; second, when this didn't work because women are stubborn creatures, by simply lying, by saying that women live only for men's love. An alteration of language, rather than of material, usually changes material conditions . . .

"Women are bitches, dog. They're the cause of the troubles between men and women. Why? Because they don't give anything, they deny. Female sexuality has always been denial or virginity.

"This's why there's no love in this world, dog. The milk in the breasts of mothers all over this world is dry; the earth is barren; monsters, instead of children, run through our nuclear wastes. In Our Bible or The Storehouse Of Language, we tried to tell women who they are: The-Loving-Mother-Who-Has-No-Sex-So-Her-Sex-Isn't-A-Crab or The-Woman-Who-Loves-That-Is-Needs Love So Much She Will Let Anything Be Done To Her. But women aren't either of these. A woman is she who stuck the stake through the red Heart of Jesus Christ. By refusing suffering, women have made armies of men into corpses. Their shut-up breasts, instead of giving men suck, brush over the once-populated Egyptian sands and the now even more decimated Russian snowy wastes where our dead bodies are lying on top of each other, unseen whites, our corpses' mouths're intertwining with each other's. This is the only love we now can know because women don't want anything to do with love.

"'What the Hell do you know!' screams Medusa. Her snakes writhe around nails varnished by the Blood of Jesus Christ. 'I'm your desire's object, dog, because I can't be the subject. Because I can't be a subject: What you name "love," I name "nothingness." I won't not be: I'll perceive and I'll speak.

"'What if,' the bitch (excuse me, dog), continues, 'by "love" you meant I was allowed to want you? Then we'd both be objects and subjects. Then sexual love would have to be the meeting-place of individual life and death.

"'Do any of you allow this transcendence?

"'As long as you men cling to your identity of powermonger or of Jesus Christ, as long as you cling to a dualistic reality which is a reality molded by power, women will not exist with you. Comradeship is love. Women exist with the deer, the foxes of redness, the horses, and the devious cats.

"'When you love us, you hate us because we have to deny you. Why? Objects can't love back. Your Man of Love is a man of hatred. Human hatred, being functionless, turns back on itself: your love has to drive you to suicide.

"'You who own this world are dead corpses: Our friends the pigs're eating your ears. The foxes're nibbling at your cocks 'n you're coming. Poor men needing mothers. Poor idiots. You're worshipping suffering, in every possible fetish, and we like our freedom. All being is timelessly wild and pathless, its own knight, free.'"

"As I have explained," Don Quixote told the dog, "there's no human suffering that humans haven't created."

HISTORY AND WOMEN

Finally Don Quixote understood her problem: she was both a woman therefore she couldn't feel love and a knight in search of Love. She had had to become a knight, for she could solve this problem only by becoming partly male.

It was necessary for her to delve deeper into this matter. Did she really have to be a male to love? What was a woman? Was a woman different from a man? What was this "Love" which, only having dreamt about, she was now turning around her total life to find?

"Therefore, who am I?" she asked St. Simeon.

"Who cares."

"Of course I'm not interested in personal identity. I mean: what is it to be female?"

"To be a bitch," the dog answered.

"If history, the enemy of time, is the mother of truth, the history of women must define female identity. The main tome on this subject or history was written by Cid Hamete Benengeli, a man. Unfortunately, the author of this work so major it is the only one is an Arab, and that nation is known for its lying propensities; but even though they be our enemies, it may readily be understood that they would more likely have added to rather than have detracted from the history.

"'Be assured,' this book starts out, 'that the history of women is that of degradation and suffering.' "True," she said to herself, rubbing her wounded cunt.) " 'Nevertheless, history shows us that no woman nor any other person has to endure anything: a woman has the power to choose to be a king and a tyrant.

" 'Let us examine this history of women in its details:

" 'The first woman recorded by human history was Amadia of Gaul. Gaul, you know dog, was an ancient city. Amadia fell into the clutches of her mortal natural enemy, Arcalaus. Arcalaus made her prisoner. Then he stuck two knives into her thigh flesh. Then he bound her to a pillar in his courtyard, for he was a rich man so he could do whatever he wanted. It's a well-known fact that he lashed her body two hundred times with his horse's reins solely for her own pleasure. A certain female chronicler, anonymous or dead as women in those days had to be, recorded how this woman, hair as white and red as the Bloody Body of Christ, left in a room alone, a trapdoor opens beneath her feet, she drops into a deep underground pit of shit. The shit smells. She finds herself again bound hands and feet. Arcalaus liked this form of torture. Servants made her drink down a bowl of sand and ice-cold water.

" " "Please love me."

" " "Why should I love you?"

" " "Hit me."

" 'He hit her hard across her face. She looked up at him with her eyes open wider than usual. "Hit me again." He hit her even harder.

" " "Oh."

" 'He slapped her face's right side twice. She wondered if there was a danger of her ear being damaged. 'I'm hitting you because I love you."

" 'Already she was in a trance in which every one of her moments was coming. She couldn't live without this pleasure: the possibility that he might love her because he was giving to her without taking. Since he wasn't vulnerable, she had no way of knowing whether he loved her."

" 'She was dangling from a long hook. She had never wanted before. "Slap." "Slap." She would do anything to make him love her.' "

"Then how have women come up in the world?"

"By magic."

"That makes a lot of sense. Magic's really done a lot for this world."

"Don't be a bitch," Don Quixote told the dog. "You only say that because the only thing you can perceive is history. History's a fiction, and, as such, propaganda. Just as death destroys pain and time memory, so magic does away with history."

The dog scratched its head. "As far as I know, the real pain is death."

"Without personal history or memory," Don Quixote explained, "you wouldn't know. Then everything would be possible. In the immortal words of Hassan i Sabbah, who was Cid Hamete Benengeli's friend, "Nothing is true, everything is permissible."

"It's not history, which is actuality, but history's opposite, death, which shows us that women are nothing and everything." Having found the answer to her problem, Don Quixote shut up for a moment.

A SCENE OF THE MADNESSS AND/OR THE DREAM
OF DON QUIXOTE

Having decided that heterosexual love's possible, Don Quixote looked up a brothel's address in the telephone book, then walked toward it. One of the madame's favorite prostitutes, seeing a woman or potential money staring at the house, ran toward her. Being female, she could see that Don Quixote was sick with love.

So she put Don Quixote in an attic and took off all of her armor. Laid her upon four smooth planks. Don Quixote had been hurt for so long, so deeply, she took pleasure in all of this. The prostitute tied a white blindfold around the knight's eyes so the night'd feel easy and learn to trust her. She covered Don Quixote's bruised body with sheets made out of saddle leather.

The madame, entering this wretched attic, was short skinny hunchbacked and one-eyed. She and her girlfriend pulled down one of the leather sheets, rubbed oil into the knight's flesh to heal the deep bruises, and covered her from her head to toe with plaster. At times, they kicked the bitch.

As the madame looked at the deep black blue and purple bruises on the knight's body, which she couldn't see cause plaster was covering them, her girlfriend explained, "She's sick from heterosexual love."

Don Quixote, being plastered, couldn't speak. Her dog spoke for her. "These aren't the marks of heterosexual love, but of Catholics. Catholics, since they're celibate, throw stones."

The girlfriend: "I prefer whips to rocks, myself." She again kicked the dog. "I often dream I'm falling down from lofty rocks, my stomach goes, but I never touch the ground, and my fear changes to freedom. When I wake up, I see I'm covered with bruises." She again kicked the dog.

The dog: "Such are the bruises of love."

The madame: "Who's this bruised-up victim?" She kicked the dog.

The dog: "A knight."

The madame: "But it's white, not black."

The dog speaking for itself: "It's the person I love." The girlfriend kicked it again.

At this point Don Quixote due to her constant habit of imagining any possibility to be true conceived of as wrong a reality as can be imagined. She imagined that the madame was beautiful and had fallen madly in love with her. For the madame had promised that night, and every night, she would sneak to the knight and lie in bed with her, so that their hearts would cease to ache throughout the long night. Thus Don Quixote spake thus (via her dog): "Beautiful lady, thank you for your treatment of me, which has been pretty lousy, which I will remember for the rest of my days. Will you marry me since I love you? I don't need to tell you who I am, so you can put the name down on the marriage certificate, because you don't give a shit. Our love, or rather my mind's idea of love, is written down in everyone's memory for all eternity; my heart through all the varying vicissitudes of life, however much we'll be parted, will adore you. I would to Bloody Christ that this love between us didn't hold me an insane captive. What are such love's laws? It scares me to love you more than to love my life. How can I live and how can I live responsibly fully when I love this way? Your eyes are the mistress of my freedom."

from *Don Quixote*

Don Quixote's mentality was so mad, she, maddened, took such mental perceptions to be facts. She had visions:

Her first vision was of human love. A person whom she loved loved her.

Her second vision was of a handsome man. This man told her that he loved more strongly or possessively or madly than she loved. If this is true, then men're more capable of love and vision and life than women. If this is true, women can survive. For, as I've said, as soon as a woman loves, she's in danger. Why? Because the man for whom she'd do anything because he beats her up makes her almost die: Because she's the one who loves, not him, from not knowing whether or not he loves her, she becomes sick, yet she can't give him up. She loves him so much, she becomes pregnant, but she can't have a child alone. Her dilemma of love or she is her abortion. If a woman insists she can and does love and her living isn't loveless or dead, she dies. So either a woman is dead or she dies. This's what the handsome man told Don Quixote.

Is it the same for a man? Men're inscrutable things.

Can Don Quixote solve this new problem? Can Don Quixote figure out how to love and live? Can Don Quixote fight this handsome man?

This is the way Don Quixote fought: "Man. I don't accept your argument. If you're realistic, I'm mad. My madness is love. It isn't possible for your Culture to judge or explain my love.

"For how can anyone judge if another person's sane or mad?"

A judge, who showed up, said that being rational he couldn't decide.

All reality and madness are trying to destroy each other. Bam! Bam! Wop! Swop. Madness, because it's a thin old debilitated aborted knight, is too weak. It had no chance of doing anything. It can't think. It fails. As it falls to the ground, the invincible reality of malehood puts his sword to its pulsating throat.

"Either become normal, that is anonymous, or die," the handsome man told Don Quixote.

"I can't be normal because I can't stop loving." *How can I stop loving you? I must stop loving you. You are my life. Please help me. I don't need help.* "I won't go against the truth of my life which is my sexuality."

In the face of her insanity, the man, being as kind as Jesus Christ, gave the woman another choice. "Become a normal person and stop having visions for at least a year. That way you'll be allowed to live."

I've stopped loving you.

All of this happened to Don Quixote in her madness which was a dream.

MARRIAGE

Now that Don Quixote couldn't love for a year, which is as good as forever, she no longer knew what to live for. It's not that she had to have a man: it's that without faith and belief, a human's shit and worse than dead. Worse than being shit and dead, Don Quixote knew she was no longer a knight but shit and dead, that is, normal. Better to be a businessman.

She decided she'd rather be dead than worse than dead.

The dog told her it could solve this problem. Since it wasn't human and didn't believe, it could believe without dying.

"What're you going to believe?" Don Quixote queried.

"I believe I'm going to die instead of you so you can love without dying."

"How're you going to die?"

"By whipping myself."

"I've no objection against that. I just don't understand how a dog can believe."

"That's why you're going to have to pay me a lot of money for me to die. How much's your life worth?"

Don Quixote, being a knight, was an idealist. "Filthy lucre has nothing to do with faith! I won't pay you a bloody cent to die. Human love occurs only when a human suffers for no reason at all. You can't give me my life if I give you anything because then you're taking, not giving."

"Thank God I'm not human and rational. Give me money or give me life."

Wanting to live, that is feel, Don Quixote agreed to pay up.

"How much?"

"A hundred."

"Five hundred."

"Two-fifty."

"Four-fifty. My life isn't dog shit, but dog."

"Four hundred. You're not a real dog. As soon as you beat yourself up so much you suffer, vision'll take over this world."

They found a powerful and flexible whip made out of a donkey's halter. That very night the dog, beginning to beat itself to death like a good Catholic, whispered, "Please beat me," to itself.

After two of these fierce whiplashes, the dog asked Don Quixote for eight hundred dollars. Suffering greatly, Don Quixote agreed. The dog began to hurt itself as much as possible, and more again, and since each lash or scratch or wound had no reason, for money doesn't exist for an idealist, each blow tore out her heart.

At the sound of its agonized wails and the thud of the cruel lash, she came running up to the dog and snatched the twisted halter that served as a whip out of its paw. "I love you too much for you to hurt yourself. If I have to, I'll be normal and dead." It was in this way that Don Quixote's quest failed.

Inasmuch as nothing human is eternal but death, and death is the one thing about which human beings can't know anything, humans know nothing. They have to fail. To do and be the one thing they don't know. Don Quixote realized that her faith was gone.

DEATH

"Thank God, I'm so happy."

"Don't you believe that humans suffer?" the dog asked.

"I don't know anything about what they're always telling me. The media. I know what's around me. All this love crap and do-good crap's an illusion. I feel great and this world's wonderful and no humans suffer."

All the people around Don Quixote decided she was mad. She was the maddest child they had ever seen. They had to get rid of her.

They tried to explain to her that human love and good deeds are good things. Humans should live for love and goodness.

"We love you." That statement confirmed Don Quixote's belief that all their statements were hot air. "In the past, romance was my joy and utter pain. Now I know it's all nothing. I have to be very precise now: I have to explain to you the exact truth. Here's my will":

Anyone who knows enough to draw up a will must be sane. Her family was willing to re-own her. They began to cry because they felt so much.

Only Don Quixote was a feelingless monster.

"Here's proof that I'm sane:

"TO THE DOG: I give my dog everything. Please, dog, forgive me for my selfishness; please, all the ways I have not understood you, for I haven't been intelligent enough and known what love is. I will the rest of your life to be very happy and, more, I know it will be, for you're strong and patient and willing to understand, more so than me, even if you are crazy."

The dog interrupted, "I don't want you to go."

Don Quixote: "We must do what we must."

The dog: "You're dying because I didn't love you."

Don Quixote: "No." Don Quixote turned back to her last will and teaching,

"TO MY ABORTED SON: If you marry anyone, male or female, who isn't totally rich, you'll be poor. Otherwise you'll be poor.

"TO MYSELF: I was wrong to be right, to write, to be a knight, to try to do anything: because having a fantasy's just living inside your own head. Being a fanatic separates you from other people. If you're like everyone else, you believe opinions or what you're told. What else is there? Oh nothingness, I have to have visions, I can't have visions, I have to love: I have to be wrong to write."

When she had finished writing down all these smart teachings, being old and worn-out, she reaffirmed her belief that human love doesn't exist and died. "For me alone you were born, and I for you. We two are one though we trouble and hurt each other. You're my master and I'm the servant; I'm your master and you're my servant. I'm sick to death because I tried to escape you, love. I yield to you with all my heart or mind. This mingling of our genitals the only cure for sickness. It's not necessary to write or be right cause writing's or being right's making more illusion: it's necessary to destroy and be wrong."

(1986)

from "Lust"

A Sailor's Slight Identity

Because he's alone, a sailor's always telling himself who he is:

Due to the increasing conservatism of this government, the cops're enforcing more and tighter restrictions on every area of the private sector. Even the hippies and punks're no longer rioting. Capture by the German cops means torture or, at best, slavery. Thus, in Berlin, I was an insect I am going to describe the life of vermin.

Burroughs said that writers are insects. Without lives. Like sailors. A writer's one type of sailor, a person without human relationships.

Cold winds sweep over our dead rats; a dead terrorists's heart sits on dogshit. Mutilated police calls, advertising leaflets spell SOS. I liked watching and reading about two men stroking each other's penises. When I reached Berlin, one morning when the street beyond my window was almost the color of diarrheic dog turd from the rain, I saw two men who were obviously a couple. One told the other, a small bastardy-looking shit, "I'll get the groceries."

I didn't leave: I had nothing better to do than wait for someone whom I didn't know to return. About two hours later, he returned with a small bag. I wanted to follow him back to his room; I didn't; I knew that following him would be useless.

Through condoms and orange peels, mosaics of newspapers floating in small pools of water and piss, down into the ooze with gangsters in concrete and pistols pounded flat to avoid ballistic detection.

I like looking at men who've got muscles. Short bodies. These men look like bastards. They're the ones who act, who can act.

They give their energy. When I look at one, I have him and I lean my head right back into his chest. Between his large hand and his stomach, there, it's warm. There I'm safe. Since he makes me safe, I'll do anything for him. I know this sexuality, who I am, is nothing to be proud of: I am almost nothing. But I can't hate myself.

The muscular man's erection was hardening. The two men kept their mouths soldered together with tongues either crushed or sharp tips in contact. A knife cannot cut through another knife. Neither dared to place his tongue on the other's cheek for a kiss is a sign of vulnerability. By mistake a pair of eyes now and then caught the other pair of eyes. Then they hid. Snakes. Tongues were as hard as metal. The pricks are harder than tongues.

If I'm to go on living, I have to accept my sexuality.

I never knew my dad. He had left my mother for good six months before I was born. He had never wanted to meet me.

Though very little of my time is devoted to fucking, often none for months, I think constantly about sex and sexuality. It was about 4:20 A.M. in a Communist Chinese hotel in Germany. Two narrow and separated beds were nailed to the floor. There was a thin gray carpet. There were two small towels. There was a wardrobe. There was a table. There were four upright chairs. There was a telephone. I had left my ship about two days ago.

A man, whom I knew slightly, a criminal type, phoned. He told me that I was lonely and he'd be good for me. I wanted to ask him questions which I was too shy to ask a stranger—

(1) Do you want to fuck me in the ass?

(2) Do you want to fuck me in the ass more than once?

Three weeks later I met this man in another town in Germany. His body was short. His muscles slightly inclined to fat. After two hours we kissed. I continued to kiss him harder faster, with rising and more cunningly, here there, quick little pecks as my tough, very wide lips moved nearer his left ear. Every animal finds a home or dies. Finally I placed my tongue in an ear which was dirty.

The tongue moved around the thick ear. I placed my cheek against his teeth because I wanted him to bite me hard. Like big warm animals hug, he held me in arms as wide as my torso.

He was a sailor.

I tried to grab his huge head and pull it down as if I were wrestling. At the same time the rest of me was pressing into him, especially his lower body, and twining my legs around his so that our genitals could meet and rub through the wool.

In this warmth which we had created we remained together. I kept kissing and rubbing the bullet head, then kissing his male skin everywhere. Rubbing the skin or mind into need.

Want rose up, the sailor.

At last I found myself about to ejaculate. I wanted to prolong this need, whose appearance was physical, into total desperation, into the most desperate need which is possible, that is, not possible. But it was impossible to remain living in the impossible.

No longer could I distinguish between lust and love. I wanted to smear KY over his, Mick's, cock. Rusty barges, red brick building, graffiti of dead anarchists on the wall, only because he was going to hurt me, I fantasized the possibility that he would hurt me. Why do I get off on being rejected? I don't care. Cut off a leg and another limb grows stronger. Our generation came out of mutilation. We wear our mutilations as badges; wearing badges is the only possibility we have for human love. I fantasized that his penis was not very long and was thick. A penis that looked like a boxer, if a boxer could look like a penis.

When I had first noticed him in Hamburg, I had been sitting next to him. I remember that I looked down and saw a large lump in old gray pants. The thighs were heavy and spread apart, as if the hill would rise up in between. . . . At the same time as I saw this, I noticed I was staring at the lump. I wouldn't have been conscious of my fascination if I had thought that there were any sexual attraction between us.

At last I found myself about to ejaculate. I let the hand that was perching on Mick's shoulder slide down his back till it reached the buttocks. The buttocks were moving. I put my hand around this quivering, still clothed flesh and took possession of it. I slipped my hand up, and under the trouser belt and the white undershirt in front. I touched the penis. I forced myself to do what I wanted to do.

I was in that being or state where only sex matters.

My other hand took hold of one of his thick hands and forced it to touch my penis. Dolphins leapt about the prow and flying fish scattered before us almost in golden showers. Mick stroked the naked penis under the wool trousers, then of his own accord unbuttoned my flap. Dead leaves falling, jagged slashes of blue sky where the boards curled as if from fire apart. Mick squeezed my penis so hard that I whispered for a suck. Mick bent down only the upper part of his body and parted his lips. Violet twilight yellow-gray around the edges, color of human brains. While he was kneeling in front of me, Mick was sucking my cock so red it was obscene.

Whereas the slums in Hamburg are the slums of its sailors, Berlin is a big slum. For everyone. Except the tourist section which is fake shit for the foreigners. Just as the USA is fake shit because of a few people's manipulations. But playgrounds die. The English Labour Party holds hands and sings "Auld Lang Syne."

The Barrio Chino, a section in Berlin only known to Berlin's dedicated alcoholics and speed shooters, is a geographical foulness inhabited, not by Spanish sailors nor by the American Merchant Marine, nor by the Turks, but by those who have been separate so long from their birthplaces or anything resembling home, they are nationless. As long as they are alive, lost. The Barrio Chino is a place for drifters. Loneliness rather than sex has become the last vestige of capitalism. Loneliness is both a disease and a cause of personal strength.

These sadistic and masochistic drifters resemble the criminals who lived in the American and German urban conglomerates prior to the emergence of crime as international monopoly before human relationships degenerated into piss. Before the filth and disorder of the Barrio Chino. Long ropes hang between sailors' legs.

Sardine can cut open with scissors . . . shoehorn has been used as spoon . . . dirty sock in a plate of moldy beans . . . toothpaste smear on washstand glass . . . cigarette butt ground out in cold scrambled eggs . . . the children of the Barrio Chino.

An apartment at no. 10-11 Bayermalle on Holy Sunday, November 10, 1974, when all the virgins were singing loneliness. Someone rang its doorbell. Through the intercom, the doorbell ringer said he was delivering flowers. (The owner of this flat, Günter von Drenkmann, President of the Superior Court of Justice and Berlin's senior judge, was celebrating his 64th birthday.) When the door was opened, one of the youths outside pushed the door wide open. Another kid shot at Drenkmann three times and hit him twice.

Then all of these kids escaped in one Peugeot and one Mercedes. They obviously had stolen the cars. The old judge died.

The first penis I saw in Berlin was so beautiful I died. Before that I had thought that I was living in boredom. With this I found a community. Penises were lice. Sometimes they were crabs through whom I could see. Water seeped through the rotting walls upward into more rotting materials. The flesh melted into ooze. I wanted to tear down these walls, the ooze, to enter fully into Mick. To mingle in the way that no flesh can mingle. Mick was my mirror, my wall. I knew for a moment I was his. But the owners of the walls, the landlords, wouldn't let us tear them down. Owners hate sailors. Even owners who believe in liberalism, for democracy's other side is crime.

Every now and then, for instance when the President of the United States came to town, the Barrio Chino held a riot. Hatred made us erect.

Mick and I lived together for six months. He wasn't my greatest fuck. But I didn't care because he was the scum I wanted. I had no family and he wasn't going to be one, but for six months I got fucked. We parted for good without a reason.

Two nights after we had parted, in a bar whose walls and ceiling were aluminum, I picked up another sailor. As the sailor was sliding a hand up to my testicles from the back, I strangled him in the bar's back room. No one in the bar cared about my strangulation. Islands isolated in madness. I watched his life ebbing (refuse) under the pressure of my clenched, tightened fingers (refusés), watched the sailor die with mouth agape (refused) tongue out (speechless), watched the crisis of my solitary pleasures (refusal). City of flesh shriveled in aluminum bars, yellow couches, tables covered in speed dust. I killed him because I needed to be rejected by you who are alive. Only then would I find a community of those who are like me.

By murdering I raise myself out of the death in which I'm living. When I murdered the sailor, a miraculous wave broke into the silence of my ears (no one to whom to talk), the silence of my mouth (no one to whom to talk): the world started humming.

At this point I had no friends. The only thing there is to talk about now is isolation. Though my murdering had come from isolation—isolation is always insupportable—my murdering also announced my isolation to the world and so provided the first step toward destroying isolation. Afterwards I could only turn to other murderers. To those who realized they were sick. We are the failures on, not the governors of, this earth. Consciousness of our failure allowed us to be friends. The diseased fear only poverty. For all else is theirs and not to be feared: isolation, the ravages of sexual needs, ravaging sexual need, misunderstanding, autism, visual and audial hallucination, paranoia.

This night which has lasted for a long time I want to say that I cannot stand isolation anymore. The only way I see out of isolation is murder. Which makes isolation. This, in a sense, is my ode to the Baader-Meinhof, a group of kids who didn't fully consider the consequences of going against the law of the land, of ownership, became mad. This endless night.

Here I am alone.

In Berlin, something beside isolation happened. In the middle of a night I drove around in a car with two other people with a cassette blaring out Marc Almond and Neubauten. In that country where the bourgeoisie are so stolid, they are immovable fairy tales: isolated from the world and from myself, doubly isolated, I found friends.

The next day the cops tried to find the sailor's, Joachim's, murderer. I didn't feel guilty because I had murdered a Jew. The cops decided that a black man, another sailor, whose name was the name of a pariah, had murdered my sailor.

Perhaps it was out of guilt that the court sentenced Jonah to an early execution. Jonah was executed.

Now, I wanted to forget. Not my murder, but the world that had wrongly condemned Jonah, the world that condemned my murder, the world that, or rather who, caused isolation. I wanted to disappear. I wanted to disappear from this world into the night. I knew that it was impossible to kill myself.

Weil er mein Freund ist, liebt er mich. The cops weren't going to learn that I had actually murdered the sailor because the cops were snouts. The next man I fucked was a cop. I insisted that what I wanted most was that he pierce my throat as far as possible and fill it with slime.

I won't kiss but I get off on sucking the prick of a man whom I detest. Because I'm penetrating myself. When I was sucking the dick's prick, I was able to go beyond myself. At the same time, I was frightened: I would lose control and bite the cock too hard, which wouldn't be a bad thing, but, on the other hand, cops are human. Sucking this hot cock made my own despair and nothingness or my death apparent to me.

How black Berlin.

While I was thinking this in the act of sucking him off, the cop moaned, "I'm a cop. I'm a cop and I'm a creep. Cause I make it with guys. *Weil er mein Freund ist, liebt er mich.* I'm homosexual. I make it with every punk I can get. Then I shove the kid into jail so that I can have him whenever I want. I put the kid in jail cause that's what I like. I like putting the kid into jail after making him do what both of us want. My hands control his mouth."

The more this cop confessed through his muttering, confessed to a sailor he didn't know, and it didn't matter in the slime of Berlin, what slime he was, the more he became a hero to me. After only a little while more I would do anything for this big man. I loved being like this. It was like being someone else. Or being someone. In an unknown place of wonder, I would grovel at the cop's feet and, then, like a puppy, try to nip the cop's ankles. Big cops wear boots because they ride BMWs. When his sperm was visible and dead, the cop and I had nothing to say to each other.

Nothing new was happening in the city. It was time to leave. It's not that the Nazis had ruined a world. The Nazis had changed nothing. Dead cops don't fuck; death breeds only death. My nostrils were stinking of the smegma in my belly and the smegma on the streets so it was time to leave.

I went back to my ship where I carried out my duties impeccably. For there's no reason not to do exactly what I'm told to do even by scum.

Back in Berlin the cop rose in his work. He became a lieutenant. Seeing that his career was beginning, finally sure of himself to be master of his doman, decay: he began to do as he pleased.

Bits of what I wrote at sea:

> I find myself alone. I'm safe because the ocean surrounds me like when I was a child. I no longer have to be an animal crazy in its foraging for food. Society appears to be largely composed of extremists and habitual criminals not normal human animals subjects or citizens of respectable states. But I have no more community here cause sailors aren't usually murderers: sailors are nothing. I have had to decide, because I'm on the edge of suicide, that loneliness, like poverty, is a test. I no longer understand anything that is happening to me.

I wrote this about my murder:

> When the grief that is beyond tears, that tears the griever apart, that grief over a human death, fades: emptiness remains. The shock that a demi-god, one to whom one has given suck, can die becomes only the shock of death: the dead person *cannot* be dead. Death, above all, is impossible. That is: unthinkable.
>
> Besides shock all the other to-do surrounding murder or political assassination is a hypocritical way of pretending that the demi-god or human cannot be replaced in our society *which is actually a world of interchangeable puppets*. Of pretending that there are still human individuals, that these individuals still make history, when in fact all that we individuals—sailors—can now do is wish to act, exert ineffective wills, talk endlessly about

human morality (do animals have morality?), when in fact the autonomous mechanisms of social repression have been and are being reproduced in every individual.

A world of interchangeable puppets . . . unless you starve . . . the autonomous mechanisms of social repression . . . unless you starve . . . inevitably reproduced in every individual . . .

. . . an eroticized state . . .

In this society of total, not so much conformity, but homogenization, pasteurization beyond what the fifties' sociologists envisaged, we're making signs to each other that we're unlike by displaying disease or murdering. It's hard to be friends. Though we both know we're evil, I wonder whether or not we'll be friends. I make mistakes, often out of impatience, by imagining that there's camaraderie when there's not.

I wrote this about romanticism which comes after murder:

I first came to Berlin when I was twenty. I found whatever I was looking for there, though I said I couldn't name it. I first came to Berlin when I was twenty for some reason which I didn't know. Before I was in Berlin, I stole motorcycles and bashed them up in Munich. They didn't like me there because I'm very quiet. Too quiet. Until they show they hate me and then my back's against the wall and then I go mad. I become violent. I hate most of all being shut up or bored. Say that I hate everyone and every social thing. Me: I believe in romanticism. Romanticism *is* the world. Why? Because there's got to be something. There has to be something for we who are and know that we're homeless.

When I returned, not to Berlin, but to Hamburg in the midst of the fog of the beginning of winter, to the road that runs right above its river and docks, a castle which never existed and a fountain which is really a sewer, a gust of wind far sweeter and more fragrant than any red rose carried the smell of shit and floating soil like a tongue into my nostril.

It was late at night. As yet there were no dreams. I wondered when dreams would come to me, when the real dreams would come, dreams of something besides sailors. I wondered where they were. Like a man who wants to sleep and can't, so tries without success to know sleep. Wondered when the muscles of my face would be released, when my eyelids would blink more slowly, when the last light would die. When soft, gentle, and not just from weariness, you would lay on your back. Still in your sailor's uniform.

Tender and gentle, you then run your hands between my buttocks as if you're loving me there. Out of modesty, a form of fear perhaps, frightened that your prick is soiled by my asshole shit, I clean it with my free hand. My other hand, already seeking your hair in order to touch it, meets the face and strokes the cheek instead.

No love can be expressed between us. Love doesn't exist between us. We know only our varied musculature which has developed out of pain. You say that only fiction or language could inform us that we love each other. Perhaps this is true. But it's for other reasons that we understand what we mean when we speak together, our grunts, our solipsisms. Without the musculature which comes from pain no one is understood. With both hands clinging, one to an ear, the other to your hair, I wrench your head away from my axis which is getting harder.

Whenever you have sex with someone, you partially become each other.

After this sailor had finished cocksucking, I strangled him. Abandoned by parents, by friends, by America, by the pricks I had sucked, I knew that above all I hated, not death, but giving up to death.

Dead People Don't Fuck

El marinero degollado
Cantaba el oso de agua que lo habia de estrechar.

There were three poets. The three poets were ugly old men. They had once been hippies, but they were no longer hippies. They thought that without their visions, this city would dissolve. Without their dreams, the city would dissolve. This city is dissolving anyway. Being into love, the poets had nothing to celebrate.

They were just like snakes who, not having anything to eat, eat their own tails. When snakes eat themselves out, they think they are the only thing there is. More and more of the people are hungry.

There was a falling-down church. The church was a hideout for Puerto Rican terrorists. A young woman leapt up from one of the church pews, there weren't many of them, as if her ass was full of tracks, but it was just tacky. She was lean and brown; her gown was pink; she began to slink just like a slinky fat rat forward and back:

I'm gwine down to de river
Set me down de ground
If the blues overtake me,
Gon' jump overboard and drown.

It was one of the weekly readings in the Puerto Rican terrorist church.
Not this.

The church was called "St. Mark's in-the Bowery." In an urban environment, a "bowery" is a bum refuge. Bums of all kinds including sexual genders lived on its doorsteps and everywhere inside and outside this church. The Puerto Ricans lived underneath the graves. Every now and then a gang of children dug up a grave. Since the bums lived everywhere in the city, they were taking over the city just like the cockroaches had already taken the walls.

One of the three old men was just about to begin to read his poetry. In his mind, or in the depths of his soul, what he was about to begin to read was jazz. Because he liked garbage, he wrote poetry by picking phrases out of the cultural garbage cans—newspapers, sex mags, TV coverage, great poems, everything else—and stringing these phrasings together according to inaudible musical rhythms. He would have been reading to a sax, but the saxophonist had died ten years before. The poet didn't notice much outside him and he didn't have opinions.

Not this.

The church's audience were friends (other old poets), students, and bums. The students weren't yuppies, but revolutionary radicals and nonrevolutionary radicals who aspired to the radicalness of bums. A few of the latter radicals had come in order to burn the church down. The bums had come in to escape the cold. The church wasn't heated. No one gave a damn about the reading.

Just as the old poet was about to read, a bum said, "Ah. Ah feels like cutting me some white motherraper's throat." For a moment, someone was silent.

"We'll burn down the church," one student whispered to another.

Not this.

"Kill all the poets cause they're dead," another student who wasn't a poet said in a slightly louder voice.

"I'll say! Cause religion sucks!"

"No, it doesn't cause poets should be crucified."

Dick, the old poet who was about to read, ignored these cat-calls, knowing he was above them, being a poet, mainly cause he was frightened. So he stammered out, "Pope . . . Pope Pius the Sixth . . . Pope Pope." Maybe he thought that he was more famous than he was.

Not this.

Then remembering, then becoming lost in the wonder of his imagination, he started reading:

give us all honest work
to fuck every girl here
Annie Joanne Suzie Bern
I suppose
the main thrust is
knowledge
Cordelia sucked off Lear
daddy came too late
death, you come
no system
above meaningless tragedy
any other organ

Just as a revolutionary student pulled out a Magnum in order to halt the advance of immoral apolitical destructive artistic nonsense, one of the other old men, since he didn't notice the gun, limped toward the podium in order to extricate his friend from the masses' growing hostility. Tall and thin, this poet, pasty-faced, three hairs away from bald, for years his mouth frozen by speed into a smile, signaled to his friend to shut up.

At the same time, a bum walked into the church.

Not this.

There were many bums in the church. That's how society is. This bum appeared visible because his right hand was holding his left hand and his left hand wasn't holding anything like an arm. He wasn't a writer. His left foot stood opposite to the way it should have stood. He walked, as much as he was able, to the backmost pew and perched up there like a great huge vulture.

Now Dick began to read a love poem to his wife:

There is no way
to find me
while I find many
cunts, my Muse . . .

The bum took out his tiny cock and began to rub its head as if it was a dog. Finally, the students noticed that something was happening.

The bum, paying attention to the attention he and his dog were drawing, cried out to Dick, "Give to the poor."

Dick was now invoking Venus for some reason or other, probably a poetic one.

Not this.

"Shit and fuck," one of the nonrevolutionary students said to another, "that's the bum who thinks he's a cop. He's always trying to arrest another bum. Here ya' go," the student threw a dead animal heart into the cop's lap.

"Come to me, my lady," said Dick.

"Give to the poor," murmured the cop as the dead heart hit his other cheek.

At this signal for war, over a hundred bums, who had forgotten to pay attention to the first signal, swarmed into the church in order to further their plan of taking over the city. Churches are major property owners. Thinking that all these new people were here to hear his poetry, Dick exclaimed:

you took my love so tenderly
with lips.

The bum in the back proceeded to show how.

Not this.

Mayor Koch, various church officials, and other government and real-estate agents were walking through this church in order to get rid of poverty and clean up the filth who were left. One of the real-estate men, casually dressed in bluejeans, said, "Poetry is shit."

The crowd agreed with him.

"Shit," yelled the members of the religious congregation.

"Shit."

"Shit."

Not this.

"Let's elect our own mayor," a bum said. Poverty changes the mind.

Cut to the quick and deeply hurt, Mayor Koch and his cohorts, criminal and otherwise, scrambled through walls of bums and ran away from the church's graves.

Now came the election of their Mayor of New York. In order to maintain democratic procedure, the students smashed one of the stained glass panels over the altar. The bums watched other people work. Whoever desired to be mayor would stick his or her face through the broken glass. The populace could choose the image they wanted to rule them.

Not this.

The poor want their own mirror. The world was created in the image of God.

Dick was reading his poetry.

"I'm just trying to sell Coca-Cola," one of the bums explained. "I'm not doing anything illegal." This bum was a big bum who once had had some muscle. Now his clothes didn't do much to hide his lack of muscles. "I dropped into this church just so I's could patronize my customers."

"You're under arrest." The bum who thought he was a cop.

"No, I ain't, cause I ain't done nothin' wrong."

Not this.

"He doesn't want to arrest you," another bum explained to the Coca-Cola dealer. "He just wants some coke to put between his girl-friend's legs."

The bum who thought he was a pig flicked open a switch and slashed the upper half of the coke dealer's arm.

The poets except for Dick left the church because they didn't want to vote.

Not this.

"Coke's an evil drink," one explained. "It destroys the human mind."

The first candidate for mayorality was sticking his head through the broken glass. He was a man. The upper half of the face looked like a fox's immediately after a wolf's eaten it. The whites of his eyes were red. The lower half was all mouth. Lips composed of red mucus membrane covered by white pustules stretched over the whole.

Not this.

Even though this one looked like a poet, the mass didn't want him. He didn't look like he had cancer.

There was some blood on the floor.

The next contestant was old enough to be a politician, so he had no sexual gender much less sex and, besides that, he, or it was dead. Just as if it had cancer. Cancer-Nose. Some uneducated bum yelled things at this face in the hope that it would die.

Not this.

"Coffin-fucker!"

"Infidel!"

Many Muslims live in New York City.

The next image was that of an English rose. The image of an English rose is more beautiful, fragile, than that of a poet, but the poet's is more metaphysical. John Donne, the poet, wrote:

Since so, my minde
Shall not desire what no man else can finde,
I'll no more dote and runne
To pursue things which had indammag'd me.

Moreover, this face was deader than the dead man's face, for this face contained a dead soul. Hippies fuck a lot. The populace wasn't bothered to vote anymore.

"She doesn't have any tits!"

Not this.

Dick, the only poet left, was so upset by the anti-feminism that he had decided to show that poetry is more powerful than politics.

cunt ass-fucking cuntface cunthead cunt-hair smidgen tad cunt-lapper muff-diver cunt-lapping cunt meat cunt-struck diddle finger-fuck quiff roundheel quim pussy pussy-whipped asstail eatin' stuffwood pussy pussy butterfly pussy posse twat box clit clit-licker button puta dick clipped dick does a wooden horse have a hickory dick donkey dick limp-dick step on it dick-brained dick head dickey-licker screw goat fuck put the screws to someone throw a fuck into someone rag curse chew the fat on the rag take the rag off the bush randy rim ream cocksucker twink skosh smegma suck suck ass cocksucker suck face suck off blow scum scumbag rubber scumsucker scupper sucker suck-and-swallow piss eyes like pissholes in the snow full of piss and vinegar not to have a pot to piss in panther piss a piss hard-on piss-hole bandit piss bones piss pines and needles piss-proud pisser tickle the shit out of someone shit crap poo does a bear shit in the woods doodle-shit eat shit full of shit have shit for brains holy shit horse shit shit-hole shit-hunter shit-locker shittle-cum-shaw like pigs in clover like shit through a tin horn like ten pounds of shit in a five pound bag piece of shit pile of shit scare the shit out of someone skin rubber condom get under someone's skin press the flesh

Though he hated feelings and cunts, he continued this poem:

O muse! Female muse!
Our children no longer see
no longer care
for dreams.
Syphilis lies on their face;
herpes on our testicles.
My heart has closed up
scared to exist.

Doe- or black-eyed prepubescent whores stood on the streetcorner outside this church, swapped obscenities with the twitching junkies. The methadone center was four blocks away. Gangs of slightly older muggers crouched in the narrow alleyways between the church and the slim buildings, not yet architecturally gentrified, but soaring up in rent every month. Pigeons died. The teenagers were waiting to rob someone, but there was no one to rob except each other and that wasn't much fun. In the gutters, young kids played "Junky" and "Whore." Uncollected torn garbage cans, rotting vegetables, broken glass, used condoms, crushed beer and Coke cans, dog and human piss and shit against the bottoms of the buildings. Big-tit moms, images of the Holy Virgin Mary, standing at the edges of the tenements, talked about God, unemployed, men, hunger disease, religion, and Jews.

Not this.

"I ain't God," a man said as he showed his face through the broken glass inside the church.

"He ain't got no tits!"

Orange hair would have sprouted out of this man's mongoloid head if he had any hair. Instead, he had a few brains. A sole strand of gray spittle fell below his chin. Just like Ronald Reagan's hair if Ronald Reagan had any real hair. Or Nancy's if she had real hair on her cunt. His face was actually ugly because it was the color of a dead person's who's been hibernating in the East River for ten days. They say that alligators crawl out of the sewers into that river and have to have their stomachs pumped. The East River's sister is the Thames and the dead are dead. Dead people don't fuck. Just like my mom when she was alive. Vomit would have been prettier than the collection of characteristics on this face. Only prettiness is no criterion for high literary quality. His was the face of a literary patriarch, for his wrinkles resembled a compilation of Mr. Reagan's, Margaret Thatcher's, and the asshole of a purple-assed baboon who's just been diarrheic. Man descended from the monkey.

Not this.

The populace of bums and students liked this one so they clapped for a long time and hard for him. In this manner, they elected their own Mayor. As soon as they had voted him in, they forgot about him which shows bums are dumb.

The living gargoyle didn't reply to any of this because he couldn't reply because he didn't have a tongue.

"Steal away to Jesus," one bum replied for him, "steal away to Jesus," as his meaty black bones stole a wallet away and then skipped the light fantastic on one of his other bones.

Not this.

Since there was a certain lack of money among all but the rich in New York City, some of the bums were female. One of the females, while she was crying, looked at a bum and said, "I've got to say how much I want someone to care for me and I thought it was you. But it wasn't. It isn't." Crying.

"Because what I want is not what you want."

She raised her bald head up. "If a person's ugly, not evil or malicious, just ugly, everyone rejects that person. Countries ban that person. West Germany, a country in which men drink piss at parties, bans that person. That person now cannot stop being ugly and so is unrelievably ugly.

"No one's ugly to themselves. Cause you don't see yourself. As far as seeing yourself goes: you're only seen. So an ugly person is ugly everywhere at all times. That's what ugliness's about."

Not this.

It seemed to the Mayor of New York that he was so ugly, he could not speak. So he looked for a shiv.

When a white student saw the black man looking for a shiv, he shot the ugly man. The ugly man's face contorted as he flopped on it into the lap of a bag-lady. His ugly face fell on her hand and bit it.

"Lesbian!" the bag-lady yelled, jumped up, and stamped on her mayor. "Perverts ought to be shot."

Not this.

Two more bums leaned down and turned the just-living gargoyle over on to his back; one tied one of his old Eton ties around the bleeding hand. The other stuck one of the pew legs in to tighten the tourniquet. The bum's other arm had been shot off.

The bum who had inserted the pew leg carefully into the hole looked up and found the bag-lady's pussy. "You're a bum."

"No, she's not," the other bum told him. "She's a he."

Not this.

At this revelation of this transvestism lying rank in their ranks, the Coca-Cola dealer stood up, though his body was tottering, and proclaimed, "Jes' sit down, folks. All of you sit down. The Coke'll be here sooner than a dead man can hear a pin drop. So everyone go back to his seat and pay up. We've called the fuzz so the Coke'll be protected."

Not this.

And the sailor moved out to sea.

(1988)

from *Empire of the Senseless*

(*Thivai speaks*)

Raise Us from the Dead

Male

As long as I can remember, I have wanted to be a pirate. As long as I can remember, I have wanted to sail the navy seas. As long as I can remember wanting, I have wanted to slaughter other humans and to watch the emerging of their blood.

Insofar as I know myself I don't know either the origin nor the cause of my wants.

It was a dark night for pirates.

Witner had approached all of us on the ship. One night whose beginning was death, three pirates squatting on the deck just like fat cunts or pigs held a consultation which lingered, like death, without becoming anything else. For one human they had taken during their last battle remained bound and gagged near the bowsprit. Their discussion became more confused, then too confused, at least for the victim who could still hear; the pirates had become increasingly drunk. A fat slob waddled over to the victim who was a child and raped her again.

She didn't struggle as the other two did the same.

"Afterwards I'd like to do it to you," the first pirate turned to the second pirate.

"No, I'm younger than you so it's possible for me to have a child. I don't want one. Just cause it's safe for you . . ."

"Not if I do it in your asshole. In your asshole you're safe."

"Just stop what you're doing. Above all I don't want to be pregnant!"

"You don't believe me. You don't trust . . ."

"No." The second one explained: "Why should I trust you? You tell me why I should trust you. You tell me why I should trust you who can't get pregnant not to make me pregnant."

The third pirate came in his pants. A round stain showed.

"Don't you believe I can fuck you and not make babies?"

Used to protecting his virginity like a girl, the youngest of the pirates capitulated. "If you let me alone I'll let you do it tonight. But you've got to promise you won't tell anyone."

Fatty replied, "I promise" since he never meant anything by these words. "But you're going to spread yourself for me now. Otherwise I want that thin trigger that thin cock you're showing me so much, I'll cut off your head to get at it." Among themselves, also, pirates're murderous. "But after I come when you're dead, you can do whatever you want."

Fatty dove in, ground and pounded his cock up into the so tight it was almost impenetrable asshole. He pound and ground until the brat started wiggling; then thrust hard. Thrust fast. Living backbone. Jewel at top of hole. The asshole opened involuntarily. The kid screeched like nerves. After a while the kid felt Fatty become still. After a few more minutes he asked Fatty if he had come.

"Shut up. Shut. Up." As it dropped out the final bit of sperm enflamed the top of his cockhole.

Barely mumbling "Now it's time for me now it's time for what I want," the pirate who had just been fucked bent over the child tightly bound in ropes, already raped. His hands reached for her breasts. While sperm which resembled mutilated oysters dropped out of his asshole, he touched the breasts.

The three pirates turned away from the child. They went back to their work of gnawing and gorging themselves on Nestle's almonds, Cadbury chocolate flakes, barbecued tortilla chips, green beans, toffeed vanilla, Lucozade, and Mars bars. They guzzled down can after can of swill.

The Captain, me, walked on deck. "What a group of pigs! Didn't your teachers in all the nice boarding schools you went to, which you never talk about, teach you about nutrition?"

"This ship isn't a public school," Fatty blurted out through show-ers of Coca-Cola mixed with beer. "This shit is a pirate ship. And this is a philanthropic association."

"Sure," Captain Thivai, me, sneered. "I'm a sweet socialist gov-ernment so I'm paying you to sit on your asses in the sun and get sun-tanned just so that you are so happy you will not revolt against my economic fascism."

Fatty dared to oppose me. "No way. This ship is our philan-thropic association, our place of safety, our baby crib. Since they have enough dough to be our charity donors, all the people outside it, all the people outside us here, are our enemies.

"Since we live on this ship, we're orphans. Orphans are dumb and stupid." Fatty was epileptic. "Since we're stupid, we don't know how to conduct ourselves in decent (monied) society and we kill people for no reason."

"Historically, weren't some of the most violent political mur-derers," the punk added, "aristocrats?"

"Do all of you have parents?" I asked my crew, for I was as-tounded. "Do you generally come from good backgrounds?"

"How can I answer a generality? So how can I answer any ques-tion?" Fatty obviously came from a superior background.

"Do you," pointing my finger at the youngest therefore the weakest of the lot, "do you, personally, have parents?"

"I don't have no parents."

"Me neither."

"Him also?"

"No one."

"None."

"No one has nothing anymore."

"Then who'd you come out of and where d'you come from?" I wasn't going to be fooled by the scum.

"That's our business. Each one of us."

The English pirate answered, "We're not used to discussing pri-vate affairs. It's not your business on whom we piss."

I had to agree with the English, for it was necessary for me to trust my crew about whom I knew nothing except that they were not the scum of the earth, they were the scum of the now scum-filled seas.

And the next day, when the ship stopped near a shore on which a bordello was stretching out its claws, I jumped ship. A cock cried on the top of a hill. Roosters' red crests jumped through the weighted-down grasses. A guard and his heavy gun descended. I hid from him.

Where there were buildings huge trees had showered dew on to their red roofs. My fear dried up my throat. My hands lay over my stomach for protection.

The sun . . .

Fear disintegrated my throat . . .

Stunned . . .

I woke. I was no longer free. Words woke me. "It's me, Xaintrilles. This afternoon the General Staff'll interrogate you. Good luck 'n all that. I'm leaving for Ait Saada."

I didn't speak.

Xaintrilles squatted down on his haunches and looked at the bars. He saw a young man spread flat on the floor, still, his knees apart, a sackcloth jacket over only part of his stomach. "Thivai, aren't you listening to me? Maybe you can't hear anymore?"

I recognized despair enough to open my senses only inside me. Lice gnawed my cropped head. Xaintrilles carried this body inside, chafed hands and knees.

In the deep river firemen and convoy soldiers washed themselves. Mud scintillated around the decaying bathhouse.

I lovingly rubbed my skull, the light wounds the hairchopper had made. "Shave me. To the flesh," I said.

The gentle haircutter, as soon as his officer had left, positioned the straight razor at the front of the forehead. "Thivai, I can't. There's not enough left."

Upon returning, the officer looked at the prisoner and ordered the barber to shave him totally.

I smiled, I lowered my head, the barber trembled, my flesh peeled off my head and the tip of my ear, the officer by his red leather boot crushed my shoeless foot; the cutter wiped his fingers on the linen knotted around my neck. Then he went back to his cutting. My hairs dropped off like flies. As they were cut, they brushed by the ears, the holes of the nostrils, caught in the eyebrows, mommy, I only went to the hairdresser to cut off a lock of hair, my matchstick, mommy's sitting in the armchair, mommy's holding my knee, mommy's picking up a magazine, mommy puts it on her knees. Véronique's behind the mirror. Véronique stands upright. Then the hairdresser pushes her down while Véronique makes signs which the mirror reflects. The cut hairs brush past the beehive I've hidden in my shirt; mommy leaves, forgetting her purse. She walks through the rain along the river. Am I dreaming? The haircutter looks around him, he puts his hand on the hot flannel of my pants, his hand climbs up my thigh, I look at Véronique, it's she who's raping me it's she who's touching me, mommy's screaming out loud and crying in the rain. Dock workers drag barbed-wire sheets through the slush. Mommy bites her soaked scarf. The haircutter's hand sinks between my knees; again I push it away; his other hand travels down my stomach; my knees hit the marble washbasin which nevertheless maintains its balance; the haircutter's hand rests openly on my obviously palpitating stomach. The hairdresser looks behind him.

Under the door, mommy's drying her shoes. She enters the room. Night fell. Her wet hands hold my small ones, I fall into the armchair; mommy pays the hairdresser; he presses me against the door.

Mommy drags me out, down black streets until we reach the river. The dock workers're trying to warm themselves by standing as close as possible to a fire made out of charcoal dust. Mommy, holding me in her arms, jumps into the thicker mist. She mounts the jetty and runs over the rocks. Snow is covering the rocks. I try to writhe myself away, but she's pressing me into her hips. So I bite her hand, while a tug boat whose bright port dead-lights are throwing glimmers on a black oily sea, moves down the estuary; mommy throws herself, . . . I bite her hand, as her arms let go, I fall down the rocks, rolling down the rocks, mommy falls into the sea (my mother's suicide), the foam finds and recovers her, I twist my body round toward the rocks. There a wave carries my mother's head. Her palms slide along a sleek, slightly glittering rock. The tug boat bears the other way, then stops; a sailor runs on to a bridge; he unfastens a yawl, runs back on board;

they row toward the jetty. Between the clouds the stars're shining. My head's bathing in a small abandoned puddle. A sailor jumps on to the jetty, lifts me in his strong arms, up, and strokes my forehead and left cheek. The other sailors ship their oars and, lifting up my mother's body, bear it over a huge flat rock. The sailor puts me to bed. From the tip of the tent's main peg a lantern was barely balancing. My blood flowed into my hands. The sailors telephoned, held my hands in theirs, covered my face, They tore the khaki posters and bills open . . .

After the jeeps and the lorries left, wounded on the forehead now by the rising sun, I placed my sackcloth jacket over my face. The rest was naked. The flies in the toilet and the wine-press the soldiers had for their own convenience were gnawing at the barrier wires' edges; they darted forward, leapt over my cock, sunk into the mop of hair below, scurted over the curly locks, so I trembled, opened my thighs. The morning breeze cooled down the thighs and the sexual mass. The flies stole . . .

Again Véronique tosses her hairs behind her; I take hold of this hair and throw my face into it; Véronique turns around and places my head in her hands:

"Xaintrilles wet-kissed me in the garden."

I throw my arms around her waist, then I eat at her mouth; revolving her thighs rub and press themselves against my stomach, though she's pushing back my arms, I kiss her eyelids; her hand rubs my back my waist; her eyelids taste of mud; the sweat wets my opened shirt.

As soon as she laughs, I turn her over under me on the armchair. The wind bangs the books on the table shut. My hand burrows like a mole in her clothes. Over a teat. Trembles. Under my hand the teat is hot. I stroke the other teat. With the second hand I unhook the dress. And tongue the teat's tip. "And me," she pants. She crushes my mouth by her breast. Wide open the windows look over the park. Xaintrilles walks through the thick grass, his gun erect.

"Don't be so hard," he tells me. "You're breaking my legs."

I crawl over him. Sirens stain the distance.

Today there's no more pirates therefore I can't be a pirate. I know I can't be a pirate because there're no more pirate ships.

In 1574 there were pirate ships.

By that time the total halt of legal, or national, European wars forced the French and German soldiers either to disappear or to become illegal—pirates. Being free of both nationalistic and religious concerns and restrictions, privateering's only limitation was economic. Piracy was the most anarchic form of private enterprise.

Thus, at that time, in one sense, the modern economic world began. In anarchic times, when anyone could become any one and thing, corsairs, free enterprisers roamed everywhere more and more . . .

Murderers killed murderers . . .

Human beings are good by nature. This is the credo of those who are liberals, even pacifists, during times of national and nationalistic wars.

But in 1574, when regular, regulated war, that is, national war, which the nations involved had maintained at huge expense only via authoritarian expansion, ceased: the sailors the soldiers the poor people the disenfranchized the sexually different waged illegal wars on land and sea.

War, if not the begetter of all things, certainly the hope of all begetting and pleasures. For the rich and especially for the poor. War, you mirror of our sexuality.

I who would have and would be a pirate: I cannot. I who live in my mind which is my imagination as everything—wanderer adventurer fighter Commander-in-Chief of Allied Forces—I am nothing in these times.

Nightmare City

1. THE PSYCHOSIS WHICH RESULTED FROM GONORRHOEA

My life began when I had gonorrhoea. I was eighteen years old. Or rather, it began when the gonorrhoea ended, if such things ever end. For the foul disease had completely incapacitated me: I became dependent on other people even for the necessities of life.

I'm now not only useless, as are all human beings and as most human beings, the ones who aren't rich, believe they are. I'm also physically and mentally damaged because my only desire is to suicide.

I'm living on Chiba. My current fuck is always telling me that I ought to kill myself but, more significantly, that everyone wants to kill me.

"Who in particular wants to kill me? Why're you always putting me down?" I know they want to kill me.

"Why're you always starting a war? A man."

"My drug supplier?" I need drugs in order to maintain precarious stability.

"A man wants to kill you," she informed me right after I had orgasmed. Then, I knew.

I didn't bother saying anything. It's a policy of mine: Don't believe in human speech as anything but a stuffer of time. I would, and I would have, run away, but there's no place to which to run, so the only safety is psychosis and drugs.

Without paying any attention to me, as if I was dead, she continued speaking. "Perception has become a philosophical problem."

Because we had become too close the fuck could read my mind. But I had an answer. "It's possible to perceive yourself just as you'd perceive anything else," I informed her. "This is how strippers perceive their bodies."

"How can you know about normal people?" Someone, probably her, had torn out the sleeves of her jumpsuit to her shoulders. The colors of her eyes matched those of her fingernails and of another part of her body.

"Before I had gonorrhoea I was normal." I thought. "But now the memory of normal living is only a dream. My business in life has become infantile neurosis. When I was young, over and over again, I dreamed I was being followed. The people following me were bad. I couldn't run away fast enough to get away from them."

I didn't bother telling her the particular dreams because she was just a fuck. Instead I watched her personality fragment, over a period of time, calving like an iceberg or space, splinters of identity drifting away, until finally I saw her raw need, obsession which is addiction. I was scared. I wanted to run away.

"How do you know they want to kill me?" I asked.

"A birdie told me."

I looked down at a head which was bodiless. Through my shock, I saw it was a head. Or, I remembered. Nothing lasts forever.

Sleep or ease is a priority the way love used to be. Before I was psychotic, before I stopped sleeping, my dreams told me someone was trying to kill me. My fuck told me someone was trying to kill me.

When I reached the bar I was accustomed to, the man behind the bar told me nobody was trying to kill me. Nothing bad was going to happen to me as long as I didn't fall asleep.

My boss didn't want to hurt me.

Then the bartender told me that the woman I had been fucking had squelched on me to the boss because, addicted, she needed the money. RAM—whoever that was—would pay her for my death. They were chasing me.

When I fuck women, they always ask me why I don't trust anyone . . .

"Why don't you trust me?" spreading her legs.

Since I'm a gentleman, I don't spit where I should. Even if I don't know who's my boss.

I walked into my apartment. Another cunt was pointing a Luger at me. They were chasing me. I could believe the actuality of hatred now it had become an actuality.

"Who are you? RAM? Are you the ones who've been chasing me? Now I know who you are," I informed her.

She told me she didn't work for any bosses, she was a free woman, her name was Abhor. Why should I believe what a cunt tells me?

If reality isn't my picture of it, I'm lost.

2. SUICIDE

My mother's always sick. She doesn't have any time for me. Nursey takes care of me by sticking a pin through my thigh. I cried so after that she didn't have much to do with me. I cried because I loved her because she was the only person, that is, cunt, who loved me.

Then, because mommy still wanted me to be dead because she was, they gave me a new nurse. Since this one was English, she was proper and didn't show (me) any feeling. I decided she was a witch.

As I approached adulthood I learned there are three types of females: dead, dumb, and evil.

My life was a life of separation. I remember. Even when I was growing up life was so boring and unpleasant that living didn't matter to me. Only children who believe in something bother being evil and worshipping Satan. But I was a good child: I did everything exactly that my English nanny ordered me.

Nanny was an alcoholic. As a child I didn't understand this. I couldn't understand why she hated my first nurse. I hated Nanny for hating nursey. I hated Nanny the way children hate: absolutely. As fire burns. Most of my conscious moments were fantasies of burning up parts of Nanny's body.

I knew I shouldn't think like this. I knew my whole mind was twisted and perverted. If becoming an adult equals the process of acquiring self-consciousness, my first recognition of my adult self was my perception of my desire to torture and kill. I hated. So they sent Nanny away; I won the first round; but I still knew (remembered) I wanted to kill.

I have preserved my memory of that naughty period.

Since she's wearing a short T-shirt and ankle socks, the beautiful naked woman looks like a child. A black leather snake which isn't moving lies on her back. She tries to roll either way across the bed, but can't because two extremely wide black leather bands, held by thick steel rings to the bedposts which are far from each other, encase her pink wrists. My sister was my real mother's and father's daughter. She tortured me by making me look at drawings depicting lobotomies. These scenes caused me horrible nightmares, for I was sensitive.

I questioned to the point of obsession whether other humans are naturally evil, and if so why.

Unable to answer this question, I prayed to God about whom they had told me. God is He Who is unknowable. My sister was so malicious and my nightmares were so violent that I knew any Creator must be a sick pig. I named God "Sickpig" and "Turdshit." Every time I saw a dog shit on the street, I thought of God. I had no idea what all this meant.

As for cripples beggars malformed bodies lobotomized women and other poor people, everytime I saw one of these living turds on the street I breathed so hard to avoid convulsing I almost convulsed.

The only thing I couldn't tolerate was being told what to do. Since beggars or anyone else who was nothing told me who I was, I couldn't bear any of them. I wanted to kill beggars because I was too scared to kill my real tormentor, my sister.

I shall now by means of my profound rational processes find the explanation for my madness, and human socially unacceptable behavior.

Once my sister said to people who were walking behind her: "Look at my little tail." Another time she told people that she liked the portrait a certain artist friend had made of her because it showed her having a tiny penis.

I felt very happy when my sister's huge hat, while we were both in an auto, flew away.

My sister and I are playing in a room. We are between four and six years old. My sister's hand takes up my cock which is so small it's almost nonexistent. She rubs the nonexistent. Then she tells me that my nurse whom I do love because my nurse loves me does this same thing with the cock of the gardener.

My sister was a tomboy and had a very high IQ, higher even than mine. Even though her IQ was high, she couldn't understand how a high IQ and the desire to be loved as a female could exist together in one body. Since her body thus had to be monstrous, she refused to go out of our parents' house. She knew who she was: since she was a freak, she was unlovable. She had to and did pay, rather my parents paid, someone to love her. She loved this paid companion because the paid companion loved her and at the same time she detested the paid companion because, since the paid companion loved her only for economic reasons, she was proved to be unlovable. When my sister suicided at the age of twenty-one I didn't cry.

3. BEYOND THE EXTINCTION OF HUMAN LIFE

I asked Abhor what she wanted with me. Did she also want to destroy my identity?

"I work for this man. I'm collecting for him." As if I understood what she meant, blindly, I followed her out of my room. They say love's also blind, but, for me, love has equalled pain.

Her boss's name was Schreber. "I've never seen you before, have I?" he asked.

"No."

"I'm going to tell you something about yourself." Finally perhaps I'd learn something about myself. "You're masochistic to the point of suicidal and, actually, physically damaged. You believe that, and the neurological and hormonal damage probably is permanent."

"Yes."

He wasn't going to let me interrupt him. "You were . . . disrupted in your childhood by the usual causes. I'm not the least bit interested in psychological interpretations. They're passé. But there's one thing."

I interrupted him. "I don't give a damn. Not only about psychology. About myself." I continued, "You're fat and ugly, sir, but I'm dead. Psychology and my psychology's a dead issue." There were a lot of dead bodies floating around the world. "All I want to know from you is what you want from me." Otherwise, I wanted to be alone.

Because, for me, desire and pain're the same.

I didn't want her. I couldn't so I didn't want. Frigidity was a way of life. I didn't know if phenomena such as desires which're fleeting even mattered. Psychology isn't here a dead issue. I decided I would keep her because I had to because she said I had to be hers.

Is reality always this unknown?

My friends informed me that the boss's real name was Schreber. Dr. Schreber. He's honest enough, they said, as bosses are honest, to pay me for my work. So I could pay off my last boss so he wouldn't off me. Of course there's no money. Money's flimsy paper people who don't have power carry on them. What they do with money I don't know. I needed drugs.

"Your neurological and hormonal damage is making you degenerate so fast, faster than if you had AIDS," the fat man informed me in front of the cunt, "that within a couple of months you're going to be a monogoloid, even stupider than a lobotomy case, due to all the hatred which is festering in you, unless I inject a certain enzyme into your bloodstream and then enable you to receive a full blood transfusion. You will get this enzyme, your savior, flea, only if you do what I want."

"What do you want?"

"For you to do exactly what I want until that time."

The trouble was I had no way of knowing if he meant to keep his part of the deal. I couldn't ask the cunt I thought I loved. Since I was thus dragging my tail through unknowable territory, my memory was useless. My memory was as dead as my desire used to be.

The next day, on a street, a garbage dump in front of the river, my former boss himself cut the throat of the fuck who informed on me in front of me. He slaughtered her because it was a practical way of making room for a fresh employee. Capitalism needs new territory or fresh blood.

I saw: blood sprayed from a jugular.

I needed my drug.

For a long time I had remained apathetic. So sure that my words meant nothing to anyone that I no longer spoke unless circumstances forced me to. So sure that my relations to the world were null that it didn't matter to what I said "yes." When I was young frivolity and trivia had been my weapons; now I did whatever I was told because I was no longer me. That is, the I who was acting was theirs, separate from the I who knew and whom I had known. Lots of eyes were watching me.

That is, the I who had SEXUAL DESIRES had nothing to do with the high IQ/understanding. This IQ used to be high but, since now was corrupted blinded covered over, wants seemed more capable and intelligent than I had known. I found myself at that point, that bottom.

I thought all I could know about was human separation; all I couldn't know, naturally, was death. Moreover, since the I who desired and the eye who perceived had nothing to do with each other and at the same time existed in the same body—mine: I was not possible. I, in fact, was more than diseased. But Schreber had given me hope of a possible solution. A hope of eradicating disease. Schreber had the enzyme which could change all my blood.

When all that's known is sick, the unknown has to look better. I, whoever I was, had no choice but to go along with Schreber. I, whoever I was, was going to be a construct.

The sky faded to blood, to the color of blood. After I left the doctor and returned home, what I called home, which was better than I had ever had, Abhor had gotten there before me and was waiting for me, so to speak. Asleep. Naked. I saw her. A transparent cast ran from her knee to a few millimeters below her crotch, the skin mottled by blue purple and green patches which looked like bruises but weren't. Black spots on the nails, finger and toe, shaded into gold. Eight derms, each a different color size and form, ran in a neat line down her right wrist and down the vein of the right upper thigh. A transdermal unit, separated from her body, connected to the input trodes under the cast by means of thin red leads. A construct.

In my imagination we were always fucking: the black whip crawls across her back. A red cock rises.

"I don't know who's backing him." Abhor turned around to face me. She must have woken up. "All I know is we call him 'boss' and he gets his orders. Like you and me."

"Somebody knows something. Whoever he is, the knower, must be the big boss."

"Look." Abhor raised herself up on one arm. She smelled warm, as if from kisses, but to my knowledge no kisses had taken place. "All I know is that we have to reach this construct. And her name's Kathy."

"That's a nice name. Who is she?"

"It doesn't mean anything."

"If it doesn't mean anything, it's dead. The cunt must be dead." My puns were dead.

"Look. All I know is we have to reach this construct. I don't know anything else."

"We have the capacities for understanding and, at the same time, we understand nothing," I replied. I understood we had to find some construct.

She told me again. "All I know is we're looking for a certain construct. Somewhere. Nothing else matters." A pulsing red then black cursor crept through the outline of a doorway. With enough endorphin analogue, Abhor could walk on a pair of bloody stumps. "You don't matter and reality doesn't matter." The road away from the airport, which became a series of roads, had been dead straight, like neat incisions, into the open body of the city. Poverty was writhing in pink. I had watched, here and there, a machine glide by, bound by fog and gray. Later on there were tenements called "council housing," walls of mottled aluminium, prison guards' cocks sticking in order to piss through unarranged holes in the brick, more plyboard and corrugated iron walls. The lucky poor had playgrounds. I remembered Abhor was a construct.

Imagination was both a dead business and the only business left to the dead.

In such a world which was nonreality terrorism made a lot of sense.

The modern Terrorists are a new version, a modern version, so to speak, of the hobos of the 1930s USA. Just as those haters of all work, (work being that situation in which they were being totally controlled; the controllers didn't work), as far as they were able took over their contemporary lines of communication, so these Terrorists, being aware of the huge extent to which the media now divorce the act of terrorism from the original sociopolitical intent, were not so much nihilists as fetishists. I had worked with them before in some way which I couldn't quite remember.

Two days after I had met the doctor, I found myself knocking on the door of a record shop somewhere. Terrorism is always a place to start because one has to start somewhere. A boy, or rather a skull, whose teeth were pointed red, as if skulls eat meat, opened the door which was falling apart so badly it was cracking open. I half crawled through a gap, half walked through the door, into a middle-sized record shop storeroom. Discs lay shattered on the floor. A celluloid nun moved her eyes horizontally as if a hand was moving her eyeballs. Smiley with one hand bone pointed me to a couch on which a freezer was sitting.

"Among the American international corporations the practice of setting up mixed affiliates if most widespread in chemicals and petrochemicals, rubber and the extractive industries. These ICs combine production on an international scale and organize the vertical and/or horizontal integration of their plants and thus, finally, control the whole product cycle . . ."

"I'm not interested."

"Du Pont and Union Carbide, Goodyear and Uniroyal, Exxon and Kaiser, for example, organize the supply of semifinished products from overseas enterprises to others on a wide scale, gain access to sources of raw . . ."

"Shut up," I said. "I need to find a code for a certain construct. I know you're planning to knock over the CIA library and the code is there."

Smiley smiled at me again. I remembered we had once been lovers; I had forgotten. We still are, I thought, in that his nastiness and inability to do anything but bite in the face of fear—any human presence triggered fear—matches my deeper nastiness. I never actually worked with the Moderns, but then I only work with people out of my need. Things are always the same.

The fact was that Moderns talked too much. Their talk, or rhetoric, was blab: they didn't care who heard them; they would happily explain anything to the tiny parrots who shitted on the record discs as they flew around. The Moderns had the same relation to their work, terrorism: they didn't give a damn. They just wanted to have fun. Like parrots, they became easily bored.

On this operation the Moderns planned with great glee to reach Washington D.C., the location of the library, via chickenwire. The chickenwire was sets of satellite and radio connectives. Like kids gone mad the Terrorists zoomed through the green purple yellow flashlights which are Manhattan, that absence of people, by using epoxy as they touched the midnight glass to control their movements. Then, over black ghettos.

Except for Manhattan, which had been left to the rich, all of the eastern American urban centers had been left to the packs of wild dogs, wild cats, and blacks who lived in and under the streets. There were no more whites there except for gays.

The library was the American Intelligence's central control network, its memory, what constituted its perception and understanding. (A hypothesis of the political uses of culture.) It was called MAINLINE. The perception based on culture is a drug, a necessity for sociopolitical control.

Being a bit behind their times the Moderns only wanted to destruct. On the other hand my construct (a cunt) and I had to find the code. The Modernists planned to shoot misinformation into MAINLINE's internal video. Due to the misinformation each video screen would strobe for twenty seconds in a frequency that would cause the constructs and other robot viewers to have seizures. Pale green apartments strobed emerald at midnight. Simultaneously the audio portion of MAINLINE's internal video, speeding double, would inform its listeners about the army's use of a certain endomorphin, at this moment being tested, to throw human skeletal growth into one thousand percent overkill. The red lights in the brothel tenements strobed blood eyes of Haiti.

The Terrorists would be happy when two minutes later their infiltrated message ended with the main system's end in white noise.

The Terrorists were happy.

In the white noise the cops arrived so that they could kill everybody. Round revolving cars emitted sonar waves. Certain sonar vibrations blinded those not in the cars; other levels numbing effectively chopped off limbs; other levels caused blood to spurt out of the mouths nostrils and eyes. The buildings were pink. Preferring mutilation the families who lived in bed-sits ran out into the streets. Outside the black ghettos, through the waters, sea-cruise missiles with two hundred kt. nuclear warheads swam like dolphins. Carrying at least twelve ALCMs on extended pylons and eight on internal rotary launchers, B-52 bombers rode on cars whose trunks held various nerve gases which seeped out through the city atmosphere at designated intervals. "Homing-and-kill" vehicles, upon sensing the presence of any living thing with their infrared sensors, unfurled two-meter-long metal ribs. Metallic weights studded the metal ribs. The insect life moved on. The cops' faces, as they killed off the poor people, as they were supposed to, were masks of human beings. And the faces of the politicians are death. A young boy who lay in the street had hollowed-out eye sockets, skinless arms, and a smile due to the large amounts of acid rain in the air. Red and black deco staircases from the magenta tops of buildings bridged building to building.

Inside the library's research department, the construct cunt inserted a sub-program into that part of the video network. The sub-program altered certain core custodial commands so that she could retrieve the code.

The code said: GET RID OF MEANING. YOUR MIND IS A NIGHTMARE THAT HAS BEEN EATING YOU: NOW EAT YOUR MIND.

The code would lead me to the human construct who would lead me to, or allow me, my drug.

Dead Love

I must have passed out because I had a nightmare: that the world is full of people who no longer feel. They are carrying on their business as usual, in fact better than usual, because they no longer feel. In the dream I felt my whole being struck still, as if I had died.

The cunt was hurt. I realized that when I awoke. The terrorists said. Six thousand micrograms of endorphin analog, however, were coming, down on the pain like a hammer, shattering it. Her back, like a cat's, was arching in convulsions. Pink warm waves were lapping her thighs.

Bodies were piled six deep in the library's halls. The latest body, shot through the neck on Black's road. But he is not dead . . .

I must have passed out because I had a nightmare: To my dead sister, dream somehow of paradise. It's the only thing that can now keep us alive. The sweetness of your mouth. Coming while not being bruised by the hatred of the one who's making you come. You no longer don't have to not exist.

Look, my sister: the eyes are gone. The suns. No one's looking. You can now do whatever you want: Crying out; teasing the thickness of thighs; smoldering by smiling. Since the world has disappeared: there's nothing; no one looks at anyone.

Since the world has disappeared: rather than objects, there exists that smoldering within time where and when subject meets object. This voluptuousness of your thighs. Odors seeping out of cunt juice and semen. Since the only mirrors are distorted; all is secret. Please come back to my arms. Without you I am nothing.

It's winter. Winter is dead time. I don't have any life now that my sister is dead. Raise us from the dead.

Raze.

But no one looks like Abhor. Everyone looks like the female who ratted on me. The boss, the terrorist leader, the terrorists—they all had the face of the female who ratted on me. It was the dead of winter. Or it was the winter of us, dead. The code I had gotten read "WINTER." It was the winter of death.

I was safe: outside. "What does WINTER mean?" I asked the Modern Terrorist leader.

"WINTER's a recognition code for an AI. This particular AI is, that is his money is located in Berne. Money is a kind of citizenship. Americans are world citizens."

"Does my boss know about WINTER?"

"Does a doctor know about death?" the terrorist replied. "Let me tell you a story:

"A certain fence was living, well, he was fencing off of the corner of Bowery and Houston Street. Around the corner from the bum bar in which the one-eyed Irish sang,

The Powers whose name and shape no living creature knows
Have pulled . . .

and then cried into whatever whisky he could beg from someone. Life's a waste of booze."

I thought about dead cunts. "Life's a waste."

"Some of the fences sold real clothing such as rubber jackets and army leather. Others, being less conventional, at least in their business, more like the bums who wipe windshields, dealt in prosynthetic limbs and other works of art. Mommy, the off-the-corner man, was an art dealer.

"There was another art dealer who had once been a bum, but now was dealing in the junk for which the rich pay a lot of money. His name was Daddy.

"Daddy came to Mommy to ask for a favor. New York City art dealers have their special codes.

"Daddy said to Mommy: 'My newest . . . supplier . . . '

"'Burglar.'

"'My newest burglar is a rat who goes by the name of Ratso. Since rats are very intelligent, Ratso has a fondness for art objects. The rat carves art. His latest work-of-art, his newest find, find-and-keep so-to-speak, is a head. Not any head. It's a dead head and death is done up in pearls. Despite the obvious value of this work of art, its humanity, not being a humanist, I advised Ratso to get rid of it. These days times are so hard that heads are worthless.

"'At that moment I remembered I knew a head freak. A head freak who was rich. And liked to spend it.

"'I accepted the rat's human head. Upon minute careful inspection, this head revealed the trademarks of the AI, American Intelligence, who're backing the AMA. Next to the military, the American medical industry take in the largest amounts of legal profit in the western hemisphere. No wonder the head was dead.

"'At the very moment I realized this, a gulag came through my door. A block, a dunderhead, a lump of cement, a lobotomized mongoloid. A man who acted like he had all the muscle in the world because he owned everything in the world. A man who didn't need to walk as if he owned the place because he owned the place. There are people like that. I don't know them. I knew he was a real man because I knew I was staring into the eyes of death.

"'The weight lifter carefully explained he had come for his head. I explained I don't give head. He explained that he thought I might be able to give it to him.

"'Not having the desire to get closer to death, though I find lack of desire strange and inhuman, I produced my head.

"'"How much does a human head cost? These days?" the owner of the world asked me.

"'I named the price of a masticated piece of bubblegum. One piece, or stick; not two. I got what I asked for. On credit.

"'Two days later I learned the rat had gotten his price. Death."

"'Extermination's difficult.'

"'Death isn't difficult. I don't know why we fight each other since we're all the same. Knowing this, I had nothing left but to understand. 'This is why I've had to come to you, Mommy, even though I'm not used to turning to cunts. Mommy, I'm desperate.'

"Out of the goodness of her heart Mommy did a little investigation. It just made her feel good to do good, especially for Daddy. But all she could learn was what she already knew: The AI control information. The AI control the medical mafia. Democracy controls its own death, its medical knowledge and praxis, just as we all control our own deaths," the terrorist said.

"I know." My love, the cunt, was dead.

"However," the terrorist told me, "there are particulars. Despite the media—not despite the media because the media exists to be wrong—democracy is an old quiet family. They don't move around much. They're stable. They're so stable, they've now got their own genetic setup."

"Who? Tell me who. Who controls himself, herself? Who doesn't feel unending pain?"

The terrorist frowned. "That's not a proper question."

"What's a proper question? Now?"

"Who can we kill?"

"I don't want to kill anyone because I don't feel anger." I felt scared.

"Look." The terrorist said to me with anger so deep that it couldn't be expressed, "Knowing much information and not feeling anything doesn't get you anywhere." He pointed his small bone at me. "The answer to your question is that democracy doesn't get you anywhere."

The cunt was dead. Afterwards I went down into the tube to wait for her. I had been a traveling man, but now it looked to me like

I was to stop traveling. Besides, the tubes didn't go anywhere. No government sinks money into dead tubes. I stood; I cried: I waited. Nothing. I cried; I cried. I would do anything to have her touch me again even though she was partially human and I hated my own wanting.

I looked for her burial place down there. I looked for the burial place of death. I looked for her whom I wanted. Because I wanted her, she was my demon. Dead and demonic.

Even though I knew she was dead—particles of soil and pieces of garbage and Thames water and whatever else humans are, that is become—I cried for her. I knew she was shit, but I cried because I would do anything to get her back!

("Oh sis," I cried in silent words which are tears, tears in the fabrics of reality, "I will become you: I will become as unreal as you.")

Pieces of chopped-up snake tail. Using my tail as bait. Fuck me so I can hate you. Children are born by being shoveled out of wolves' bodies, but who does the shoveling? Are all wolves, therefore, females; are all females, therefore, as vicious as wolves? Tell me, my heart, what reality is.

When I got home, which was like every other home, my love was waiting for me. She wasn't dead, yet. She looked like a piece of red and dead meat. It was St. Valentine's Day.

She wasn't dead. "I'm on your meat line now," I told her.

"You're what I make you," Abhor said.

(1988)

from *In Memoriam to Identity*

The Last Days of Rimbaud

Men always understand each other.

"... Solitude is a bad thing in this world. Personally, *personally*, I regret only two things. Not being married and not having children. I am living out the worst punishment: being without other people, being an outsider. What is the point of this atonement if I cannot, one day, before I'm too old (and old age is coming up, sitting on this shoulder), settle down in a nice, middle-class neighborhood and have a family of my own, mainly a son to whom I'll devote the rest of my life by raising him in accordance with my etc.

"You see," said Rimbaud.

"See what?" said Father. Speaking because he wasn't totally inebriated yet. Men always understand each other. Or: males.

"That I shouldn't be here with a drunk and a whore too young to be a virgin, that I'd be with my son if there was any justice in this world."

"There isn't," Paw himself explained. And took another drink. "Haven't I explained this to you over and over again? Man is always fooling himself; maybe he's on earth to do just that."

"Yeah," Rimbaud said, "God."

"Not God, but man. Man fools himself that he or God exists."

"Well, since she doesn't exist," pointing to an imaginary woman, "maybe she should at least learn to act decent." Rimbaud's voice rose. "Do you know what your daughter does?"

"She's not mine," said Paw. "She's not no man's."

I know that.

"She's now doing what bitches do and she's going to end up the way bitches end up if one of us doesn't do something about it."

"Her mother ended up," Father replied.

"That's what I mean. And they leave younger bitches."

Father started crying. "I'm just a trouble and a burden to you."

"I ought to know that. And you're a man. Or you were before you started on that stuff you use as a substitute for your mother's nipple. But your daughter's worse. There's no telling what she's likely to drag in here. She's a whore, but her mother the bitch couldn't even get it up to teach her that whores are supposed to earn money.

"So I'm supporting all of you.

"She takes anything in and when it leaves, bawls a little like a dog who's been kicked. You know why you kick dogs who stink. Where she takes anything in," Rimbaud stated, "is this house, plus she's wearing her cunt out which should be virginal. No man will ever want to take her away from us and impregnate her. Work saves."

"Given the welter of femal emotion, the female is unable to know or to value work." Father.

"She's your own flesh and blood."

Childhood was an education in how adults treated flesh and blood.

So the only thing for a man to do is to settle down with a wife and have children, the most rigid setup possible, to counter his natural tendencies toward disorder even suicide. "Sure," Rimbaud said aloud, "that's what I'm thinking about. Flesh. It's her goddamn flesh. There's something the matter with it. It's hot. Like nuclear energy run wild. I think either we do something with her immediately and that something can't have anything to do with schooling cause she'll just fuck everything male there, or else throw her out on the street and let her survive like the wild cats do."

"It's not right, Rimbaud, for our own flesh and blood or for someone's flesh and blood to be out on the streets." Father sobbed a second time.

"I should have been a poet, but I've the burden of this decadent family. I am forced to concern myself with money, with no help from either of you. I who hate the musk like garbage that rises off of female flesh."

Those were the days in which there was the smell of something other than human desperation.

"Either lock her up in this house yourself," my older brother continued, "or hand her over to me and I'll get the shit out of her."

Father protested, though he didn't care what he said, that I was still a child. As if anything could matter.

Rimbaud knew a slut who'd never be loved. We'd be better off rid of her, thrown out onto the streets, but then he should have been a poet.

"Nothing *can* matter," Father said, "because no man can do that which matters and he knows matters."

Jason or Rimbaud went out and got me. Out of the outside. I had been drinking coffee because I couldn't get booze because it was too early in the morning though I didn't like the taste of booze.

Inside, the sun was shining through two kitchen windows as yellow as piss. "That's what they should have named you." Rimbaud's fingrs were on my arm.

I looked up from them as much as I could, through the hair over my eyes as if all the world and I were a mess. But my eyes were so big, I could see through all that hair, eyes too big to be scared.

Quentin when he had loved me had said I looked like a victim.

"OK. I'm late I've got to be going."

I could feel his eyes.

"I'm going to school."

"We're gonna fix that right now."

"I'm vulnerable and I survive."

"Come here." The fingers didn't move, but tugged.

"I'm not going to go anymore near you. I'm going to school."

"You've been handling men ever since you were ten and blood traveled down your legs, but you're not handling me." His fingers were as white as the skin under them.

"Mother's dead," I said.

"You sluts always want to get your way. You act like babies, thinking we're stupid. You've made a mistake this time, haven't you?"

"Mother made the mistake;" I said, "mistakes are human. Not finally irremediable."

"You're going to school," he replied, "and afterwards it's time to learn something from me and it's about being hurt." Rimbaud had been hurt when he had been a kid. "Either you'll do what I tell you or you'll get hurt."

"Hit me," I said, just like Verlaine had pleaded to Rimbaud in my literary book.

"You don't think I'm going to hit you."

"Father became drunk so he could manage Mother, and he didn't manage her. No one manages death."

"But I'm your brother," Rimbaud answered, while he let me go so quickly I stumbled, in their house, against the wall near the stairs, trying to keep my kimono shut. "I'm going to teach you to not be a slut."

I've always wondered how some people teach other people. Death and blood transfusions teach. Quentin, at least, had gone to Harvard to learn and had learned about Freud whereas Rimbaud was part of America who know that book education has nothing to do with experience. When I looked up from the stairs, I saw Father watching his children. The first time I had dreamt about Father, I had dreamed that a huge, translucent worm with opaque teeth and no other features was chasing me. Never again I kissed Father. "Do something." I always wanted my lovers to be my father. "Do something."

Father smelt. "I'm watching," he answered. "Nobody's going to hurt you. Not in this family. Capitol."

I threw Rimbaud's arm against the wall behind it with a strength whose source was unknowable and then I ran up those stairs. To where the bedrooms were.

"Capitol."

"Capitol."

I could hear both of them from the beginning of the black iron fire escape in my bedroom. I finished climbing out the window; the window slammed down; got out.

Father a kind, gentle man, and a wimp, because he couldn't stand up for himself, believed in the American values someone or some people had taught him. Honesty and hard work. If a man's honest and works his butt off, his life will be valuable, but my father's life wasn't valuable. "The present is always grim, and the future is supposed to be worse."—Father.

I don't know whether or not Rimbaud and Dad noticed that I wasn't there anymore though they say that men run the world. The feminists. The feminists say, too, that women, unlike men, are good because women don't have aggfression in them. My problem is, that given my circumstances, that is my family, I don't have enough aggression in me.

"I guess love must be based on absence."—Rimbaud.

Though Father was saying about me, "Rimbaud, she wants something."

"She's going to get something. 'Bout time." Rimbaud had a faraway look in his eye just like a visionary.

"You don't understand her. You're never understood anything about women. She's not bad: she's sick. Women're always sick with wanting to eat up your soul. It's all in *Jane Eyre*." Father read books. I inherited his love of reading which proves that inheritance is important for human beings. A huge inheritance can make a miserable person's life happy. "A man has to keep himself away from women, cold and hard."

"Speak for yourself, drunk,"—Rimbaud. "Mother ate you up, but there was nothing to eat. Women's lower mouths have bad taste or taste bad."

"Never had to taste one," replied Father. "I've never abided perversion. If a man's going to have anything to do with a woman, he has to destroy her."

"Why that's what I aim to do with . . ."

"I don't actually mean make her into a whore or a physical corpse. By *her*, I mean *wanting*. Without their wanting, women are nothing like everything else."

"Well, what's your fucking problem? Rhetoric and booze?" asked Rimbaud. "I know how to take Capitol in hand and I'm willing to do it and save you all the effort so you won't have to look at the blood on your hands and you're crying again."

Father couldn't stop crying, so Rimbaud left the flat to find me. He knew that the most likely place for me to be, if I was alone, was in the motorcycle garage to the left of the apartment building. Crouching in one of the back corners like an animal who's frightened. Knows it's about to die. Fear smells like cunts do. All over. I was scared all the time; when the fear came up, grew, it took me and made me absolutely passive. I always do whatever anyone tells me to do even if I hate the person's guts. All of their guts. At the very same time there's a spot between my legs since it's almost burning up is almost my consciousness. Since it involves another person, sexual need looks like fear. I don't see any reason not to play my fear out, not to swing it in their faces like a live cunt.

Rimbaud thought, our whole fucking family.

Sure I was where he thought I'd be. Into a corner, on the ground, all the time as low as she can get. Jason or Rimbaud was thinking. And that's where she wants to be that's why she's there that's what she wants to be cause she's a whore. Our whole fucking family. They might as well have committed a lot of murders their genes are so bad.

Despite all I got myself off the ground. I was once as low as you can get and I changed myself into a successful businessman. Now they all depend on me as if all I am is strength. Since the act of poetry's weakness, it's disease. I am proof, Americans, that a man who is low and filthy even perverted in his very mind can become the acme or acumen of American cleanliness.

[Looking at Capitol.] Look at what the fuck I'm responsible for. A cunt who spreads the legs attached to her for anyone cause she's too stupid even to know what a sexual disease is.

I had crouched down lower so my legs were spread out and my ass was in the center of a used tire. "Didn't your mother teach you how to be a whore like the whore she was before she died?" Now there was a question. The garage had fleas for light. "You aren't naked enough to be a whore, but you've got more gook on your face than clothes."

"I do what I want. Just like Mother. But unlike Mother, nobody really touches me because nobody means anything to me nobody will ever have anything to do with me again now that I've been perverted into a monster by Mother's suicide, so I do exactly as I want." As I spoke, I pointed my right middle finger at my chest and thumped into there as if it were a weapon. I don't know why. I was angry. And I had no intention of suiciding or even of hating myself now that Mother had suicided. "And do you know what I can do, if I feel like it, with these things which you don't even call *clothes?*" With my hands, I tore at my green dress though it wasn't my green dress that I was tearing.

"You don't even know how to do that." He kicked me. "Maybe you need a man to help you." Father would have said that people are only the repositories of their inheritance if Father had been sober enough to put mind to lips. By rending my dress, Rimbaud was carefully informing me that I depended on him because he had paid for my clothes. Family education is a sound, unforgettable education. I've been educated to know that truth, that I have been brought up as a whore to be a whore. If poetry is the salt of this earth, females by education or economic training are more poets than males. I told Rimbaud this while he was ripping up my clothes.

But. Only poetry is rebellion and Rimbaud had gone, rebelled against his inheritance in order to make himself into a businessman. He was still a poet. A dead poet. Dead poets don't have ears.

I put one of my fingers up my cunt, withdrew it all white wet, and said "See" while I showed it to Rimbaud.

"See."

"I've seen what you are, slimy slut, and I'm going to whip it out of you."

"Whip? Like you're a slave trader? Go on. Big boy."

"Like my own flesh and blood."

I knew a poem by the original Rimbaud:

In olden times animals came as they ran
Glands larded with shit and blood, not the curse.
My father himself proudly displayed his member,
His sheath's wrinkles and the grain of his purse.

. . . Not having loved women—although his cock was full of blood—he had trained his soul, his heart, all his force, to strange and sad errors or wanderings. Following dreams—his loves—which came to him by chance, both their beginnings and endings. Since this bizarre suffering possesses its own unquestionable authority, all of you must hope that this soul, wandering and lost in the world, and who, it seems, wants to die, will right now find value and real consolation in suffering.

Jason or Rimbaud hates when I say things out loud, especially the things he wants to repress. He says I'm scared all the time cause he's scared. So, out of the garage, I stood on the street and said in as loud a voice as I could, "These are the boys and men in this town who I fuck," and started naming names. Quentin's name wasn't among these names. Since most of my clothes were still in the garage, people were staring at me.

"You do a thing like that again, I'll make you sorry you ever drew breath." Rimbaud hit me.

"I'm sorry now," I said. I was beginning to be sorry I was me and I didn't know where to go with or in me. When a man loves you, you wake up like plants out of the earth, and I was dead and perverted. Both my soil and my blood are sick.

Rimbaud's poem continues, somewhere, "Truth: this time I wept more than all the children in the world." Keeping hold of my hand, my brother dragged me into his Ford which was parked on one of the corners. The left side of my face was still smarting. I didn't care about anything anymore. Except I didn't want to be Shirley Temple. I didn't want to be myself. Sure I got into the Ford with him. "I'm going to hell, Jason. Do what you want with me. Rape me. Lobotomize me into a good little doll. I'm going to hell. I'm bad and I don't give a goddamn. You'll never touch my brains and my heart. I'd rather be in hell and be hell than wherever and what you are. Brother."

He turned to me, and, even though he was driving, smacked me. "You'll be in hell even more," he muttered, "when I've finished with you."

He could have run someone over while he was hitting me. Men don't have any sense of responsibility.

When he had driven some way and turned, came back to the apartment building, rich, ugly as his bearded face, he opened his car door.

About three months before she had offed herself, Mother had told Quentin and me that she had a boyfriend. The boyfriend worked in Father's show company, the company into which Father had married.

The day after I saw Mother's dead body, I phoned the company. I asked to speak to the boyfriend. I told the boyfriend Mom had just died.

Boyfriend didn't know about whom I was speaking. But don't you know Father? I asked. Of course he knew Father cause he worked for Father.

The boyfriend asked me to convey his condolences to Father.

I decided that I had to learn why and how Mother had died so that I could know what it is to be a woman. To be me.

If memory is a tool by which I'm making myself, why do I make painful, even deadly parts of myself? I'm not sure who's in control. I spent most of my childhood fighting against parents and men in order to control what I call my life.

Perhaps it'd be better if I do nothing. I miss the swans and plants grow. Do memories spring up like plants?

Thinking about what he had to do with me though he didn't want to be thinking about me, Rimbaud drove on to his office. A man named Earl was already there. They left the building together.

Earl was a Jew; Rimbaud said that didn't bother him. Perverts were worse. Jews and Italians were into the pornography business in this part of Connecticut and Italians didn't let anyone into their part. History always repeats itself.

"I don't have a Jewish accent," said Earl.

"I don't hold a man's religion against him or a man against religion. I asked you to have lunch with me cause I need the advice of an expert." R never had any expression on his face and he was thin. "What do you do with a slut?"

"You don't know?" asked Earl. He reached over for a ketchup bottle.

"When she's your sister and she advertises her sluttishness all over town."

"It shouldn't matter to a man what a woman's doing. They don't have any brains to make their doing noticeable. If she's a slut, make your money that way."

"Money," R replied.

"Americans got out of England so they could make money any way they pleased." Since Jews have brains, they know history. "You going to be told what to do by a woman . . ."

"Girl . . ."

". . . or are you free to do with her as you need whatever the hell she does?"

Father had said, "History always repeats itself, at least in blood." We knew.

R opened a pack of cigs. "I'm not paying for your goddamn lunch for philosophy. How do I sell this bitch?"

"They've got a lot of religion in this country now?"

"So? Religion doesn't have anything to do with me."

Earl looked at R funny. "This government loves religion. They're not going to let the only way poor people can now make money alter their new shiny religious surface, the screen behind which they can now hide their criminal doings. All they're doing is trimming a sucker like everyone else, but they are and they can be better at it."

"They believe in Christianity." Rimbaud had never known if he was Christian or not.

"Why shouldn't they? The Haitians believed in the white missionaries who showed up with black books; the Haitians knew power when they met it."

"So what am I supposed to do? Lobotomize the slut's clit into a Bible so she can go around begging righteously for more of my money?"

"She wouldn't stand a chance against the TV preachers."

"Listen," R said. "Sex is a sucker game unless a man keeps a continuing, expanding profit. I don't want to be in a high-risk business."

"I don't mean to put you off," Earl answered. "If you can learn to keep your head down (your name out of the papers), sex is the surest business there is."

They were sitting in a drugstore, at one of the Formica-topped tables next to a large glass-paned window. Through a fence across the street, Rimbaud could see grimy kids. That, somewhere in his memories, returned him to himself as a boy, doing something in the haze of pollution like mauling and being mauled. He was now no longer part of their world, misfits losers vulnerable fucked-over; he was never going to be fucked again.

He'd do something about Capitol.

Earl swallowed a bit of the lukewarm coffee. "I can put you in the way of a little business. The kind of business you're looking for. Sure."

"It's not that I give her anything." R explained. "It's that she won't believe she's nothing. And she's costing me."

"You're a businessman," Earl. "Money has no value. If you want to go into this little business I'm talking about, family business, you know that it's going to cost you. You have to spend money to start a good business. Like a car. You wouldn't run your car without gas and oil, would you?"

"She's been running me."

"Well, you have to set her up properly. A woman will do what she's told if she's been told clearly. It's when they get confused, they act up. Women aren't your problem, Rim. Sex is good for business otherwise it doesn't matter anything."

Rim agreed. "So how much money do you think it's going to take to set her up?"

"The thing you've got to learn," Earl, "is that to set up business, you've got to spend money like a whore. Funny, how things go. You see, every dollar a whore spends, she spends double in her own flesh. Pockmarked, junked. And that's your profit."

"That'll teach her."

"She don't exist. I'll tell you about moralism and religion. All the jazz the politicians're now saying. Every whore gets junked then the holey cunt finds religion—you might say she's supporting our government—and when she dies, she'll find out religion's nothing."

"Money in my pocket," Rim. Not my brother's mind, but rather his flesh held a memory of love. The second a human begins loving, he or she is better off dying, the memory whispered. Flesh is always whispering and it hurts, itself and others, when restrained. Mass murdering. "For those who love." Rim was looking through the fence at the kids who believed that this parking lot full of rubbish and half-dead dogs was their playground.

Once upon a time he too had hated his mother whoever she was but now he had forgotten for a long time.

As he walked over to the real parking lot where his Ford was, he congratulated himself for growing into responsibility. Finally. Taking care of his family. Providing for the goddamn sons of bitches. Son of a bitch and bitch. They were his family so their beauty was foul. He was keeping this circus, bitch and son of a bitch, together. When he got some money stashed, he'd get him a decent wife, a non-bitch or a nothing, and then they'd have a son whom he could teach properly, to have his values.

You can't teach a bitch nothing because bitches live in blood. He had always known that. He hadn't changed.

There was poetry somewhere.

Pieces of a dream unreeled down the back of time.

"Our Fathers," Father had said, "had their children to support them in times like these."

These are the times when we no longer have the myth of escape. Go to the multinationals, think tanks for your myths of information, but never look to the home.

What is it? Shards.

"What time?" asked the man who had once been a poet.

The poet had sung for a bit until what seemed to be the causes of his singing frightened him into failure. Reaganite failure. Shelley sang though, now the scholars say, he had been a shit. To women.

Shelley isn't a shit to me and if men aren't shits to me, they don't exist. Is that true? Shards of memory. Father was trying to not exist; Rimbaud, unlike Quentin who had disappeared from me would disappear for me.

Either Mother had never had a boyfriend and had been mad (loneliness, sexual deprivation, thwarted ambition) or her boyfriend had lied when I had informed him of Mother's suicide and, perhaps, had killed her.

I didn't see any other possibilities.

Was the latter true? Why would he have killed her? Because

she gave him money? At her funeral, the family lawyer had informed me about a million was missing. The only people I knew who carelessly murdered were the rich people I read about in newspaper stories.

I want to know who I am and I don't know what's real.

Yesterday over the phone a friend told me that when she was living in a seaside resort, she noticed that a whore was working out of the flat next door to her accommodation.

Shards of memory. A sailor whore port town. One night, my friend (an actress) was walking home through the early hours of the morning. Leaves fell into an ocean which didn't exist. Noticed one shadow among all the other shadows. As if noticing a memory. Rushed to get her door open, inside, where she'd be safe from.

As her door finally was opening, the shadow emerged into a woman. "I haven't talked to anyone in three weeks."

I could have said that.

The actress went with the whore.

Entered into the whore's flat, her world. This world was one room which was empty except for a mattress on a floor and a lamp with a red light. Sailors get serviced easily. I don't remember.

The whore took one of the actress's hands into her own. "I've seen that ring before." Rings are for marriage, belonging to the world. Shards of memory.

I will remember so that I can dream.

There were empty bottles pyramid-packed into one corner. My father was a drinker. "I remember," the whore said. "I hated the person who wore that ring. It doesn't have anything to do with you. Have something to drink, dear."

The actress had two tumblers of whiskey. Into the waters of the nonexistent sea.

This is between women.

"What's your name?"

"I knew a woman with that name. Hated her hated her." The whore said.

Since my family are dead people, I know that dead people never win and live in the bottom of the sea.

Wanting to abandon the mad whore, the actress looked ahead of her, then saw the shoes the whore had on. Men's oxfords.

"I'm dressed as I used to dress in England."

The slut had a man's voice, but wasn't a man. My friend said that women are strong, that when they act as men, they become fragile.

The whore screamed for help.

When Rimbaud entered the apartment, he walked past Father, ignoring him, up the stairs to his workroom.

I opened that door he was looking at his watch as if the goddamn watch which every businessman wears was going to tell him something about life. "So you've come back," he said, but his eyes didn't move from the watch. He knew damn well and I didn't have to tell him nothin' that I had nowhere to go so there was no coming back because (I thought—they had taught me) no human wanted to have me. At the dinner table, Rimbaud had said no man would have me no matter how much I spread my cunt lips—

("How I spread my cunt lips," I inserted.)

(If I could, I would have fucked over every man.)

("Childhood. The whole of poetry is there. I have only to open my senses and then to fix, with words, what they've received.")

He asked why I had been knocking on his door. I asked him if he had gotten a letter from Mother.

"Were you expecting one?" He wasn't interested. "Were you expecting the dead to tell you what it's like there so you can have a new place to spread your cunt lips?"

"Just tell me, Rim."

"Tell you? Tell you what? That Mother's dead because she suicided? That she suicided because she was female or mad? What could I possibly tell you? That all that you have, that all that anyone in this family has, in possibility, is what I give you. What are you looking for now?"

"Money."

"Eat it."

"Just give me some money. Some of it's mine. I'll do anything you want if you give me a bit of money. Please. After that you can think and say what you want about me."

Rimbaud, after his experiences, knew a whore, a girl desperate for money without a chance of getting it, when he heard one. But he hadn't made me low enough yet. To suit his weakness, his insecurity, his inability to do anything but attempt to control. *He was the first sane member of our family.* He thought that poetry is dead in this modern world.

"I need some money now," I begged, "because. I owe it. To a friend and I can't hurt a friend."

"What's the friend's name?" He knew that everyone who knew me in my school (but I didn't care) hated me.

"It's a girl. In school." I couldn't tell him that I was pregnant cause then he'd do something horrible to me. All of them knew I didn't have any friends my own age.

"You know that our mother's dead and every penny I make goes on supporting you?"

When you don't eat your dead meat, a child in China starves. "Yes." But even then I knew I was going to be like Mother. No matter what men did.

Let the children in China starve. "Now, get out of here." He didn't hand me any money.

I knew that he was planning some new business in his mind and that business had to do with me. I knew as if we were born to get married to each other cause I can hear blood, power. I knew that this brother had never taken care of me and that now he was going to take care of me. All I had to do now was find out the details of caring or maybe I didn't care, maybe I should get the hell out of there.

Rimbaud came down behind me on the stairs, placed his hand on my shoulder so that I had to turn around into his face, and gave me a fifty. Said, "I'm taking care of you."

Since he had a beard and skin that was all wrinkled like a sailor's, he looked old. Something to do with memory.

"Childhood. Innocence. Innocence is the plague. O Nature, O Mother."

Father was resigned to Rimbaud's haphazard, violent aggression, but Father was financially dependent on Rimbaud. He didn't seem to like his son, but he didn't seem to like anyone.

"I'm dying," Rimbaud said, "rolling in platitudes, nastiness, and grayness. What do you expect, I persist stubbornly to worshiping full freedom."

ODE TO ANONYMITY
Four young girls lean against the wood bars horizontally crossing a gym wall. All of them wear black cotton sleeveless blouses and black cotton full skirts. One girl leaves the group by herself and half walks, half struts, very slowly, across the floor. Her strut, as her head falls toward the floor, turns into a swirl. Falling without falling. All the girls are moving, alternately lifting skirts and showing their white underpants, or stepping high, as they've been taught is proper. They can be good and they can be bad. They forget their roles and just move. They rest in the center of the gym, out of breath. I am not one of them. Me: Capitol.

All my brother cared about was money. Business. His money. He didn't care whether I was a slut. He had stopped drinking, though he didn't believe in Jesus Christ yet. "I want to," Rimbaud said, "slowly, carefully, climb up the ladder of common sense. I don't depend on anyone but myself." He depended on one body. My body. I was so fond of my body, and dumb about what men do, I let him think this. I let what happened, happen. You might say that *dumb* means *fond of the body;* I will never let this go.

Rimbaud intended to reach and cling to the topmost rung of success on the ladder of my body. I remember that what existence was for me was that there was nowhere to escape.

Rimbaud walked past. Then I heard his and Earl's voices together in the living room below.

"Been much busy?"

"Not much. Not since I talked to you."

They were talking about me. I walked down into the living room. Rimbaud told me to get out. I got out and I didn't think I had anywhere to go.

I went up the stairs. I could still hear them talking.

Mother had hated me despite her slight and unexpected change of heart a few months before her death. She had made Rimbaud the sole trustee of the scrap of money she had left for my education.

"She's just a girl." Rimbaud.

"You need capital before you can use her or anyone else."

"That's what I'm saying. She's a girl."

"Since women don't think, women don't know how to think," Earl added.

"I haven't beat that out of her."

Since I'm not dumb, I knew what they were talking about. I knew only a few facts. Mother had deliberately checked into one of the hotels which was around the corner from the hotel in which her mother lived the day before my mother died. I didn't know if she had planned to suicide when she had checked into that hotel. If she had checked into that hotel in order to meet a man, she probably (I didn't know this for certain) wouldn't have checked into a hotel next to her mother's hotel. She could have checked into the hotel for some other reason and by chance eaten too many pills.

My mother's mother had been the family money supplier. Father was a dildo and a hanger-on. Who isn't a hanger-on of the rich? Mother's mother had adored Mother.

After Father had turned to drink to the point of death, Mother took more and more of her mother's money. Then, she stole the most valuable of the diamonds. When Grandmother had learned about this theft, a week before Mother had checked into the hotel, she had cut the economic umbilical cord. Hanger-on of the rich.

Time goes forwards and backwards. Time is only material and I'm only time, their time when a child. My older brother wanted to prostitute me. I couldn't be what I was. Time and in time.

Quentin said that when there's no solution, you can't try to find one, you have to wait.

After my brother had finished with Earl, he came up to my bedroom to talk to me. He didn't bother knocking.

I don't say useless things.

"You don't need to cry about a woman who couldn't tell her cunt from a toilet."

If I had been another person, I would have mashed his face into red. Like some girls want to become ballerinas or have babies, I hoped that one day I'd have the ability to be totally independent and then I'd never again have to be nice to anyone or see anyone. Not someone who's a creep.

Money is only one of the means (power) of freedom (for me) and I wanted the money Mother had left me which I couldn't put my hands on. Everything disappeared in that house.

If one bit of what I was feeling had appeared, I and the whole world would have exploded with it.

"I'll tell you about your mother. When she took one drink of alcohol, she turned into a bitch. Sharper than the razor blades she used on her white legs. And then she turned into a dog, on her hands and knees, and moved to the nearest man's legs. Waggling her rump."

"I never saw this."

"Women need men. As soon as she reached the man's knees, she rubbed herself against them as if she was not only a bitch but in heat."

"Father didn't fuck her."

"So if one of you doesn't get fucked, for one second, you're so hot for it that you have to crawl over to every form of man you can smell? And she complained about Father being an alcoholic."

"You murder people."

"I'm telling you about your mother. The one you keep mourning for. The bitch who gave you bitch blood and made you the whore you are."

"Who was she?" I asked. I'll ask anyone. No one including me cares whether I cry.

"She never loved you, Capitol. In fact, she hated your guts because your real father left her because she was pregnant with you and she just wanted to fuck, she didn't want a kid."

"I know," I said to the only brother who remained.

"The dead are just dead," he said.

But if there weren't any dead in our lives or our living hearts, what could life be? "I'm not Quentin. I have to remember. I want to remember."

"Then remember how much she loved you. Remember when she sat on her bed all the time, naked; talking away on the phone to her friends. And you'd come into their room, tentatively, frightened, to ask her something that meant a lot to you. Without leaving the phone, she told you to get out because you were bothering her."

I knew how to remember. "Whenever I took a shower, as soon as my eyes were blinded with liquid, she'd come into the bathroom to toss a glass of cold water over my body."

"You know who you are? Capitol. You don't know what you want or how to ask for it. All you know is the smell between your legs."

I could hear the affection in his voice. My blood is infected. I don't know why I bothered explaining to anyone. "Maybe I make up my mother in my head and what I make up keeps me alive." My blood's infected.

"Your mother was crazy and she suicided. Capitol. You can feel and believe whatever you want and it's you who lives the consequences." Rimbaud knew what those consequences were. "Since you have her blood, why don't you make some money off of it."

I fuck every boy in town.

As for leaving I didn't need to live on the streets to know what it was to live on the streets R had instructed me. It was time for dinner. My body.

Better than dog food.

There was a cocker spaniel left over from the old days. What old days nobody knew. Maybe American history. This cocker spaniel, black and white as proof of the existence of Good and Evil or morality in early American history, ate anything. He was subconsciously trying to bury his pedigree to show his superiority to the English. Ate chocolate wrappers floating in toilet bowl water; ate the white toilet paper wrapped endlessly around my used Kotex pads, presents to the Virgin, so that no man would be inflicted with or remember that carrot juice was now dripping down between my legs. Father: "Women are freaks." This dog had one flaw: an insane lust for dead meat. He couldn't forget his lust. Every night when I placed the hamburger steak or lamb chops, Father never ate anything else; on the small round dining room table, I had to guard the dead meat with my life.

We ate for a while. I love the blood that drips out of dead meat. Father always mumbled before he ate his food; Mother taught us not to listen to him. After a while, Rimbaud said, "If I'm going to maintain your support, you're going to have to do something back. You're now too old to live for free."

"I can leave."

"I'm preferable to the streets," he said.

I was beginning to learn who I was.

Rimbaud: Oh you bitch I said females can't change I said once that thing between your legs gets walking.

I knew who she was who my sister was even if no one else did. They all wanted to sleep with her, the males, some of them thought they really loved her. But it had nothing to do with love. It was because of what she really was.

It wasn't that thing down there, it was what she had inside her that made her what she was. Build makeup on her face so her face would look and smell like what she had down there.

My regular business was trade. The main income was small arms and ammunition. We had a few stores in town which we used as outlets. But I wasn't earning enough. I couldn't figure out why. Every penny I got I saved so I could some day know I was rich. So I could have. It's not as if I disliked my own fucking sister.

The convention forbidding slavery had simply rendered this trade more lucrative.

Father was mumbling, "I've done my duty by you; I've done all that anyone can expect of me and more than most parents do; I've done my duty I don't have any more money you know I don't have endless money."

"What do you propose we do with her?" Rimbaud inquired.

"We could send her to the state loony bin," Father said.

We all ate for a while. I remembered that there had been a man, a brother, who had cared about me; I wondered how long I could remember a memory.

And what would there be when there are no memories to re-member? Someone said. We would be sailors. Sailors are helpless when they're not at sea.

I knew and I didn't know why Quentin had to fuck a lot of people and he didn't care about sex. I didn't know anything anymore.

I wanted him back with sheer desperation and I didn't know if I wanted him back.

England is worse than America cause the people in England who are oppressed don't even know they're oppressed. If there's no memory, is there anything? In England, they've internalized their oppression for so long that the only revolution they can conceive is to become their oppressors. There, a populist movement is one in which the members of a poorer class defy their limits and climb into the class above them. You eat the shit you live in. The English internalized class consciousness or class torture to such a degree that their mouths no longer open naturally. Those who weren't educated properly (in torture of the body) can't *speak properly* cause they're poor. The poor don't know what art is so they hate it. And rightfully. The whole country stinks of its own prison which it keeps making smaller. "You don't eat your own shit," I said to Rimbaud, "because your mouth's too small." I didn't excuse myself. I left the dinner table.

I wasn't used to eating their blood.

I went up to my bedroom, though I wasn't being punished. I was going to run away from here. The problem of where to run wasn't a problem anymore cause my mind was made up. In order to run away, I needed to have money. Mother had left me some money. I hadn't hated her as much as she had hated me. Rimbaud had taken this money. Legally, but *legal* is *illegal* to me. It's all the fucking same. It's not my decision. Their systems. In my nation, people say "Up yours," fought for self-determination, and whether this is historically accurate or not, we believe it happened. Is. I will not give up memory. "He's also your brother," Mother had explained. "When I'm gone, he'll take care of you."

Through the one window in my bedroom, which only dirty white blinds which were now open sometimes covered, I could see through the gaps in some wire. A dying animal lies under rubble. A small bakery sits in a white building. There's a cake in that bakery; thirteen different animals ride around its top. It had been my birthday and Easter so Mother couldn't get me a real birthday cake. So the next year, she got me the animal cake. The girls in my class at school came to my birthday party. Each of them was given a different animal and then there were no animals left for me. I wanted what was remembered.

Father had said to Quentin, *because he understood him,* that a man has two instincts, *eros* and *death.* The natural conjuncture, in the male, of these two drives bends him toward brutality and violence. Sexually and nonsexually. Is there a difference? He asked. A man can try to kill himself, but it's useless to try, for he'll always kill another person.

That's what he was saying before Mother suicided.

I knew I had other instincts.

Just as the desire to suicide easily slides into murder, so my hatred of family and men also had to be hatred of myself.

Down there, Father was giving out his rare words of wisdom. ["If conscience had to drink, it'd be another animal. There's no difference between love of family and business like there's no difference between honesty and dishonesty."]

"*Her*—" Rimbaud pointed at an imaginary me. "She's running around the streets and making them stink with that thing between her legs and this family is so rotten that her parent isn't doing anything about it. *Her.* All that I want in life is to have a good life and raise my son and how can I do that when this family represents an unholy cross between hell and the abyss?"

"No man should care for a woman."

"Mother destroyed you. You know that, don't you, you drunk? Mother despised you, looked down on your intelligence, said you didn't have a cock. She taught us to do the same. It was the same thing as destroying herself."

"They all do it. They have something between their legs."

I would have to get to the next town's shipyards. Since I was under eighteen, I would have to sneak aboard the ship. Once out to sea, they couldn't send me back to my family then I would use my feminine or masculine charms to persuade the captain or a sailor to keep me. If I were a boy, it would be easier.

Rimbaud. "The point is that someone has to pay. Her upper mouth is at least as hungry and devouring as the cavern below it. Either let the state asylum take care of these holes or let them earn money. If blood flows out, history is the flow of human blood."

"Do what you have to." Father explained, "Nothing matters. Women cling to that myth called *meaning* cause their flesh's a repository for life and death. They say we're scared. But we know the world doesn't care about us. Finally."

Maybe he was right. Maybe I had no relations to men. Maybe that's why I could fuck so many of them at once.

I didn't remember nothing. I didn't remember Quentin.

I realized I needed R. Quentin was gone; Father as good as dead; I needed a dream of love. Love can not exist, but if the dreaming of it dies, there's no more love. This brother wasn't going to abandon me. He was a creep, but he was stable. I would hold on to him.

Rimbaud wants me to be a whore, I said. My mother was always happy. Laughing. These are some of the things my mother loved: clothes, books, pornography, new places, canned kangaroo meat and chocolate-covered ants, gossip, gambling. Her eyes were a wild cat's. She adored her own flesh. She stuck a piece of raw chicken under the broiler until the skin turned black. And then she ordered out for the largest, most expensive lobsters she could find. With chocolate-covered bees. The kitchen was the smallest room in the house. I don't care whether you eat or not. She knew how to use a phone who needs to cook she had a big, strong man to take care of her, a former football player. American hero. It doesn't matter what you feel about him because he's going to take care of you forever and ever. Men aren't important, she taught us. She always taught us while she was sitting naked on her bed. Father's bed, twin, sat next to hers. Like in the movies. Objects. "Look at your father," she said. "He's sleeping again." He was sleeping. "He never does anything because he's stupid. Tell him he's stupid." I always did what I was told. I told Father he was stupid and woke him up. When I was older, I learned that Father is kind and gentle. And there's no need to laugh at kindness, gentleness. He had started trying to drink himself into death because he couldn't be what she wanted and no man could. An American hero is a man who's made American history and American history is myth.

Doomed to be unwed.

Two days before this conversation, I had been outside, not in school. Walking through some alleys that were repositories for bums' piss. Only if you're paranoid, you're scared of a bum. Rimbaud spied me.

My skirt was half over my ass and there were no underpants, just a hand, a few fingers of which had disappeared into me. It didn't matter who the guy was. I can never remember whom I've fucked. How can I be my memories? I can't remember and yet genital touching means everything.

Men told me they remembered whom they fucked: they brought out memories for display, notches cut into a belt, to name identity. Being female I didn't and don't have to prove that I don't exist. Maybe the guy who I was with looked like Quentin.

Rimbaud walked right up to us and hit the left side of my face. He told the boy or man to get out. (Of me or out of the bedless street.) (As if he didn't exist. Only Rimbaud and I existed.)

"Even if you don't have any respect for me, Cap, couldn't you remember your father and respect him?"

Before he could say anything else, I ran out to a car, dodged behind it, swiveled around up a smaller alley. The boy or man with whom I had been was waiting in his car, a beaten-up brown, at the end of the lane. I got in.

Uncle Maury was another man in my family. Was a geologist who had worked on the hydrogen bomb. Went the myth. When young, he had wed a nice Deutsch girl who went mad. Maybe because she was no longer in Deutschland. Married a second again nameless girl, and, when she hanged herself in a closet, re-wed the Deutsch girl. We are German Jews. He lived on one floor of the mansion he owned near Harvard University and she lived on another. They didn't meet. There were three children. One of the males suicided; the other weighed three hundred pounds and was a violin prodigy, was about to die. The girl was a successful modern dancer. A few months before her death, Mother had begun to see Uncle Maury frequently.

Nameless at birth and already doomed to be unwed.

"Fuck me," I whispered to the bimbo in the car. "I don't like preliminaries."

But he was going down on me.

"If you touch my clit, you hurt me. Fuck."

He did what I told him cause he liked what I like. I felt good for a few moments.

Rimbaud must have found us in the car while we were fucking. The sun was sitting inside his head to his blood felt inhuman, as if the sun had escaped humanity. Pass out. He thought the city was exploding. Just as he was about to stick his hand through the car window, the bitch's fuck having partly pulled up his pants, the car burst into speed.

"Try to convince Father that I haven't seen what I've seen."

Come was dripping down between my legs (onto the car scat). I felt good. For a few moments.

I told the bimbo to take me home. Home was a weak father and a dead mother. There is nowhere else to go. I have to go somewhere, I said to myself, therefore there has to be somewhere.

Perhaps outside where the swans are sitting are the cunts of the night. Perhaps where the heat of human flesh is a song that's being sung by the winds who will never be even slightly human.

Once-almost-red reeds crossing once-almost-blue weeds stood half upright over dark-gray water. Above them, an occasional gull was a black shape in a darkening blue sky. (The buzzing in the head comes from wanting to suicide; when you've got a bad family, you're bad. So all humans hate you.)

(Inside the apartment, Father would be sitting in his black leather chair by a semilit or unlit window. He wouldn't care.)

(I had decided to pick up a man the way men pick up, are supposed to pick up, women to show I could do it. I went out with two gay friends of mine. We met a sailor in a gay bar. Neither of my friends wanted him because they smelled trouble, but I was so determined to prove something, I forgot to smell.

(The sailor took me to his room. All I remember is a large bed. He told me he fucked men and women. The day he had married his wife, he had tied her to the kitchen table and fucked her without stopping for three days. When I gave the sailor the underpants I was wearing, he let me leave his room.

(Back in my parents' house, I looked at myself in a mirror. Black-and-blue marks stained most of my body.)

Two days later, I was up in my room and thinking about how Rimbaud wanted me to be a whore so he could make more money.

We're all how this society makes us. R, in his way, was still pure, a poet. He didn't give a damn about God. About what people thought about him. All he cared about was money. He was the only one of us fit to live in this world. *R was the last romantic,* for he had totally made himself, except for his dislike of me, so whatever I felt about him or whatever he felt about me, I looked up to him. I can't live without having someone to look up to.

Mother had suicided. I knew I had to stop needing him, but I didn't know how except by suiciding and I wasn't going to do that.

I went downstairs to inform them I was getting married so you can't talk me into white slavery I said to Rimbaud. You saw him in the car the other day. By the way.

Why?

Why what?

"Why're you getting married, Capitol, are you . . . ?" (Men can't say this word.)

"I have problems Dad [though I don't bother to speak to my father] OK you don't know anything I just slit my wrists." I showed my wrists which didn't have any marks on them. "Maybe women get married because they're in love."

I can take care of it answered Dad.

Go to the doctor said Rimbaud.

I'm suicidal I repeated.

"Don't talk about nasty things at the dinner table," Father added and took another swig just like a writer. In a sexist culture particularly threatened by its sense of its own coherence or its hypocrisy, the prostitute assumes the mythic figure, CRIMINAL. DESTROYER OF SOCIETY IN FEMALE FORM. Better dead than red, said Mom, and I was lying when I said there were razor marks on my wrists.

A prostitute is restless reckless feclesss, worst of all sexually demanding, homeless like a bum only she's worse she goes from one *man's* bed to *another's*. Not even her own body. RUINER OF SOCIETY. Did my brother want to make me a criminal or a revolutionary?

"This author has concluded that prostitutes are essentially over-sexed pseudomen." I reported or repeated to Father.

"Women. I guess a man like me doesn't know women because no man knows anything."

"That doesn't matter." R. *He was the only one of us fit to live in this world.*

I knew Father didn't want to make me into a prostitute cause he believed in American morality so I crumbled a biscuit I had found onto the table and asked if I could be excused cause I wanted to see the swans.

Rimbaud said we'd talk about marriage later.

When I looked at him, his eyes were those of a small animal, a ferret who's trapped and knows it and is righteous in his knowing. Every time I looked at him and bit through my lips, I made them more tender. Soon I would poison my own blood.

"Blood is thicker than water." Father before he became an alcoholic. Father didn't matter. *"Just let me go," I told Rimbaud.*

"He's taking care of us." Father.

"If I'm bad, it's because I have to be. But I won't kill myself. You've made me so disturbed, I don't know I'm anything. You've made me hate everything. The world. Me."

"Fecund for it," Father.

I ran upstairs and slammed the door on them.

"She didn't go to school today, did she?"

I had closed the door so that I could be safe. Downstairs they could say anything about me, do anything to me. Downstairs wasn't me. ("I'm not a sadist. I don't want control over other people: I believe in love.")

Fatherless nine months before my birth, and already doomed, and knew it, to be unwed from the instant the dividing egg determined its own sex.

"How can you know?" Rimbaud answered Father. "How can you know anything that goes on even in your own family?"

"I know. My daughter." [Father was a wimp. Father was kind, gentle.] He did because he had once given me fifty dollars when I had begged him for it and the next day my mother had instructed me that if I didn't instantaneously give it back to him and apologize to him, I'd have to leave their home forever. I wish all humans were dead because they rot, but I'm never going to die.

Perhaps the feminists are right when they say that all power's evil, but don't think so because I had to fight for my power in order to live. Father had no power and he was kind, gentle.

"How can you know anything," R said, "but alcohol? How can you know your daughter's a slut?"

"I just want my children to get along."

"I followed her. Someone has to follow her. Someone has to take care of her."

"I'll take care of her," Father whined.

Rimbaud didn't bother to answer the drunk.

"Schopenhauer said. Sure Capitol wants her own way, just like her mother did, but Caddy was one of the happiest women anyone ever's seen, so wanting her own way's not . . . "

"She's dead."

"Dead?"

"Dead as that river." Pointing to the outside. "Why don't you cry more about love? Who're you going to tell me to love next?"

Father looked down at the steak fat on his plate.

Fatherless nine months before my birth.

The next heart attack would be the one that killed him. End of some American un-dynasty. "Your sister doesn't love me because she doesn't have any love in her. Just like Quentin. She and Quentin. He's no son of mine; riffraff; he's probably shooting drugs in some alley, scum. My family is decent. [Honest, American] And Capitol's taking after him. He poisoned Capitol with ideas he learned in that university [it's good you didn't go to university] and filth. He's filth. He no longer exists in this family."

"Forget about Quentin. He's not taking any money away from you."

"I won't pretend I'm anything but a weak man, but I know family matters. Quentin and Capitol never learned this. [They're sick.] Maybe if they had grown up somewhere where there's no crime."

"You've got me. That's more than most people have these days."

I could hear everything. I could hear the feathers on swans' wings brushing over each other in an orgy. Of pride.

"You've got to love Capitol for my sake."

"I'm going to take care of her," said my last brother and then I heard him call my name up the stairs.

I heard Father yell goodnight.

The key turned in the outside lock of my bedroom and someone shambled off down the upstairs hall to sleep, way past my bedroom. To whatever those who are drunk call sleep and I don't know it is hell.

A good night.

Fuck them and fuck them again because even carnage is holy. I don't know what's out there in the night because *all I will be is lonely*. Maybe swans know. Night is what is to come.

Mother didn't put her cunt around loveliness and she suicided. Loneliness isn't alienation, I said, I hate the alienation of those men downstairs, shopping malls, their city. The court. I've been a child and I've been taught and shown meaninglessness and despair, but I don't dream that.

Not emptiness, monsters sit in flesh's halls. I know monsters and loneliness and they keep me alive.

"Experience," Father said, "only reveals to a man his own folly and despair, and victory is an illusion of philosophers and fools."

But there are wonders out there. Maybe all the sailors smell my cunt. I was crying.

The last of my family. Fatherless and doomed to be unwed from the instant the dividing egg determined its own sex. Who at seventeen, on the one thousand nine hundred fifty-ninth anniversary of someone's Lord perhaps the Lord the blacks in the United States resurrected into a human caring force a discusser of freedom according to James Baldwin, opened the one stinking window in the room they had allotted to be her bedroom, implying that she had free choice in their house, her own bedroom, and climbed over its black dust sill onto a blacker iron fire escape.

But had not immediately left their household premises because she was not about to go into loneliness without a weapon. There might be right and wrong, but it certainly isn't what they teach you. Had semi-

leaped, no just thought her way, onto the fire escape on her left so that she could clamber into R's room where she knew he wouldn't be, yet (he spent more and more time poring over his business books in his study, figures accounts savings, every penny put away noted counted again and again, sometimes he would fall asleep over what he called *real poetry*). Wanted to get to that large pale blue and red tin box in which she knew he kept the remains of their mother's life, her will, her own father's soft gray fedora. The documents of the money and actual money.

I wanted the truth. Scared he'd catch me, but all there is to be scared of in this world is that one of your relatives will get you. Entered the window and with a chisel I had kept in my room broke up the lock of the tin which should have been filled with cookies and took her will (as evidence, unknown of what) and all the money that was there (almost $7,000), not because it was mine but because it was my method of penetrating him. Inserting myself into the only thing he cared about. You will not whore me. Which I knew he could never forgive because insertion wounds, because wounds leave scars. A child who did it in a way at one blow certainly at the end of her tether, hardly knowing what she did, not even knowing what would actually be there except something called the truth (the only truth was her action—the one thing), that her mother had left her money, and that truth is loneliness.

Let all men dream about her afterwards.

I climbed down the black fire escape in the dusk and leaped, another leap this one partly premeditated, into the car in which Rimbaud had seen me fucking. Let them all see me fuck. Leaped not quite into the arms of the car's occupant; using him to get away. Knowing he, since he was married, would be easy to leave. Using him to get what was at the time the nearest thing to love: human help. For it, loved him in return. Until I vanished. From him. Never took money from a man that wasn't mine.

Fatherless from birth and already doomed to be unwed. Afterwards vanished, but no more to myself.

(1990)

from "Low"

Hansel and Gretel

FAMINE

There was a great famine in the land. The nation had begun economically disintegrating. A certain father who could no longer provide for his family muttered to his wife, "What is going to become of all of us?"

The mother answered, "Let's take our children to a forest so thick, no one who doesn't know how can escape it, and let's leave them there to die."

"I don't think that's a good idea," said the man.

As if she hadn't stopped talking, the mother replied, "If we don't kill our children, we're all going to die. In a period of famine, two deaths are better than four."

The father wept because he pitied his children. Abandoned children, abandoned only to death.

INNOCENCE

Through the walls, the children could hear their parents planning their deaths.

"We're going to die," said Hansel.

"What's death?" inquired the girl.

"I'll save you."

In order to rescue himself and his sister, Hansel went out into the night. In that night, he stuffed his pockets full of stones. Back in his parents' house, with pockets weighed down by worthless pebbles, he told Gretel that they were saved. "God is protecting us."

The Little Boy Lost
The little boy lost in the lonely fen,
Led by the wand'ring light,
Began to cry, but God ever night,
Appeard like his father in white.

He kissed the child and by the hand led
And to his mother brought,
Who is sorrow pale, thro the lonely dale
Her little boy weeping sought.

                                        William Blake

ABBREVIATED JOURNEY INTO THE FOREST

"Get up, brats. We're going to the forest."

The brats woke up and their parents accompanied them into the forest.

While they were walking deeper and deeper, the boy secretly dropped stones. In the middle where the forest was so dense nothing could be seen but a chaos of wood and leaves, mother told her children to wait.

The children waited and slid into dream.

When they woke up, there were no parents.

No longer knowing how to leave, where she was, if there were paths, anywhere, parents, home, the girl became hysterical and nauseous. Hansel tried to calm her down by telling her to be patient until the moon gave them some light.

When the moon was so high that bits of its white penetrated through the leaves, Hansel saw his stones and followed them through the forest and out until he and his sister safely reached their home.

The Little Boy Lost
Father, father, where are you going
O do not walk so fast.
Speak father, speak to your little boy
Or else I shall be lost.

The night was dark no father was there
The child was wet with dew.
The mire was deep, and the child did weep
And away the vapour flew.

William Blake

THE INNOCENTS ARE FREE AT LAST

The country became poorer. The father feared that they were all going to starve.

The mother said, "This time let's take our children into woods so black and pathless, they'll never escape their deaths."

The father loved his children, so he persuaded his wife to give them each a last piece of bread before they were led to death.

The brats were still listening through the walls to everything their parents said. They knew their parents wanted to kill them.

When Hansel tried to leave the house, he learned that his mother had locked the door.

In his innocence Hansel told Gretel that they were safe because God would protect them.

This time on his way through the forest Hansel dropped the only thing he had. Crumbs of his piece of bread. Better to escape from the forest than to eat.

The mother led her children into a part of the forest where they had never been in their lives.

Then the parents ordered them to wait until evening. When the parents would return. Then it was midnight and there would never again be parents.

Infant Joy

I have no name
I am but two days old.—
What shall I call thee?
I happy am
Joy is my name,—
Sweet joy befall thee!

Pretty joy!
Sweet joy but two days old.
Sweet joy I call thee:
Thou dost smile.
I sing the while
Sweet joy befall thee.
                    William Blake

EATING

Hansel searched for breadcrumbs, but now there was nothing. The birds had eaten everything.

He said to his sister, "We'll find a way out." But there was no way. Wandered in circles and spirals. The children were hungry. Walked for three days in desolation.

On the next morning, the sun was dazzling away its own color and somewhere in that light a bird was singing. When Hansel and Gretel looked up, the bird started flying. Soon they could see it.

They followed the bird until it stopped in the air and hovered over a house constructed out of food. All the foods about which the children had dreamed.

Hansel stated, "God has saved us."

While Hansel munched on a roof, Gretel licked a window.

Twinkle, twinkle, little bats,
What the hell you nibbling at?
Rats get eaten by big cats
After God has shat.—
Up above the world so high
There or in hell you're going to die.

The female voice who sang these words asked why they were destroying her house. "Who are you?"

Hansel and Gretel didn't answer the voice, but went on chomping.

One of the uneaten doors opened and a woman too old to be human hopped out. She told the children that they shouldn't be frightened: she was going to take care of them.

Inside her home, the witch fed Hansel and Gretel German food and then she tucked them into a bed of gigantic mattresses and comforters. Finally the children felt safe enough to dream again.

Witches resemble animals in eye color and smell. They perceive, not by sight, but by smell. This witch, Queen of the Forest, was a cannibal and she preferred children.

Next morning, Witch locked up the boy in an animal-restraining cage.

When the girl awoke, she was informed that she was to cook and serve food to her brother so that he would become plump enough for the witch's digestive needs.

While Hansel ate and drank the richest foods in the world, Gretel was fed on burnt matchsticks and diseased pig teeth. (The witch wasn't a feminist.)

Because Gretel was female and also wasn't a feminist, she cried a lot. Her tears made her brother's food so salty, he became fatter.

Every time the Wicked Witch of the West spied Gretel sobbing, she'd make the girl cry harder by describing exactly how her brother was going to feel when the oven's huge flames touched each part of his body. When hot peppers were rubbed into the mucous membranes as they started to split up and ooze liquid.

"If you don't stop bawling," announced the inhuman Queen, "I'll feed your brother to all the starving children in China." (Witch never read newspapers because she didn't trust reporters.)

Morning, afternoon and evening the girl did the maid's work. One dawn, while she was doing something too disgusting to name, the witch ordered the child to come to her.

"Come."

Gretel came.

"Climb into that oven."

The child didn't want to climb into the oven because the oven was too hot.

"You stupid brat, that oven isn't hot. That oven is cold. That oven is a virgin oven just like you."

The girl protested that she was scared of fire. Since fire terrified her, she loved to play with matches.

Witch replied that is was no longer cool for women to be weak. Frightened all the time. "C'mon, sister. Get into the fuckin' oven."

Gretel sensed that there was something wrong with this argument.

"If one woman can do it, all women can do it," announced the Queen of the Forest and climbed in.

Gretel quickly shut the door, shoved a refrigerator against it, so the witch burned to death.

There was a smell.

INDEPENDENCE

"C'mon, Hansel. You're free!" She opened the animal-cage door. The children were now free to be as they wanted in the world.

Like lovers they held on to each other.

The pebbles had become precious jewels. They ran through the forest until its end and then they walked back home. Their parents were dead.

(1990)

from *My Mother: Demonology*

My mother began to love at the same moment in her life that she began to search for who she was. This was the moment she met my father. Since my mother felt that she had to be alone in order to find out who she was and might be, she kept abandoning and returning to love.

My mother spoke:

Into That Belly of Hell Whose Name Is the United States

ONE: MY MOTHER
I'm in love with red. I dream in red.

My nightmares are based on red. Red's the color of passion, of joy. Red's the color of all the journeys which are interior, the color of the hidden flesh, of the depths and recesses of the unconscious. Above all, red is the color of rage and violence.

I was six years old. Every night immediately after supper, which I usually was allowed to take with my parents, I would say, "Good night." To reach my room, I'd have to walk down a long dark corridor that was lined with doors on either side. I was terrified. Each door half-opened to unexpected violence.

Morality and moral judgments protect us only from fear.

In my dreams, it was I who simultaneously murdered and was murdered.

Moral ambiguity's the color of horror.

I was born on October 6, 1945, in Brooklyn, New York. My parents were rich, but not of the purest upper class. I'm talking about my father. At age six, I suddenly took off for unknown regions, the regions of dreams and secret desires. Most of my life, but not all, I've been dissolute. According to nineteenth-century cliché, dissoluteness and debauchery are connected to art.

I wrote: *The child's eyes pierce the night. I'm a sleepwalker trying to clear away the shadows, but when sound asleep, kneel in front of their crucifix and Virgin.*

Holy images covered every wall of my parents' house.

Their house had the immobility of a nightmare.

The first color I knew was that of horror.

Almost everything that I know and can know about my preadult life lies not in memories but in these writings.

Religion:

Days and nights all there was was a sordid and fearful childhood. Morality wore the habit of religion. Mortal sin or the Saint of Sunday and the Ashes of Wednesday kept on judging me. Thus condemnation and repression crushed me even before I was born. Childhood was stolen from children.

Never enough can be said, muttered and snarled, when one has been born into anger. THEIR criminal hands took hold of my fate. HER umbilical cord strangled me dropping out of her. All I desired was everything.

Listen to the children. All children come red out of the womb because their mothers know God.

The night's replete with their cries: unceasing flagellated bowls that are broken by the sound of a window slammed shut. Harsh and drooling screams die inside lips that are muzzled. We who're about to be suffocated throw our murmurs and screeches, our names, into a hole; that hole is everywhere. They laugh waterfalls of scorn down on us. If any speech comes out of us, it appears as nonsense; when the adults answered me, I puked. My few cries, like dead leaves tumbled by winds, climbed out of my body and vaporized.

It is a very Parisian garden that I found for hiding myself.

My mother was a great lady. Whenever she walked into the local grocery store that the neighborhood rich used, she'd order whatever young boy she could find to fetch the various items she happened to desire and to bring them to the taxi waiting for her. It didn't occur to Mother that she might have to pay.

If it was my misfortune to accompany her, I'd crawl behind her, trying to be invisible. I didn't know her. Me, an orphan. As soon as she was about to leave the store, as quickly as possible I'd pay the man behind the counter. My face flamed as if struck by sun. I don't know what happened when I wasn't there to pay: at that time events I didn't perceive didn't take place.

At that time I thought, Let them all go to hell.

It's entirely possible that I wasn't the only person who knew that Mother could always do as she wanted. The Queen of England never carries her own money. Someone's money.

Three or four times, trying to escape her, I ran away. Since my father was so gentle that he was subservient to Mother, I also had to run away from him.

I climbed down their back fire escape to the street below. Walked down streets till there was nowhere to go.

There's a white man behind the spindly trees. He leans into the sky to grasp at the wood and falls down on all fours, a dog. On pebbles. Now he's crawling across the street, stretches out one hand as if it's dead. Trying to become a wall, I hide against one. Sooted ivy and begonias are crushed. Another man rises up; his face, burning, and lips too red. He walks toward me, hand touching his cock, and another man, aghast, leaps out of a window. His arms beat against the sky as if he's a windmill. Through the froth on his lips he says, "They've stolen me."

Walked down the streets until there was nowhere.

A lying, hypocritical society turns around the grave of the holes in the garden of childhood.

I had to return home.

I didn't want to escape my parents because I hated them but because I was wild. Wild children are honest. My mother wanted to command me to the point that I no longer existed. My father was so gentle, he didn't exist. I remained uneducated or wild because I was imprisoned by my mother and had no father.

My body was all I had.

*A a a a I don't know what language is. One one one one I shall
never learn to count.*

I remained selfish. There was only my mother and me.

Selfishness and curiosity are conjoint. I'd do anything to find
out about my body, investigated the stenches arising out of trenches
and armpits, the tastes in every hole. No one taught me regret. I was
wild to make my body's imaginings actual.

And I knew that I couldn't escape from my parents because I
was female, not yet eighteen years old. Even if there was work for a
female minor, my parents, my educators, and my society had taught
me I was powerless and needed either parents or a man to survive. I
couldn't fight the whole world; I only hated.

So in order to escape my parents I needed a man. After I had escaped, I could and would hate the man who was imprisoning me. And
after that, I would be anxious to annihilate my hatred, my double bind.

This personal and political state was the only one they had taught
me. *I'm always in the wrong so I'm a freak. I'm always destroying
everything including myself, which is what I want to do.*

Red was the color of wildness and of what is as yet unknown.

As my body, which my mother refused to recognize and thus
didn't control, grew, it grew into sexuality. As if sexuality can occur
without touching. Masturbated not only before I knew what the word
masturbation meant, but before I could come. Physical time became
a movement toward orgasm. I became sexually wilder. I wanted a man
to help me escape my parents, but not for sexual reasons. I didn't need
another sexual object. Mine was my own skin.

Longing equaled skin. Skin didn't belong to anyone in my king-
dom of untouchability.

I hadn't decided to be a person. I was almost refusing to become
a person, because the moment I was, I would have to be lonely. Con-
junction with the entirety of the universe is one way to avoid suffering.

*Today I don't have any friends. Mother's critized everyone I've
tried to know as being "nouveau riche" or "not pious enough." This
idiot finds it normal to run to a priest to ask him whether it's all right
for me to play with whatever friend I'm lucky enough to have. No
one's ever good enough for her or her priest.*

Mother just hates everyone who isn't of our blood. She uses the word blood. *She hates everyone and everything that she can't control: everything gay, lively, everything that's growing, productive. Humanness throws her into a panic; when she panics, she does her best to hurt me.*

I've taken refuge in the basement. In its stale air. Jesus sits dead in its windows.

I found safety there, sitting on a horse who was rocking on decaying moleskins or crouching on a red cushion that needed to be repaired. There I told myself story after story. Every story is real. One story always leads to another story. Most of the stories tell how I'm born:

"Before I was born, I lived in Heaven. There the inhabitants spend their time imagining a sweet white Jesus who kills figures such as Mitterrand, or a golden Joseph swaddled in velvet who plays heavy metal. There're dolls everywhere. But I owned a cap gun that I used to blind pigeons, and minutely examined my body. Then I entered a world in which, since God sees everything that happens there, I had to become curious."

God followed me into the basement. Though I was curious, He frightened me. I decided that curiosity has to be more powerful than fear and that I need curiosity plus fear, for I'm going to journey through unknown, wonderful, and ecstatic realms. If there is God, the coupling of curiosity and fear is the door to the unknown.

For a while there was no one in my life.

I became older.

I adored the maid, who was younger than me. One day she told me she was planning to get married and have a child.

"I'll dress my baby only in white," the maid said.

"You can't do that," I replied, "because you're poverty-stricken."

Her face turned the color of my cunt's lips. It was she who was red, not me.

"I'm not poor. I work, and my boyfriend has a steady job with the subway."

The word work *meant nothing to me; I continued to try to teach her that she was too poor to afford a baby. That she couldn't clothe a baby.*

In desperation, Henrietta (the maid) couldn't find any language; finally she located the word evil. *I was "evil."*

This word evil *made me begin to think.*

I remembered how Mother calls her "the girl" and talks about her in the third person even when Henrietta's in the same room. Whereas if I show the slightest disrespect to any of my parents' friends, I'm severely punished. I see that I'm being trained to want only the girls who come from the wealthiest and most socially powerful families at my friends. I see that education is one means by which this economic class system becomes incorporated in the body as personal rules. The world outside me that's human seems to be formed by economics, hierarchy, and class.

I'm anything but free.

I want Henrietta to explain to me the degree of filth proper to each class.

After that, I fell in love with the gardener. Eight years old, I was no longer human.

There's the country. I'm learning the names of the flowers of night and those of water, heliotrope and Saint-John's-wort, water lilies and all the sorts of roses. I know that there are birds of the evening and those of the night; bats, screech owls, and baby owls fallen out of their nests and drowned in a pail of water haunt my dreams.

The summer air in the grotto, like a blind cat, walks down my stomach. I had to disappear finally. I pressed myself between a gray-red wall and its ivy growing up from the ground. In there I became many-legged, a spider, a hedgehog, a raccoon, every animal I'll ever want to be and every animal that is.

This is what God saw when He followed me into the basement.

I observed wheatfields, cornfields, clover the colors of flesh, poppy and huge cornflower fields, fields framed by weeping willows and poplars.

Behind Mother's kitchen, a plain which is sparkling in the sun appears. Cricket-rustling and fat-bumblebee-buzzing. Filthy flies are fertilizing its pastures. In the full of noon I walk out here. My head bare to the light, the hay scabbed my knees. There was a new taste on my hot lips, lavender and burning skin. I'm journeying in order to know vertigo and enchantment.

My father showed me all of this and more: dragonflies, the king-fishers, and wrens, the day-flies and all that glistens around them; wild ducks, turkey hens, and all the fish. Daddy taught me the trees and the seasons, tar, the forests and fire.

Now and forever, I no longer care about religion.

No religion: this is the one event that'll never change. No religion is my stability and surety.

Mother's demanding that I see her priest.

I couldn't escape my family because I still didn't know a man who would help me.

For reasons other than escape, I wanted this man to be wilder than me.

When I was twenty-three, it began to be possible for me to escape my parents. I started to remember directly, not just through writing, all that happened to me. A sailor is a man who keeps on approaching the limits of what is describable.

I was wild. My brother was the first man who helped me. I spent an increasing amount of time in his apartment.

It was the days of ghosts. Still is. Not the death, but the actual forgetting, even of the death of sexuality and wonderment, of all but those who control and those and that which can be controlled. Since an emotion's an announcement of value, in this society of the death (of values) emotions moved like zombies through humans.

At my brother's house I met artists. Romare Bearden. Maya Deren. This hint that it was possible to live in a community other than my parents', a community that wasn't hateful and boring, one of intellectuals, by opening up the world of possibilities, saved me from despair and nihilism.

I still couldn't break with my parents' society on my own.

There Paul Rendier took my virginity. Fucking enabled me to cast off my past; red gave me the authority to be other than red.

Once I had fucked, the only thing I wanted was to give myself entirely and absolutely to another person. I didn't and don't know what this desire means other than itself.

In me dead blood blushed crimson into the insides of roses and became a living color that's unnameable.

When Rendier left me and I didn't know where he was, I had to find him, because all that was left of me, all that was me, was to give myself to him.

In order to run after Rendier, I had to break with my family. My father was already dead; he had left me enough money so that I no longer economically needed a man. I know that women need men not just out of weakness. I escaped my mother because sexuality was stronger than her.

Then I found Rendier. We lived together one year.

After Rendier, I threw myself onto every bed as a dead sailor flings himself into the sea. My sexuality at that time was separate from my real being. For my real being's an ocean in which all beings die and grow.

The acceptance of this separation between sexuality and being was an invention of hell.

Searching I traveled to Berlin. There I lived with a doctor named Wartburg whose apartment I wouldn't leave. I never saw anyone but him. I had wanted to give myself to another and now I was beginning to. Wartburg put me in a dog collar; while I was on all fours, he held me by a leash and beat me with a dog whip. He was elegant and refined and looked like Jean Genet.

At that time, *nobody was able to look for me, find me, join me.*

What dominated me totally was my need to give myself entirely and absolutely directly to my lover. I knew that I belonged to the community of artists or freaks not because the anger in me was unbearable but because my overpowering wish to give myself away wasn't socially acceptable. As yet I hadn't asked if there was someone named *me.*

At this time I first read de Sade. Perusing *The 120 Days of Sodom* exulted and horrified me; horror because I recognized my self, or desire.

Living with Wartburg ended; I had no money nor friends in Berlin. All I wanted was to be entirely alone. I had strong political convictions, so I took off for Russia. There I couldn't speak any language.

Loneliness, and my kind of life, in Russia physically deteriorated me to such a point that I almost died.

From that time onward I have always felt anxiety baseed on this situation: I need to give myself away to a lover and simultaneously I need to be always alone. Such loneliness can be a form of death. My brother found me in Russia and brought me back to New York.

I first attempted to dissipate my anxiety by deciding to fuck and be fucked only when there could be no personal involvement. I traveled on trains, like a sailor, and made love with men I encountered on those trains.

My attempt failed. Friends said about me, "She's on her way to dying young." But I wanted, more than most people, to live, because just being alive wasn't enough for me. Wildness or curiosity about my own body was showing itself as beauty. My brother placed as much importance on sexuality as I did. When I met Bourénine at one of the orgies my brother gave, I was ready to try again to give myself to another, to someone who was more intelligent than me and a committed radical.

Anxiety turned into a physical disease. Bourénine said that he wanted to save me from myself, my wildness, my weakness. He made me feel safe enough to try to give myself to him.

I became so physically weak that I stood near death. When Bourénine believed that I might die, he began to love me. I began to hate him, yet I worshiped him because I thought he protected me. My gratitude has always been as strong as my curiosity, as is mostly true in those who are wild.

Even then I knew that most men saw me as a woman who fucked every man in sight. Since Bourénine wanted to be my father, he didn't want me to make my own decisions. I saw myself as split between two desperations: to be loved by a man and to be alone so I could begin to be. When I met B, he was married. I didn't mind because I didn't really want to deal with another. Since B immediately saw me as I saw myself, I saw in B a friend and one who wouldn't try, since he was married, to stop me from becoming a person, rather than wild.

From the first moment that B and I spoke together in the Brasserie Lipp, there was a mutual confidence between us.

I had pushed my life to an edge, having to give myself away absolutely to a lover and simultaneously needing to find "myself." Now I had to push my life more.

Bourénine's inability to deal with what was happening to me turned him violent and aggressive. During this period, B and I met several times and discussed only political issues. As soon as I began speaking personally to him, we commenced spending as much time alone with each other as we could.

Wildness changed into friendship.

I had already written: *No religion: this is the one event that will never change. No religion is my only stability and security.*

Mother insisted that I see her priest, to such a degree that I had to.

Let me describe this Director of Human Morality. (One of the Directors of Human Morality.) While his hands were sneaking everywhere, all he could see in my words was his own fear.

Right after I saw him, I wrote down in my secret notebook: "Religion is a screen behind which the religious shields himself from suffering, death, and life. The religious decide everything prior to the fact; religion's a moral system because by means of religion the religious assure themselves that they're right.

"From now on I'm going to decide for myself and live according to my decisions—decisions out of desire. I'll always look ... like a sailor who carries his huge cock in his hand. ... I'll travel and travel by reading. I won't read in order to become more intelligent, but so that I can see as clearly as possible that there's too much lying and hypocrisy in this world. I knew from the first moment I was that I hated them, the hypocrites."

As soon as I had written this down, I knew that I was dreadfully and magnificently alone.

I am now seventeen years old.

All around me are termites, familial households without their imaginations. They would never rise an iota above their daily tasks, daily obligations, daily distractions. Everyone who's around me has lost the sense that life's always pushing itself over an edge while everything is being risked.

So now there's going to be a war! Hey! Finally something exciting's going to happen! The United States's coming back to life! The government of the United States is realizing that someone's angry about something or other and's descending to offer its people a target for their bilious bitterness. O emotionless sentimental and sedentary people, because your government's a democracy and responsible to you, it is giving you a whole race to detest, a nation on which to spit, a religion to damn, everything you've ever wanted. You're incontestably superior to men who wear dresses. Again you will become important in the eyes of the world.

You Americans need to be right. This war will not only be a pathway to future glory: once war's begun, you'll feel secure because you'll no longer have to understand anything else. You will again know what good and evil are.

Tomorrow you're going to give your sons joyfully to the desert, maybe daughters if you're feminist enough, because you're emotionless and, in war, you can be so emotionless, you don't have to exist. Therefore war allows people to surpass themselves. The English know this full well. As soon as you have tanks and dead people all around you, you'll be able to feel alive, once more powerful, magnanimous, and generous to all the world.

All that your grandparents and parents, educators, and society showed you, the triumphant road, the right way, the path of true virtue—the RIGHT, the GOOD—is only Liberty mutilated and Freedom shredded into scraps of flesh. The raped body. A man's a child who walks down the right road—a street thoroughly carved out and signposted—because all he can see is the word danger.

(1993)

from *Pussy, King of the Pirates*

The Pirate Girls

King Pussy's Story
Pussy, Who Always Lives Inside Her Own Head . . .

Childhood ended when Pussy learned that she was pregnant. It didn't matter to her, at that point, who the man was. Or it did.

NAMING:
All that she knew was that he had come from across an ocean. After she had fucked with him twice, he had mentioned to her that he was on methadone. But he had run out, or else he was kicking it, therefore he couldn't fuck her anymore.

Since Pussy was a nice girl, she offered him her apartment, or hole, as a refuge; she offered herself as a friend. Three days later, she asked him to get out of her home . . .

In those days, Pussy made meager amounts of money by being a performance artist. That's what it was called. After the flight of the stranger, she went on the road.

It was during the second week of road work that she remembered that her period was a day late. It was the first time in her life that it ever occurred to her that she could become pregnant.

The possibility had never before been a possibility. As soon as it was possible for her to be pregnant, Pussy was sure that she was. She was definite that she must get an abortion as soon as she got off this road, and even sooner.

Before this time it hadn't been possible for her to be pregnant, because she hadn't wanted a child. She had no idea why she didn't want a child, because all women want to bear children.

Pussy got off the road.

She ran to see a gynecologist whose name she had found in the telephone directory and then she informed him that she was pregnant.

The clinic in which she had found herself seemed to be devoted to abortions. The gynecologist, who was actually a nurse-practitioner, informed Pussy that she had to be pregnant for a full six weeks and then her baby could be aborted.

Pussy *waited,* as if *waded,* rather than lived, through the remainder of the full six weeks. During this *period,* according to Pussy, her body became alien to whatever was her, because her breasts turned so painfully swollen that she could no longer sleep in her usual positions, because she was simultaneously and continuously hungry and nauseous, because she wanted the child to remain alive.

She didn't know whether or not to tell the stranger that she and he could now have a baby; she decided not to bother him, because by not disturbing him she was being polite.

"I can't have a baby," she told herself. Since she could, she made up reasons why she couldn't. She couldn't bear her child because she had no money, because there was no way in the future for her to earn money. Because the child wouldn't have a father.

A week lay between this conversation with herself and the abortion. Her only hope, though she didn't know what *hope* could mean, was to stop being pregnant naturally. Her immune system had never operated in regard to pelvic inflammations and abortions lead to such infections. Pussy drank cup after cup of pennyroyal tea until she almost puked. She waited a few hours, then began the process again.

After three days of pennyroyal tea, nightmares rather than swollen breasts kept her awake. The final nightmare, she murdered her daughter.

Upon waking or leaving the nightmare, she realized this was true. Her doctor who wasn't a gynecologist agreed with her. "After your abortion," he said, "you are going to have to pay."

Since Pussy never had thought, nor would she think, that women shouldn't have abortions, she had to come to terms with the realization that to be human, and woman, includes the possibility and even the act of murder.

Nothing but abortion was going to work.

The night prior to the suction, the stranger phoned her. He hadn't contacted her since she had been on the road. "You're going to be a father." These words fell out of Pussy's mouth before she knew about them. She was out of her mind.

He wanted her to bear his child. He replied. He began to talk. She was the fourth woman he had made pregnant. For the first time, he wanted one of his children to become alive. Perhaps this desire was a sign that, now, he was adult.

"I can't afford to bring up a child."

"I'll help you out financially if you need it."

"You can't 'help me out financially.'" For the moment Pussy forgot his name. "Since you're the child's father, you're as responsible as I am in every possible way.

"But you can't be the father, because we don't have a relationship. We knew each other only for a week."

"I agree with what you're saying."

"The question of responsibility's complicated. I never knew my father and look how fucked-up I am. Not knowing my father fucked me up my whole life. Because I never let people get close to me. I won't do that to a child; I won't give my child my childhood."

Pussy didn't tell the stranger that she was going to have the abortion the next morning.

NOW I TELL THIS STORY THE WAY I SAY IT

That night, because after I got pregnant it was always night, one of my girlfriends led me through whatever city I was living in.

To an antique store. I didn't want to go *there* because antique stores are graveyards for all those who are dead.

This one was located behind a street. When we found it, it was shivering like a dying animal behind iron bars. Dead clothes filled it up. Dead clothes, the parts of the skin that have been used and used until they're flaky and yellow.

For weeks I needed new clothes. The city had been turning colder. Holes had crept into all of my wool clothing. I had searched for sweaters. Here, in this store, for the first time, were the sweaters I craved, sexual ones, the kind that aren't manufactured anymore. I tried one on. Two of them. Sweater after sweater. Each one softer, more developed than the last. No two were ever the same.

My guide must have been a guy because he was trying on men's clothes.

I hate it when I can't fuck, for whatever reason, someone I want to fuck. I went back to whatever stood for a dressing room. In the back of the store, in a corner.

A red velvet curtain, rather than a door, obscured whatever lay inside.

In there, I looked at myself in a green sweater whose hairs were so long that they curled around each other. Green glass jewels hid in this hair. Its huge collar didn't imprison me, like most collars. Watching myself in a mirror that was older and taller than me, a mirror that was also outside, I realized I was beautiful.

The second sweater I put on, though black, was so thin that I could still see my own breasts. They had no nipples. The more naked that I became, the more beautiful.

Sweater after sweater.

I wanted to own every single one. I couldn't afford this. I arbitrarily decided on number four. Abandoning the four I had chosen, all of the sweaters I had tried on, heaped in turds upon the floor, I went back into the dressing room, which I thought was empty.

My boyfriend was in there.

When we were inside, he told me and the girl who was with me what I had never known, that he was going to abandon me.

Right then, everything, or the world, stopped.

This was how MD, who was my girlfriend, and I started our journey through this forgotten city.

Its streets were more crowded than I remembered. I don't know who was driving that car we were in.

... As yet I didn't understand that I was in the city's heart ...

... I saw women, dressed in black, standing on a sidewalk. They were milling, that is, not yet in a line, around, under, a bright pink movie marquee ...

... The color of all the streets was brown ...

... The street down which we were driving connected the two ends of the city ...

... I saw a poster on a wall that was the color of the streets. It read "Maya Angelou." Then I looked down an alley: all of the buildings down that tube were brownstones. In that street, the sky was that gray which is perpetual and never devoid of light. When I looked again, the women under "Maya Angelou," now even more of them, dressed in black, stood in a line.

I didn't understand what I was seeing. But I couldn't have been hallucinating because my girlfriend was seeing what I was.

"Why are so many women wearing black waiting for Maya Angelou?" I asked her.

We were driven the same distance we had been driven. Again, I looked down an alley. Here the perspective reminded me of a world in a Renaissance painting: the condition of the space, especially in regard to infinity, depended on its perceiver's seeing.

I saw a line of women which extended down that alley as far as I could see, turned the corner, beyond my sight. All of the women I saw wore nun's habits.

"They're imitating Coffee," remarked MD.

"Coffee?"

As soon as I responded to her, in my mind's eye I saw a novel by Chester Himes. I had no idea what Chester Himes had to do with Coffee.

"Coffee's a huge draw," Marguerite explained to me, "because the people who live in this neighborhood hate PG&E." PG&E was the local gas and electric company.

Though I detest every gas and electric company I've ever encountered, I didn't rationally understand how Coffee connected to hatred for PG&E. But nonrationally I understood.

MD explained further: "When Angela Davis appeared downtown her audience was tiny."

I agreed. "And, unlike Maya Angelou's audience, none of the women in the former's audience wanted to be her." Then I began my analysis of mass and media culture: "There are far more women who want to be Coffee than there are Angela or Maya Angelou wanna-bes, but we don't know who Coffee is."

MD remarked that Angela read downtown and that downtown is where the art venues and rich whites reside. "No one goes there anymore."

Instead of saying this, she actually said, "No one goes down now."

We went down to where it was no longer poor.

Here streets were dark from the color of rain. The same color I saw fall in Berlin.

"Pussy, pussy," I called.

We were walking away from the antique store filled with dead clothes, and a little cat was prancing ahead of us over the light gray concrete. She darted between my legs, raced around behind me, leapt ahead of me. Until she no longer could be seen.

In all that half-light and half-dark, I said out loud, "Pussy."

Every time I called her, she returned to me. Then scooted even faster between mine and my girlfriend's legs, around and around our feet, until the world was a tangle. Just at that moment, she extended one of her paws. As if she was going to bat.

It was the only way that she could touch me. She was just like me.

The cat said to me, so that I could understand her, "I'll never leave you." As if I had been instructed in a more secret language, I then understood that, according to her nature, she goes wherever she wants whenever and at whatever speed, often disappears for days, and that if I welcome this, she'll never abandon me.

I liked this.

This was how I got my name.

TURNING INTO A CRIMINAL

Pussy met her gynecologist for the first time on the day of the abortion. Since he was sporting a ponytail, she decided that he must have once been a hippy. She was high on the pills that they had fed her.

They blabbed for an unknown amount of time about the nature of poetry and then Pussy asked when her abortion was going to begin.

The hippy answered that it would soon be over. She felt a twinge which was almost painful.

The abortion was over. Just before the end of this world Pussy hadn't known a thing.

There is no master narrative nor realist perspective to provide a background of social and historical facts.

Two weeks after the abortion, Pussy returned to the clinic for her routine checkup. A nurse-practitioner, who might have been the first one, informed her that she was still pregnant.

"I don't feel pregnant."

"Some women even bear a child after they've had a termination. But we're not sure you're pregnant."

Pussy asked when they might know positively what she was. She, or her body, was confused.

"Why don't you relax for two weeks? Forget that any of this happened. You'll probably get your period before the end of two weeks and then you'll know for sure that you're not pregnant."

The Time of Possibilities was the name of these two weeks. Sometime during this time, the nurse-practitioners and the doctors—there seemed to be two of each—speculated that Pussy might have a tubal pregnancy.

Two weeks had passed. No period was anywhere to be found. So they decided to test her to find out if anyone or part of anyone was living inside her.

They photographed the insides of her uterus. The photos showed uterine insides. There was nothing else. But the quality of the photos was poor.

They, and in this world *they* always means *medical people,* then extracted blood from Pussy. The blood told *them* that Pussy was pregnant.

"This means," one of the nurse-practitioners explained to the female, "that you might be pregnant and you might not be. If you are pregnant, we don't know where . . ." she hesitated, ". . . it's . . . hiding." She consulted a calendar. "If *it's* hiding inside a tube, that tube by now should be broken, so the tube must be about to break."

"What're you saying?" Pussy was in that state in which anger resembles stupidity.

"Tonight or at any other time after this, if you faint, go directly to the nearest hospital."

Do not pass Go. Instead of adding this, Pussy explained that she didn't know anything about the hospitals in the city, that she thought all of them were sites in which people were murdered. She didn't have any medical insurance.

"Go to a hospital for children."

They discussed that point.

Later in the night, Pussy phoned one of the doctors.

He was in his car, or one of his cars; the static from the car phone was louder than his voice.

"Is there any way that you, that anyone in the world, can learn whether or not I have a tubal? I have lots of money," Pussy explained.

"We'll learn whether or not when one of your tubes bursts open."

Later Pussy would remember that it was at this very moment that she forgot to be moral, especially to be moral about abortion.

For the next few days, she kept phoning the doctors.

Finally, it happened. "We've decided how we're going to know whether or not you have an ectopic pregnancy. We'll give you a second abortion. If that abortion works, you won't have an ectopic pregnancy."

The logic made as much sense to Pussy as anything else in the world.

Pussy ate their painkillers; she had what seemed to her to be the same abortion as she had the first time; again, she asked whether she was still pregnant.

The doctor who did the suction replied that this time something had come out, but he didn't know what it was.

In order to find out what it was, *they* were going to extract more blood from Pussy. In a few days, the new blood would be able to talk to them.

The blood announced to everyone that Pussy was no longer pregnant.

NOW I TELL THIS STORY THE WAY I SAY IT

Since I was poor, I had to prove to myself that I was rich, so I began to haunt clothing stores.

What I wanted was a black dress.

Two pools sat in the middle of the store *where I had once seen a black dress.* One of them was smaller than the other.

A man who was tall and thin was spooning black liquid into small vials, which he then gave to people to drink.

Like ink, the liquid tainted whomever it entered.

One of those who were infected was a girl with ebony hair.

Inside the store, there was no natural time. One day, or night, the tall thin man saw a girl who resembled the ebony-haired one, whom he had infected, to a T. For this reason, he fell in love with the black-haired girl. He fell so thoroughly in love that he stopped feeding people liquid, he left the store, he desired to go off with her for all that would remain of time.

I was in that store. I didn't have any money nor any capability for earning money in the urban society and I wanted that black dress badly, so I walked off with it. I didn't run; I didn't want to make a spectacle of myself, of my guilt. Walked out of that store.

This was how I began the occupation that I would later become.

Stealing was part of the city. Every city is born, continually being born, out of configurations of minds and desires: every city is alive. This city was patriarchal, that which allows the existence of none but itself, for it had arisen and was arising only out of the rational, moralistic bends of minds.

Patriarchal, it expressed its unbearability: for years, the economic power had lain in white liberal hands. The money was now coming from the Hong Kong immigrant community. Many of the children of these close-knit families clustered themselves into street gangs. In the lowest loins of the city, these boys engaged Hispanic and black gangs in more violence than any could handle. The white liberals who hadn't as yet abandoned the city knew nothing of this because they didn't wish to know all, in the city, that lay outside their control. They pretended that they could control gang warfare: passed laws which, they claimed, would put an end to all violence. Protect the kids. The laws defined the children who were members of gangs as hardened murderers and so turned them into lifelong criminals. The search for all those who had been tainted began.

Even though the urban arena was becoming more nonwhite than white, liberals and other whites decided that those who had been infected must be destroyed as efficaciously as possible.

Lest evil spread her wings. The evil of those who have drunk black.

The search narrowed. Soon the identities of all those who have been polluted will come to be known. Soon we'll know where all the evil in this world resides. I realized that I hadn't been touched. I was clean. Then I knew that a speck inside me, something as much like a trace as a memory, a memory of my lips brushing the black liquor, was tainted.

Immediately I thought: It really isn't anything. I'm not a sick one. I'm not one of the monsters. I thought: I'm passing for normal; I'm as normal as any moral person.

Their search narrowed further. I returned to the store where I had stolen the black dress.

It was here that the creation of the world had begun.

When I was finally inside the store, I saw that the ebony-haired girl who had escaped from here hadn't died even though she had drunk some of the black liquid. Perhaps instead of dying she had given birth to three freaks. I saw this. Three children, or things, scampering around a room now so large that it was the back of a clothes store, where its designers work and live. No longer the actual clothes store.

Everything in this room was messy. Heaps of clothes and cloths in no possible order.

Chaos had once been a clothes store.

One of these children was so tall that the body below his head was a stilt. The head was falling off, almost separated from his neck. A midget sat around the neck. Tiny legs hugged a beanpole of flesh, as if they were fucking it.

The existence and appearance of these freaks announced the revelation of the mystery. Thus of all mysteries. As if *to find out* was simply *to see,* I found out that I'm one of the tainted. *To see* equaled *to accept,* because the object of my sight was exactly what I was now forced to accept. That I'm going to die.

Now I realized that no one and nothing will ever escape the chains of cause and effect: I'd stolen a dress; I had to endure the consequences of my act. I'm going to die.

I knew I couldn't escape my death.

I looked around at everyone in the room. At the man who had spooned liquid out of the pools. At the ebony-haired woman. At the half-human half-stilt. At the mongoloid midget. At all who were stranger or more monstrous. I couldn't tell which one I was. I kept looking and looking, but I could no longer find myself.

I realized that I'd escaped my death because I no longer knew who I was.

NOW I TELL EVERYTHING IN MY OWN LANGUAGE
Ending the Memory of Childhood
There will be no more abortions. Criminality will no longer be connected to unfortunate consequence," I said.

I had just left the hospital; I was still in those environs. I looked down and into my underpants.

The underpants resembled the white cotton ones schoolgirls used to wear. Now they don't wear anything. I saw blood flowing over one of the white sides.

In order to handle this situation, I fashioned the following plan: First, I'd leave my boyfriend. Prior to the plan, I didn't know that I had a boyfriend. Second, since the pads, once as white as the panties, that were sitting one on top of the other upon the cloth crotch, were holding more blood than they were capable of storing, I'd find a place where I could be alone. There I would change.

I began looking for the place where I would change my blood.

Within the city of dusk, the only house that was real was hidden. It was wood.

Inside this house, I found the room I was looking for. The place for change. It was partly open, partly closed, like all the other areas in the house. If it had been normal, it would have had a door. There was no wall where a door should have been.

327

Despite all the openness and vulnerability, everywhere was dark. The décor of this room pirated that of a 1950s New York City apartment: roses papered its walls. All the antiques were green.

As if I were outside the room and looking in, I remarked, "The lamps are especially beautiful this time of year."

And as if that sentence had just carved out a space in which something could take place, a man stood in front of the wall that wasn't there. His hair was punked up.

I couldn't change my bloody rags while a strange guy was watching me so I told him that he had to go away now. "Go away. Shoo."

I couldn't explain myself.

When he replied that he would go, I felt guilty.

As soon as he left the room, I moved left, around the bit of wall that jutted out of one of the principal ones. Within the recess that was there, I found a bathroom. The room must have been designed and decorated at the same time as the one of roses. A charming bathroom, for all of its furniture—toilet in white, white bathtub with rose-streaked curtain—its very space, were slightly too small to accommodate an adult human.

Nevertheless I managed to throw my used Kotex wrapped in toilet paper and the plastic wrapping of the new pad into the miniature wastepaper basket that was sitting under the sink . . .

. . . It was time for me again to change my pad. As if I had never before changed, I no longer knew where I could go.

Free from abortions, I had nowhere to go in the world.

I wandered, without knowing where, through that house whose insides were lightless. I came to a bedroom. Its huge door was open. I looked into the openness and saw a man. I knew him, he used to be my best friend before I had gotten a name.

I believe he was still a poet. He was sitting on a bed and talking on the phone. He used to talk on the phone so much, when we had been friends, that I would have to tell the operator that I was making an emergency call whenever I wanted to contact him. Since he was on the phone, I knew that he wouldn't catch sight of me. I didn't want him to because the fight that he had picked with me and that had ended our friendship had wounded me.

During this quarrel which had taken place just prior to my abortions, he had told me that he was one of the few men who understands what it is to be a woman.

I still had to change my Kotex. So I walked into the next bedroom.

Two men were sleeping inside there. Two narrow beds which didn't touch each other.

I couldn't change my pad because there were men everywhere. But if I didn't throw away the old blood, something dreadful, like rot or disease, was going to touch my body.

I just stood there, in front of all those men. I no longer cared whether they saw me. And changed the pad in the hallway.

Childhood was officially over.

HOW I TRIED TO BECOME PART OF SOCIETY

As soon as I was clean, again I started haunting clothes stores.

I went back to the store in which the strange people had lived. In amazement, I saw upwardly mobile heterosexuals, coupled.

I no longer belonged in that store where I had found the black dress. Black, androgynous.

But all the clothes I was seeing belonged on the bodies of secretaries or security guards, men in offices or officers.

All I wanted to do was escape what had once felt like home. The only possible home during the days of abortions.

But if I didn't buy something, I would have nothing. I thought: I have to buy something, I do, I do, even though I've almost no money.

I've to find that one object I might want to own.

Thus, I defined the word *clothing* for myself.

The only thing I came upon I wanted even a little bit was a gray catsuit. I didn't really want it. The breast said, "Gaultier." I looked at the rest. A white tag said, "$300."

My eyes sat on it, stroked it, even though I didn't want it. I knew I had to want something.

In order to make myself want that which I couldn't have because I was poor, I began feeling up clothes I would never wear, clothes I would never go near if they paid me.

Short wool coats that my grandmother had forced me to wear when I was a child.

A salesgirl, doing her job, started telling me what I desired. I knew that she was trying to brainwash me by talking me into wearing a straight-woman outfit.

I was so disgusted that I was about to leave, but instead, I went the other way. Backwards. Into a dressing room. Back there where I had left all my clothes.

There wasn't anything anymore.

"Where are my clothes?" I asked the salesgirl who despised me because I wasn't like everybody else.

Bitch informed me, with as much brevity as she could get up, that she had stuffed my "things" into a plastic bag. "Other people have to use this dressing room."

"A plastic bag" means "a body bag."

She handed me a brown paper container.

Inside, a pair of wet shoes.

I was now so poor that I no longer knew what to do, so I did the only thing I knew. I went back to my mother.

She wasn't as poor as she used to be. Now she was living in a large house in the suburbs. When I was a child, she never let me near her. Perhaps it was because she was living in affluence that she let me come into her house and stay.

I was surprised. By this time I had accepted, though with agony, that she hated me.

Living in her house with her, I felt safe for the first time in my life. So safe that if the world, which lay outside the house, was going to die, I would be in that house and nothing would change.

In the days before the beginning of seuxality.

I was inside, separate from what was outside, so I looked out one of the picture windows. When I stuck out my head, I saw that a man was standing on the ledge.

I knew that he was about to break in. As if I had never seen any man before. There had been no men when I was a child. My skin was prickling; my nose smelling my own sweat: all that my mother feared, which I had learned to take inside, was now outside the window. This man or image formed by the meeting of interior and exterior fear was about to shatter the clear glass.

Thus, the image had two names: *criminal* and *motherfucker*. The motherfucker—that's what men were in those days before the pirates again came—was doing whatever he was doing so that he could break into me. I knew it. *To know* is *to cause*. Knowing he was about to come in me, I screeched.

After that, there was something evil inside my mother's body. For her house no longer was safe. It had become open to every fucking stranger, to anyone who just wanted to enter for any reason at all. This is how the world really is. I screeched. Everyone's penetrating and coming. I was all alone. Inside. There would never be anyone to help me.

No one's going to help me.

Mommy's always been gone. She never wanted anything to do with me. I'm alone for the rest of time and after that. As soon as I realized as completely as it's possible to realize that I was alone, I knew that I could no longer survive on my own. I have to be with another. Because of all this openness.

As if the walls were coming down, then it started to rain. Rain seemed to be coming through those windowpanes, it was seeping through the cracks. Of my mother's fucking body. My mother's body fucking. There were no longer any differences between inside and outside. There were no curtains over the windows, so everybody could see everything.

I didn't know how to be a woman. I couldn't make a curtain. A curtain or shroud for the body of my mother.

She hadn't been there.

In all the growing terror, I looked through the window and saw people walking on a gravel path. This sight, this act of seeing, was the clue to how I could escape the house of fear. If I could reverse inside and outside, then I'd be outside, on the black gravel path down which people were walking safely to a river.

The man I'd seen on the ledge and a boy were in the house, stealing. I reversed interior and exterior: I joined them. We began to steal from my mother.

They didn't steal because they wanted anything. They wanted to trash.

Me too. I'm going to trash the house of childhood. Which had been unbearable.

I wanted to remain forever with that man and boy.

That's how I got outside.

We lounged next to her house. We kicked over some dead grass. There weren't any dogs. My mother drove by us in a car. She took a potshot at us from the car window. I saw it was my mother though she was a man.

A bullet entered the chest of the Mexican, the boy.

I went away from my mother forever. I lived with the boy. He was the only one I had ever had and all that I would love.

The bullet that was sitting in his chest made him sicker, so I took care of him. Even though it wasn't in my nature to care for anyone. Since he was sick, we were two children goether.

One day he said, "Pussy, we're going to go shopping."

I was so excited that I jumped up and down.

We decided we were going to find underwear. I would try this underwear on in a dressing room whose curtain would be open, just enough, so that everyone who was outside the curtain could watch his hands pinch my nipples, then the tips of his fingers in my crack, partly obscured in black hairs. They could watch me come. Or else I'd take off as many clothes as I could just so I could try on underwear, in the center of the store, so everyone would see everything that is me.

The store would be an antique store full of dead clothes.

Despite all our fantasies, we found ourselves in a department store. Fluorescents overlit a large room. The kid—that's what I called him—rather than me, was trying on shorts, boxers so bright blue-green that fish were swimming in them.

I wanted two other pairs of boxers and planned to buy them for myself. Because I was a selfish bitch. OK, one of them would be for him. I told the kid that one of them was for him.

Then, I looked at him more closely. Now I was frightened.

"How do you feel?"

He was becoming thinner and thinner.

My boyfriend went downhill. All the way. During this period, we moved back into my apartment. There we lived as if we were never going anywhere again. The bed where we lay was against a wall. A small, square window hung over the mattress.

The boy phoned someone and asked whoever it was to come to our house because he didn't want me to be by myself. His request terrified me. For being lonely is what scares me most in the world.

I attempted to analyze why I was frightened. *To be lonely in the world,* it seemed to me, *is to be solely with my mother.*

After that, I wanted my boyfriend to touch me and never to stop. To do what I believed he was always doing. To slither his cock between my legs. Which was to stick his fingers into my skin. I knew that he would never do this because he was only becoming weaker.

We would no longer have sex together, but we could lie in bed. As if a bed was a sky. All that was inside us was lying outside.

On the bed I told the Mexican boy, "I have never loved anyone but you."

I GO TO THE BOTTOM OF THE WORLD

After the boy left me alone, I got on my motorcycle.

I had already placed my stuffed white cat in one of its saddle-bags and made sure that she'd be comfortable.

Together, we took off. We wanted to go to the country.

I was traveling down what appeared to be a country road: a thin layer of snow, hard and dirty, almost completely covered rich brown dirt; thick white stripes separated the whole into four tracks. On each side of these four tracks, but only here and there, one- and two-story suburban houses half-sunk below the snow.

Looking down below my front wheel, which was rotating I saw there was no more road under the hard snow.

I was aware I wasn't going to crash.

In this manner, the country ended. I was at a big, black tunnel. I had no choice but to enter it.

All light was black. Walls began to curve left while floor descended; walls were now curving so sharply that when I looked ahead, I thought I was going to slide. Turning was easier than seeing.

At the bottom of these turns, still in the tunnel, orange-and-white barriers stood in a jagged row across the black floor. Here my journey ended. The barriers forced me to make a U too sharp for my bike's turning capacity, but I turned without falling.

And parked by one of the orange-and-white barriers. Opposite the only parking lot, there was a street scene: a concrete sidewalk. A building wall. Behind windows in that wall, movie posters. As if I myself were in a film.

I wanted to attend the fun fair that took place behind this façade, but in this dead time of the year it had been shut down.

All there was was time. Face-to-face with time, I had to act: the only thing there was to do, in this dead town, was go to a movie.

I returned to those windows and looked inside them. The only movie playing was Hollywood. Too stupid to see.

There wasn't anything for me. Here, in the total bottom of the world.

I must have walked away from that entrance, for I found myself climbing up the stairs of a huge redbrick school building. Inside, a movie was about to be shown.

It wouldn't cost anything.

Wooden folding chairs had been strung across a room.

The movie began in the dark.

In the film, some of the homeless went about their lives. Watching the nonsensationalized, or non-Hollywood, details made me realize that I was like that. Never before had I known that I was homeless.

The film ended: again it was dark.

At one point during the playing of the movie I learned that this was its first screening, for government officials had been keeping it from the public.

A strange girl asked me where everyone had gone.

While it had been running. I hadn't noticed that anyone had left the room, so the only answer I could come up with was that her mind must have stopped for several minutes while the film had been playing.

And then I couldn't tell the difference between her and me. Between the disappearance of her mind and of mine.

And then, since *to understand* is *to learn,* I understood that consciousness isn't the mind and that it's consciousness, not the mind, which dies.

There was no more movie. It was time to go.

My new girl and I walked down one of those long halls.

I don't know how long it was before I realized that I was in a world dominated by the visual.

Paintings covered as much as possible of the walls of the hall I was in or of the room so open to that hall that I thought it was a hall.

Either these paintings had been made by children or they were in naïf style. I could take anything I wanted. For it was the world of the visual.

I walked up to each painting, peered at it closely. I didn't want any. This was when I began to want.

In the room next to the front door, streamers hovered in the air. Between these party objects, I saw, through an open doorway, a smaller room:

Racks of clothes occupied its center. Everything was hung for sale. Just as I had walked as far up as I could to the canvases, I now approached the clothes the same way. I looked at them. But I didn't want any rags, simulacra of the ones sold on Haight St. Haight St. in Hippyville. The only half-bearable one was a replica of a blouse I already owned.

Paintings crammed the walls of the room of streamers as much as they had the hall down which I had journeyed with my girlfriend. That strange girl. Paintings were no longer on canvas, but were comic books, books hung on the walls. Books I had never before seen, entrances into wonder.

Into the geographical wonders of the world known only to sailors.

It was here, in wonder, in this bottom, that I met the punk boys.

I had learned how to travel through my dreams.

(1996)